Cross Crease

ON THE EDGE
BOOK THREE

ELIZABETH HARTEY

LIMITLESS PUBLISHING, LLC

Cross Crease

Copyright © 2019 by Elizabeth Hartey.

All rights reserved.

First Print Edition: August 2019

Limitless Publishing, LLC

Kailua, HI 96734

www.limitlesspublishing.com

Formatting: Limitless Publishing

ISBN-13: 978-1-64034-866-0

Dedication

To all my girls for their unending support.

Cross Crease

cross crease
/krôs/ /krēs/
Noun

The crease is the area of ice directly in front of the net: the goalie's turf. It is very difficult to score on a top-level goalie unless someone obstructs his vision and shoots a cross crease pass to get the goalie out of position.

Prologue

HEAVEN

"Hey, brat. What's up?" The screen on my laptop fills with my brother's taunting face.

"Hey, doofus. Not much. Same old same old. School, studying, school. One exciting thing after the other. How 'bout you?"

"Same. Except throw in some hockey in the middle of these crazy ass courses I'm taking." The close-up on his face is unforgiving. He looks tired.

"No infamous Friday night house parties this semester?"

"Not so much during hockey season. But occasionally, if we have a free weekend. I try to steer clear though if I can. I need as much quiet study time as possible."

"Wow. Who are you and what have you done with my pain in the neck brother?" I laugh. Dak not wanting to party with his hockey bros? His classes must be harder than usual. "Tough classes this semester?" I close the anatomy book I was reading, happy to have the reprieve from my own studying.

"Yeah. This graduate course I convinced the Dean to let me take may have been a mistake. It's really..." Dak's voice fades when he drops his head to adjust the noise canceling headphones covering his ears.

The living room behind him comes into view. It's apparent he's sitting at his kitchen table with his back to the living room. But the room isn't the thing distracting my attention from Dak. My eyes snap to the vision on the sofa: *Damon Wolfe*.

My Karmic punishment for having spent the past ten years telling my brother how much I hate hockey players. My fantasized-about-to-the-point-of-distraction bad boy who can turn my otherwise adequate brain into stupefied goo with one glance and a sly grin.

Dak lifts his head, blocking the view behind him. "Thankfully the professor paired me up with a genius girl. She's agreed to tutor..." He drops the pen he's been tapping on the table and bends over to pick it up, giving me another Wolfe-filled bird's eye view.

His head is tipped back, his long hair spread out around his face along the sofa back. He must be sleeping.

Dak sits up. "...in exchange for me doing a skating routine with her in the Winter Fest." His face fills my screen, bringing my attention back to his conversation.

"Wait. What did you say?"

"I said, she agreed to tutor me in exchange for me skating..."

"That's what I thought you said. What do you mean? Like *figure skating* skating?"

"No. Like we're going to do a hockey skating routine." Dak shakes his head and purses his lips to one side. "Of course, I mean figure skating, dummy. It's the Winter Fest."

"But you haven't figure skated in years. Not since you got into hockey full time. What makes you think you can still do it? And a pairs routine, no less. You're crazy. This girl must be something special to get you to agree to figure skate." I quirk my brows up and down. "You're going to break your pretty face just for her pretty face."

"You're the crazy one. You just watch me, brat. I've..." A loud moan coming from behind Dak pulls my attention away from his absurd protestation concerning his ability to do a pairs routine in a show. Dak can't hear the curious groaning coming from the living room because his headphones only allow him to hear me, nothing else around him.

Maybe Wolfe is having a nightmare. I strain my head from side to side, as if it will allow me to see around Dak's giant head—the head which is growing larger by the second as he touts his imagined ability to figure skate. I'll admit he was good when he was twelve, almost a decade ago. Now the only skating he excels in is hockey.

"You know it's true. Right?" Oops. I have no idea what he just asked me.

"Huh?" My brilliant response.

"You're not even listening to me. What the hell are you looking at?" When Dak turns around to see what I'm craning my neck to get a look at, we simultaneously see the tableau occurring on the sofa.

"What the fuck?" He rips his headphones off his ears. "What the fuck are you doing, dipshit?"

Wolfe isn't sleeping. Without Dak obstructing my view, I can see the blonde head bobbing up and down at a frantic pace between Wolfe's legs.

Holy smokes! Wolfe is getting a BJ right out in the open in the living room where everyone and anyone can see. The way his eyes are clamped shut in a frown and the muscles in his neck are taut and straining it almost looks like he's in pain. But I'm reasonably certain he isn't moaning in agony, at least not *painful* agony.

Meanwhile, I can't pull my pervy, voyeuristic eyes away from Wolfe's not-so-private porno show. I'm definitely going to need a panty change and a very cold shower.

"My sister is here, asshole. She can see you!" But Dak's anxiety-ridden announcement concerning my digital presence doesn't deter Wolfe from his mission. In fact, I'd say it encourages him.

"Heaven?" He moans my name as if it's my mouth wrapped around him. He turns his head, and forces his eyes open just enough to stare directly at the computer. *At me?* I'm sure he's looking at *me* with his lust-filled eyes and pulling me into their vortex.

He threads his fingers through blondie's hair and directs her movements without taking his eyes off the computer. "Heaven," he groans again. *Oh my God.* I'm two seconds away from slipping my hand into my sleep shorts when Dak yells out, reminding me it's not my mouth pleasuring Wolfe and we're not alone.

"Seriously, dude? I cannot fucking believe..." My

screen goes black when Dak apparently comes to his senses and slams his computer closed.

But Wolfe's heated gaze is still burning inside my head. There will be no more studying this evening. Placing my computer on the night table next to me and reaching into the drawer, I retrieve the black silk bag nestled in the back—where my mom is least likely to find it. Flicking off the light and kicking my books off the bed, I snuggle down under the covers. It's going to be another night with my battery-operated friend substituting for the goalie who has been my obsession since I was fourteen years old.

Chapter One

HEAVEN

Ten Months Later

See the girl stretched out on a blanket in the sweltering California sun? The one reading and sighing out in frustration every few seconds? That's me, Heaven Andersen. Other than surfing, reading is my passion. Or should I say it's my substitute for passion?

The book's not very good. I should know. It's my gazillionth romance novel. I'm an expert on romance. No. I'm an expert on romance *novels*. I don't know one darn thing about real-life romance. The sad truth is, the swoony books I've read are my entire—totally desolate—exposure to lovemaking.

The only consolation; at least they're diverse. Instead of one guy, I get to experience—in my mind—what having sex with hundreds of different lovers would be like. Does admitting my fantasies make me a paperback slut? Not sure if it's better or worse than being an eigh-teen-year-old—nineteen in a few months—virgin.

My bawdy romantic story? There isn't any. Unless the world is looking for a new romance genre—the unhappily ever after, the story of a pitiable girl who never gets laid. If I were an emoji, my current mood status would be extreme frustration. So why, you ask, am I bothering to tell you my boring, unfulfilled tale? Because all that's about to change. I'm on a Devirginize Heaven mission. And here comes the *not* so boring means to accomplish my mission, right now.

"There's my Pip! Damn, girl, did it hurt when you fell from heaven?" Wolfe delivers the line with his tilted grin and velvet voice. It sends pebbled chill bumps over my skin even in the scorching heat. He could be a char-acter right out of the book I'm reading. Reeking of confi-dence, Wolfe saunters toward me carrying his surfboard, like the sun, sand, ocean, and me were put there just for him.

Slamming my book closed, I heave out another huge, exasperated sigh. Ever since our first meeting four years ago, we have this unknowingly-provocative-on-Wolfe's-part-game we play exchanging cornball pick-up lines. After Wolfe playfully teased me with one the first time I met him, I decided I wasn't going to stand there like some star-struck little fangirl when he taunted me. So, I honed my cheese whiz pick-up line skills and gave them right back to him.

"Hey, D! Guess what I'm wearing?" I quip, standing up on the blanket as he walks toward me. His wry grin morphs to a wide-eyed, shocked expression before it's quickly replaced by his usual indifferent smug look.

"W...what are you wearing?"

"The smile you gave me." I hold my arms out in a ta-da position as I deliver the corny line.

"Holy shit, Pip. When did you grow tits?" He smirks while shoving his board into an upright position in the sand

"Right about the time you were away at school learning to be an even bigger ass." I tilt my head and smirk right back at him.

"Real nice. You kiss your mother with that mouth?" He pulls the elastic from around his man bun and flops down on his back on the blanket next to me, stretching his arms over his head. His chest muscles ripple causing my heart muscle to undulate like a series of corduroy ocean swells. I clench my gaping mouth closed and swallow the gasp I refuse to let him hear.

Ugh. The present man candy dominating my panorama is too much. As I lay on my side on the blanket facing Wolfe, my hip pressing into the soft sand, my thoughts drift to him. My body temperature soars, not from the blazing sun or the warm baked sand, and not even from the steamy sex scene I was reading. It's the red-hot images smoldering through my mind—all the things I'd like to be doing with *him*, which have me panting.

Truth is, I've loved him ever since I was fourteen. Not in the biblical sense, merely in the swoony, my body aches for him sense. He didn't then—nor does he now—know I exist. Correction. He knows I exist, he just doesn't care, at least not in the swoony achy way. Here comes another frustrated sigh.

Wolf's beauty is other-worldly: long wavy hair, carved muscle, bronzed skin like an ancient Egyptian prince, chiseled cheekbones which could cut glass, pillow lips I'd like to sink my teeth into. He's unlike any guy I've ever seen, unlike any *human* I've ever seen.

Raising his head, he tosses his hair out before returning to the stretched position on his back. Seeing his gorgeous hair spread out around his face, I shrug. It's a bit disconcerting when the guy you're lusting over has hair more beautiful than yours.

"Yes. I do kiss my mom. Regularly." I flick my chin up in satisfaction. "But never mind about my mother. I wonder what my *brother* would think if he saw you ogling my boobs?" I remind him my brother, Dak, is only a few yards down the beach watching us.

Wolfe is the goalie on the Bernard University hockey team—the team on which my brother is the captain. Wolfe is also the beyond-bad-boy team member. You've heard the term MVP? Well, Wolfe is the MIP on the Bernard team—Most Infamous Player. He is also Dak's friend and roommate.

Consequently, whenever Wolfe is within a five-mile radius, Dak is on full alert. He never takes his analytical eyes off us. He becomes my nosey, super over-protective big brother.

"I'm not ogling your boobs." D clicks his tongue but at the same time gives a nervous glance down the beach in the direction where Dak is teaching his girlfriend Tracy to surf. "I was only commenting on their existence.

And I'm not the one Dak needs to worry about. What the hell was he thinking letting you go out practically naked?" He jerks his head toward my loving brother, who does indeed seem to be glowering at us as he glides to shore on a wave.

"Doesn't he know the dirtbags hanging out on beaches won't know you're a vir...I mean they'll think..." He hesitates.

No way. He's actually going to throw my virginal status in my face. I confided in him only because I thought, as a well-practiced friend in the field, he could give me some pointers on what I needed to do to attract the opposite sex. Okay. Maybe I was hoping I'd get the inside scoop on what attracts *him*.

Even though we're friends, I've never actually come out and said 'take me, I'm yours.' And he's never offered his assistance to deflower me. In Wolfe's mind, I merely exist as his best friend's baby sister. But not cool if he's been discussing our private conversations with Dak. Or worse, maybe he's had a good laugh concerning my virginal handicap with his other teammates. It's completely humiliating.

"*Who* will know and think what, exactly?" I hold back my seething irritation.

"They might think you're...available," he scoffs.

That's it. I'm annoyed and not holding back. "For your information I *am* available. *And* I would appreciate it if you wouldn't discuss my...experience with my brother and the troglodytes on your hockey team. Also, Dak says *you're* a dirtbag." *Whenever your name comes up in our conversations.*

11

"I think what you meant to say is your *inexperience.* And I haven't been discussing it with anyone but you." His flat tone makes me want to yank out his lustrous hair. Maybe just one handful. But I suppose hair pulling wouldn't bode well for my trying to prove to him how grown up and ready I am to do the deed.

"You can be such a pain in the arse sometimes."

"Arse? Have you taken a trip to merry old England recently?" He chuckles. Sometimes while I'm love-lusting him, I'm hating him.

"Arse, ass, if the label fits you, *wear* it. As I was saying, Dak says he loves you like a brother, but you're still a dirtbag when it comes to women. You know after having lived with you for four years, he's well aware of your dirtbag status." I mimic his apathetic tone.

Just because I see beyond Wolfe's whorish exterior and know the right woman could melt his cold, cold heart—the right woman being me—doesn't mean I'm going to get all sappy about it.

"Can't argue with my man there. When it comes to women, I'm as dirty as they get. I'm no gentleman and never claimed to be. But I've never had any complaints from the ladies so far," he says through his infamous tilted grin. There's a strange clenching in my stomach.

"Anyway, no worries. You're not a woman." He fidgets, burrowing himself and the blanket further into the sand. "You're...you're Pip." He waves his hand up and down in my direction "Exactly why you shouldn't be parading around in that getup." Shielding his eyes from the glaring sun with his hand, he scowls at me.

"Oh, I'm not a woman, huh? Should I stand up again so you can get a better look?"

What does he mean I'm not a woman? Maybe he hasn't noticed I'm no longer a gangly fourteen-year-old girl who's built like a ten-year-old boy. The dental braces are gone, I've grown into my lanky limbs, and I if I do say so myself, my boobs are rather spectacular. All things considered. There isn't a speck of synthetic gelatin keeping them perky.

Since my dad's a cosmetic surgeon in Beverly Hills, I have inside knowledge concerning the polymer goo used to keep his celeb patients up and running. But I digress.

"No. No need to go displaying your almost naked ass around again," D snarls.

What business is it of his if I display my naked ass... wait. What? I'm not naked. I'm wearing the fantastic hot pink bikini my mom bought me, and I'm pretty sure I don't look like a...a non-woman in it.

I think he needs some affirmation of my new and improved enticing *developments*. He only sees me as the little girl I was four years ago when my parents and I were moving Dak into his college house—the first time I met Wolfe, the first time his bewitching eyes cast their spell on me.

The house was thick with hockey players and their bulging biceps. Who cared? With a brother who had played hockey since he was five, I'd seen my fair share of the cave dwellers.

When Dak played in high school, his teammates swarmed all over our house on a regular basis. Hanging out in our home gym, lifting and pressing weights, challenging each other to see who could do the most push-ups or pull-ups, bragging about who got laid the most and who had the biggest...muscles.

I'd seen their sickening macho behavior enough to make me want to stay as far away from the nearest hockey jock as possible, except for Dak. Loving one's older brother like crazy, even when he's the person driving you crazy, is a given.

Anyway, the day we moved Dak into his college house, I couldn't care less about the radioactive levels of testosterone saturating the air. I ran up and down the stairs without a concern in the world, helping to carry things into Dak's bedroom, my long, gangly legs taking two steps at a time.

Then Wolfe walked into the hallway with his shoulder-length, kissed-by-the-sun chestnut hair, features chiseled by Michelangelo's ghost, and wintery, almost silver wolf-like eyes. The blankets I had in my arms drifted to the floor like I was in a dreamlike fog.

My imagined dream boy come to life: dangerous eyes, panty dropping perma-scowl with occasional ovary exploding barely-there tilted smiles. I stood there grinning like a fool with more metal and wires in my mouth than the San Francisco Bay Bridge.

"Hey, pip-squeak." He flicked his chin up with a wry grin, and I died. "Excuse me, I think you have something in your eye. Nope, it's just a sparkle."

A few simple words. Then Wolfe ruffled his hand through my messy hair and floated down the stairs. At least in my mind, he floated—like a vision. I swore I would never rewash my hair.

I was a complete goner. That was it; the very minute I fell in lust with the goalie who with one sentence had stopped my heart and caught it in his hand like the ten-thousand pucks he had interrupted on their way into hockey nets. Teen Heart Interrupted, perfect title if I ever write my memoirs.

"What are you doing, doofus?" My annoying brother came from his room and interrupted my fantasy.

"Nothing. Get lost." I scowled, scooped up the blankets, carried them into Dak's room, and flopped back onto his bed.

As I lay on the unmade mattress, my mind filled with images: Wolfe's magnetic eyes, alluring mouth, and sultry grin. My imagination churned.

Unfortunately, I would soon come to learn, the guy I was fantasizing about would only ever see me as 'pip-squeak' or 'squirt' or some other equally humiliating pocket-size person.

Thus, began my journey on the road to unrequited love. From then on, whenever I visited Dak at Bernard, it took a concerted effort on my part to keep my tongue from hitting the floor, cartoon style, every time Wolfe walked in the room.

And although he continued his bad-boy-couldn't-give-a-crap-about-anyone attitude, I suppose, since I was his team captain's *baby* sister, Wolfe was nice to me—

even though I beat him at every *Super Smash Brothers'* challenge.

Once, when Wolfe threw the game controller down in frustration because I beat him for the fifth consecutive time, Dak came in the living room and commented, "You don't have to babysit my annoying little sister, bro." I was so mortified I wanted to wrap the game controller wire around Dak's neck. Lucky for him the controllers were wireless.

Wolfe laughed, tugged me into his side in a headlock and assured my brother, "Nah, man. It's cool. Pip's the only one who can beat my ass at Super Smash Brothers. I like the challenge." I'm surprised he didn't tickle me under my chin or scratch behind my ears like he would a playful puppy.

Four years later I would almost settle for a squeezing headlock just to have the opportunity to press my nose into Wolfe's hard body. I have no self-respect whatsoever when it comes to wanting this guy. Whatever. Wolfe's body is amazing. I can sacrifice a little self-respect.

"Your quad muscles are looking tense." I shake my thoughts away from my little-girl memories and direct the conversation to something other than his disapproval concerning my bikini-clad body before I actually resort to yanking out his hair. "I could help work out some tension for you, help make you even more flexible." I offer my assistance with calculated indifference.

"Stop being weird," Wolfe scoffs. He drapes his arm across his face like he's trying to block out the sun but I choose to believe what he's really trying to do is keep himself from looking at my spectacular boobs.

"I will not. Weirdness makes life far less boring, Jerkface."

"Jerkface?" He chuckles. "What're you, five?"

"As a matter of fact, I'm going to be *nineteen* soon," I emphasize my age.

He lifts his arm for a second and glances at me. "Oh, yeah." He lowers his arm again and mumbles from under its protective shield, "I forgot how *old* you're getting to be. And for the record, I didn't call you weird. I said you were *being* weird."

"For the *record*," I imitate, "I love and embrace *all* my weird. Anyway, in this case, I wasn't being weird. I'm starting my undergraduate Physical Therapy courses in a few weeks. I'm majoring in strength and conditioning and sports therapy. I figured I could get a head start on acupressure and trigger point therapy. Strictly for educational purposes." *My sexual education.*

"Ah huh," he continues to talk into his arm. "My quads are fine and don't require any massaging from *you*, Pip-squeak. Talk to me in a few years when you're all grown up and have your doctorate."

He's infuriating. "I wasn't offering a massage, Sicko. I'm going to be a DPT, not a stripper."

"*I'm* the sicko?" He peeks out from under his arm and smirks. "I'd say all those sex books you read are giving you a one-track mind. Does Dak know you read those things?"

"Number one, they are not *sex* books. They are *romance* novels. Number two, my mother gave me this one after she was done reading it." I wave my book in his face. "Most importantly, number three. Who cares what Dak knows?"

"Hmm." He lifts his arm. *The Duke and the Parlor Maid*. Sounds riveting," he comments in a bored tone and goes back under his arm cover.

"You'd love it, I'm sure. It could be your biography, the eighteenth-century version. Maybe the scoundrels they write about in these books are your ancestors." I stick my tongue out at him while he's still undercover. Again, I'm supposed to be showing my maturity. Don't want to give off any terrible-two vibes.

As you can see, D doesn't reciprocate any lust-filled yearnings for me. He's become my D, short for Damon and I've become his Pippa or Pip, short for Pip-squeak. When he looks at me, he only sees his innocent, sometimes snarky, friend. Although I'm almost nineteen and all grown up and legal—legal in the sense I can join the armed forces or...have sex with *members* of the armed forces—things have not gone the way I hoped they would with D.

After another visit to Bernard and a weekend marathon *Smash Brothers* championship, in which I once again beat Wolfe at every game, we became long distance, digital buddies. Our 'wi-friendly' connection began when Wolfe asked if I played *Grand Theft Auto*. After telling him my team kicked butt every time we played, I got a late-night text.

WOLFE

> Hey, Pip. I'm putting together a team
> for GTA tonight. You interested?

Well, not exactly the late-night text I was hoping for, but at least he was thinking about me.

> It's Saturday night. I was thinking
> about going to a party.

There's no way I was going to the party. I would much rather connect with D all night even if it was only through data bytes rather than through flesh bites on a date. But I didn't want to sound too excited about a silly multiplayer game.

> No sweat. Have fun. Whose party?

> The quarterback from our high school
> team is having a celebration for the
> big win they had today. BTW. It's late
> there. Didn't you have a game
> tonight? Shouldn't you be out
> celebrating?

Feathery hope tickled my heart. He wasn't out celebrating with the guys or rocking some other girl's world. Instead, he'd rather stay home and play with me. So what if three thousand geographic miles were separating us and he was holding on to a game controller rather than my hips. Technically, we would still be playing something.

> Quarterback? WTF? You hanging out
> with douchebag football players now?

He's not a douchebag.

He was totally a douchebag. Biggest man-child whore in the school who kept trying to get into my pants and couldn't seem to take no for an answer.

I think I need to have a talk with you concerning the perils of associating with the teenage dick for brains male adolescent. Especially dickhole football player jocks!

From then on, we kept in touch, not only talking while our team kicked ass in GTA, but video chatting and texting.

Wolfe somehow became my surrogate big brother-protector which, unfortunately, has put the brakes on any bedroom antics between us. He asks about my "teenybopper crushes." I don't tell him about my biggest crush. He doesn't know how every nerve ending electrifies in anticipation whenever he's near me.

As I said, he doesn't share in my electric infatuation. What he does share with me, ad-nauseum, is brotherly advice and judicious opinions on who, or it seems more important, who *never ever*, to sleep with. In return, I keep a stiff upper and lower *everything* and continue my frustrating friendship with him.

"Anyway, your quads may be okay, but there's a good chance you're going blind if you can't see I'm already *quite* grown up," I say with a haughty glare toward his arm-covered face.

"*Pip-pa*," D drones a warning.

"Whatever. It's your loss...or your quadricep's' loss." I hmmph to accentuate my so-there statement. D turns his head and scowls at me from under his bulging triceps. "Anyway, how's your last spring break before becoming a big famous pro hockey player?" I ignore his exasperated glare.

He tucks his arms under his head and does a crunch sit up to look out at the ocean. *Sweet Jesus!* It is not normal human anatomy for his ab muscles to be doing what they're doing. I bet I could bounce a coin off his stomach and it would jump like a slinky down each glorious eight pack rectus abdominus section.

"It's only AHL for now, but I'm looking forward to getting started on my career and moving out here to LA."

"Huh?" I lose focus on our conversation for a second, blinded by the mouthwatering manscape display.

He lays flat again. "I said it's only the AHL but..."

"Oh. Right, right." I wave him off. "Don't give me that feigned humility, D. You and I both know you'll be moved up to the NHL in no time."

Besides having bitchin' looks and rumored bedroom skills, D is the best goalie in Division 1 NCAA hockey. Everyone knows his stint in the AHL is only until the Winds goalie retires next season and then he'll be moved up to the Santa Ana hockey team. We'll practically be next door neighbors.

He'll be graduating in a month and moving out to Los Angeles and I'll be doing my undergrad and graduate studies right here at California State. Needless to say, I'm more than thrilled we're going to be living near each other.

"Whatever. I always play my best. If the Winds don't move me up, some other team eventually will." *Hmm. Did I say confident? Maybe I should add the word cocky to my ever-growing Damon Wolfe Pros and Cons* list. "I've worked my ass off for this opportunity. I've been waiting for it my whole life. But I suppose I'd like to be here in LA rather than anywhere else."

"Really?" My question comes out sounding a little too enthusiastic.

"Yeah. This place is fuckin' lit. I'd like to get a place on the ocean."

"Oh, right." It has nothing to do with me living here. I push the disappointment back down to the pit of my stomach where it lives.

"Something like your parents' place, right on the beach. By the way, don't forget to thank them for letting us stay here."

"I will, but they were happy to have you guys staying here with me while they're away."

"They were happy to have a bunch of hockey slobs staying with their little girl?" He quirks a brow.

"I told you, I'm not such a *little* girl anymore," I hiss back at him.

"No." He props his elbows up behind him and gives me another squinted sideways glance. "I suppose you're not, which is all the more reason not to be alone in a house with hockey sluts," he mumbles.

"I'm pretty sure my overrated virtue is safe. Dak's there with his tyrannical vigilance, and there's you keeping an eye on me." My voice drips with sarcasm because I *know* he was ogling my boobs.

"Right. There's me keeping an eye on you. No fuckin' worries." He scrubs a hand over his face.

"Anyway, my parents aren't worried. They know I hate hockey players."

"Right. Sure you do," he sneers. *So cocky.*

"I'm beginning to hate them more by the second." I wrinkle my nose at him and purse my lips to keep myself from sticking my tongue out at him—again.

"*You're* a little liar.' He flops down and retreats back into his arm-covered shell.

He's right. I am a liar. As I glance over at D lying next to me on the blanket, all beautifully bare-chested, it isn't hatred which has every hormone in my body racing to an aching spot between my thighs.

I stand up and blow out a big breath. I have to get out into the waves: burn off some adrenaline, get my mind and other areas off Wolfe's body and my prolonged virginal status.

"You are an exceptionally cocky ass today. I'm heading out." I grab my baby blue board. "Surf looks good. More fun than *you*."

"Fuck yeah! Let's do this." He completely ignores my sarcasm and rolls up into a standing position. There go his ridiculous ab muscles doing things which make me cross my legs and squeeze my adductor muscles together. "I can't wait to beat *your* snarky ass in a race to shore."

Frustration washes over me, pulling me down. He's only excited about another competition with me. Rather than his play*mate*, I've become his play*date*.

"You ready, Pip-squeak?" He pinches my cheek. Actually, freakin' pinches my cheek! My adductors unclench with a silent, mortified lament.

"Ready?" *If you mean am I ready to relinquish my lily-white chastity? I'm totally ready.*

"You ready for me to beat your ass to shore?" My dirty mind prefers to misinterpret his suggestive question and remains groveling in the gutter, while warmth and frustration travel from my nose to my toes at my own improper thoughts. But frustration or not, I'll never let him beat me to shore.

Chapter Two

WOLFE

"Ha. Just because I've given you a few lessons, you think the student is ready to beat the teacher, Grasshopper?" Pip laughs.

"Hell, yeah I am."

"How about we make a bet? Loser buys lunch at the yummy café down the beach."

"You're on. Hope you brought your debit card because I'm really in the mood for some surf and turf: fresh whole lobster with a nice twelve-ounce filet on the side." I smile and lick my lips to demonstrate how I'm already imagining eating the expensive lunch she'll be paying for.

Her gaze lingers on my mouth for a few seconds before she clears her throat and says, "Don't get your hopes up, dude. You know you can't beat me at anything. And *I'd* say the question is more like, are *you* ready for me to beat your *cocky* ass to shore?" She smirks, one hand propped on her hip.

Is she kidding? "You're kidding, right?" I shake my head in disbelief.

"We'll see. How's your balance and endurance?" Pip continues to taunt me with a smug little grin.

"Never had any problem staying erect for as long as necessary." Her whole-body blushes pink at my suggestive play on words. But she doesn't get flustered and sends the teasing right back to my court.

"Can't wait to see that."

"Okay, smart ass. Now you're really going down."

"Am I?" She quirks a brow and my dick twitches. *Fuck.* She wins this round. Enough double entendre wordplay.

"Let's go, Squirt. The student is about to decimate the teacher."

"My goodness. Someone's extraordinarily arrogant today. I think you need to practice vibrating higher." She sticks her board back into the sand and bends, flipping her long, silky hair over and tugging it into a ponytail.

"I need to do what now?" I suck in my bottom lip to keep from smiling and adjust myself when my dick begins to salute at the sight. Not only am I picturing what I could do to her in a bent over position, she's fucking adorable when she's talking about her cosmic bullshit.

"Vibrate higher." She stands up and flips her head back. "It's a real thing. Something people do to get closer to a more harmonious, peaceful existence. Lately, my mom even has my dad doing meditation and yoga trying to reach Cosmic Consciousness, or...Nirvana, or...Tahiti. I don't know—*someplace* blissfully wonderful. I think you should try it. You need it."

She pivots in the sand and struts away carrying her board under one arm. *Christ Almighty.* It's. A. Mother. Fucking. Thong. The ability to breathe is gone, along with all logic, all sanity. I stop in my tracks, willing my legs not to buckle and leave me on my knees in the sand. Talk about vibrating? She looks like 1000Hz of energy, and I want to fuck her so bad it hurts. Damn. When did I become a creepy cradle robbing perv?

Let's get one thing straight. I'm not a saint. The farthest thing from it. Any other time, with any other woman, I wouldn't think twice about getting busy worshipping at the altar of her pussy. It's a gift knowing how to worship a woman's pussy in a way she'll never forget, and I've been blessed with the talent. And I never have to work at finding a willing recipient. The right glance and in no time some chick is riding my dick like a world-class rodeo champion. Don't start with the 'cocky jerk' comments. Women love me, and I'm not ashamed to say it.

I'll also admit, without shame, I like having sex anytime, anywhere as long as it's with a consenting woman—sometimes more than one consenting woman at the same time. But never more than once with the same woman...or women. There's a planet full of hot choices out there. I'm not about to dine on the same meal every night, if you get my meaning. Maybe it sounds cold to you ladies. I make no apologies because I always make sure the women I've fucked walk away—

with some difficulty—feeling like queens. But the game rules are, they *have* to walk away.

I'm not interested in long-term unless it's a hockey contract. I excised emotional sensitivity and monogamous devotion from my DNA a long time ago when it became a necessity for survival. Sex had only been a means to survive in the past, no emotions, no attachments. Just payment for services rendered. Sex for me now is the same, minus the payment: numb brain and heart but fiery physical release.

Getting attached to someone else, expecting them to be there for you is for fairytales, not real life—unless you don't mind being screwed over and crushed. I mind. Been there. Done that.

Now, to get back to the hot little firecracker strutting down the beach. Pippa. Dak's baby sister. Although, at the moment, she doesn't look like anyone's *baby* sister. The teeny weeny almost non-existent bikini she's barely wearing is showing off all her newly acquired, brain-stupefying curves and long tan legs which would feel perfect wrapped around my waist while I pound into her. Fuck. Everything I'm thinking is so wrong—even for me. I may have been blessed by the gods in certain areas but that big of a dick I'm not.

"Keep up, loser. Or are you chickening out?" Pip turns and continues to walk backward as she taunts me.

"Loser? Don't worry, sweetheart. I'm coming," I yell back. But if I *were* coming, she'd be the one screaming my name and dropping over the edge so hard she wouldn't be able to walk, let alone keep up.

What the fuck is wrong with me? I have got to get my

blood cells to take a return trip from my dick back into the head on my shoulders. This can never happen between us.

I've known Pip was crushing on me for years. It was apparent ever since the first time I met the nervous little girl when we were moving into our college house four years ago.

I remember thinking she couldn't be real, just a beautiful figment of my seriously deranged mind. A storybook princess, all silky dark hair, golden skin, and intense turquoise eyes which sent the demons in my soul running away in fear. Who the hell has turquoise eyes? Something about her rocked my world. I had to say something to her. The cheesy line I teased her with shocked me even more than the way I was drawn to her.

But Heaven was just a kid back then, and she's still just an innocent kid, even if she is going to be nineteen soon. I know all about her innocence because she confides in me during our late-night texting or video chat sessions. It's devilish irony I should be the one she examines her virginity with...well, not *examines*. I don't *examine* her virginity. I *talk* to her about it.

Ever since she turned eighteen, she's had a single-minded vocation—to get laid. She asks for advice about who she should sleep with and what to do the first time. My advice is always the same. Don't sleep with anyone...*ever*. At least not for a long, long, *long* time.

I can't take my eyes off her as she wiggles her sweet, round ass with confidence down the beach—all while carrying a surfboard. If things were different, I'd love to help her out on her quest to lose her virginity. But that can never happen. Pip is off-limits, forbidden territory, a big loud no-no.

What the hell is wrong with Dak? Why would he let her go out in two threads imitating a bathing suit? I wasn't kidding about the scumbags hanging out on beaches who will see her and only have one thing on their minds. Like the one thing on my mind—tearing those two little strings off her and burying myself so deep inside her I'll be lost in Heaven, literally.

Jesus. I don't know how things between us have gotten to this place. This isn't my usual MO when inter-acting with people, especially not *female* people. I don't spend time conversing with them, befriending them, or trying to analyze them.

The only things worth analyzing, besides which way a puck is going to come careening toward the goal, are mathematically definitive computer codes. They can't hurt you, deceive you, or leave you broken.

But with Pippa, everything's changed. I want to breathe her in, get to know everything about her. I don't know how to explain it. She brings something to my life I've never had, a luminescence wiping away my dark past.

Believe me, I know how this sounds. A few months ago, if I had heard any other guy spewing this schmaltz, I would've hurled my most recent meal and called him a little bitch. Hell, I did call my teammate, Dalt, a vagina back when he was getting all moony-eyed about Nik, and she didn't want anything to do with him.

Now? Let's just say I understand his predicament. I want Pippa like I've never wanted anything or anybody. Problem is, although Pip claims she's only looking for a quick deflowering, I know she's girlfriend material with a capital G.

I. Am. Not. Interested in having a girlfriend, in case you misunderstood my previous confession. Never had one. Never want one. By now, you must see where this is going.

But to be clear, let me reiterate. Pip is a girl and she's a friend but with a big slash between the two words. She is, in fact, the only girl/friend I've ever had. I enjoy hanging out with her like I would any guy friend. Except, in Pip's case, a small problem has developed. Or should I say, a rather big, *hard* problem? I don't drool over any guy friends when they're walking down the beach. I don't get hard every time I think about one of them, or dream about pounding balls deep into them. *Eww. There's a thought I'll never be able to erase from my mind.* See my dilemma here? To say the friendship lines have been blurred when it comes to Pip is the understatement to end all understatements.

I knew I was in trouble when we got to the Andersens' Malibu house the other night and I dropped my bags in the room which was going to be mine for the week; the room right next to Pippa's.

I could hear the water running in the bathroom which adjoined our bedrooms.

I hadn't seen her in person for months, but all I could picture was her standing naked in the shower, lathering her glistening skin with soap. In my mind, I could see the bubbles and water streaming along her curves and sliding down between her thighs into her sweet pussy. As I listened to her humming, I closed my eyes, imagining stripping off my clothes and stepping in behind her in the shower.

As she moaned and arched back against me, I pressed my hard cock between her ass cheeks. My arms wrapped around her, one arm holding her firmly against my cock as the fingers on my other hand plunged into her and fucked her into ecstasy. I stood there, my eyes closed, having my pervy wide-awake dream. In my imagination, Pippa's humming had changed into pleasured moans.

Just as I slid my hand into my sweatpants to stroke my hard as fuck cock into a much-needed release, Batt, my step-brother and hockey teammate, came barreling through the door.

"What are you doing, fucktard? We're waiting for you to go to dinner."

I pulled my hand from my pants with such a quick tug it caused the elastic to snap against my skin. Batt's whole face pinched into a questioning frown. At the exact same time, Pippa began singing Pink. And in its full a capella glory, she sounded a lot like Julia Michaels. I'll never forget the way Batt's mouth dropped open in shock. But I don't think his shock stemmed from Pip's impressive voice. He glanced back and forth from the closed bathroom door to me.

When his eyes finally stayed locked on me, I could almost feel the punch emanating from his narrow-eyed glare. "Are you fucking kidding me? Really, bro? Heaven? Come on, dude. She's Dak's little sister. Tell me you're not hittin' that."

"Fuck. No." I faked a laugh because even my vocal

cords knew I was full of shit. If Batt hadn't walked in, I might have kicked in the bathroom door and tried to fulfill my dream.

"It's nothing like that." I ran my frustrated fingers through my frustrated hair because for the past few months and the way I'd been thinking about Pippa every night, I couldn't find satisfaction with any other chick.

"I hope not, bro. Because it's seriously fucked up, even for you. She's not your usual hook-up material. She's young and innocent. Besides, it's not cool to hit on a hockey bruh's sister without talking to him about it first." He shook his head.

"I know, bro. It's all good." It was completely not good. In fact, the whole situation was sheer badness and all I had been thinking about every night for months while jacking off to imaginary Pippa-riding-me-visions and then dreaming about pounding into her in ways that would make the Kama Sutra's author blush.

*"Dak would never give you the go ahead anyway. Your reputation for the **unusual** ways you hook-up with women precedes you. He's not about to hand over his baby sister to the lecherous wolf." Batt snorted a chuckle through his nose.*

Dak didn't know everything about my former life. But he saw my current life enough to know I wasn't a nice guy.

Batt, on the other hand, knew all about my tarnished past because it was his dad who found me living on the Brooklyn streets when I was fifteen—no, not living, surviving. If the Battaglias hadn't taken me in and helped me turn my life around, I wouldn't have gotten as far as I am today. But even though they loved and supported me like no one else in my life ever had, not even they could erase all the scars on my heart.

Just then the water in the shower turned off. I glanced over to the door. I swear to God I don't know why I fucking licked my lips.

"Oh man, bro." Batt dropped his gaze to the floor and pinched his brow between his fingers. "You. Are. So. Fucked."

Before the door even closed behind Batt, I knew he was right. I was fucked. I had to stop thinking about Pippa the way I was. Because I couldn't dispute the way Dak had assessed my reputation with women and I wasn't about to make Pip another one-night conquest.

"C'mon, D. The tide's going out," Pippa drones in annoyance from down the beach, reminding me she's waiting.

As I look up, I tell myself she's not just some nameless chick. She's an angel, a sweet innocent *baby* angel.

"Be right there," I call back. I watch as Pippa drops her board in the water, stretches onto it and begins to paddle out.

After this surfing competition is over, I need to find one of those long-legged blondes who walked by and gave me the 'let's fuck' eye, earlier. I gotta get laid. It's been too many days.

What can I say? It's a guy thing. You ladies don't get

it because you don't have the same equipment. Try to cut us some slack. Us guys are zoned in on our dicks 24/7 and when they don't get any attention for a while—like a whole week—and then a pretty ass wiggles at us, it's like dangling water at a man who just came off the desert.

It has to be the reason I'm reacting the way I am to Pip because there is no way my dick should be doing what he's doing right now or *ever* when thinking about her. She's a princess and...I'm no prince.

Chapter Three

HEAVEN

Two Years Later

"Wolfe is looking really good," Nikki leans in and yells over the crowd.

I'm mesmerized watching him. It's such a rush seeing the way he moves on the ice doing the thing he loves most in the world. My mind drifts, imagining how his flexibility would translate to the bedroom—someplace it shouldn't be drifting.

I'm well aware it's ridiculous and stupid to be lusting over my textbook bad-boy friend because there's no doubt he's broken when it comes to affection. Anyone who looks beyond his gorgeous exterior and amazing athletic skills could see it. Although I must admit, it's a challenge to look beyond his magnificent exterior. This struggle has resulted in a small dilemma: whenever I'm around him, I'm not sure if it's my heart or my vagina beating in overdrive.

I've been at every home game since they brought D up to the Winds after their first-string goalie was injured. D doesn't play every game, but when he does, he proves he's an armed guard at protecting the net. Like he's doing tonight against the Knights. I always sit with Nikki—Dalt's wife—and their two kids, if they're with her. We prefer to sit down near the ice adjacent to the Winds' bench, rather than in the suite they have reserved for the players' family members and friends.

Nikki's sans kids tonight. Dalt insisted they hire a nanny to give him and Nik more alone time. Nikki said she tried to explain to him, more alone time was only going to lead to more little intruders. But in reality, I think they're happily working on their own homegrown hockey and soccer teams.

Dalt was the left-winger on the Bernard team and another roommate in the infamous Bernard U. house. He was also drafted to the Winds and totally stoked when D was brought up to the team.

"He really knows how to use his *stick*. Don't ya think?" Nikki nudges my leg with hers, reminding me she's here—along with fifteen thousand other people.

"What? Oh...yeah. He looks amazing." My voice is a little too breathy when I confirm her assessment.

During the brief timeout, D's bouncing up and down like a spring, keeping his legs buoyant.

"And his gameplay doesn't look too bad either." She purses her lips and quirks a brow.

I sit up straight and flip one side of my hair back over

my shoulder: the universal female move for 'I'm telling the absolute truth' or 'fuck off,' depending on who you're talking to.

"I don't know what you mean. I was totally talking about his gameplay."

"Uh huh. Sure you were." Nikki shakes her head. "Heaven, I heart you like a sister, that's why I'm going to come right out and say this. When the fuck are you going to stop chasing after that lucky SOB and finally let him catch you?"

"Humph. It's not like I haven't tried. I mean...it's not like that." I add a forced laugh. "D and I are just friends."

Besides being Dalt's wife, Nikki is also Tracey's best friend. Tracey is my brother's girlfriend. She and Nikki lived together while attending Bernard. Now we all live in Cali, and I've gotten close to both Nikki and Tracey. They know all about my White Swan status and my desire to trade in my boring white wings for the Black Swan's dirty girl more exciting ones. But although they suspect my less than pure intentions toward D, I haven't confirmed it. I don't want Tracey to feel the need to keep secrets from Dak. She knows Dak would lose a nut if he found out what I was contemplating.

Dak never misses an opportunity to tell me about D's less than stellar reputation for having been the biggest manwhore on the Bernard hockey team and current first place contender for the title on the Winds. But I don't need his lectures.

I'm more than aware Wolfe's rep matches his predatorial name. It goes beyond whoring around. He's...um... shall we say, somewhat primal with his hookups. Dak isn't quite so polite when classifying Wolfe's liaisons. 'Fuck 'em and dump 'em,' is how he summarizes Wolfe's harlotry.

In college, he had a thing for getting it on in public places like empty classrooms, bathroom stalls, cars in parking lots, and as I'm painfully aware, in the living room—no matter who was around. Anywhere I guess, other than his own bed. His relationships—and I use the term loosely—have a one-night or day run only. Evidently, whenever the opportune moment avails itself.

But Dak doesn't have to worry about *my* relationship with D. Nothing much has changed in Wolfe's one-night public liaisons and he still isn't spending any one of those sleepless nights with me. He simply refuses to have any discussion which revolves around his being my devirginizing knight in shining armor. He says we're friends and he doesn't want to do anything to ruin our friendship. Blah. Blah. Blah.

I don't see why it has to ruin our friendship. It's just two friends helping each other out.

I can help D thaw his frozen damaged heart, and he can help heat my cold, lonely V-jay. A therapeutic exchange—tat for *tit*, so to speak. No one gets hurt.

I have to get D to see me as something other than his competitive, Lilliputian friend. It's taking longer than I thought it would to bring him to his knees—pun totally intended. Haven't given up, though. I'm still working on it.

"I call bullshit. Never try to kid a kidder." Nikki's loud remark pulls my focus back to our conversation and the crowded arena. Guess my attempt at keeping my intentions on the DL didn't fool her.

"Is it that obvious?" I shrug.

"Only when you breathe." She laughs. "And only because I've been there. Not with Wolfe, of course. But Dalt and I had our own problems for a while. Don't worry. Things have a way of working out the way they're supposed to."

"Thanks, Nik. And I heart you like a sister too." I don't get a chance to continue our conversation because the cheering in the arena raises to a deafening decibel.

All hell has broken loose at the crease. D is using every weird contortion he has in his arsenal to hold the Winds' 2-1 lead. Somewhere in the mad scramble, he loses his stick. He spreads himself out like a starfish to block the first two shots. In a blink, he's up into a butterfly stance to prevent the third and fourth shots. He's like a flexible cement wall until the whistle finally blows, ending D's successful defense and the Winds win the game.

"You and Wolfe practically burst into flames whenever you're near each other," Nikki yells over the celebrating fans and our own loud clapping. "You guys better do something about the slow burn going on between you or when you finally get together you two may combust into a zillion scorching embers."

But Nikki's observation is wrong. D isn't smoldering for me. The heat from the hot Winds goalie *is* blowing in my direction, but I seem to be the only one in slow-burn mode.

Nikki and I make our way to the locker room door to congratulate the guys and wait for them. I'm at the door every home game, whether they win or lose. If I'm even one minute late, D texts me to see if I'm okay.

Ever since he moved to Los Angeles, we spend more time together hanging out rather than texting or video chatting. We meet for lunch at least three times a week and go surfing on the weekends when he doesn't have games. He's almost gotten good enough to beat me to shore, but not quite. Sometimes we go to the movies or hike up Runyan Canyon. Even though we see each other much more now, we remain in the best friends-who-hang-out-category.

The strange thing is, although we have no problem hanging out in public places, he avoids being *alone* with me like I'm the original Ebola virus carrier. Outings, in public places, are a regular occurrence. But if he comes to pick me up, he never comes inside. He'll call or text to tell me he's outside and he'll wait in the car for me. Same thing happens if I go to pick him up at his new condo. When I get there, he tells the doorman at the desk to let me know he'll be right down. And at night? Like when I hang out with him after games? He makes sure there's an entourage going with us. He's sure to have some super model type or other draped over his shoulder at all times. He never does a repeat performance with whichever flaw-less beauty is decorating his arm. But it's still enough to break my heart a little.

And every time he does it I tell myself it's time to

forget my silly schoolgirl mission. To accept the fact D is never going to agree to take my virginity because we're friends and I'm Dak's little sister.

I'll be starting my Physical Therapy internship next week. Maybe it's time for new beginnings in every way, time to reconsider my options.

"Hey. Do you work for NASA? Because you're out of this world." I smile and wrap him in a tight squeeze.

Pressing my cheek against his jersey—wet with sweat and oozing his manly, soapy scent—there's a familiar swirl in my stomach. I'm beginning to question the funny pick-up lines game we've played forever. It was cute when I was fourteen. But now, every time he innocently teases me with one, a strange aching twinge zaps my heart.

"Do you work at Starbucks? Because I like you a latte." He chuckles and squeezes me back. I inhale him and remind myself this is just one friend greeting another, the same way we've done a million times in the past. Nothing more.

"Eww. You're sweaty gross," I cringe, and push away from him. I don't really care about the sweat. I'd stay wrapped up in his arms forever, sweat and all, if he showed the slightest indication he wanted to stay wrapped up in mine. "And I didn't think you could get much cornier, but that was pretty bad." I disguise my hurt by teasing him.

"What? I thought it was pretty clever. Besides, it's true. I do like you a lot," Wolfe's voice softens. For a moment our eyes lock. His silver eyes seem to sparkle just for me.

"C'mon, bébé. Everyone's waiting. Hurry and shower." Miss Swimsuit Edition cover model breathes her thick, French-accented request into D's ear and breaks my greedy moment. He takes a step back from me at the interruption.

This is crazy. These ping-ponging thoughts and actions have been going on for two years. It's exhausting. I'm not some starry-eyed teenager anymore. I don't need the ooey gooey, crazy-in-love thing. I just need to get laid by someone who doesn't see me as a fragile porcelain doll, someone who can vanquish my virginity. I want it to be D, but maybe it's time to forget my teenage obsession with my best friend.

"Yeah. Be right out." D holds a wait a minute finger up to Frenchie but doesn't take his eyes off me. "We're headed over to the Flying Puck. Dalt and Nik aren't going because they want to get back to the kids but you're coming, right?"

"No. I...I..." I glance at the long-legged, flawless beauty tugging on his arm and she flashes a perfect, white-toothed smile at me. I smile in return before she walks back to the group waiting for D.

I suppose some women might want to scratch out the woman's eyes who will be with their man, but I'm determined to face reality. D's not my man, and he never will be. Reality sucks big time. She's the type he wants: gorgeous, glamorous, exotic. It's not her fault she's...perfect.

"Give me a minute, Gigi. You okay, Pip?" And there it is. I'm Pip, and she's freakin' Gigi.

"Yeah. I mean no. I'm...I'm not feeling too good. I'm

going to head home. I just wanted to say great game tonight. You were on fire out there." My eyes are starting to burn as I hold back the imminent tears.

Dammit. I will not cry. Why *now* for Pete's sake? I've been lusting over this big dope for seven years, I have to pick this place and time to have a complete meltdown? I turn toward the exit. I have to get away from him.

"Wait, Heaven." He grabs my arm and stops me from walking away. I can't remember the last time he called me by my actual name. It should make me happy but instead, being the muddleheaded little fool, I am, it only makes me want to cry more.

He closes the space between us and says softly, "What's wrong? Did something happen tonight? Who do I need to crush?"

His lips are so close to my face, I can feel his warm breath feather my cheek. If I turned my head our lips would be touching. This is ridiculous. I'm trembling like a love-struck puppy.

I'm a twenty-one-year-old woman who has never let another man get beyond a few kisses and awkward fondles because no other man has ever compared to the man standing next to me. This has to stop. I'm sure I'm the only twenty-something virgin left in LA, maybe in California or on the planet! *Who do you need to crush? How about yourself? You big dumbass.*

"Nothing happened." I pry his hand off my arm. "Nothing ever does. That's the problem. I...I mean...I have to go. I have a date." The lie falls from my mouth.

I don't know why I said it, but I like the way it makes his expression change from concerned big brother to angry...I don't know what, but he looks angry. At least anger requires more passion than brotherly concern.

"A date? I thought you said you didn't feel good? What do you mean you have a date?" His thick brows pinch, making him appear even more intimidating than his dark features and six-foot-three frame usually do.

"You know. A *date*? The thing two people who like each other do. They go out *alone*, have fun, maybe go home *alone* together and...well, you know. Like what you'll be doing with *Gigi* tonight in some bathroom stall somewhere."

His silver eyes darken to a stormy grey, making him look even angrier. I don't feel like crying anymore. I'm bold, empowered. Sass is my bitch. I start to walk away, but he grabs my arm again, this time a little tighter.

"The hell you are," he snarls.

"Excuse me?"

"You are not going to do what me and Gi...I mean... who are you going out with? We never talked about this." He raises his voice. The crowd waiting for him stops conversing. Every head turns to see what's going on.

"Stop it," I whisper. "You're making a scene. What will your friends think? And since when do I need to talk to you about who I'm going out with?"

"I don't give a fuck who hears us." He glares at the stunned group waiting for him. Apparently, his wordless stare sends the message to disregard the crazy man still decked out in his goalie uniform yelling at his friend. Every head turns at the same time and resumes their conversations, ignoring me and D.

He opens a nearby door and tugs me inside. It

45

appears to be an equipment closet filled with hockey sticks, nets, buckets, and other things I don't have time to process before D drops his helmet and gloves and pushes my back against the closed door. He stands in front of me with barely enough space between us to keep us from touching.

"What are you doing, Pippa?"

"What am *I* doing? What are you doing? You're not my father, and I don't need another big brother getting all up in my personal space. And stop calling me Pippa! I'm a twenty-one-year-old woman! I'm not your Kewpie doll." For a fleeting moment, his brows twitch in questioning sadness.

"What the hell does that even mean? I never thought you were my fucking Kewpie doll," he hisses back at me, his angry scowl returning. "I'm just saying, we've always discussed who you date and how you want to wait for the right guy before you...before you..."

"Before I what? *Fuck*?" I snap back. "You're right. I'm certainly *not* your *fucking* Kewpie doll. Also, I'm pretty sure my waiting for the right guy was your fucked-up idea, not mine."

"Don't. You never talk like that." He shakes his head and runs his hand back over his sweat-slicked hair.

"No, I never talk like that, and I never *do* it, either. But it's going to change. I guess I'm going to have to start looking for the *right* guy. Apparently, he isn't going to come knocking on my door. Seems to have worked out pretty good for Dak and Dalt. They fucked all over the place before they found their Ms. Rights and now they're living their happily ever afters. And look at you. You've got a new woman every few days who's willing to humiliate herself for you. Why is it okay for you guys, but not for me?"

"I'm not looking for a fucking happily ever after, and besides, you just said it. We're guys!" He punches the door behind me.

"What!" I smack my palms against his pad-covered chest. It's like smacking a brick wall. "Don't even go there with the 'we're guys' crap. I'm not looking for a forever after, either. I just don't want to do this anymore." I wave my hand between us.

"Do what?" he says in a quiet voice and steps closer.

"Beg you for something you're not willing to give me."

"Don't do this, Heaven." He closes what little space is left between us, towering over me. My small body is enveloped by his massive, strong presence. My breasts squash against his chest protector.

"Don't fuck some random guy." His soft words ricochet off every sensory nerve in my body. I involuntarily arch into him. Even through all his pads, I feel the rumble in his chest as the growl moves up and out of his throat.

"I don't want to fuck some random guy," I whisper. "I...I want it to be you. You know I've always wanted it to be you." I close my eyes and part my lips, waiting. Waiting for the inescapable kiss he seems to want as much as I do. But then the weight of his glorious body is gone when he steps back. I'm left cold and trembling against the door, alone. Alone, like I am every time he walks away from me.

"I...fuck. No..." He shakes his head. "Don't be a little fool." He dips his chin and doesn't look at me.

"A little fool? I just told you I want you to fuck me and your only response is to call me a fool?"

"I'm not what you need," he mumbles, glancing up at me from under his long, dark lashes.

"You're exactly what I need, D," I state, my voice adamant and strong. "I'm twenty-one, a graduate student in a doctorate program. I can recite every muscle in the body with origin and insertion and how those muscles respond during sexual exertion. I have the useless knowledge to describe the way the blood flows and which hormones are released during an orgasm. But I've never had a chance to *experience* what happens emotionally and physically between a man and a woman during sex."

He shakes his head like he doesn't like where this is going and wants me to stop. But I keep right on telling him like it is.

"I don't want to know the *science* of sex, D. I want to feel it." I lower my voice to a velvet whisper. I'd like to be touching him with my hands, but since he's still covered in protective hockey pads, I'm going to use my soft words to caress him. "I want to feel the trembling excitement when a guy undresses me. I want to feel the warmth rushing through me when he runs his hands down my body and touches me in secret places, places where he can feel what he's doing to me. I want to smile in satisfaction when I stroke him and realize the power I have to make him respond. I want to explode into white-hot flames and lose all control when he pushes into me and takes me over the edge." If he touches me in secret places now? No amount of protective gear is going to keep me from touching him—*everywhere*—in return.

He groans and runs his fingers through his hair again. "Pip. Please," he begs me like my words are causing him pain. But I show no mercy.

"You're right. It shouldn't be with some random guy." I place a hand on his cheek. "And despite what you think, I'm not such a little fool. Who better to share a first-time experience with than my best friend? A friend who cares about me."

He's looking straight into my eyes when I finish explaining all the reasons why he should be the one to deflower me. I can almost see flames in his half-lidded, covetous gaze. I'm confident he understands. But then he shoves my hand off his face and closes his eyes.

"I...damn it. I can't." There's such grit in his voice, for a second I think he's going to punch the wall again. Instead, he blows out a huge breath. His voice drops to a whisper. "I *do* care about you. You're...I'm...I have to fucking go. Gigi's waiting."

"Gigi's waiting? Really? You really are a jerk. You know that?" I huff out.

"What the hell are you talking about, Pippa?" The angry tone returns to his voice. No one is whispering now. *He's* angry with *me*. I'd laugh if I weren't so flattened by his response. "Why are you doing this? You know we can't. We're friends, and you're Dak's baby sister, for chrissakes."

"I'm no one's baby anything." This time when I

49

shove him, he loses his footing and steps back, giving me time to yank the door open.

"Maybe not. But you *are* my best friend," he says in a hushed tone.

"Yeah. You're my best friend too," my tone matching his. "But sometimes...I really hate you." I turn and run from the closet and down the hall. This time he doesn't stop me from leaving.

—

My shiny white Audi convertible glistens under the LED lighting in the VIP lot outside the players' entrance. I drop into the driver's seat and grip the steering wheel in an attempt to keep myself from sobbing. I will not fall apart.

D doesn't come after me. I didn't expect him to. *Gigi* is waiting. *Dammit. I should've known better.*

Ironically, Wolfe's so-called reprobate status may have been the very reason I fell so in lust with him and chose him as the designated recipient of my V-card. Well, besides his model face and Mr. Olympia body.

My dad says I'm a sucker for taking in strays. A broken things collector, so to speak, confident I can help them or fix them: cats, dogs, birds, turtles, and even people.

I'm obviously no expert on damaged, beautiful bad boys, but in my opinion, those guys weren't born bad. Something happened to them somewhere along the way which froze their hearts inside those picture-perfect exteriors.

I don't mean bad boys who are robbing banks or selling drugs on street corners. I'm talking about the guys who *think* they don't want any long-term commitment or affection and definitely aren't interested in giving any. The guys who don't have to work at being attractive. They nonchalantly ooze sex from every pore, and the ladies flock to them. They use those willing women one after the other and then discard them with a casual 'see ya.' I mean, what is it with these guys? They have the power to turn intelligent, level-headed women into quivery, giggling idiots. And I've joined the ranks. It's infuriating.

I push the ignition button and then the button for the power roof. It's a warm September evening in Santa Ana...although, I'm shivering like it's December in Aspen. I tug the elastic band from my wrist and wrap it around my hair in a ponytail. Even though I'm shivering, I relish the brisk wind blowing across my face as I fight the traffic leaving the arena and drive the few miles to my bungalow in Long Beach. I can't wait to get back to the tranquility of waves crashing onshore. Maybe the repetitive sound will lull away the mess going on inside my head.

My phone buzzes in my pocket. I take it out and throw it onto the passenger seat without looking at it. I don't want to talk to anyone right now.

I almost wish my date lie wasn't a lie. Having a meaningless someone to screw me senseless would be a welcome distraction, wipe D from my mind.

The phone vibrates against the leather seat with another incoming call. I'm stuck in jammed up traffic trying to exit the stadium, so I pick it up. The screen lights up with Wolfe's stunning face. His eyes are looking directly into my camera lens with a slight squint, giving him a real wolf's dark, predatorial appearance—the one it gets when it's ready to overwhelm its prey. I took the photo a few weeks ago when we were walking down the beach after surfing.

It's unsettling as I stare at the screen and recognize the power Wolfe's face has to destroy all sense of self-preservation. He has a face no woman can resist. The kind which looks like he's had the best freaking orgasm of his life—or he's about to give you yours. Sultry wolf eyes which say, 'I'm going to devour you' and full plump lips which silently say, 'let me.'

In the photo, he has a Winds cap turned backward on his head, and his long hair is hanging to his shoulders, the salty ocean water making it even more wavy than usual. His tanned muscles are glistening with water droplets, and the way his sexy glare pierces right through the screen shoots aching sensations down to my core.

I swipe the decline button, turn the ringer off, and toss the phone onto the seat again.

I can't avoid him forever. I'll have to talk to him eventually, but not now. I'm not ready to have a sensible non-emotional conversation with him.

When I get back to my house, I drop my keys onto the kitchen counter on the way to my bedroom. Before putting my phone on the night table next to the bed, I notice there are several messages and two more missed calls from D.

I can't deal with any more D drama tonight. I don't know what to say to him. Offering him my V-card and him turning me down yet again, like I'm a fangirl puck bunny begging for some action, is about as much humiliating rejection as I can take for one night.

Stripping off my Wolfe number 30 jersey, jeans, and bra, I drop them where I stand and grab a t-shirt from the folded clean laundry—still waiting to be put away—piled high on my Narl chair. Only after I slip it on do I realize it's a Winds t-shirt with Wolfe's name on the back. *Gah.* All my clothing is branded with his name. Just like my heart.

In the bathroom, I splash water on my face and give my pearly whites a quick brush to pretend I didn't skip one, obligatory three-times-a-day brushing.

At last, I can climb into bed and get myself into a cozy, protected, fetal position under my puffy bubble quilt and sheets. I'm pleasantly cocooned under my bedcovers when I think I hear a knock at the door. Since the sheets are rustling around my head, I'm not sure if I imagined it.

I lie still for a moment, then shake my head at the deafening silence. *You're really losing it.* But then another louder, more frantic knocking on the door confirms I haven't lost my mind and I'm not imagining it. Sitting up, I glance at my phone. Who the hell is knocking on my door at eleven thirty at night?

I stomp toward the door like a grizzly bear who's been disturbed from her winter's hibernation. It's not until I have the door halfway ajar I realize I didn't bother to check or ask who it was before opening it.

When I see Wolfe standing there, all desire to growl is replaced by an immediate urge to purr. He's gorgeous, standing there in a plain white V-neck t-shirt stretched across his broad chest, accentuating his bronzed skin and dark features. His distressed washed out jeans hug his bulging goalie thighs.

"Well, here I am. What are your other two wishes?" With one look at his sly smile, I find myself crossing my legs again.

It's ridiculous. I'm like Pavlov's dogs—the human, sexual version. One look at him, one cheeseball pick-up line, and I'm throbbing with desire. Positive note, with all this clenching, I'll never have to exercise my thigh muscles at the gym again. Negative note, every particle of my soul screams at me to slam the door. But I don't listen.

Chapter Four

WOLFE

Damn. She's got my t-shirt on. Nothing else. And it looks hot as fuck on her. I clamp my eyes closed for a second, but I still see her: tropical ocean blue eyes, plump lips, long legs. She's in my head, every day, all day.

Coming here unannounced might have been a bad idea, but I have to make this right. I tried to call before coming over. She wouldn't answer her phone. For once I'm trying to do the decent thing, trying to do what's best for her.

"Well, I'm here. What are your other two wishes?" I open my eyes and deliver the dumb line to ease the tension. When I look at her again, I notice her long dark hair is tousled like she's been satisfyingly fucked. *Fucking hell.* Did she do it? Is the dickwad still here?

"What are you doing here?" Her curt tone says she's not amused by my funny line. She leans from side to side looking out into the street behind me. Maybe the dickwad isn't here yet, and she thought I was him. *Too bad.* I'm not leaving.

"That's it? What am I doing here? You can do better than that."

"No. I can't. I'm tired and not in the mood for any more stupid games." Ouch. She usually giggles at my cheeseball pick-up lines, and I look forward to whatever cheddar she comes up with in return. It *is* a stupid game, but it's *our* stupid game, the one we've shared for years.

"Where's *Gigi*?" She spits the name out as if a bug flew into her mouth.

"I took her home. I wasn't feelin' it tonight." I shrug.

"Wow. The great sloot slayer wasn't feelin' it tonight?" Uh oh. She air quotes around the words 'feelin' it.' I know when Pippa starts air quoting, she's pissed. "I'm shocked. Word on the street is D. Wolfe is *feelin'* it somewhere with someone *all* the time."

"A little harsh, don't you think, Pip?"

"No. I don't think, and I told you to stop calling me Pip."

"No, you didn't. You told me to stop calling you *Pippa*." I smirk. She did, in fact, tell me to stop calling her Pippa, not Pip. But the semantic truth doesn't stop her from trying to slam the door in my face. I hold my hand against it to stop her.

"Can I come in for a minute? Are...are you alone?"

"Am I alone?' She hmphs through her nose. "Yeah. I wasn't '*feelin'* it tonight.' She slaps my words back to me. I know she's angry. But anger or not, her snarky state-ment is a relief and I regain the ability to take in a breath.

"You want to come in here?" Her voice raises an

octave as she jerks her thumb over her shoulder. "You actually want to come into the lion's den all by yourself?" she scoffs.

"C'mon, Pip...uh, Heaven. Give me a break. I just want to say sorry about what happened earlier."

"What exactly did happen earlier, because I'm confused." She quirks a brow and crosses her arms over her chest. I want to grab her and kiss the smug look off her face, but I don't dare because I'll never be able to stop at a kiss.

I blow out another huge breath. "Can we talk about it inside?"

Without saying another word, she steps aside and waves me into her house.

The arched oak-plank door, which looks like it belongs on a elves' cottage, opens directly into the small living room. The house smells like her; caramel and vanilla. I close my eyes again and take in a deep breath, adrift in intoxicating Heaven. The door slamming behind me snaps me from my euphoria.

Even though I've never seen it before, I knew her bungalow would look like this. It has Heaven written all over it. Sky blue walls with vivid white molding surrounding the windows, floor, and ceiling. Her baby blue surfboard is propped against the wall next to the door. Framed artwork and photos cover the walls: breaking waves, surfing action shots, some anonymous people in various states of exercise.

It's the perfect house for Pippa: small bungalow beach house, sunny and inviting—even though it's close to midnight and there's no actual sunshine contributing to the cheerful vibes. Nor—at the moment—is the mistress of the house.

"Welcome to my spider web," she snarks. I guess my avoiding coming inside her house hasn't gone unnoticed. It's not that I don't want to be alone with her. On the contrary, *all* I want is to be alone with her. And that's the problem.

I inexplicably care about Pip to the point I can't allow her to become another notch on my hockey stick. This is all new territory for me. I've never turned down a ready and willing woman. Pip's a girl/friend I've watched blossom into the most gorgeous, amazing woman I've ever known. She is also a friend who has told me a hundred times how she's saving herself for the right guy. As much as I want to help her out with her current desires, and as many times as she's suggested *I'm* the right guy, she's wrong. She's waited this long. No sense in giving in to misplaced hormonal urges now. But Christ, when she was describing what she wants earlier tonight, I wanted to tear her clothes off and take her right there on the closet floor.

But Pip deserves way more than a quick fuck on a closet floor. She *does* deserve the right guy: the guy who's going to worship her, love her, be devoted to her. Sure as hell isn't me. I'd take what I wanted and walk away like I always do. Obviously, something you don't do to a friend.

"Have a seat. I promise I won't bite, *bébé*," she puffs out in a resigned tone, mimicking Gigi's term for me— and anyone else she's conversing with.

"Thanks." I run a hand down the back of my neck.

Damn. I don't want things to be awkward between us. I don't want to lose Pip as a friend, which is precisely why I can't fuck her.

I have to set some clear boundaries and stay within those lines. I have to stop thinking about her rosebud lips, spellbinding turquoise eyes, perfect handful size tits, fuckable ass. Right. Seems I'm off to a shit start.

I walk between the two large, teal blue pod chairs and around the coffee table to take a seat on the small bright yellow sofa against one wall. It feels like it's been stuffed with clouds. Under the coffee table is a rainbow-colored rug. The pattern resembles colorful abstract waves. The room screams beach, sunshine, and Heaven.

It's only after she sits next to me I realize I should've sat on a chair rather than the sofa. Her leg brushes against mine when she sits. I'm hyper-aware of the sensation shooting straight to my balls.

"I like your place." We both make an awkward shift, trying to create some space between us. But the sofa is small and soft, and I'm...not. Not with her this close. *Boundaries.*

"Sloot slayer," I taunt to distract my suddenly attentive dick. "Where'd you get that? Have you been perusing the Urban Dictionary again?" I hold back the grin from spreading across my face. She's so damn cute when she's being all feisty. She's like sunshine with a little bit of hurricane.

"Oh. Yes. In all my virginal spare time I memorize the Urban dictionary so I can communicate with *you* in the coolest way possible."

She's not too far off the mark. Not about communicating with me or memorizing the dictionary, but about spending her 'virginal' spare time reading tacky romance novels when she's not studying or surfing.

"I know you don't do it to communicate with me. But it wouldn't be the first time you surfed through the Urban Dictionary to find out what the quirky terms mean they use in those trashy books you read."

"You're ridic..."

"How about the time you looked up the word 'robo-coitus' because you didn't know it meant having video chat sex?" I chew on my lip to keep from smiling.

"When I asked you, you didn't know what it meant either." She crosses her arms over her chest and flops back onto the sofa.

"Oh, right. I'm a computer geek in *my* spare time. Of course, I knew what it meant. But you wouldn't believe me. You said I was wrong, had a one-track mind, and you were going to look it up. I remember how much you hated having to admit I was right."

"Well, I wasn't wrong about you having a one-track mind." She tilts her head and smirks. "And the *romance* novels I read are *not* trashy. They're beautiful stories about love and devotion."

"Sure. You read two a week because they're such a huge contribution to the literary world of art and love." I give her a crooked smirk right back. "Not what you said when you were reading the chapter to me last week on the beach. You know, the one where the guy was standing behind the girl, ripped off her panties and..."

"Whatever." She waves me off. "I think they're an enormous contribution to bringing more love and happiness into the world." Her voice softens. "And I also read them because they're good learning tools: references on the hottest, most pleasurable ways to have sex."

Fuck. Her voice may have softened, but I didn't. Her words succeed in wiping the smirk off my face and dropping my thoughts right between my legs. *Boundaries*.

"Um." I shift again and attempt the impossible task of making the sofa stretch a few inches. But in shifting, my leg brushes hers again, and we jump like we simultaneously stuck our fingers into an electrical outlet. "Which brings me to the reason I came over tonight."

"To read swoony sex scenes and get some pointers?" she teases, stretching her long, toned legs across the antique trunk which serves as a coffee table.

My gaze follows her legs and then drifts up to where her t-shirt has shifted a little higher on her legs. My cock twitches in expectation. *Down, boy. This is Pippa.*

"We've never had a problem being straight with each other. Have we?" She shakes her head and nibbles on her thumbnail. "So, let's be honest now. I know what you want. I mean, I get it. Maybe I can help."

"Really?" She pops up excitedly and tucks her legs under her. Lunging toward me, she wraps her arms around my neck. "I knew you wanted this too. This will be perfect."

Climbing onto my lap and straddling my hips, she grinds down on my more than eager cock. *Christ almighty.* They both seem to be misunderstanding my intentions since they didn't give me a chance to finish my statement.

"I promise I won't get all clingy or expect anything

61

from you. I just don't want to be the first one in history to start graduate school as a virgin. There's no one else I'd rather share my first time with."

I lean away from her, but my back hits the sofa arm. There's nowhere to go without throwing her off me. She presses herself against me and crashes her lips onto mine. Her sweet lips are soft and delicious. When her tongue traces the seam of my lips, game over. I may be experienced, but I have no experience whatsoever in practicing restraint.

I open and delve my tongue into her mouth: probing, investigating, tasting her, my tongue dancing with hers. I grab her plump little ass and pull her further against my hard-on. Her shirt is pushed up to her hips. The only thing separating my fingers from the woman I've been fantasizing about for so long are her satin panties.

I can feel her moist warmth through my jeans. Moving my hand down between us, I stroke her through the wet fabric. She shivers in my arms. I move the meager obstacle to one side and run my fingers over her soft damp curls before sliding one finger inside her. She lets out a gasp and clenches around my finger.

Damn. She's so tight, and her silky warmth is dripping for me already. *Fuck.* I want her so bad I'm ready to explode. But this is her first time. I need to make this special for her.

She whimpers when I circle my thumb over her throbbing clit. I continue stroking her gently and wonder if any other man has ever touched her like this. I push her back onto the sofa and stretch out over her. She hasn't said one word, just keeps making soft mewling sounds. Thrusting up into my hand, she silently begs for more, as I continue to tease her clit and fuck her with my fingers. She bites down on her bottom lip like she's savoring every sensation. Her eyes are pinched shut, but my eyes stay fixed on her. I'm enthralled. I've always thought Heaven was a beautiful girl but at this moment, flushed in longing, she's the most stunning woman I've ever seen.

Her eyes open in a drowsy, half-lidded gaze. The sparkling eyes which stopped my heart the first time I saw them are darkened with lust, pleading for something I know Heaven has never had before. My cock thickens against my jeans, aching to be inside her. As I reach down to unzip my pants, she whispers, "Mmm. Are you a campfire? 'Cause you're hot and I want s'more." Only when she purrs out the silly pick-up line, do I snap back to my senses and down from my Heaven. Literally.

"Wait. Heaven." I slip my fingers from her warm, clenching pussy and stand up so fast Pippa nearly topples off the sofa.

"What...what's wrong, D?" Pippa's voice quivers. "Did...did I do something wrong?" I want to kill myself for putting the insecure quiver in her sweet voice.

"No. No. You didn't do anything wrong. You're... I'm...I'm sorry. This...this is a mistake. Fuck!" I scrub my hands down my face. *What the fuck am I doing?* "You... you misunderstood what I meant by 'help you.'"

"Misunderstood?" Her shirt is pushed up, revealing her tiny waist and tanned, flat stomach. Her skin is covered in goosebumps, and she's trembling. I can see her dark curls glistening with juices from the unfinished arousal I caused. Her chest is heaving up and down with every breath she takes, offering up her puckered nipples through her shirt.

I want to bend down and suck one of those taut buds into my mouth right through the thin fabric and then continue down to lick and suck those sweet juices. Finish what I started, send her into a sensual delirium, make her feel all the pleasure she's been longing for.

This is Pippa. Boundaries. My self-inflicted safe words pound over and over inside my head, matching my manic overexcited pulse. *How the hell did I let this happen?*

"I...I didn't mean *we* should...*I* should..." I try to explain through my sexually muddled brain.

Blowing out a big breath, she adjusts her skewed panties, tugs her shirt down to her knees, and sits up so guardedly it appears to be slow motion. She tilts her head, and her angel-like face scrunches into a perplexed look.

"You said you wanted to help me," she whispers, as those shimmering, questioning eyes drill right into my heart

"I did. I do. But not...not like this." I run my hand down the back of my neck again and will myself not to reach out for her. *Fuck.* What a mess!

"No? It certainly looks and *feels* like you want to help me like this." Looking straight into my eyes or maybe it's straight into my soul, she leans forward and runs her hand down the hard shaft pressing against my jeans. My throbbing dick doesn't want to accept the abort message from my brain. He has no experience whatsoever in restraint, either.

I place my hand atop hers to stop her from stroking me. I can't take much more. I'm trying to do the right thing, be the good guy for once in my life. But I'm no fucking saint. "Listen to me, Pip."

"Oh, we're back to the innocent baby Pip thing again, huh?" She lets out a frustrated sigh and flops back against the sofa.

"You're always going to be my innocent, sweet Pip," I confirm, as I sit down next to her and reach over to brush her hair behind her ear. But she slaps my hand away.

"Sorry." She shakes her head. "But I need you to stop touching me." I understand. Now more than ever. Every time we touch, I never want to stop touching her. I want to run my hands down her body and light her on fire with every stroke.

"If you didn't come here to help me retire my V-card why did you come?" she asks in a frustrated voice.

"We're friends, Pip. I don't want things to be weird between us."

"I don't want things to be weird either." She shrugs and grabs a throw pillow, clutching it to her chest. It has the words *If it swells, ride it* printed on it. Jesus. I know it's in reference to surfing, but I have to reach down and subtly adjust my very hard, resolute cock at the double entendre.

"We've always been able to talk about everything and help each other figure things out. Right?" This is nuts. We're both still sizzling from my foolish actions. How the hell am I going to explain this to her in a non-hormonal, non-crazed way?

"I guess." She puffs out another big breath.

"I can't...you know...we can't..." I wave my hand back and forth between us, but I can't bring myself to say the words. Just the thought makes me harder.

"Fuck?" Pippa doesn't haven't any problem spitting the word out. I close my eyes and bite my lip at her straightforward question. "What? You said we have no problem talking about things. Why should this be any different? I get it. You don't want to fuck me because you're not attracted to me in that way."

"No...I mean yes...I mean...I think you're really cute. I..."

"Cute! Like a puppy? Gee thanks." She pouts.

"No. Not like a...fuck. I'm not good at talking about this stuff."

"No. I suppose not. I never heard anyone accuse you of being an amazing *talker* when it comes to this stuff." She's right. Talking has never been my forté when it comes to *this* stuff.

I scratch my head to give myself a minute to think about how to say what I need to. "You're beautiful, Pip. The most beautiful girl I've ever seen. If things were different...I mean any guy would be lucky to...to..."

"To fuck me?" She tilts her head, bats her lashes, and flashes a devilish grin, driving me wild. She's not so innocent, after all. She knows exactly what she's doing to me.

"Yeah. That. Even though you're being a little jerk right now."

"*I'm* being the jerk?" She quirks a brow.

Before I have a chance to respond, a grey scraggy fluff ball pounces onto my lap and scares the shit out of me. I jump about a foot into the air and stretch my arms out in either direction, so I don't touch the bizarre looking creature.

Yet another relationship I've never indulged in—owning a pet. Who the fuck wants to be saddled with the commitment pets require?

The cat—at least I think it's a cat—is pretty nimble for only having three legs and he's purring so loud he's vibrating against my chest like a lawnmower. The thing keeps rubbing against me and has apparently decided I'm his new best friend.

"Uh, who and what is this?" I shift from side to side to keep the thing from licking my face without having to use my hands to touch it.

"Stop it, Hal." Pippa scoops *Hal*—I'm thinking Quasimodo would be a more fitting name—off my lap. "You picked the wrong person to fall in love with. This guy doesn't like to be cuddled," she informs the creature in baby speak while pouting her lips. The way he's rubbing against her tits, and she's nuzzling her nose into him while scratching his belly, I'm getting ready to yell, "yes I do. I love being cuddled." Maybe in my next life, I'll come back as a cat.

"What the hell happened to him?" I ignore her remark and brush off the fur gifts Quasi deposited all over my shirt.

"He was hit by a car. I found him by the side of the road and took him right to the vet. Dr. Sharon managed to save him, but couldn't save his leg." She plants a kiss on the top of his head and I'm captivated by her tenderness.

"Hmm. That's...uh...that sucks." Christ. I'm jealous of a fucking mutant cat.

"It's okay. He's adapted. I don't think he even notices he's missing a leg anymore." She bends and gingerly places him on the floor. "Okay, baby. Go find Sheldon and snuggle with him."

"Sheldon?" *Who the hell is Sheldon?*

Pippa doesn't have time to explain before another malformed being lumbers into the room. This one appears to be a dog—a one-eyed dog. The beast looks to be a mixed breed Pug with a hair wisp growing from the top of his head. And it has to be the ugliest damn dog I've ever seen.

"This, I take it, is Sheldon? Interesting name."

"I named him after the Sponge Bob character. You know, because he has one eye," she whispers, as if *Sheldon* can understand what she's saying and would be devastated to find out he's disfigured.

Fuck knows why, but *I* whisper, "Did Sheldon get hit by a car too?"

"Oh no. He was an abused rescue baby. I got him at the shelter where I was volunteering." She bends over and scratches Sheldon's head, running her fingers through the bizarre wispy, disheveled fur. This girl is pure love. Now I know for sure what I have to do. I have to make sure she finds the right man to share it with.

"You volunteer at a shelter?" I glance around, expecting to see a menagerie of aberrant animals.

"I used to. I had to give it up because of my classes

and internship. There just isn't enough time." She shrugs a shoulder. "It's probably for the best, anyway," she adds, like she's trying to convince herself. But the sadness in her voice is obvious. "I wanted to adopt all the abandoned fur babies, and I don't have enough space for them here."

"Are...are there more?" I give another nervous glance around the room.

"Just one. Would you like to meet him?" Her eyes are sparkling again with excited anticipation.

"Sure." I'm not about to disappoint her one more time or take the twinkle from those beautiful eyes again. The least I can do is take a few minutes to meet her adopted beasts.

She stands up and reaches her hand out to me. I wrap my hand around hers. The instant warmth which flames through me is startling. She stands still for a moment, gazing first at our entwined hands, and then up into my eyes. She was right. It's better if we don't touch each other. But somehow, I can't let go of her hand. It's so...good.

After the brief silence, she leads me down the hall toward what I assume are the bedrooms. I'm actually shaking like it's the first time I've been led to a woman's bed. I know if she brings me to her bedroom, I won't be able to stop myself this time.

She stops at a door, pushing it open and leading me inside. The warm air in the room in contrast to the cool temperature in the hall is like a punch in the face.

"I have to keep it warm in here. He likes it around eighty degrees."

"He?"

She drops my hand and walks over to an aquarium. Even in the heated room, I'm left with the cold loss of her warm touch.

"Come here. He won't bite. He's very sweet." She gestures for me to look into the huge glass encasement. The aquarium is on a long table and is about five feet in length. "He's a box turtle. I'm helping to rehab him. Since I can't go to the shelter, I'm doing it here."

When I look into the aquarium, I almost want to laugh at the pathetic site. I mean I'm not a cruel SOB... well, maybe I am. But in this case, the reason I'm holding back a chuckle is because the poor guy has what appears to be a modified sanitary napkin taped to his shell. Other than the humiliating circumstance, he seems to be living in luxury in his glass condo. He even has his own gray pottery mini pond.

"What happened here?" I bite back a smile.

"He was also found on the side of the road. We think a dog got to him. But he's been all cleaned up and taped. He's healing, really coming along." She takes a banana from a bowl next to the tank, peels it, and breaks off a piece. Reaching down into the aquarium, she holds the banana out. The turtle lumbers over and grabs it from her fingers.

"Yes. you're doing great now, aren't you, Wolfe?" Apparently, smooshy baby talk is the only language pets understand. *Wait. What did she say?*

"Did...did you just call him Wolfe?" No way she named this pitiful turtle after me.

"Oh. I...um...well...yes." She doesn't look up at me

when she answers, and she doesn't offer any further explanation.

I push for one. "Why?"

"I...I just did. What difference does it make? Let's go. It's too hot in here." She turns and leaves me standing there staring down at my absurd namesake.

I follow her back into the living room, but she's not sitting on the sofa. She's standing in the middle of the room, her back to me. She brushes her hand across her face. Fucking hell. Is she crying?

"Hey. Are you okay?" I come up behind her. When I touch her shoulder, she jumps as if I hit her with a branding iron.

"I'm fine." She moves a few steps away from me. "I'm just tired. I think you better go." She turns and slowly brings her gaze up to mine. I see all the sadness and disappointment I assume *this* Wolfe and not Wolfe, the turtle, is responsible for.

"Listen to me." I close the space between us. Putting one finger under her chin, I tilt her head up so she'll look at me while I talk to her.

As soon as I look into her glistening eyes, I know I've made another mistake, and I pull my hand away. I'll never be able to explain anything if I'm this close to her. I take a step back, and she lets out a shuddering sigh.

This is fucking killing me. I want to push her to the floor and rip her t-shirt off her body, give her everything she needs and take what I want. I want to taste her, devour her, pound balls deep inside her. But this isn't about what I want.

"I know you think I'm being an asshole, but I'm

doing my best not to be. You deserve a guy who can commit, fall in love with you, be devoted. I can't give you that. I have the life I want, the one that suits me, doing what I want when I want. No commitment, no answering to anyone, or having to be responsible for someone else's feelings."

"I didn't ask you to marry me, D. Just devirginize me." I'm sorry I made her look at me. I can't handle the gleam in her eyes.

"Jesus, Pip." I grip my neck and tug in frustration. "I can't fuck you and walk out. I care too much about you."

"So, don't walk out." She lifts one shoulder like it's simple.

I shake my head at her naivete. "I'm the wrong guy for you, Pip. The things you need? I don't have them to give."

"Hmm. I'd say your feelings are showing. I thought you said you don't do feelings."

"This is different. You're my friend, for chrissakes! And I want to see you find the guy you deserve. Maybe I can...I thought...maybe I can help you find him."

"You...what now?" The quizzical pinched look taking over her face suggests she's thinking the same thing I am. *I've lost my mind.* I can't give her what she needs, so I'm going to help her find another guy and hand her over?

"You're not the kind of girl who sleeps around with random assholes." *Including me.* "You've always said you're saving yourself for the right person. And I think it's a good plan, a smart plan. I'm going to help you find him."

"Are...are you kidding me right now?"

"No. I get it. You need...I don't know...to experience...ah..."

"Sex."

"Yeah. That." I continue to rub my neck. "But you also need a good guy. Not some dickhole. I can introduce you to some good dudes."

"You want to introduce me to *other* guys." She says it like I just told her I want to introduce her to the male residents at Folsom State prison. "Other guys for me to have sex with?"

"Not *guys.* Just one guy to have sex...to date. But you might have to meet a few before you find the right one."

I don't even know what I'm saying anymore. Can your brain freeze along with your balls? Because I think I'm in some kind of blue-balled stupefied state. I'm spewing these bullshit words from my mouth, but my stomach is in knots thinking about my Pippa with another guy.

No. This is right. I look down at myself. *I can't hurt her. I have to step aside and let it happen for her.* Christ. I have officially lost my mind. I'm reprimanding my own cock.

Pip cartoon shakes her head like she's trying to clear it. She's staring at me in wide-eyed confusion. But not because she noticed me staring at my crotch. "You really want me to sleep...to go out with someone else?"

This. Is. Fucking. Killing. Me. But it's the right thing for her. I'm not. It takes all my resolve to answer her. "I would prefer you wait another ten or twenty years before you sleep...go out with someone. But since we both know it isn't going to happen...yeah. That's what I want." *The hell you do, you fucking dumb ass.* I'm pretty sure that's my frustrated cock reprimanding me right back.

Pippa sucks her full top lip between her teeth. For a moment I think she's going to burst into tears, and if she does, I'm going to wrap her in my arms to soothe her. And if *I* do, I'm going to comfort and soothe her every way I know. And I know lots of ways to soothe a woman. I'm a professional. Or at least I was.

But she doesn't cry. In fact, she doesn't shed one goddamn tear. What she does is stand straight, brush her hair behind her shoulders, and fuckin' smile.

"Okay. Sounds like a plan."

"It...it does?" She could have at least argued with me a little.

"Abso-frigin-lutely! You know a lot of hot hockey players. How 'bout Sanders? He's so hot he melts the ice when he's on it. Jesus. I saw him walk out of the locker room without his shirt on the other day and I almost got pregnant. He'd be per..."

"Fuck that shit. He's a bigger whore than me. And since when do you ogle shirtless guys?"

"Since I've been hanging around outside your locker room." She plops down onto the sofa with a frisky bounce. For chrissakes, this girl has more mood swings than Tiger Woods' golf club. "I never appreciated the testosterone levels swirling around all those hockey boys, but I do now. And I think your plan is fantastic. If not Sanders, how about Carson? His biceps alone are enough to make me come in my pants." She fucking sighs.

"Okay. Enough. I'm not fixing you up with any manwhore hockey players. If I wanted you to fuck some dickhole I'd..."

"You'd what?" She purses her lips.

"I'd nothing. Forget it. And forget hockey players."

"Really? Darn." She pouts those luscious lips. I'm about to say fuck it and suck her teasing lips into my mouth and face fuck her with my tongue until she forgets every other hockey player on the planet. "I hear hockey guys have amazing stamina and enormous..."

"Forget fucking hockey players!"

"I wasn't planning on fucking *every* hockey player, just *one* particularly well-endowed specimen." She blinks her long dark lashes again and smirks.

"Stop fucking with me." I run both hands back through my hair. Little monster.

She's trying to make me jealous talking about getting it on with some other guy. And it's working. Thinking about any one of my teammates getting close enough to her just to breathe in her scent makes me crazy.

"I'm not fucking with you, D," she sing-songs, taunting me. "Exactly the problem."

Fucking hell! I begin pacing the floor. I should take her in my arms and give her what we both want.

Instead, I stop and turn to her. She has to see how crazy this is. "I can't do it. I can't risk hurting you."

"Why would you be hurting me? It's just one friend helping out another. No big deal."

"No big deal? You don't believe that. If it wasn't a big deal to you, you would have slept with someone a long time ago. You wouldn't have thought twice about waiting for the right freaking guy. And I'm not him. Think about it. You don't know...I mean think about how I am. You've known me long enough to know my MO. What happens when I pop your cherry, get up, stick my dick back in my pants and walk out? Are you going to want to go have a pizza with me the next day? And what are you going to do when I fuck some other chick afterward? Will you want to hang out on the beach with me? Go surfing like nothing ever happened? You don't want this, Pip. I'm not a good guy. And I don't do the whole virginal chick thing because it can get too complicated. It requires sensitivity I don't have to give." She doesn't say a word through my rant. She's staring at me through narrowed eyes like she's trying to process everything I'm saying.

"I think you're more sensitive than you realize," she says in a soft voice.

"I'm not. You just see what you want to see. You only see the good in people."

"I see the good in you." She blinks back the unshed tears glazing her eyes.

"No. There is no good to see!" My words come out harsher than I intend, causing her to jump. I sit down next to her again, but I don't touch her. I can't touch her without losing the determination to protect her from me. "Sorry. But you have to understand. The only good thing about me is my friendship with you."

"That's not true. You're a good friend to your teammates, an amazing goalie, and you read computer code like it's your first language. Those are good things."

"Right, and the only reason I have those skills is

because Batt's dad rescued me from the streets and took the time to help me. There's nothing deeper in me waiting to be discovered or saved. Everything else is toxic waste, and I'm not going to contaminate you with my noxious existence."

There's complete silence for an uncomfortable moment. Then Pippa clears her throat and says, "Okay." She blows out a big breath.

"Okay?"

"Yes. I already told you, I won't beg you for what you think you can't give me." Standing up, she walks across the room and opens the front door. "But you do realize you're being ridiculous, right? You'll never be able to fix me up with another guy." She holds the door open.

I stand and walk toward the open invitation for me to leave, stopping in front of her.

"I know. It's going to be the hardest thing I've ever done." I reach out once more to brush her hair behind her ear, but she steps back away from me.

"No." She shakes her head. "I don't mean because I'm so irresistible. I mean because you don't know anyone other than hockey guys and you already declared them off limits. *Sooo...*"

"Bull. I know lots of other guys." I don't know any other guys but manwhore hockey players.

"Like who?" She crosses her arms over her chest.

"Like...um...I need time to think about it." I scratch my head. No way in fucking hell is there anyone out there good enough for her.

"Don't worry about it. I got this." She grins and tilts her head toward the empty street outside her door.

"What do you mean you got this? Wait. Tell me you're not going to sleep with some random asshole."

"Not cool, D." She shakes her head. "Or fair. I don't ask you about your innumerable hookups."

"Yeah. But I'm a..."

"Uh. I wouldn't revisit your chauvinistic beliefs at this particular time. I'm not feeling very forgiving." She twists her pursed lips to one side.

"I was just going to say I'm an asshole and you're not." I lift one shoulder in a slight shrug. She's right. I was going to give her the bullshit 'I'm a guy' reasoning again. But what I should be saying is, I'm a *broken* guy with a messed up broken past, and she's...perfect.

"Can't argue with you there." Her mouth tips up in a sweet grin. I want to wrap her in my arms and bury my nose in her hair. I'd be happy just holding her all night and breathing her in. *Jesus.* Since when have I ever wanted to hold a chick without doing anything else? And all night, no less!

"Can you get out now, please? I'm exhausted. I can't talk about this anymore."

I start to walk out the door but stop. Even without touching her I feel the warmth emanating from her body and the light radiating from her soul through her beautiful eyes. I don't care what she says. I'll never let anyone use her, hurt her. Including me.

"I'll call you tomorrow," I whisper but keep my hands fisted at my sides to stop myself from reaching out for her.

"Don't." Her curt tone shocks me. "I need some time to think about stuff and get my head into school."

"Then I'll call you this weekend. The surf's supposed to be..."

"No. My internship starts in two weeks. You have a road trip with a string of away games coming up. I need time to prepare for working at the clinic. I'll call you when you get back."

"Are...are we okay?" In trying to do the right thing, something I've always been shit at, I may have lost her anyway.

"We're good. No worries. I'll call you." She smiles and flicks her chin toward the lonely street. As my legs carry my protesting dick into the dark, desolate night it occurs to me, if I've lost her, I may never have sunlight in my life again.

Chapter Five

HEAVEN

One Month Later

I didn't call D when he got back. I couldn't. When you practically beg a guy to have sex with you, and he stops mid-foreplay and says something like, um, let me find someone to take care of this for you, it's a teensy bit humiliating.

I pretended I was okay with the whole awkward scene, even going so far as to suggest he hook me up with a teammate. But what I really need is to distance myself from D and try to cleanse my system from all Wolfe-related desires.

Wolfe does things to my hormonal levels which are lethal. I can't seem to stop myself from wanting my lecherous friend. He's like a drug I need just to get through the day, even if there are dangerous side effects as long as my arm. I haven't even gone to any Winds games since he's been home. It's too difficult to see him and not crave him.

Making my way into my house after a long day in the clinic I drop my keys and computer bag on the coffee table and collapse onto the sofa. Hal jumps into my lap, whining in my face for attention. Sheldon saunters into the room and sits obediently at my feet but barks when he doesn't get the recognition he wants fast enough. I bend to scratch his head while holding Hal under one arm.

We were extra busy today. Every muscle in my body aches to the point where I should have been the one to climb onto a treatment table. As I sit up and let my head drop back onto the sofa, a muffled rhythm beats inside my bag. It's D's ringtone—the one I downloaded: *The Wolfe.* If you listen to the song, you'll understand why I'm sure The Spencer Lee Band must've known D when they wrote it.

D keeps calling and leaving voice messages and texts. I answer his texts and make some excuse about school or interning. I don't answer his calls. I can't hear his deep, velvety voice without getting a weird ache between my thighs. The stupid thing is, as much as I want to shun my *attraction* to him, I miss my friend. I can't keep avoiding him.

Pushing myself up and placing Hal on the floor, I slip the phone from its designated pocket in my computer satchel. I'm met with Wolfe's orgasmic face. My finger hovers over the screen; my heart and vagina are doing battle with my brain. My brain's too weary to fight and loses the battle.

"Hey, D. What's up?" I simulate my cheeriest, most aloof voice.

"Geez! Did you drop off the planet? I thought you said you were going to call me when I got back?" I close my eyes and drink in the intoxicating voice I've missed so much.

"I know. Sorry. This internship is killing me. I thought I was in pretty good shape, but I didn't realize how physical this job was going to be. I'm using muscles I didn't know I had."

"You need a break. It's Friday night, and I don't have a game. I'll pick you up in an hour."

"No!" I blurt out, all attempts at indifference lost. "I mean, no." I soften my protest. "I'm too exhausted. I'm just going to sink into a hot bubble bath and then climb into bed." D doesn't answer. In fact, his silence makes me think the call has disconnected until I hear a sound like he's clearing his throat.

"Are you still there?"

"Yeah...um...yeah. Still here. But you're going to need to eat dinner. I'll bring the cardboard tasting vegan stuff you like." He chuckles, and the sound hits me like a lightning bolt to my heart.

"No. I'm even too tired to chew. I'm skipping dinner tonight. I had a late lunch anyway. But thanks for the thought. I'll take a raincheck. Okay?"

"Okay. How about tomorrow morning? I'll take you to breakfast. I have practice at six but don't have a game till eight. We'll have the afternoon."

"Wish I could, but I have a ton of notes to catch up on before Monday."

Part of me is wishing he'd ask me once more and insist on coming over—the bad girl part. She wants to say, "The hell with it. I don't care if you get up, walk out, and go screw every other woman in LA," but I know the truth. If we had sex, I wouldn't be able to stand by afterward and witness his innumerable, somewhat peculiar indiscretions and remain his bemused friend. Guess I'm not as freethinking as my mom.

I've never been a very good bad girl. Ironically, it's sort of my mom's fault. She cursed me with the name Heaven Lee. Say that once, fast. See what I mean? I feel compelled to live up to the label. If Mom had realized the enormous V-jay blocking mistake she was making, she would have named me Jezebel.

In fact, if she knew I'm still as unexplored as the newly discovered ETNO planets, she would most likely start pumping a love potion herbal concoction into me. Not kidding. She has an herbal concoction for just about every situation in life. With love and sex being two things topping her list for happiness, *Love Potion Number 9* could be her theme song.

I realize a mother being dismayed because her daughter is a total stuffed shirt yet remains as unstuffed as possible by any human male is a tad unconventional. That's my mom, an unconventional anachronism right up to her eyelids: a beautiful, happy, loving, born too late, flower child. She believed in marijuana's therapeutic properties long before it became fashionable. Now, CBD oil, non-GMO food—predominantly kale-based—home birth, naked yoga, healing crystals and free love with organic condoms, are her formula for a blissful, fulfilled existence. The key word there being, *love*.

The day I got my period for the first time, Mom announced it was time for our "mother-daughter talk"—as if I wasn't traumatized enough by the bloody river gushing from my body. She tenderly went on to explain —along with the sexually graphic description, which I can never unhear—as long as you *love* the person you're with, having sex is a beautiful thing. Seriously. Stephen Still's *Love the One You're With* is her *actual* theme song. Well, it's her actual default ringtone. I'm thinking she might've misunderstood Stephen's meaning.

Nevertheless, based on Mom's interpretation, she assumes I've '*loved*' at least one person somewhere along my young adult journey. I hate to disappoint her by telling her I'm still as pure as the newborn babies she delivers in homes all over LaLa Land. Did I mention she's a midwife? *How can I be the daughter of LA county's love guru and still be a virgin at twenty-one?*

"What?" D chuckles and blasts me from my inner turmoil. Oh boy. Did I say that out loud? The cricket silence on the phone line after my excuse for not going to breakfast with him, allowed my mind to drift.

"Huh? I...I said...um...I was just wondering how I got so behind in my work. I have twenty-one chapters to read." Hang up before you say something else super stupid.

"Hey, Squirt...you...you avoiding me?" If he *did* hear my actual question, he doesn't let on. Instead, he asks *his* faltering question.

"Of course not," I lie "I just really need to focus on this internship right now."

And I need to focus on the guy I had lunch with. A guy Dak introduced me to. Dr. Joshua Littner. He's a theoretical biologist who specializes in conservation biology. He works at the Marine Institute with Dak and Tracey and has become my brother's latest bromance and current hero.

Dak couldn't stop jabbering over what a great guy Josh is when he was insisting I go on a dinner date with him. After the night at my house when D stopped mid...uh...when D turned me down, I decided it was time to quit fooling myself. Time to put myself out there and make an effort to meet someone else. I agreed to meet Dr. Littner for lunch. Somehow it felt less familiar, not as intimate as a dinner date.

Josh is fantastic: smart, interesting, funny, attentive. And although I was expecting him to be stuffy and professorial in appearance, turns out theoretical biologists can be fun and HAF.

I'm going to give this new relationship a chance and I can't while spending time with D. Maybe after I figure out what's happening with Josh I'll be able to be around D without getting all warm and gooey; be able to enjoy him as a good friend and nothing else.

But I can't explain everything to D yet. I don't know why. It seems weird to talk to him about another guy after what we did or should I say, what we *almost* did. It's not like I have a relationship with Josh yet, anyway. It was only two casual lunch dates.

I'll continue using my new internship as an excuse to

keep my distance from D for a while without having to go into the dirty details. I know I should be honest. But what am I supposed to say? "Sorry, D. I can't be near you without wanting to tear your clothes off." Please allow me to hold onto at least one shred of my dwindling dignity.

"They're transferring me to another clinic in a few weeks, and they say it's going to be even more intense than this one. I need to be proficient in everything before I'm moved to wherever they're sending me. Soon as I get into the rhythm of things, I'll have more time to hang out and surf. I miss being in the water. I need to get out there in the waves before I completely lose my mind."

"Yeah. I miss...surfing too." If I didn't know better, I'd say his quiet tone sounds sad, but this is D. He doesn't do sad. He does disgusted, pissed off, sarcastic, but I've never seen or heard him do sad.

"You know you don't need me to surf, right? You've gotten really good. You can go by yourself now. Or you could teach someone else like...how about Gigi? I'm sure she could handle a surfboard." And all kinds of other big things between her legs.

"Who?" Jesus. He's forgotten Miss Frenchie Swim-suit Model already? Okay. I'm *kinda* happy he doesn't remember her. But she was gorgeous and nice, and she was clearly into him. What more could a guy want? I'll never understand these manwhore hockey players.

"Oh. Yeah. No. I haven't seen Gigi since the night I came to your place and we...um...since that night."

"Really? I'm sorry." Not sorry at all. "I hope it wasn't

because of me." I hope it was totally because of me. "She seemed so nice." And gorgeous and French and perfect.

"Nah. She was...well, you know me. I don't go back to the scene of the crime more than once." He snickers but it sounds more gloomy than happy.

"You okay? You sound strange."

"I'm good," he says, failing at his attempt to be convincing. "Just being my broody self when I don't get to see my sweet little Pippa." Of course. What he's missing is his little doll to joke around and hang out with, someone to keep him smiling—like a court jester.

"Right. Well, it won't be long before I see you. We have Dak's and Trace's rehearsal dinner and wedding in two weeks. I hear the place is phenomenal. I can't wait to have a few days to relax and enjoy some party time with everyone."

My brother and Trace finally decided to tie the forever knot. They're getting married and having the ceremony and reception at a resort vineyard which overlooks the ocean. The venue is supposed to be spectacular and impossible to book. But since it belongs to an old family friend of Dalt's and he's Dak's best man, he hooked them up.

I'm thrilled for my brother, getting to marry his soulmate in a dream location. But selfishly, I'm not looking forward to being partnered at the romantic, lovey-dovey wedding with the groomsman Trace chose for me. Something tells me it wasn't a coincidence I was paired with Wolfe. I'm sure Tracey and Nikki put their beautiful, conspiratorial, matchmaking heads together to plot the pairing. But since Josh is on the guest list, I'll be able to focus on him when all my wedding party duties are fulfilled and keep my mind—and hands—off D.

"The wedding's not for two weeks," he repeats what I just told him.

"I know. Tracey must be frantic. Even with a wedding planner, the final two weeks must be…"

"We're not going to see each other for another two weeks?" He interrupts my try-to-change-the-subject ramble about the wedding. "What the fuck? I thought you said we were good?"

"We are good, D. In fact, you'll be happy to know you can stop looking for my Mr. Right."

"Yeah? Why's that?" For the first time since I told him not to come over, his voice is back to its usual confident tone.

"I'm dating someone—a doctor, an animal conservationist. He's a great guy. I think you'll like him. You'll get to meet him at the wedding." So much for not wanting to tell him about my non-relationship yet. But why should I feel awkward telling him about Josh? D's the one who said he wanted me to date someone else. At least it's better he finds out now, rather than waiting to surprise him with Josh at the wedding.

"You're bringing a date to the wedding?" His question is so quiet I almost can't hear it through the phone speaker.

"No. I'm not bringing him. He's on the guest list. He works with Dak, and he's his friend."

"Dak introduced you to this…this…guy?" He snarls the question a bit louder but doesn't wait for me to answer. "He must be a great guy for Dak to give him the green light to fuck you," he sneers, his voice no longer soft or sad.

"Are you mad at me? I thought you would be happy. Isn't this what you—"

"I have to go. I'm meeting a chick at Pelican Hill. I'm late," he interrupts.

"You're meeting someone at a hotel? But I thought you..."

"Yeah. She's a great girl. I think you'd like her. Mile-long legs. Sweet ass. Gorgeous tits. And she knows how to use them, if you know what I mean. Maybe I'll bring her to the wedding so you can meet her." He's never talked to me like this. I know he has the ability to use his words like arrows to shred his target. I've heard him do it more than once to other people. But never to me. He's trying to hurt me with his vicious words. But no way does his mean boy act fool me.

"Wait. Could you speak up a little? I can't hear you over the noise of the spaceship."

"What are you talking about? What spaceship?" D hisses into the phone.

"The one filled with aliens who just laser fried your brain." I can't resist taunting him about his ridiculous behavior.

"Hardy-fucking har. You're a laugh a minute," he says, but he isn't laughing.

"You think? Because right now you seem to be the one joking around. I don't believe you have someone waiting for you since you asked to come here with dinner for me. And even if there is someone, since when do you describe your skanks' geographical topography to me and what you do with all their hills and crevices?" Also, if you bring her to the wedding, I may have to strangle you with the bride's garter. I keep that one to myself. "What's wrong with you? Why are you being so cruel?"

"Cruel? I'm not being cruel, Pip. I thought you'd be happy for me." Mimicking my words, he emphasizes the word happy. "You know. Because I found someone who has everything I need, everything I want."

He's lucky I can't transport myself over the cellular pings, or I might have to strangle him now instead of waiting for the wedding day.

"Gotta go. See you in two weeks." He disconnects the call.

Does his apparent anger and cruelty upset me? Hell no. I'm enjoying this. Am I being self-centered relishing my best friend's distress? I guess. Do I care? Ahhh. Nope.

What do ya know? The infamous Damon Wolfe, biggest off-the-ice player in hockey land, may be a little bit jealous. What I'm sure must be a huge, smug, Grinch-style grin crosses my face. But even while I'm basking in D's anguish and even though Josh is going to be there, if D brings a Miss Tits and Ass to the wedding, I'm seriously going to follow through with the strangling thing.

Chapter Six

WOLFE

I can't stop glancing over at her. Pippa's sitting next to me; not because she chose to but because the place card directed her to. She's fucking luscious in her strapless azure blue mini-dress which succeeds in intensifying her eye color. The reflection of the twinkling lights on the ceiling glistens throughout the waves of her long dark hair as it tumbles down her back. The candlelight from the centerpieces on the table reveals the touches of shimmering copper strands left by the sun.

I want to run my fingers through it. I want her on her hands and knees while I pull on it and drive into her from behind. Fuck. I have to stop thinking about her as a woman...I mean...as a fuckable woman.

I haven't seen her in almost two months, which might explain the reason I can't stop looking at her. But I have no excuse for the way my dick jolts every time her arm or leg brushes against mine.

My suit is beginning to feel like it's suffocating me, restricting me. If I keep thinking about being between Heaven's legs, I'm going to rip out of my suit pants. Thank fuck we're at a ranch combination winery resort and the ridiculously expensive wine and bourbon keeps flowing. I'm not going to be able to get through this weekend with a clear head.

The Santa Barbara five-hundred-acre ranch is extravagant. I wouldn't expect anything less from the Andersens and Haywards. Money flows through them as freely as the wine is flowing from the bottles tonight.

The rehearsal dinner is being held in an outdoor covered patio overlooking the ocean. Although the temperature isn't what any other American would consider chilly, Californians think anything below eighty degrees frigid. Since temps are threatening somewhere in the low sixties tonight, the massive stone fireplace in the center of the wall to our left is in full swing. With the cool breezes drifting in from the ocean, the atmosphere is what I'm sure anyone with tits would describe as *dreamy*.

The wedding party is seated at one table, and the family members and friends who arrived early and are attending the rehearsal dinner sit at several others. We're all staying at the resort for the extended weekend celebration.

Dak and Trace are glowing like they just shoved sunshine up their asses and it's beaming out of every pore on their bodies.

Two hockey bros down for the count: first Dalt, now Dak. All wrapped up in love's sweet embrace—or the old ball and chain, depending on your perspective. I suppose it's cool—for them. They've got awesome women. But the whole till death forever thing isn't for me, awesome chick or otherwise. It's the reason I can't take my friendship with Pippa to the next level.

She's a diamond girl: shiny, flawless, perfect, daddy's little girl. The kind of girl who deserves all the promises. And I'm going to make sure she gets them by keeping my dick away from her. Even though my dick and I almost made the mistake of getting to know her—intimately. And even though I acted like a complete douche when she told me about the guy she's dating.

I get sick to my stomach thinking about her with someone else. But I can't tarnish her with a one-night learn-to-fuck lesson and then get up and walk away. And I would. It's what I do. It's what I trained myself to do all those years ago on the streets. I don't know anything else. I don't feel anything else after I've elicited the last blissful scream of my name from whoever I've just been inside of, balls deep.

"Hey. Do you have a library card?" I come up with a cornball line and finally make my mouth move.

She turns to me and rolls her eyes. "Why?"

"Because I'm checking you out."

"Yes. I noticed. But you should really eat something and stop staring at me and slurping down the bourbon." Pippa's flippant comment confirms my sly attempt at sideways ogling is an epic fail. "This salad is incredible. It has crab, lobster, shaved truffles, and even a bit of caviar in it."

"I'm not staring at you. Well, I *was*. But only because I was admiring that color on you." I don't usually notice the color of the clothing I want to tear off a woman. But Pip looks hot as fuck in the blue dress.

I push the lump of caviar to the side of my dish. I hate that shit.

"Oh. Okay. Mr. Vuitton. You were only admiring my dress color." She smirks, scoops the unwanted pile of caviar off my plate, and shovels it in her mouth. *Blech.* At least she succeeded in temporarily obliterating any desire to kiss her.

"I just wanted to say I'm sorry about the other night on the phone. I was overtired from the trip and unusually grumpy."

"*Unusually?*" she teases, but stays focused on her disgusting seafood salad. "So, where's Miss T and A?"

"Who?"

"You know. The skank with the Olympian tits and ass. You said you were bringing her." She doesn't look at me, just keeps eating her fucking salad like she's never seen food before.

"Um...about that. There was no Tits and Ass. I made her up." The humiliating admission is as far as I'm willing to travel on the honesty train.

I'm not about to tell her, in fact, there hasn't been any T and A since the night at her house and our curtailed orgasmic interaction. Two months without so much as a ground shaking blow job because all I can think about, all I dream about, is Pippa and her immaculate pussy.

"I know." She turns to look at me.

"What do you mean, you know?"

"I told you. I knew there was no one waiting for you

because you had called to get together with me. What I don't know is why you were so angry you felt you had to lie to me."

"I wasn't angry I was...I was...pissed off about you dating someone and not telling me about it."

"I *was* telling you about it, and you got all territorial and crazy. *I* think you were jealous." She shakes her fork at me.

"I wasn't jealous! I was concerned." I manage to turn the hushed private conversation we're having into a public outburst when I yell out my declaration. Pippa sucks in her lips to hold back her devious little smile.

"Hey! What's going on with you two?" Batt, who's seated to my right, asks. "You having your own private romantic event over there?"

"Yeah, right. Heaven and Wolfe having a romantic conversation," Dak laughs. He tips back his bourbon on the rocks and takes a long swallow. "Not likely."

"Why not likely?" Trace interjects. "I think they make a fabulous couple."

Dak chokes on the spicy liquid sliding down his throat and sprays it out all over his salad. "A couple? Are you kidding? Heaven's a...a...and Wolfe, he's a...a..." He flails his drink around in the air like the words, 'virgin' and 'whore' are somewhere in the air waiting to fall into his glass.

"What exactly are you trying to say, Dak?" Pippa demands.

"I'm not trying. I'm *saying,* if the thought even crosses one of Wolfe's brain cells to get with you he's going to be the only goalie in the NHL with a hockey stick rammed up his ass." He lifts his glass to me like I'm supposed to toast his ridiculous threat. I put my glass down long enough to answer his toast with two very erect middle fingers.

"Fuck you, asshole." I pick up my glass and raise it in my own crappy toast.

"Yes. Dak. Fuck you," Pippa adds and clinks her wine-filled glass to mine.

Everyone at the table stops drinking or chewing and looks at Pippa in wide-eyed shock, and then at Dak to see his response. But Pippa doesn't give him time to respond.

"What? There comes a time in every girl's life when she just has to let the 'fuck yous' rip."

Heaven is a unique girl. She doesn't indulge in cursing because she thinks, *"It's lazy. There are better ways to use one's words to express emotion."* An exact quote. Shit you not. I teased her and said that was *"fucking bullshit."* She punched me in the arm. Anyway, it's the reason everyone is so shocked to hear her demonstrative comment to her brother.

"I'll fucking kill him if he thinks he's..." Dak pushes his chair back, ready to stand and take me down at the suggestion of my hooking up with Heaven. No worries. He isn't thinking anything I haven't thought myself—a million times. I'd kick my own ass around the block if I had a one-nighter with Pip.

Trace grabs his arm to keep him from standing. Batt intervenes, reminding us where we are.

"Now, now, boys. You know I love all you assholes dearly, but remember where the fuck we are and why we're here. Reel in your dueling dicks for the weekend and let's celebrate this special occasion." He raises his glass. "To Trace and Dak. May you have a long, happy and healthy life together cleaning up all the world's oceans and having lots of your own little tadpoles!" He extends his glass toward me, and I don't hesitate to clink to his toast.

Even though Dak and I aren't on a hockey team together or aren't housemates anymore, I still love the pain in the ass like a brother. And Tracey is one of the finest women I know—other than Heaven. I'm happy he's found his happily ever after, even if I'm not looking for one of my own. I also understand and respect his wanting to protect Pippa from me. I don't blame him. I wouldn't expect anything less. It's exactly what I'm trying to do.

"To Dak and Trace," I reiterate Batt's toast. "Still not sure why she decided to marry this big windbag instead of me but I guess I'll have to learn to live with it." Everyone laughs as I raise my glass to Dak.

"Yeah. Right." Dak smirks and touches his glass to mine from across the table. "Trace is way too smart to be interested in a player like you, bro." He glances at Heaven. The responding 'oh sures,' 'ah huhs,' and 'rights,' ripple through the people seated around the table.

"Oh no. You weren't a player at all," Trace teases. "It wasn't a naked girl sprawled out on top of you when I walked into your room while we were dating."

"Oh. Yes. I seem to remember something like that," Nikki continues to taunt Dak. "I'm not sure, but wasn't Dak lying on his back naked while the lady in question—

and I use the term loosely—tried to ride him like a cowgirl?" A unison of agreement is heard around the table.

"I *clearly* remember Tracey was a basket case when she came home for the holidays after that little *misunderstanding*," Sloan, Trace's sister, sneers. She doesn't seem to be enjoying the memory as much as everyone else.

Her Guccified boyfriend seated next to her—who looks like he's in a constant pose waiting for the next photographic shoot—lets out an evil sounding snicker. Sloan picks up her wine glass and takes a long swallow without acknowledging her date's strange display of malevolent pleasure at Trace's distress. In fact, the only person at the table other than me who seems to have noticed the guy's strange response is Batt, who's leering at him like he's about to rip his head off. Since we're technically stepbrothers, I figure we may have developed similar radar when it comes to picking up on dickhead vibes. We make no comment on the guy's strange reaction.

"Oooh. I have one," Heaven calls out, pulling my attention back to the current group task of busting Dak's balls. "Remember the time you thought Mom and Dad were away for the weekend, and you brought those two girls home and..."

"Okay. Enough," Dak interrupts. "We all know the episode with Bri was a misunderstanding. Since the first time I saw Trace, I haven't laid eyes on any other woman. She's the love of my life." He leans over and kisses Trace on the cheek.

"Aww, that's sweet, bro. But it wasn't your *eyes* you

were laying on Bri," Dalt laughs. And Trace pushes Dak's face away from her in a playful rejection because the whole Bri event was resolved between them a long time ago.

"Nice. To my best friends in the whole world and my loving, devoted sister," Dak raises his glass this time. "I just want to say fuck you very much for being here on this special occasion." Everyone laughs and raises their glasses in a toast.

"But seriously," Dak continues. "Thank you all for being here and sharing this weekend with Trace and me. I don't think she would have taken me back and said yes to being stuck with me forever if it hadn't been for you guys. You're our family forever, and we love you." The 'awws' make their way around the table this time.

I glance over to see Pippa brush a tear off her cheek. I hold myself back from running my thumb under her eye to catch a tear.

The main entrees are served amid our toasts. They're the most decadent, delicious looking burgers I've ever seen made from Wagyu beef and foie gras topped with truffle sauce and shaved black truffles, all served on a brioche bun. Everyone goes back to eating when they're served.

"Oooh ma gawd," Pippa moans through a mouthful of burger. "Sooo good."

"You do realize there's a vegan option on the menu, right?" She's been driving me crazy for months with the disgusting vegan restaurants she always wants to go to for lunch. I mean seriously. What the fuck?

She wipes her mouth with her napkin after swallowing the huge burger bite she was moaning over. "Of course I know there's a vegan option. If there wasn't, my mom would have to eat the floral centerpieces." She goes back to drooling over the lavish burger on her plate.

"So why are you eating seafood and meat? I thought you never touched the stuff."

"D," she sighs out my name like I'm too naïve for her to waste her words on. "I've been eating vegetarian or vegan food my whole life. It's what my mother served us, the only thing we ever had in the house. I'm a big girl now, making my own decisions. There comes a time in every girl's life when she has to say fuck it and enjoy diverse choices, tastes." She purses her lips and gives me a narrow-eyed glare.

"Huh. Seems to be a whole lot of things a girl has to say 'fuck' to this weekend." I smirk.

"Exactly. And I intend on doing just that." She quirks a brow and then goes back to chomping on her burger.

Damn. I don't think we're talking about food anymore. Sounds like she's planning on fucking Dr. Douche this weekend.

"Speaking of which, where's Dr. Do...the infamous doctor tonight?"

"He's not here yet. He had lab hours. He'll be here for the wedding, Saturday."

"How fucking awesome for you," I mumble under my breath.

"What?"

"Huh? Oh nothing. Can't wait to meet Mr. Wonderful." I polish off the last swallow in my glass and raise it to the waitress to signal for another bourbon.

"What can I get you, sir?" the perky blonde asks as she bends down to shove her ample cleavage in my face—cleavage I'm uncharacteristically not the least bit interested in.

"Michter's Sour Mash. Double. Straight up." It's going to be a long fucking weekend.

Chapter Seven

HEAVEN

I don't see D all afternoon on Friday. Dak and the guys hang out doing whatever it is guys do the day before a wedding. We girls go to the beach and then spend the rest of the day being pampered in the spa with massages, facials, mani-pedis, and never-ending champagne. By the time we all meet in the bar later in the evening, I'm rubbed, scrubbed, and blissfully floating on champagne dreams.

The cozy ambiance in the lounge immediately makes me feel as if I've stepped back in time. The entire repurposed building was built with huge stones like an old castle. The stones make up the interior lounge walls, as well. Roughhewn beams cross the ceiling. The crackling flames dancing in the fireplace and the flickering candles encased in sconces on the walls make their sultry swaying impression, adding to the old-world charm.

My gaze settles on the bar along the back wall. The

well-stocked bar, with its high-priced beer, wine, and liquors from around the world, belie the room's seventeenth-century ambiance.

But the trendy bar isn't what's holding my interest. The too-beautiful-to-be-human leaning against the bar looks good enough to eat in a silver-gray sports jacket with a black t-shirt underneath and black jeans hugging him in all the right places. D's wavy hair is hanging loose on his shoulders. His chiseled cheekbones are even more prominent as his sly grin holds the attention of the person sitting on the barstool to the left of him. *Crap.* The person holding his attention is the stunningly beautiful blonde who was our waitress at the rehearsal dinner. Is it surprising it took him only hours to find someone to hook up with? Not at all. Do I hate her with every fiber of my being? Almost. But I can handle this.

"I'm a strong, powerful woman in control of my own destiny." I chant aloud the mantra Trace has been reciting to me ever since I've known her. She said her mom recited it to her almost like a lullaby from the time she was a little girl and it got her through some tough times.

"What? You okay?" Nikki asks as she follows my gaze across the room to where Blondie has her hand running up and down D's arm.

"I'm fantastic." The mantra works in making me feel empowered and happy with the world. Or maybe it's the champagne bubbles. Whatever it is, I tell Nikki I'll catch up with them in a few and approach the bar like a woman on a mission. My mission—to squeeze into the right of D and order an AMF, aka Adios Mother Fucker.

Trace let Dak pick the signature cocktail for their

wedding since he wasn't allowed to choose anything else. He claims he chose it because it's the same color as a beautiful Caribbean ocean, which is also the same color scheme as the wedding. But I'm sure he picked it because it has an obscene name *and* it's made with equal parts vodka, rum, tequila, gin, and blue curacao. It's a celebratory-to-the-max-drink waiting to happen. My brother may be a crude jackass, but in this case, I'll cut him some slack. The alcoholic content is precisely what I need to get myself in a party mood.

"What can I get you, sweetheart?" the hot bartender, with his tan skin, disheveled blond hair, and inviting blue eyes leans in to take my order, and while doing so gives me an obvious up and down scan. I think I hear Wolfe growl. I ignore him.

"Could I get an AMF?"

"Sure thing, Gorgeous." Am I loving the fact D is standing there listening to every flirtatious word the bartender says? C'mon now. Of course, I am.

I've read more than romance novels to learn all about the sexual attraction between humans. My analyses have also included all the most pertinent research studies out there: *The Kinsey Report*, and Masters and Johnson's *The Human Sexual Response*. I've even read Helen Gurley Brown's *Sex and the Single Girl*.

I didn't get all buffed and shined to have no one notice me. Unfortunately, the cute bartender wasn't the one I wanted to notice my spruced-up chassis. But there's nothing wrong with testing my newly acquired seduction engine until the right guy does notice.

"Whoa. You better take it easy on those things, little

girl. They pack a punch. And I heard it on the DL you ladies have been sucking down Mimosas all day," D offers his uninvited, annoying advice.

"Excuse me? *Little* girl?" I turn so he can get a good look at the black halter dress I'm wearing.

The front of the dress is covered in floral sequin designs. They are strategically placed to cover my most intimate parts. Surrounding the designs are black mesh cutouts. The dress's design doesn't allow for a bra, but since I'm not as voluptuous as the woman sitting on D's other side, I can pull it off without any wardrobe malfunctions. Judging from the way D's jaw is clenching, I'd say he gets my not so *little* girl status. But just to be sure, I turn my back to him and call for the bartender's attention again.

"Make that two, please."

"You got it."

It gives D a chance to get an up close and personal view of the backless dress. It's cut down to the small of my back, and the stretchy black fabric hugging my ass leaves nothing to the imagination.

"Holy fuck," D gasps.

"I'm sorry, did you say something?" I turn to him.

"That dress is...it's..."

"Something a *little* girl shouldn't be wearing?" I help him finish his sentence since he seems to be somewhat tongue-tied.

"I was going to say, it's amazing." He moves closer and brushes up against me. Or rather his obvious erection brushes up against me. *Did I do that?* My heart catapults inside my chest. "And you look amazing in it."

"Thanks. But since you made it abundantly clear you have no intention of using that," I glance down between his thighs, "at least not on *me*, I think you better back off." I smile sweetly and flutter my lashes at him. But he doesn't move.

"I'm sorry. I don't think I met your friend." I lean into the bar to look past him, so I can see Blondie. I will not give in to the hormonal siege going on inside my body in response to him. I will not behave like a drooly lovestruck fool. Been there. Done that. And I was left bare-assed and humiliated. I inhale a calming breath and take a napkin doily from the bar to wipe my mouth. Whatever. It's only one *small* drop of drool.

"Hi. I'm Heaven." I stretch my hand out toward the beautiful girl.

"Hi." She extends her hand out for mine. Since D's in between us, we shake hands in front of his glorious erection. On second thought, maybe *she's* the cause of D's excessive...zeal.

"Oh. Sorry." D decides to back up a bit after all. "This is...um...Heaven, this is..." Oh boy. He can't even remember her name. If I wasn't so happy he can't remember her name, I'd have to agree with his hockey mates, D is a dick when it comes to women.

"Alison," the girl blurts out in frustration.

"Right. Alison this is P...Heaven." He turns back and forth between us. I'm sure the fact he's sandwiched in between two attentive women is right up his whoring alley.

"Nice to meet you, Heaven. Beautiful name. So

unusual," Alison comments in a somewhat mocking tone.

"Thanks." I don't react to her snarky comment because I mean, really. What *were* my parents smoking? "Can't take credit, I'm afraid. All my mother's idea." Meanwhile, D keeps looking back and forth at us like he's at a ping pong tournament.

"Sheesh, D. Are you having a senior moment?" I decide to let the poor boy know I remember he's here. "How could you forget such a beautiful woman's name? I have to apologize for him. He can be such a *guy* sometimes." I roll my eyes to emphasize my feigned disgust.

"Have you known Wolfe long? You seem to know him so well." We continue to converse past D, while I do my best to ignore the way my body is heating and my pulse is racing in double time from his close proximity.

"Oh, I've known Heaven since she was just a little squirt. She's Dak's *baby* sister. You know, the groom?" D interjects with his snide comment.

"Oooh. So, you're old friends through your brother. Makes sense," Alison says in a relieved tone. What does she mean 'makes sense?' Why couldn't I be more to D than a friend through my brother? Do I look like someone he could never be interested in as more than a friend's baby sister?

The hot bartender delivers my drinks. I gulp the first one down in one long swallow.

"You're with the wedding party right, sweetheart? Should I put that on their tab?"

"Yes. I'm..."

"What's with all the sweetheart bullshit? Show some

respect, asshole, or I'll have to come across this bar and teach you some," Wolfe snarls.

"Sorry, dude. Just being friendly. Didn't realize she was with you. I thought you were with Alison."

"He is," I quickly offer. "I'm not *with* him. He's just a self-appointed bodyguard. I'm Heaven." I extend my hand to the bartender, who's looking more attractive with every gulping swallow of AMFs.

"You certainly are." The smooth-talking bartender takes my hand in his. "Beautiful name to match a beautiful lady. I'm Matt."

"Hi, Matt. So nice to meet you."

"I can understand why you need a bodyguard. That body definitely requires guarding. I get off at ten. Are you staying in a guest cottage?" The somewhat fast moving, beach boy mixologist seems to have no intention of letting my hand go until D pulls my arm away and closes his massive paw around Matt's in a handshake.

"Nice to meet you, Matt." By the grimace on Matt's face, I'd say D is greeting him with a vigorous grip. "You better get back to tending bar. There are a lot of people waiting to be served and my friend, Heaven, isn't one of them. Understand where I'm coming from, dude?" D asks while continuing to hold Matt's hand in a vise grip.

"Su...sure, man. I...I get it," Matt stutters as his knees begin to buckle under him.

"So, we're clear?" D leans in, while at the same time pulling Matt halfway across the bar.

"Com...completely clear," Matt, in obvious pain, strains out the words.

"Stop it, D! What's wrong with you? You're behaving like a Neanderthal." Would I mind D behaving all territorial and possessive like a caveman protecting his woman? Um...well...no, if I *was* his woman. But since he made it clear it's never going to happen, he needs to stop the whole vagina blocking thing, or I am going to be the Virgin Heaven for the rest of my life. And while the name has a lovely spiritual ring to it, it sounds boring as hell to me!

D lets go of Matt's hand. "Good. As long as we're clear." D rubs his hand down his pant leg like he's wiping off the toxic waste he squeezed from Matt. Poor Matt shakes out his arm like he's trying to get the blood circulating down to his fingers again.

"I'm so sorry, Matt. I..." I begin to apologize for D's boorish behavior.

"Yeah. Whatever. Crazy fucking asshole," Matt grumbles as he makes his way down to the other end of the bar still massaging his right hand. He whispers something to the gray-haired man tending bar in the other section. The man makes his way down to our end of the bar, apparently trading workstations with Matt.

"Well, that was interesting," Alison says, reminding me she's still there. "It's sweet how protective you are of your friend's little sister. And kind of hot," she whisper-breathes like a serpent into D's ear. It's loud enough I can hear her seductive hiss.

I've had enough. This on again off again hot and cold game D keeps playing with me is ridiculous and... hormonally confusing.

"Yes. D can be so sweet when he's behaving like an

idiot," I mumble into my glass before gulping the last swallow of my second AMF.

The drinks are sloshing around in my stomach like a perfect storm. It's my cue to call it a night and head back to my cottage if there's any hope I'm going to be able to get up bright-eyed and bushy-tailed in the morning for my brother's wedding.

What I really want to do is drag D away from beautiful Alison and pull him all the way to my cottage. Unfortunately, I'm not feeling AMFing brave enough to act on my desires. Even if I were drunk enough to be uninhibited, it still wouldn't make me brave enough to be able to handle another possible rejection from D.

"I'm outta here." I wave my empty glass in the air like I accomplished an amazing feat. "Don't shtay up too late, Mr. Wolfe." I waggle my finger at him. "Doing whatever it is people get to do when shomone doesn't ruin their evening." I can't seem to get my tongue to work properly. "Remember we're having breakfast at my parents' cottage bright and early tomorrow morning before we join the cel...celbratory lineup." Mom insisted me and my designated groomsman should have breakfast with her and Dad before the wedding.

I have a sneaky suspicion she's getting desperate and joined the Trace and Nikki Matchmaking Incorporated team. I thought Mom would be thrilled when she called me last week and I told her I started seeing Dak's friend Josh. But all she did was mumble, "the auras aren't right" and hung up on me.

After offering my unsolicited advice to D, I take a step away from the bar and stumble.

"Oops. Maybe I chugged those Mother Fuckers a little too quick." I giggle until I realize D has his arm wrapped around my waist. "Get..." I push his arm away from me because I can't handle the tingly goosies running up and down my body his touch elicits. "Away." In the process, I stumble over my feet yet again.

D reaches out for me once more. I hold my hand up like a traffic cop to stop him. "I'm good. Perfectly fine. Good night beautiful, very blonde Alishon. Good night V-jay blocking Wolfe. 'Good night, good night! Parting is shush shweet sorrow.'" *Oh God. I'm drunk quoting Shakespeare. Bedtime for sure.* Don't know where Nikki and the girls are but I'm sure they'll understand if I don't say goodnight.

"Wait, Pip. I'm going to walk you back to your cottage," D informs me.

"No no. No ashistance required." I turn and trip on the barstool and fall against D's lovely granite-like chest. "Jeez, what did they do, put shom kind of no walking formula into those AMF's?

"And some kind of no pronunciation formula too, it seems." D chuckles. "I'm walking you," he insists. "Bartender?" He holds a hundred dollar bill out to the guy who took over Matt's station. "Give the lady anything she wants." He tips his head toward Alison. "And keep the change."

"You're leaving?" Alison spits out the straw she was twirling her tongue around. I'm not into girls, but I have to admit she has some provocative skills at the whole tongue twirling, seductive sucking on a straw routine.

"Sorry, hon. Can't be helped. As you can see, something's come up."

D takes my arm and starts to walk me away from the bar just as Alison adds, "Something's come up with the sugary little virgin? Huh. Going to end up being quite a frustrating night for you, sweetie," she sneers.

"Heyyy," I spin around D like he's a pole and point my finger right in Alison's stunning flawless face. "Who you calling a virgin? Bet I could show you a few moves..."

"Okay, Dr. Ruth. That's it. Let's go." D steps between me and the latest woman willing to give up all self-respect for him.

"And do me a favor...ah...ah..." He turns to say something to Alison but apparently is once again having trouble remembering her name. I want to wrap my arms around his neck and give him the biggest thank you kiss in the whole world, but instead, I help the big jerk.

"Alishon," I loud whisper in his ear.

"Right. Alishon...uh...Alison. Here's the thing. If we're going to continue to be chums for the weekend, don't talk shit about Heaven." D doesn't wait for her to respond. He takes my hand and leads me out into the balmy, beautiful Santa Barbara night.

Chapter Eight

WOLFE

"There is absholutely no need for you to walk me back to my cottage. I told you I'm fine." Pip continues to protest in slurs but doesn't take her hand from mine.

"If you think I'm going to let you roam around alone at night in that dress with the masses of horny, tanked-up, predatorial hockey players here for the bachelor party and wedding, you're even more sozzled than I thought." I know what these scumbags are looking for. After all, I've been a brother scumbag my whole life. There's no way I'm letting Pippa traipse around the torchlit, silvery moon-shining resort all by herself like shark bait.

"I am not sozzled. I'm pleasantly numb. There's no need for you to go out of your way to walk with me," she scoffs.

"I'm not going out of my way. My guest cottage is right next door to yours." I shrug a shoulder like it's a big coincidence. She doesn't need to know when I checked in I greased a few palms with some hefty tips to make sure we ended up next door neighbors.

"Really? What a co-inky dink! Then I'd say you're the only predatorial hockey player in the immediate vicinity." She waves her hand out over the darkened horizon. Have to admit she might be right.

I don't remember ever having such a sensorial awareness of the environment all around me. The flaming torches are the only light guiding our path other than the full moon, which looks bigger and fuller than I've ever seen it. Its reflection fluoresces a shimmering pathway over the ocean. The resort sits atop a cliff and the waves crashing on the beach below sparkle with every lap onto the sand. There's a faint perfume of lavender and grapes carried on the warm breeze. *Jesus. I might be growing tits.* I'm sure my newfound poetic vision has something to do with my companion, even though she's being all snarky and not the least bit romantic.

"Anyway, I told you a thousand times, I hate hockey players." She sticks her chin out and smirks, blasting me from my sappy reverie.

"Right. Except for Carson with his babymaking pecs and Sanders with his orgasmic biceps." I haven't forgotten the way she salivated while describing my teammates.

"Don't be silly." She waves me off.

"Me? You're the one who used the overzealous descriptions."

"I mean, don't be silly. It's *Sanders* with the babymaking pecs and *Carson* with the orgasmic biceps." She glances at me sideways and giggles.

I stop dead in my tracks, Pip is tugged backward by my abrupt stop. "You aren't such an angel after all. You really are an evil little monster, aren't you," I tease and tug her into my arms.

"I'm not the one who totally cockblocked *you* tonight." She tilts her head and wiggles against me. *Jesus Christ.* The teasing little minx has no idea what she's doing to me. Or maybe she does.

"I believe it was *you* scaring away *my* prospects," she adds and pushes away from me and keeps walking. "What's your problem?" She stops short, turns and pokes her finger into my chest. "When did you become the stuffed shirt in this duo?"

The poking transforms into her running her hands up and down my chest. Every muscle in my body tenses. I'm about to scoop her up in my arms and carry her caveman style back to my cottage. But then she stops feeling me up and jolts me back to reality.

"Not me. This weekend I'm letting go," she chants while stepping back, spreading her arms and spinning in a circle. "I'm vibrating higher." I reach out and catch her arm when she stumbles, too dizzy to recover from the spinning.

"I'd say you better go low key on the vibrating high for the time being. At least until the AMFs wear off." I bite back a smile.

I didn't think it was possible, but she's even more adorable in her tipsy state, and at the same time exquisite, standing here with the torches illuminating her in glimmering firelight. My pulse is in overdrive watching her. With all my past experience, I've never felt this raw, insatiable need to touch a woman. Is it the fact she's off limits? Wanting her is driving me crazy.

"Pfft." She pushes my hand off her arm and continues her unsteady walk down the path to her cottage. "Speaking of which, you are free to let go and return to the lovely, waiting and willing Alison. This is my cottage." She stops at the white guest cottage with a gated arbor. The eight-foot-tall gate is ajar enough to see the wildflower garden beds surrounding the front terrace.

"Christ. You left your gate open. I bet you didn't even bother to lock your door."

"Really. What is with *you* tonight? We're at a five star fabulously exclusive resort. I'm pretty sure no stalkers are going to be hiding under my bed."

"Just to be sure I'm coming in with you." I walk ahead of her through the open gate and onto the terrace. Sure enough, when I test the knob, the door swings open. I turn and shake my head at Pippa for her lack of discretion. She's standing next to me with her spiked heels dangling off her fingers—the heels I've been imagining draped over my shoulders all night.

"What? I was in a hurry. No biggie." She pushes past me and drops her shoes as she continues toward her bedroom. "I'm ex-haust-ed," she calls from the bedroom, accentuating each syllable.

She'll probably be asleep the second her head hits the pillow. I walk around the cottage and then out onto the private patio, checking to make sure everything is safe and secure before I leave. Yes. I am definitely going. Even if I convinced myself I should do what she asked me to do, I'm not a big enough scumbag to fuck her in the condition she's in right now.

I don't hear Pippa walk up behind me because the water jets gurgling in the sunken hot tub on the patio are too loud. The tubs are an added luxury in all the private cottages at the resort. They can be set with timers to have them bubbling and warm whenever the quests get back to their rooms.

"Are you a pirate? Because I'm wondering where you got that booty." I jump a mile when she delivers the corn-ball line behind me. When I turn, I almost swallow my tongue at the sight. She's leaning against the door frame in nothing but her lacy, black, see-through panties.

"I'm going to take a dip in the hot tub before bed. Care to join me?" Pippa declares in a nonchalant tone like it's customary for her to be standing in front of me practically naked.

"Jesus fucking Christ, Pip! What the hell are you doing?" I drag my fingers back through my hair and tug.

This girl is my karmic payback for the shit life I've led in the past and the current one I'm still living: doing whatever and whoever the hell I want whenever the hell I want. The universe taunts me every time I see Pip because now all I want is her and I can't have her. My dick strains against my jeans. Her perfect tits in the moonlight are begging to be touched, licked, nibbled on.

"I told you. I'm going in the hot tub." She stumbles past me and steps down into the steaming water.

"Might not be such a good idea," I warn her through clenched teeth I'm gritting so hard I may crack one.

I imagine all the things I could be doing to her in the heated, bubbling water and how she'd be moaning my name. I'm resisting giving in to my demanding dick. Closing my eyes, I fist my hands at my side to stop myself from ripping off my restrictive clothing to join her. Pippa moans in a not so pleasurable tone. I snap my eyes open to see if she's okay.

"Dizzy. Too hot," she groans.

"I told you it wasn't a good idea to mix the alcohol effects with the hot water." I reach into the tub and lift her into my arms, cradling her against me. "You're so damn stubborn. You never listen." She nuzzles her nose into my neck.

"Aww. Don't be mad at me, D. Love me. Just love me," she coos. Holy fuck. I have a nearly naked Heaven in my arms begging me to love her. My body trembles like an inexperienced teen as she nestles further into me. My cock swells against the unyielding denim.

I grab a towel off the rack next to the hot tub and carry her into the bedroom. Standing her up next to the bed, I wrap the towel around her. She throws her arms around my neck and stares up at me with a big-eyed questioning gaze.

"Well?" She tilts her head and waits for me to answer.

"Well, what?" I drag my gaze away from her sweet questioning face and focus on keeping the towel around her while using it to rub her dry before she gets into bed. As I stroke her, my skin gets hot, and I get harder. I'm sure every ounce of my blood is headed straight to my dick.

"Are you going to love me?"

"What are you talking about? You silly pip-squeak. I already love you." I make the mistake of looking into her dangerous cerulean eyes without the safety of body armor. Her yearning gaze shoots rockets straight to my heart. Then they ricochet and shoot straight to my thickening cock. "I...I always have," I mumble, trying to get my brain to focus on something besides the gorgeous-naked-woman-in-my-arms sensations.

"Poo. You know that's not what I mean." Pippa pulls the towel off her and slides her thumbs into the sides of her wet lace panties. Wiggling them off, she lies back onto the bed. "I mean, I want you to touch me."

Bending one leg up, she slides a hand down between her thighs and touches herself and then pushes one finger inside the exact place I'd like to have my fingers, the place where I'd like to have my face buried, where I'd like to be licking and sucking and devouring her. "I mean, I want you to fuck me," she moans as she pleasures herself.

"Fuck, Heaven," I groan. I should look away. I should run away. But I can't. I can't stop watching her finger fuck herself.

"Yes. Fuck me, D," she moans. Dropping her head back, she arches up, pushing against her own hand.

I have never in my life done what I'm about to do. Not even when I was being paid for my services. Watching her writhe against her hand while making soft whimpering sounds, I unzip my jeans. My cock lunges free, straining out the top of my briefs like it's gasping for air. Yanking my underwear down, I run my thumb over the tip of my throbbing erection, using the precum lingering there to moisten my length. Wrapping my fist around my shaft, I slide it down in a long, slow stroke and then back up again. I let out a moan. Pippa opens her eyes and stares at me through half-lidded eyes clouded in a sexual haze. When she sees what I'm doing, desire flares even hotter in her eyes.

"D, don't stop," she moans.

"Jesus. Fuck." My cock jerks and somehow grows even harder in my hand.

Our gazes lock. Pippa pushes another finger into herself, her thrusts becoming more urgent, more wild. I can see the juices glistening on her fingers as they thrust in and out. Her other hand grips her tit, and she begins kneading it. Even though she's pleasuring herself, she keeps begging me in tormented groans not to stop. I'm lost in a sexual fog, my eyes focused on the breathtaking image in front of me.

I begin to stroke myself in a feverish rhythm to match hers. When Pippa lets out a pleasured scream, every muscle in my body goes rigid. I let go, releasing violent hot jets into my hand. A feral growl pushes out of me when I shoot into my fist. I have never come as strong or hard, and I wasn't even touching her. What the hell would it be like if I was?

For a moment I stand frozen in place. It takes only seconds for reality to sink in. What the fuck just happened? What did I do? I swipe my sticky hand down the leg of my jeans as I tug them up. Shifting my dick back into place, I zip up my pants. He's not happy about it. Even though I just came with hurricane force, he's still semi-hard and wants more. Hell, we both want more from the goddess stretched back on the bed.

"Pippa. I'm...are you..." I don't know what to say to her. Should I apologize or will acting like it was a mistake, yet again, only make it worse?

But while I'm groping for the right words, I realize Pippa is making little snoring noises. In her AMF'd, hot tub inebriated state she had fucked herself to sleep. Another first for me. I've never had a woman fall asleep after an earth-shattering orgasm. Then again, it wasn't me giving her the cataclysmic orgasm. It was her own hand. Huh. Who knew? My little virgin can be a wildcat.

I head into the bathroom and wash the evidence of my erroneous actions off my hands, stomach, and shirt before returning to Pippa's bedside. She looks like a dark angel lying there naked, in a peaceful slumber, her long, raven hair splayed out around her head. She's the most gorgeous perfect thing I've ever seen. Tugging the comforter and sheets out from underneath her, I lift her legs and turn her, placing her head on a pillow. She lets out a little protesting moan as I reposition her.

"Shh. It's okay, baby. Everything's going to be okay." I pull the covers up to her chin and tuck them in around her. "You sleep and tomorrow your prince charming scientist will be here, and I'll never go near you like that again."

I bend and give her a soft kiss on the forehead before making my way to the door. I check after closing it to make sure the automatic lock clicked into place. My head is pounding in thought, and my dick is still throbbing as I make my way down the path the few feet to my own cottage.

When I get inside, I head for my bathroom, stripping

my soaking wet clothes off as I walk. Turning on the surround shower jets, I step in before the water has time to warm up. The initial icy blast pelting my body is a relief. But it's not enough. As the water begins to warm, my cock thickens at the mental images of Heaven writhing and moaning across her bed while finger fucking herself. I drop my head back and close my eyes.

She's no longer little Pippa—that's for fucking sure. Visions of Heaven continue to fill my thoughts. I make a fist around my hard length and stroke up and down, imagining it's her touching me, caressing me, stroking me. My engorged need for her is almost painful. I continue to work myself faster, up and down, jackhammering at a frenzied pace, chasing another desperate release.

When I reach the agonizing blissful pressure point where I let go, I cry out her name in a beseeching groan. The relief I'm seeking doesn't follow because it's not her. It's not Heaven. It's not the woman I'm craving with every thought in my head and cell in my body.

Chapter Nine

HEAVEN

"Oh God. Just take me now," I groan as I sit up in bed. Have you ever banged your head against a wall in rhythmic time to a jazzy tune? Me neither. But it's exactly what my head feels like right now; like a thousand Oompa Loompas are doing a tap dance on my brain. I will never, ever, *ever* drink again. When I stand, I almost lose my footing and fall back onto the bed. Doing my best to stay upright, I shuffle my way to the bathroom. I have to pee so bad my bladder is in imminent danger of exploding.

"Yikes! *Who* is that?" Gaping at the reflection in the wall-size mirror over the sink I find myself wondering who the heck is looking back at me. Surely some hungover wretch found their way into my room. I blink a few times to clear my vision. Nope. The naked wretch whose reflection looks like who did it and ran is me. Where the hell are my clothes? I don't remember taking off my dress or my..."Oh God, no!" The memory of last night's antics hits me like a sledgehammer. "No! No, you didn't! Heaven, you stupid, stupid girl," I groan and push my fisted hands against my smudged eyeliner and mascara encircled owl eyes. No need to judge. I'm self-judging enough for everyone. I'm officially too humiliated and too ridiculous to ever interact with another human being again as long as I live.

"Don't look at me like that," I scold the disheveled mess in the mirror. "This is all your fault." I know. I'll change my name, dye my hair, move to Antarctica, join the witness protection program.

"That's right. I said the witness protection program." The unruly girl in the mirror scowls at me like I'm crazy. "Because I witnessed the murder of a beautiful friendship," I explain to the imp in exasperation. Ugh. Not only am I a hungover slut, I'm talking to myself like a lunatic.

Except I can't change my identity today because it's my brother's wedding day and I'm a bridesmaid in the happy event. And oh, fuckity fuck! I'm supposed to have breakfast at my parents' cottage *with* D in...I run to the nightstand to check the digital clock. Twenty minutes! I have twenty minutes to metamorphosize from last night's hussy into this morning's angelic bridesmaid.

I take the much-needed pee, which uses up two ticking minutes and jump in and out of the shower. After towel drying my hair, I pull it up into a wet mess on my head. Tracey has a hairdresser coming to her cottage later to do everyone's hair and makeup, anyway.

And there's certainly no sense in doing anything to make myself look more presentable for D.

He saw me at my absolute most desperate point last night. There's no coming back from it. I tug on a pair of leggings and a loose t-shirt, which were *supposed* to be my sleeping attire before I decided to become Santa Barbara's Mata Hari. Slamming the door behind me, I hurry out the gate, only to run smack into D.

He, of course, looks like the gift from the gods he is, all gleaming skin and rippling muscle. His beautiful hair flows in perfect waves down to his shoulders, his silver eyes are bright and sparkling in the sunlight. There's just enough scruff on his jaw to make him look even sexier than usual. He couldn't be more gorgeous if he were already wearing his tux rather than low hanging black sweatpants and a white muscle t-shirt. Does he seriously wake up like that?

He flashes his panty-dropping grin. "Hey, you can call me Enterprise 'cause..."

"Don't." I hold up a hand to stop him right there. "I can't with the stupid pick-up lines this morning."

"Look. About last night..."

"Don't say another word," I interrupt him again. "It happened. I did what I did. I can't take it back. It's in the past. Let's just forget it. No need to analyze and discuss it." I continue to walk past him toward my parents' cottage.

"What *you* did?" He catches up to me. "It wasn't just you. I think I was an active and willing participant in our...um...joint effort."

"Joint effort? Nice way to put it." I shake my head

and keep walking without looking at him. I can't look at him without picturing him stroking himself and groaning in pleasure.

"How would you put it? Hand fucking ourselves into ecstasy while we watched each other?" He smirks. I come to such an abrupt stop, my flip flops get stuck on the damp grass and slide off my feet.

"No. I wouldn't put it that way." I turn and glare into his heart-stopping eyes. "Can we not put it any way at all? I don't want to talk about it or think about it ever again. It was another mistake. I'm sorry. I assure you it will never happen again. Now can we go have breakfast with my parents and get through this wedding and the rest of this freaking weekend, please?" I'm glowering at D with such projected anger, I don't miss the way he takes a step back from me. But the anger isn't for him, it's for me.

"Sorry. Can we just go eat and not talk?" I attempt a smile.

"Sure."

I slide back into my sandals, and we resume walking. "But...Pip?"

I let out a sigh, not wanting to hear what he has to say about my behavior.

"You have nothing to be sorry for."

The remaining walk down the path to my parents' cottage is spent in silence. Even though I said I never want to think about last night again, all I can do is think about it. How it felt to plunge my fingers inside myself in front of D while imagining it was his fingers caressing me, fucking me. And then seeing him stroke his hard length while watching me with his hungry eyes. My leggings are soaked just thinking about it.

When we get to my parents' cottage door, I can hear the Snatam Kaur music Mom streams when she does yoga. Guess room service hasn't delivered breakfast yet. I did manage to get myself together in record-breaking time and get here a few minutes early. Could be a good thing. Maybe some relaxing Kirtan music is exactly what I need to calm myself from this frenzied humiliated state. I don't bother to knock because I don't want to disturb Mom's yoga session. D walks in behind me.

"Wow. It's sweltering in here. Isn't it?" he comments and wipes his brow.

"Mom must be doing a hot yoga session. She must've turned the heat up." *Jesus. It's unusually humid and sweaty even for Mom's hot yoga.* "Mom? Dad?" I call out as we walk into the small foyer. No answer.

Walking into the living room I'm surprised not to see my mom in some contorted position on her yoga mat. But then I hear it. Husky strained grunts and the bubbling hot tub jets coming from the patio. When I walk a little further into the room my eyes are zinged with a sight I'll never be able to erase from my brain as long as I live.

"What the hell? Mom? *Daddy?* What are you doing? Oh God. Unsee. Unsee. Unsee." I turn, scrub my closed eyes with the heels of my hands and beg my brain to abort and erase the vision.

"Hi, honey. Breakfast should be here in a few." Mom raises her head from my dad's crotch and greets me like everything is perfectly normal.

"Holy shit!" D is standing next to me staring out to the patio. "Your parents are a trip."

"Heaven! What are you doing here? You're early," my dad grunts from the base of the inverted two-person yoga pose he and Mom are holding.

"Dad! What is going on?" I ask without turning around to look at the sight which may have scarred me for life.

"We're having a hot yoga session, honey," Mom answers like it's the most normal thing in the world. I can tell from the strained sound of her voice she hasn't moved from her upside-down position against my dad's thighs with her face pointing straight into his package.

"You. Are. Naked." I state the obvious.

"Fucking amazing. It's like a live version of the Kama Sutra," D mumbles and tilts his head like he's trying to adjust his gaze to get a better look at the naked crazies. There's a shuffling sound, but I don't turn to see what's going on.

"I know! I find it's so much more freeing. Allows for a much higher vibration. You should try it, sweetheart," Mom chirps.

"With the *Haywards*?" I screech at a decibel I didn't know my voice could reach.

"Well...no. You don't need to do it with the Haywards." She hesitates like I'm the crazy one here. "I was telling Terace about it at the rehearsal dinner, and she was anxious to give it a try. So, no better time than the present. Speaking of which, don't be rude, Heaven. Say hello to the Haywards," Mom calls out, her voice sounding clear and sharp like she has finally decided to stand the hell up.

"So that's how you reach the higher vibration you were telling me about." D smirks, while still gaping at the freaky family tableau on the patio. "You're right. I'm definitely going to have to try it."

"Do you think you could turn around now? That is my mother and Mrs. Hayward you're gawking at," I admonish D.

"Your dad and Mr. Hayward are there too," he points and adds in a matter-of-fact tone like it makes his gawking perfectly okay. "I didn't even know your parents and Tracey's parents were such good friends." I punch him in the shoulder. "Ow! *What?* It's true."

"Turn. Around," I demand through clenched teeth while stomping my foot. He does. "Dear God. First, I masturbate in front of you and now this. My family has officially reached creepy perv status." I cover my face with my hands and groan through my fingers.

"Nah. I think your family is fucking awesome. I especially enjoy the way you masturbate and the sounds you make when you're doing it."

"Stop!" I shove a finger in each ear. "La la la. We agreed to never talk about last night again," I singsong in a loud voice to block D's words.

"Hey." He tugs my hand away from one ear. "You brought it up." He shrugs a shoulder.

"Hi, Heaven." Mrs. Hayward beats me to the awkward civilities, causing me to glance sideways toward the patio where she and my mom are still proudly displaying their sweat covered gorgeous bodies in an Extended Mountain stretch. "Are you excited for your brother's big day?" she asks without moving out of her stretch. Before I get a chance to answer, Mr. Hayward and my dad scurry by with towels wrapped around their waists.

"Hello, *Mr.* Hayward," I scoff.

"Heaven," he answers without stopping to look at me. "Wolfe. Nice save last game." He flicks his chin at D.

"Thanks, Duke. Appreciate you watching the game." Oh, yes. Just because Duke Hayward is an ex-hockey pro, now is a perfect time to discuss game highlights—after he just exposed *all* his highlights to us! I shake my head at D but don't comment.

I glance back to the patio. "Ah. Mom?" I tilt my head toward D to make her aware of the six-foot-three massive hockey player standing next to me, in case she didn't notice him.

"Oh goodness." Mom reaches for a towel and wipes her face. "Look at me. I'm being just as rude. I didn't even say hello to you, Damon. How are you, hon? Enjoying the resort?"

"Yes. Thanks, Mrs. Andersen." D nods. "More every minute I'm here," he mumbles. He does an awkward half turn toward my mom. I punch him again. "Ouch! Geez. You're gonna leave a bruise."

"I'm going to leave more than that if you don't stop eyeballing my mom and Mrs. Hayward."

"I am not eyeballing them. They're moms, for chrissakes." He scowls and shakes his head at me.

I'm about to apologize. It's not his fault my parents have completely lost their minds and are prancing around naked with Tracey's parents. "But for older women, their bodies are fucking amazing." I punch him again and don't apologize.

"Room service!" Someone knocks on the front door.

"Get that, will you, sweetheart?" Mom requests as she and Mrs. Hayward walk by us toward the bedrooms. At last, they have towels in their hands. Unfortunately, they're using them to dry their boobs and arms instead of covering themselves.

Jesus. Will this weekend from hell never end?

Chapter Ten

HEAVEN

We don't stay for breakfast. There's no way I can sit at a table with my parents, the Haywards, and D after the yoga exhibition. Between the disturbing demonstration and my queasiness from last night's adventure, I don't think my stomach could hold the food.

We make our awkward goodbyes. D says he forgot he had promised some of the other guys he was going to work out at the resort gym with them before the wedding and I say I promised Nikki to help her get Trace ready—which isn't a lie because I did tell Nikki I would be there after breakfast to help.

I head toward Trace's cottage for the bridesmaids' beautifying session and D heads for wherever Dak and his groomsmen have been banished so he won't see Trace before the ceremony. I'm relieved to have the day to figure out how I'll ever be able to spend time with him again after the past two days.

I consider walking right into Trace's cottage without knocking but decide it's better to announce my presence after the previous surprising fiasco. I knock, and it takes Nikki about five seconds to open the door.

"Hey, girl. You're early. Thank goodness. We could use...what the hell happened to you?" Nikki asks as I walk past her into the cottage. "You look like the way I felt the morning after I drank too much Jägermeister and fucked Dalt's brains out in his car. The *last* time I ever drank Jägermeister, I might add. *Although*...it wasn't the last time I fucked Dalt's brains out." She wiggles her brow up and down. Nikki's delightfully unfettered.

"In my case, it was AMF's," I moan.

"Christ. I hope you're not in the same condition I was. That was the night I got pregnant with Chloe. I mean, I love Chloe with every fiber of my being, but you're..."

"Relax." I crash onto the pearly white sofa. Everything in the bridal cottage is blindingly white. "I'm still as snowy white as this sofa." I'm not ready to confess the previous night's antics.

"Champagne and strawberries!" Tracey chants as she enters the room with a tray. "Uh oh." She stops short when she gets a look at me. "I'm thinking maybe you should stick to sparkling lemon water. What happened to *you*?"

"AMF's," Nikki enlightens her.

"Oh God. I'm going to kill Dak for making it our signature wedding drink."

"My brother *is* as annoying as hell, but in this case, it's not his fault I jumped into the AMF vat right after floating in Mimosas." *Eek.* Just admitting to my overindulgence has my stomach turning.

"No worries. Nina will be here in a few minutes. She's a beauty sorceress. She'll have you looking like a movie star in no time," Trace assures me while putting the tray down on a table across the room. Guess she's decided to keep the champagne-filled flutes far away from me. But she doesn't have to worry. Not wanting to repeat my Dita Von Teese performance tonight, I'm more than content to stick with sparkling lemon water.

Sloane arrives about fifteen minutes after me. Nina comes flying through the door a few minutes later laden with satchels filled with beauty magic. We spend the next few hours being primed and coiffed by Nina and her wizard-like abilities.

By the time she's finished, I'm beginning to feel like a presentable human again. I nibble on the delectable hors d'oeuvres the resort has provided since my stomach is reminding me I haven't eaten anything today. Nina shakes her head and tsks at me because after I'm done chomping the finger food, she needs to do another meticulous lipstick application.

I wait to slip into my bridesmaid gown to avoid any wardrobe disasters while eating and being beautified. All the form-fitting dresses are the same Caribbean blue color, with cut out midriffs and slit skirts but they have slightly different necklines. Nikki's is a halter top, Sloan's is strapless, and mine is one-shoulder style.

When I stand in front of the full-length mirror in the

room, I'm shocked by the transformation Nina has managed to achieve. My makeup is flawless, not a trace of last night's escapades remaining. My hair is pinned to one side, soft waves cascading down my shoulder. Trace was right. In my case, Nina was a sorceress.

Although, no sorcery was needed to transform Trace. She's stunning in her off the shoulder embroidered lace and layered tulle Elie Saab ball gown. But then, she would be stunning in a canvas bag. I'm so happy for my brother. He went through some tough times in college. He's a lucky man to have come through it all to find a woman as beautiful, smart, and genuine as Trace. And I'm a lucky girl to have her as my future sister—the future being in about a half hour.

We pile into the two horse-drawn carriages waiting outside the cottage and are whisked off to the chapel, like Cinderella and her entourage.

The quaint stone chapel has been transformed with enough flowers to rival the Royal Botanical Gardens. As Sloan, then me, then Nikki, walk up the aisle behind Chloe—Dalt and Nikki's little girl—I glance to the front of the chapel and see Dak standing at the altar with Dalt, Batt, and Wolfe. I've never seen my brother so happy. Tracey and her *fully-clothed* dad follow us. I know the second Dak sees her. His face lights up like he's seeing sunshine for the first time in his life.

Dak and Tracey share their self-written vows with each other. At that moment, listening to their tender words and promises, I can't help but dream of someday having someone love me the way Dak loves Tracey. I know. I'm a hopeless romantic.

My eyes drift across the aisle where Wolfe is standing. I find him staring at me, his direct gaze so intent it's a bit unsettling. His silver glare holds me, pierces me, wraps around my heart and squeezes. The rest of the world dims in my periphery. He's looking at me like he did last night when I was stretched across the bed naked. It's as if he can see right through my dress.

Oh God. My body is responding to his hungry glare. All my sensitive spots are rekindled with last night's memory. My eyes flutter closed. Desire overcomes reason. Without thinking, I spread my legs a little in a reaction to the inexplicable tingling going on between my thighs, causing one leg to jut outside the slit in my gown's skirt.

Applause and whistles jolt me out of my extremely inappropriate trance. My eyes snap open in time to see Dak and Tracey kiss. Apparently, Reverend Daniels has announced them husband and wife and given them the official clearance to kiss. I scoot my leg back undercover, squeezing my thighs together in an attempt to stop the imprudent throbbing in my core. What am I doing? Josh is sitting somewhere out there, hopefully somewhere in the back where he couldn't witness my unfitting behavior.

When I glance at Wolfe, my face flames red in embarrassment. His half-lidded smiling eyes and devious grin tell me he knows exactly what's going on between my legs and how pleased he is with himself at having been the stimulus.

The beaming bride and groom turn to make their way down the aisle and out of the chapel. And one by one, just as we rehearsed, the bridal party pairs off and follows them out. When Wolfe joins me center aisle, I try to avoid looking at him. I can't believe, with one *penetrating* glance, he almost had me moaning and coming in my thong in the middle of a church wedding!

"You look like a Grecian goddess," he leans in and whispers. "The blue matches your eyes." His nose brushes my hair as his warm breath feathers across my cheek Mmm. He smells amazing, all male and him. I'm getting tingly again.

His mere presence has been affecting me for years. But now? Ever since our telegraphic interaction last night? I'm lit up, ready to let go from one glance, a whiff of his scent, a whisper of his breath.

I force myself back to earth. "Stop it! We're in church," I side whisper, not wanting to risk looking at him.

"I'm not doing anything." He chuckles. "Just sayin' how much I love that dress on you."

"Thanks. Now, shh." Tracey and Dak have stopped at the chapel door and are being greeted with congratulatory hugs, which has blocked the exit for the rest of the wedding party. Which, in turn, means I'm unable to hightail it away from Wolfe's narcotic temptation to find Josh in the crowd.

"Of course, I would like it much better off you. I've become partial to the way hot tub bubbles look on you."

"What are you doing?" I turn and hiss at D a little louder than I intend. Even though we were moving at a snail's pace down the aisle, my halt is abrupt. Nikki and Batt, who were behind us, almost plow into our backs.

"What's going on, children?" Batt taunts.

"Another one of those combustible interactions we were talking about the other night?" Nikki raises a brow.

"Ruh-roh. Another smoldering tiff brought on by unrequited yearnings." Batt laughs.

If looks could actually kill, I'm sure my saber-sharp glare would have my dear friends pushing up daisies.

"Sorry." Nikki takes the hint and looks down at the floor.

Batt holds his hands up in surrender and lets out a whistle of air. Wolfe doesn't say a word, just stares straight ahead with a smug look tipping up one corner of his mouth.

Dear God. I've unleashed the wolf. What is it they say about being careful what you wish for?

Chapter Eleven

WOLFE

I know. I know. I'm being a total dick. I can't help it. After promising I would never go near her again in a sexual way, after all the banal lectures I've given Pippa about not being the right guy for her, not wanting to ruin our friendship, and then going as far as to stop our foreplay—mid finger fuck—I've been flirting with her all day and fucking with her head. This whole thing is fucking with my head too.

Watching her dance with Dr. Douche across the room, my brain is doing battle with my dick. She looks happy. She's having fun, enjoying herself. Do I want my friend to be happy? Of course, I do. Do I want her to be happy without me—with some douchebag? Fuck. No. I. Don't. And that's the whole cluster fucking problem.

This guy may be right for her, good for her. He's a scientist, an animal conservationist. The dickwad couldn't be more perfect for a smart, future doctor like Pip who, in her spare time, wants to save all the animals. But when I look at her, laughing and dancing with him, I don't give a fuck about what's right. All I can think about is last night. The vision of her stretched out naked on her bed plays on autorepeat in my head, causing a very uncomfortable, continually stiff dick.

Earlier, the wedding party was seated at a long table in the front of the room, Pippa sitting next to me. But as soon as Dalt and Sloan finished giving their toasts, Pip left the table and never came back. She didn't even sit at the bridal table to eat. She slid an extra chair next to Doctor Dickhead and ate dinner at his table. I moved to the bar after she left, in an attempt to quiet the confusing battle going on inside my body by drowning it with a continuous deluge of bourbon. It's where I'm seated right now, watching her.

As I look around the lavish room with its gold leaf chairs, parquet floor, gilt plaster cherubs, and garlands lining the white ceiling, walls, and massive arched windows, I'm reminded why I'm not the guy for Heaven. A place like this—with this caliber of clientele, especially female clientele—would have made for a very successful, lucrative evening back when I was fourteen or fifteen.

After my mom died when I was nine, my father opted to spend his days at the bottom of a whiskey bottle rather than wasting his time with me. Dear old Dad blamed me for the car accident we were in one night when Mom came to pick me up from hockey practice.

The only advice my father ever shared was to tell me over and over I was a "pretty boy." He never hesitated to reiterate, "Even though you're a good-for-nothing, useless piece of shit, responsible for your mother's death, the ladies are going to love your useless pretty boy ass."

That was his crap idea of fatherly support, to harass me with abusive taunting. Eventually, he stopped coming home at all. I don't even know what happened to him. The authorities tried to find him. They gave up after a few weeks. I'm sure they had better things to do than search for some old drunk in an alley somewhere. Didn't matter. I wasn't sorry to see him go.

My first hellish experience in foster care confirmed there was no way I was going to stay in the system. That's when I took my absentee father's crap advice and went out on my own. He was a shit parent. But he was right. The ladies loved me.

It didn't take me long to figure out I had something wealthy women were more than happy to pay for. And for two years, they did. I looked older than my fifteen years when I began working the bars and nightclubs with my fake ID. Countless lonely women with names and faces I've long since forgotten, or never knew, came and went. No attachments. No feelings. A means of survival.

Until Batt's dad saw me playing hockey one day at Chelsea Piers in a city league I had gotten into. It was the only thing in my life I looked forward to, the only thing I cared about, weekly local hockey games.

Mr. Battaglia stopped to talk to me after the game, commenting on how good I was and asking what school I played for. I told him I dropped out of school, without any further explanation.

He came to watch me play several times in the weeks

that followed, always taking the time to talk afterward. When he found out why I left school and how I was living, he took me into his home and family, got me into the high school Batt was attending, and helped me get my life back on track. The rest is history. But even now, sitting in a room like this, overflowing with decadence and wealth, I'm reminded how I would've been trolling for clientele not all that long ago.

Shit. I'm supposed to be celebrating my friend's wedding, not wallowing in my sordid past. My gaze drifts back to Pippa. She's still dancing and flirting with the douche. The music stops long enough for the wedding cake to make an entrance.

It takes four people to roll the damn thing out. Everyone moves off the dance floor to make space for the gargantuan, ocean blue cake. It has edible white starfish, seahorses, and coral all over it and there's a good chance astronauts can see the fucking thing from space.

The crowd gathers around to watch Trace and Dak feed it to each other. From my perch at the bar, I can see them being all lovey-dovey and sweet when they gently place a bite in each other's mouth. How fucking boring. My man, Dak, is missing the opportunity to smash it all over Trace's face, neck and chest just to have the excuse to lick it off her. When they're finished making nice, the cake is rolled away to be cut and served.

The band begins playing again, this time some of the cutesy sixties' music Dak and Tracey are into. They move back onto the dance floor along with the rest of the wedding party. Dak is serenading Trace as they dance, singing along with the band to the sixties' song,

Tracey. Everyone else on the floor joins in, singing at the top of their lungs, jumping up and down, having fun. Pip is singing her heart out and laughing with Dr. Cum Stain.

What the hell is his real name, again? Jason? Jonah? Jackoff? The mood changes when the music slows and the band begins playing *Dancing with A Stranger.* The dickhead pulls Heaven into his arms and nestles his nose in her hair like he's breathing her in. He dips his head and places his lips next to her ear to say something. She looks up at him and gives him a sweet smile.

When the vocalist belts out something about *what you made me do*, I can relate. Dr. Dick for Brains puts his hands on Pippa's ass and pulls her closer against his groin. I'm ready to blow a gasket. It hits me like a lightning bolt. I don't give a fuck if Dr. Shithead is right for Pip. She's mine. That's *my* sweet smile she's giving him.

Then, as if I willed it to happen, the song ends, and the band starts rocking the song, *The Wolf.* I snicker. How fucking perfect. It's my ringtone on Pippa's phone. Everyone on the dance floor goes wild, everyone except Pippa. She pushes out of dickhead's arms and slowly turns in circles, searching the room. I know she's looking for me. When our eyes lock, I can tell she's pissed. I put my arms out on either side, palms up and shrug, miming the fact I have no idea why they're playing the song. Her narrow-eyed glare and pursed lips tell me she doesn't believe me.

"It wasn't me," I mouth while shaking my head. Meanwhile, the fuckwad starts grinding into her from behind in the guise of dancing. Pippa jumps in shock, turns, and glances down at his crotch. I'm going to pummel the motherfucker all the way back to his rat lab.

When the suggestive song ends, the music slows. The lead singer begins rasping out the lyrics to, *Say You Won't Let Go*. It's like this song set is a musical journey through the bullshit Pip and I are living.

Fuck it. It's time for me to get in there. I gulp down the last three bourbon shots lined up for me on the bar and make my somewhat whiskey-labored prowl across the dance floor. Pippa has her back to me and doesn't see me approaching. She's all nestled in the bastard's arms. His fucking eyes are closed, while I'm sure, his hard-on is pushing into Pippa's leg.

I tap her on the shoulder. When she turns, the shithead opens his moony, motherfucking eyes. Not waiting for a reaction, I push him away from Pippa. "I think this is my dance." I wrap an arm around her waist. "You don't mind. Right, pal?" I give zero fucks if he minds.

"Oh...I...uh...Heaven?" He glances at Pippa and gives her an is-this-okay-look.

"Josh, this is Damon Wolfe. Wolfe, this is Dr. Joshua Littner." Pip fidgets with the bracelet on her wrist when she makes the awkward introduction.

"Of course. The infamous hockey player. Don't really watch the game. Never really got into the sport. But I've heard so much about you." He extends his slimy hand. I don't take it.

"Too bad. You don't know what you're missing." The loser's probably never gotten into any sport. Too busy playing with lab rats. Not wasting another second talking to the asshat, I sweep Pippa away, swaying in time to the music. At least I'm trying to sway to the music. The excessive bourbon isn't conducive to non-wobbly dancing. Pip stiffens in my arms. She's probably annoyed at the way I treated the dickhead. I'm not apologizing.

I pull her in close. The evocative song lyrics swirl around us. "This is our song," I whisper in her ear.

She lets out a sigh. I can feel her tension evaporating as she settles into my arms. I bend my head down to nestle it next to hers.

"Jesus. What is that smell?"

"Are you saying I smell?" She stops short, causing me to stumble and step on her foot. "Ow-wah?" Damn. Great way to kill the mood.

"I'm *trying* to say you smell like something I want to eat." I focus on the music and resume swaying in slow, seductive movements.

Once more my comment distracts her long enough for her to forget her anger. "Oh, that's my Bum Bum cream," she answers.

"Your *bum* smells like caramel and vanilla? Now I *know* I want to eat you." I nuzzle my nose into her neck.

"Not my *bum*. My...and you smell like a distillery." She stops dancing again. "How much have you had to drink, D?" She pushes my head up.

Uh oh. She remembers she's annoyed with me. Still, I didn't miss the way she trembled when I mentioned wanting to eat her.

"Not enough to make me think this is a good idea. But enough to not give a fuck." I pull her against me to make her *feel* how much I don't give a fuck about doing the right thing.

ELIZABETH HARTEY

She gasps. "What...what's going on, D? What are you doing?" she asks, as we stand frozen in place on the dance floor. Has to be a rhetorical question because she can't miss what my cock is doing. "You've made it more than clear what you think about us getting together. I told you I was sorry about what I did last night. And now..." She takes a quick glance down.

"Forget everything I said. What I'm trying to do *now* is show you how much I want you, how much I want to touch you, taste you, be inside you, make you scream my name." My words come out in a raspy growl.

Her legs give out under her, and she falls into my arms. Closing her eyes, she lets out a long calming breath. I'm as shocked by what I'm saying as she is, but I can't stop myself from expressing what I've been thinking for so long.

When she finally opens her eyes, she keeps them focused on the floor while asking, "Are you trying to get back at me for last night?"

"Get back at you?" I chuckle. Placing a finger under her chin, I tilt her head back to look into the eyes that have held me captive for seven years. "Okay. If that's what you want to call it, let's get *back* at each other like we did last night."

Someone bumps me from behind. In my unsteady state, I lurch forward and step on Pippa's other foot.

"Ouch! May...maybe we better sit down before I end up with a broken toe." She smiles up at me. God, how I love that smile.

I take her by the hand and lead her toward the bar.

The room continues to spin even though we're not dancing any longer. "Let me get you a drink."

When Phil, the bartender, sees me he places a double bourbon on the rocks in front of me. "Thanks, man." I pull out a barstool for Pip and offer to help her up before sliding or should I say nearly toppling onto mine.

"And for the young lady?" Phil asks.

"What's your poison tonight, Pip?"

"Water with lemon, please. I drank my yearly poison limit last night, if you remember," she says and slides onto the stool next to me.

"You can bring me another one of these too, Phil." I chug down the bourbon.

"Comin' right up, Wolfe." Phil scurries off to get our drinks.

"I do remember last night. You were amazing." I run the back of my hand down her silky cheek. She gets chill bumps at my touch, while at the same time her face warms in a pink flush.

"I want to be the one touching you tonight. I want to put my hands and lips all over you." I lean toward Pippa to continue whispering seductive suggestions into her ear.

The earth seems to tip off its axis. I topple off the barstool. Falling into her, she gasps when my weight hits her. My face is pressed against her neck, my lips tasting her sweetness and somehow my right hand has landed on one of her boobs. It feels perfect in my hand. I swear it was an accident.

"That's it. Time for bed." Pippa pushes my hand off her boob but not before I feel her nipple tighten.

"Exactly what I had in mind." Even in my alcoholic haze, I know this is insanity. I'm being an asshole. But my whole body is longing for this woman. "Is your name Jasmine? Because I'm about to show you a whole new world."

"I *meant*, it's time for *you* to go to bed. Alone. What is going on, D? You're behaving like fifty shades of crazy right now." She waves away Phil and the luscious amber liquid he's carrying toward me.

"I'm fifty shades of crazy for you, sweetheart." I try to touch her again, but she pushes my hand away.

"No. No more touching and definitely no more bourbon. It seems neither of us can handle our alcohol when we're around each other. We become sloppy, horny drunks."

I'm about to protest, tell her how much I've wanted her long before I had one sip of bourbon. But then, for fuck's sake, the douche shows up.

"Everything okay here?" Jackoff asks in his sickening cheery, prep-boy voice.

"Everything's just fine, Jacob. No worries. Just having a drink with my girl." The dickhead's eyes widen as he looks back and forth between Pip and me. *That's right, asshole. She's mine. Back the fuck off.* "Don't you have some endangered slugs you need to rescue or something?" I feign a smile.

"It's fine, Josh. D's been celebrating a little too hard. I'm going to take him back to his cottage so he can sleep it off." Pip slides off the barstool and brushes a kiss across the shithead's cheek. I'm about to flatten the guy, until the damn room starts spinning again.

Maybe I have overdone the bourbon a bit. I don't usually drink this much hard liquor. I had my father as the perfect fucked up role model to remind me to stay away from it. Add on the fact it's hockey season and this attempt to numb my brain was an all-around bad idea.

"Let me help you," the douche offers his assistance to Pippa while moving toward me. "He looks pretty unstable."

"I wouldn't do that if I were you, *buddy*. At least not if you like your arm attached to your body." I wave him back.

"D!" Pippa scolds me. "I'm so sorry, Josh. I'll be fine. Let me take him. I'll be back in a few minutes."

"You sure? He looks kind of...big." I swear the asshole looks at my crotch when he says that. Poor bastard. He'll probably have an inferiority complex for the rest of his life. "He might be too heavy for you to handle." He keeps talking to Pippa like I'm not standing right here.

"No need for you to worry about how she handles me. I'm going to teach her everything she needs to know." My intention is to tap him on the shoulder, but the tap turns into more of a shove.

"Maybe someone needs to teach this hockey barbarian some manners." For a smart guy, the prick's pretty fucking stupid. He actually pushes me back. I take a step backward but keep myself upright and move toward him. I'm going to pulverize his scientific ass.

Pippa comes up behind me and wraps her arms around my body to keep me from moving. I could easily get out of her hold to deck this bastard, but I like the way she feels wrapped around me.

"I'll be fine, Josh. I'll bring him to his room and come back. He just needs to sleep this off. I'll text you when I'm done."

"Text me if you need me," he says to Pip as he glares at me.

Pippa takes my hand and drags me away from the bar. "She won't be *needing* you," I yell over my shoulder to the asshat.

"Shh. Quiet. What has gotten into you?" Pip says in a hushed tone. *Nothing. But wait till you see what's about to get into you.*

"What did you say?" *Shit. Did I say that out loud?* "I think we need to make a deal. No more AMF's for me and no more bourbon for you. *Ever.*"

"Aw, but I love the way you look after you've had a few AMF's, all flushed and *pink.* But then I love the way you look all the time." I'm leaning against Pippa. She's half dragging me, half walking me as we make our very long journey to the guest cottages.

"Never mind how I look. I'm never drinking again if last night is any indication as to how I behave. This helping each other walk our drunk asses back to our rooms is getting to be a bad habit."

"I think you mean how you *mis*behave. Did I mention how much I loved the way your drunk ass looked last night when you were misbehaving?" I nuzzle my nose into her neck.

"Stop it, D." She shoves my head up.

"And anyway, everyone says 'I'm never drinking

again' the day after until the next celebration rolls around." *Where the hell is my cabin? Did they move it? I don't remember it being so far away.*

"I'm serious. Never again. And you definitely shouldn't either," she insists.

"Another thing they all say." I try to wave her overused vow off, but when I move too fast, my head spins. I think I'm going to pass out. For a second, I forget where I am.

"It's okay. We're almost there." Pip's sweet voice reminds me whose arms are wrapped around me keeping me upright. The lust surges through me, jolting me awake.

"Here we are." She clucks her tongue when she turns the doorknob on my cottage and the door swings open. "Look at that. You didn't lock your door. How careless of you. Don't you know there could be some crazy fangirls hiding under your bed waiting to have their way with you?" I think she's teasing me with the same warning I gave her last night.

"There's only one fangirl who's going to have her way with me tonight," I mumble as I step into the cottage. Stumbling toward the bedroom, I keep tearing my clothes off as I go. I have to lay down before I fall down.

"Oh? And who would that be?" Pippa trails behind me, picking up my discarded clothes from the floor.

"C'mere. I'll show you." I push out the words as I flop back onto the bed.

"You couldn't possibly be referring to me. Because

I'm no fangirl of yours, especially not after tonight," Pip scowls as she tugs my shoes and socks off.

I managed to get my jacket and shirt off. I'm still working on the damn belt buckle to get my pants off. I can't feel my fingers as I attempt to tug open my belt. Suddenly, I'm enveloped in a swirling haze. It's like a black vortex pulling me in, swallowing me.

Chapter Twelve

HEAVEN

"D? Are you okay? D? Guess not." He's out cold. "Hmmph. Here, let me help you. What was that? We're completely wrong for each other?" I continue to taunt the unconscious pain in my ass stretched out across the bed while unbuckling his belt.

"You're no good for me? I should find the right guy for me, you say?" I gibe as I lean over D and struggle to slide his pants down off his legs. "What's that? Oh, *now* you want me? Want to taste me? Be inside me? Sure. No problem. So what if you're the most annoying, infuriating...oh...oh my."

When I look up, I realize as I was sliding D's pants down, his briefs slid down with them. Apparently, his penis hasn't gotten the we're-stone-cold-cataleptic message. He's in full-on erect mode and peeking at me over the top of his briefs.

Other than the long-distance blurry-eyed view I had

last night during our remote interaction, I've never seen D...um...in his entirety. And his entirety is pretty darn impressive. A little *too* impressive for a girl who hasn't had anything inside her besides two fingers and a tiny Lelo vibrator.

Who in the world has a vagina big enough to accommodate that thing? And why am I being such a reprehensible perv and staring at an unconscious man's penis? The polite thing to do is slide his briefs up. I mean, I can't leave him lying there with the elastic around his shaft all night. It might cause physical damage.

"'Kay. Here goes." I slide my fingertips into the waistband of D's briefs and stretch it to clear his massive erection. When I do, his colossal penis boings toward me like a pogo stick in flight. I stop short and hold my breath, waiting for him to wake up and ask me what the heck I'm doing. When he doesn't, I begin breathing again— although I can't seem to manage more than short, quick breaths. As I begin to slip his underwear up with a gentle tug, a large hand wraps around my wrist. The feral growl coming from the formerly sleeping giant sends sparks shooting through my body. The next thing I know, D yanks on my arm and I'm sprawled on top of him.

"No. Let *me* help *you*." The raspy voice sweeps over me like a hypnotic command.

He finds the zipper on my dress and begins to slide it down but stops when I ask, "What are you doing? Has the bourbon pickled your brain?" I'm looking directly into his alluring eyes. We're nose-to-nose. Our lips nearly touching. But I'm determined to remain aloof and in control.

"The bourbon has told my brain to shut the fuck up for a change. I want to feel you naked against me. I want you more than I've ever wanted anything in my life but if you tell me to stop I will," he whispers, his bourbon-laced breath a magical aphrodisiac. My body is shaking in an intense hormonal dance. So much for aloof control.

"You've had a lot to drink. What about everything you've said? I don't want you to regret..."

"Regret?" He takes the wrist he's still holding and places my hand over his shaft, which seems to be even harder and bigger than it was a moment ago.

"Feel that? Feel what you do to me? What you *always* do to me? I think I knew from the first time I saw you this was inevitable. We belong together."

"You...you did? That's how I felt too. But I didn't think you..." He crushes his lips onto mine, swallowing my uncertain sentiment.

He tastes like a mixture of whiskey, mint, and answered prayers. My mouth opens with a gasp for air. He invades it with his tongue, tasting me, teasing me. It's the kiss I've been waiting years for. Not gentle. Hard, almost cruel, devouring away all my indecision. I return his savage hunger, my tongue warring with his. His hard shaft throbs against me.

Breaking our kiss, he whispers against my lips, "I don't want to risk ruining our friendship, but I want to show you how good this can be."

"Risk it. Show me." My blunt commands are all I can manage. My body is on fire. I'm going to burn up in his arms. I had no idea it would be this intense.

He continues sliding my zipper down. It opens in an

effortless glide as if offering its assistance to render me naked in his arms. He finds the looped buttons holding the one-shoulder strap at my neck and with a quick flick pops them open. His fingers aren't having any problem maneuvering buttons or clasps now. The top of my dress falls, exposing one side of my strapless lace bra and the eager puckered nipple pressing against it.

Lifting his head, he runs his tongue in a circle around the responsive peak. He rewards its attentiveness by savagely sucking on it through the fabric.

"Oh, God." I grind against him with a wanton need. "Please," I beg him, but I'm not even sure what I'm begging for.

"Please what? What do you want?" He continues to tease me with his tongue.

"I think...oooh...you know exactly...exactly what I want. I've been begging you for it for four years." My answer is a breathy moan.

Gripping his fingers through my hair, he gently tugs my head back. His predatorial glare pierces me. I feel it right between my legs. "Tell me what you want. I want to hear you say it." His words are a gravelly demand.

"You, D. I want you," I give him the straightforward answer. "Stop teasing me and just do it." If he's expecting me to be some scared little rabbit, he's going to be disappointed. I've been waiting years for this, for him.

"That's one needy little pussy. Isn't it?" He sits up further and licks the length of my neck.

"Mmm. I su...suppose it is." I tremble in an attempt to form logical answers with a brain that's in full on shut-up-and-fuck-me-mode. "I want you inside me."

The only response I get is another feral growl as he nearly tears my dress off and throws it across the room. My lacy thong doesn't fare as well. He rips it off. Evidence of my neediness covers his legs in wet desire as I writhe against him. Reaching behind me, he deftly unclasps my bra. It falls to the side.

I find myself wondering if his ability to shake off his intoxication, to perform in apparent routine dexterity comes from his experience with countless women. For a moment I panic, remembering I have no real experience. Will I disappoint him? Hell. Will he even be able to get that enormous thing inside me? At least I was smart enough to have continued taking my birth control pills. Even though my prospects were looking grim, I never gave up hope.

He must sense my apprehension. "You okay, baby?"

"I'm...yes...but I don't know..."

"Don't worry. Relax. I got you." He flips me over onto my back. He's stretched out over me, supporting himself on his forearms on either side of me. I've never felt so vulnerable, so open to someone else, so ready to be taken, heart and soul.

Will he break me? Destroy me? No. This is D. We've loved each other for years, even if it was as platonic friends. It was a considerate love. He would never hurt me. We would never hurt each other.

"I think I've been waiting for you my whole life. I..." he begins, but then stops and shakes his head like he's trying to clear it.

"Are *you* okay?" For a moment he looks...different, his brow pinched in confusion. Almost like he's lost.

"I'm...I'm good." He looks straight into my eyes like he's seeing me for the first time. "Are you really here?" he whispers.

"I'm right here. I've been waiting for you my whole life too. I've wanted you for so long, wanted this for so long. Please, D."

With a groan, D kicks his briefs off, lines himself up at my center, and with one hard thrust slams into me. I gasp at the invading thickness tearing through me, filling me. I suddenly know the meaning of seeing stars as pinpoints of light explode behind my eyelids. The pain surges through me. I swallow a scream. This isn't right. This isn't how it's supposed to be. It should feel...good. He said he would make it feel good. Instead, he's tearing me apart. He's too big. I can't be stretched this wide. He's going to split me in two.

"So fucking tight," he growls. He doesn't seem to notice my discomfort and he doesn't slow down. He pushes up onto the palms of his hands and continues to plow in and out of me, each time deeper, more ruthless.

"D," I manage to groan out his name. I want to tell him to stop. But when I moan his name in agony, his thrusts become harder, deeper, more intense. The stinging pain becomes overwhelming, affecting my ability to do anything but whimper. I can't manage to speak. He's slamming so deep inside me, he's touching places I didn't know it was possible to touch. He's shredding me to pieces. It's so unbearably painful I think I'm going to pass out.

I open my clenched eyes enough to look down between us to confirm what he's doing to me, verifying through blurred, tear-filled eyes the way he's impaling me, driving into me with animal fierceness, almost like he hates me. Is he trying to prove to me I was wrong to ask him for this? No. I'm losing my mind from the pain. I remind myself this is D pounding into me with hard, rough strokes. He cares about me. It's his wild need for me which has him behaving like this.

"Fuck. So good. So good. You're so fucking tight," he groans his filthy endearments. "Fuuuck. You feel so fucking good." His brow pinches and his face and neck muscles strain. Every muscle in his body stiffens, and then with one more bone-deep growl he lets go, bursting into me with a violent release as unrestrained as his thrusts.

"Christ. I'm coming so hard." He keeps filling me with burning hot jets as his cock continues to pulse inside me.

When he's done, he drops his weight onto me and groans into my neck. I wipe my wet cheeks with the back of my hand and try to will the hurt away from between my thighs. But D's still inside me. The unrelenting stinging is impossible to alleviate with his merciless thick shaft filling me.

I want to say something but I'm not sure what to say. He told me he doesn't fuck virgins. He warned me he had no sensitivity to give and I begged him for this anyway. Why doesn't *he* say something?

But then empty words become unnecessary. With a grumble, D rolls off me onto his back, yanking his somewhat still firm cock from me. It causes yet another hurtful sensation and a rush of warmth to drip down my thighs, soaking the sheets. His chest rises up and down in long breaths. D's snoring. He fucked me and passed out without saying a word other than declaring the strength of his orgasmic release.

I'm confused, crushed, feeling as discarded as my torn panties. Taking a deep breath, I remind myself this is what I wanted, what I asked for, a quick deflowering and we would be done. It was nothing. It means nothing. I promised him it would mean nothing.

I have to get out of here, go back to my own cottage, not let anyone see me leaving his room. I thought I would be walking on cloud nine after giving my virginity to D. Instead, I'm facing a walk of shame I'm not prepared for. God. If Dak finds out about this, he'll be feverish with anger. He already threatened to kill D if he came near me. I know he didn't really mean he'd kill him, but I don't want to ruin his wedding weekend with any drama. *You're so stupid, Heaven.* D was right. I've been nothing but a little fool.

I slip out of D's bed and quietly gather my clothes. Stepping into my disheveled gown, I take one last look at D. I cringe at the sallow crimson stain left on his sheets; humiliating evidence of what happened here. D, however, is in a deep contented sleep, not a care in the world.

As I climb into my own bed, I can still feel D inside me, stretching me wide with his fullness. My shredded core continues to pulse in discomfort as manic thoughts swirl through my head. He didn't force me. I asked him to have sex with me. I expected him to be gentle, knowing it was my first time—at least, *somewhat* gentle. Instead, he hurt me, physically and emotionally.

He warned me. He warned me. The reproach thrums in my head. All the misgivings I should have had before having sex with him join my frenzied thoughts. He had way too much to drink. He wasn't coherent. I should never have gone back to his room with him alone. I should never have agreed to sex. I knew he was drunk. *I* should have been the sensible one.

And here I am, hurt and broken, making excuses for D yet again. Can I blame him, though? He's been nothing but honest with me. He never promised me anything. Always admitted the way he is with women. I was foolish or arrogant enough to think he would be different with me.

Time to grow up, Heaven. Time to stop being the headstrong little girl who always thinks I can fix everyone and everything. D is who he is. He has no desire to be anyone else. He's told me as much a hundred times.

Things will be different, awkward now. He warned me about that too.

I roll onto my side and punch the pillow. I'm so angry with D—with myself. But I have to stop this, stop blaming myself, stop blaming him. I'll drive myself crazy second guessing what I can't change.

I'll talk to him tomorrow. As I glance toward the window, I realize the sky's soft pink glow is evidence it's already tomorrow. My body is spent and begging for sleep. But the chaos inside my head refuses to be quiet.

I promised D I would make it work between us after we slept together. But I've had so many foolish-girl fantasies. Now I'm discovering it's more complicated than I thought it would be to abandon them—to not be overwhelmed by these broken, empty feelings.

Chapter Thirteen

HEAVEN

Not having my mom's pain-relieving herbal potions, I resort to taking two aspirin and a cool shower. With the dull pain going on between my thighs and the lack of sleep, I'm a hot mess when it comes time to meet everyone for breakfast.

Tracey had planned for everyone to meet for one last breakfast in the patio restaurant before heading home. The uneasy thought occurs to me, D might stop at my cottage to get me since he passes it on his way. I'm not sure if I'm relieved or upset when he doesn't. I reluctantly head over to the main building.

The lobby is bustling with wedding guests checking out and family members sending them off with hugs and kisses. When I walk in the door, the first person I bump into is Josh. The shame washes over me when I realize I never gave one thought to him. *I'm a horrible person.* I left him at the reception and didn't return, even though I said I would. He must know why I didn't return. I'm mortified.

"Hey, you. What happened to you last night? I tried to call you, but it went straight to voicemail. I figured you were tired and went to bed. I didn't want to bother you." He greets me with a kiss on the cheek.

Between no sleep and the residual distress, I didn't think to check my phone this morning for missed calls or messages. Josh isn't even mad at me for ditching him the way I did. Now I feel even worse. *I'm going straight to hell for my appalling behavior.*

"Oh. Yeah, I...I was really exhausted, I decided to go straight to bed. I'm so sorry. I just didn't have the energy to walk all the way back here." He doesn't question why I didn't take a minute to call him and tell him I was going to bed. And now, I'm not only a wanton, bruised, one-night stand, I'm also a bold-faced liar. What's the alternative? 'Sorry about that. I decided to let my intoxicated best friend take my virginity and tear me to shreds?'

"No problem. I'm sure after having to drag Wolfe back to his room you were beat. I should have insisted on helping you. He's pretty big. He must have been a lot to handle for you." Of course, my dirty little mind drops right into the gutter. I think about my inability to handle D's gigantic penis. The response going on in my aching morning-after core has me clenching my thighs together.

"Um...yes...I mean no, he was fine. I mean, it was fine. I mean...it's been a long weekend. I was exhausted." I can feel the warm blush creeping up my neck. Hopefully, Josh doesn't notice.

"I'll forgive you if you promise to make it up to me

by taking a trip with me up to San Francisco next weekend. It could be really nice. A quiet weekend, just the two
of us and lots of marine life." He chuckles and reaches
for my hand, entwining his fingers in mine.

He's the sweetest, most perfect guy: handsome,
smart, interesting. Why doesn't my heart beat in triple
time when he walks into a room? And why isn't there too
little oxygen whenever I look into his piercing eyes? And
where are all those annoying fluttery things sending my
insides into a giddy convulsive dance from the inability
to breathe whenever I'm near him?

"San Francisco? That's a long way to go just for a
weekend trip, isn't it?" He's still holding my hand, and
I'm still feeling like an awkward, terrible person.

"Actually, I have to go up to the Marine Mammal
Center to check on some sick sea lions that washed up on
shore. I thought maybe we could combine business with
pleasure."

I glance around the room, trying to look anywhere
but at Josh, certain there are big scarlet letters flashing in
my eyes, and he'll know what I did last night. My attention is immediately drawn across the room where D is
leaning against a wall, hands in his pockets, legs crossed
in front of him. His gaze locks with mine, like a magnet
to steel, as if he willed me to look up and see him. He
begins to make his way toward me. I reflexively yank my
hand from Josh's.

He runs the hand back through his hair. "I understand if you're busy. This is short notice for a weekend
getaway."

"Hey, Pip. You staying for breakfast?" D interrupts

the conversation before I have a chance to answer Josh or explain why I can't possibly take a weekend trip with him.

"Um...I think..."

Alison appears out of nowhere and interrupts me. "Hey, Wolfe. You ready? I'm starving," she whines her greeting and slips her arm into D's. I'm sure the way my jaw drops to the floor is apparent to everyone within fifty feet.

"Oh...uh...Pip, you remember Alison, don't you? From last night? At the bar?" D tugs on his ear. Maybe he's searching for the mind I'm sure he's lost.

"Alison...of...of course I remember her," I answer, politely stunned. But I want to scream, why is she pressing herself against you and running her hands up and down your arm?

Josh extends his hand to the beautiful woman whose hair I want to tear out by the roots. "Hi. Nice to meet you, Alison. I'm Josh."

"Nice to meet you, Josh." She giggles. What the hell is she giggling about when my heart is a shredded bleeding mess along with my vagina?

"Crazy night last night, huh?" D rubs the back of his neck.

"Stark raving mad, I'd say." *On my part.* I didn't expect him to marry me or even apologize. But it's been a handful of hours, and he's shoving another girl in my face.

"I guess I overindulged in the bourbon last night. I couldn't even remember how I got back to my room until Alison knocked on my door this morning. I could barely drag my bourbon-soaked ass to the door. When I told her how out of it I was and how that's never happened to me before, she explained it was her that helped me back to my room and..." He clears his throat. "And helped me out."

"Alison did?" When I look over at the heroine in question, she gives me a smug grin and shrugs one shoulder.

"I think you're mistak—" Josh interjects, trying to set the record straight.

"Wasn't that sweet of her?" I interrupt Josh. "Good thing she was around to *help* you."

I think it's time for me to take up cursing. And right this minute all I can say is, you have got to be fucking kidding me. He doesn't remember? He doesn't remember it was me! How did he explain the big red blood stain on his sheets? Surely, he's not naïve enough to believe Alison was a virgin.

"Yeah. She rushed in the room and shoved me into the shower. Said I would feel better after a long hot shower. She even had room service bring me a morning after smoothie and take care of my room while I was showering."

That's why he didn't see the sheets. She took them off the bed before he noticed. But what about the things D said last night before he plowed into me? He said he had been waiting for me his whole life. Did he think he was saying it to Alison? Maybe he uses the same sleazy lines on all his one-night stands. Screw Alison! No. Screw D! And every other whoring hockey player on the planet. But not literally. Never screw them literally. They will rip your heart out and toss it around like a hockey puck—right after shredding your V-Jay.

Maybe I'm still sleeping. This has to be a nightmare. This is much worse than I even imagined it was going to be. Beyond his indifferent aggression, he doesn't even remember it was *me* he was pounding into.

"No. I'm not staying for breakfast. I have to get home. My new internship starts tomorrow. I have to get myself ready. I'm going to be super busy for the next few weeks." I turn and walk away from D, Josh, and cunning Alison. D deserves her. Let him believe her lies. I'll apologize to Josh later when my head stops spinning.

"Wait! Pip!" D runs after me. I keep walking. I think I'm going to be sick and I don't want to throw up in the lobby.

"Wait." D grabs my arm and stops me as I step outside. "What's going on? You're not mad about me hanging out with Alison, are you? I figured I should thank her for looking out for me last night and this morning. I offered to buy her breakfast. No big deal."

I suppose the adult thing to do here would be to tell him it wasn't Alison, it was me who helped him back to his room last night. It was me he fucked. But there's something a tad demoralizing when a guy doesn't remember it was your virginity he was taking with disregard, while he was balls deep inside you. Humiliation at that level has a way of bringing out the thirteen-year-old broken-hearted drama queen. And ta-da! Here I am.

"Huh. That's a new one, Damon Wolfe sticking around long enough to buy his one-night stand breakfast. Seems like a big deal to me. Quite a breakthrough in your I-don't-give-a-shit-existence."

"Wow. You *are* mad." He blows out a big breath. "I won't have breakfast with her then if it's a problem. Doesn't matter to me one way or the other."

"How gallant of you." I mean, I *don't* want him to have breakfast with the deceiving be-otch but as far as he knows she was his fuckable Florence Nightingale last night.

"Tell me what you want, Pip." My stupid body warms at the memory of his voice giving me the same sultry demand only a few hours ago. "If you're mad about me hanging out with her, I won't. We can leave right now."

I stare at him for a moment. This has to be a joke. Maybe he remembers everything and he's teasing me like he always does. He has to remember. But he doesn't give me the usual 'just kidding, you silly Pip-squeak' line he does when he's taunting me. Because he idiotically really doesn't remember having his gigantic dick inside me.

"No, I'm not mad. In fact, I'd say I've finally come to my senses." I continue to walk toward my cottage to collect my things so I can get the hell out of this nightmare.

"I thought we could ride back together." D catches up to me and walks along with me. "You don't have a car here, do you? I have the Bronco. I wanted you to see it. 412 MotorSport did a phenomenal job refurbishing it. You're going to love it. I took your advice and went with the candy apple red exterior."

I stop, turn to him, and shake my head. He's incredible. He basically just told me he had sex with Alison last night. He has somehow blocked the memory of our being together and his aggressive behavior and now he wants to discuss his vintage car.

"You're right. I don't have a car here, but I don't need a ride. Maybe you should give *Alison* a ride in your shiny refurbished car."

"Will you just stop for a minute?" He grabs my arm with a bit more force and jerks me back. "I don't want to give Alison a ride. I told you I don't care one way or the other about her. I want you. I mean...I want to ride home with you."

"You sure about that? Because it seems like you've already given her a *ride*." I glance down at his fingers still curled around my arm in a tight hold. "Could you let me go, please? I need to get my things."

"No. I can't let you go. Ever." He tightens his grip.

"I'm afraid you're going to have to. Josh is waiting for me. I'm driving home with him," I lie in a smug tone, hoping it will mask the sound of my heart shattering. Apparently, Alison isn't the only one who can lie to get what she wants. Or in this case, what I don't want.

I don't want to be around D, Josh, or anyone right now. I'll Uber my way home. It will give me time to cry my eyes out without anyone witnessing my meltdown except for the poor, unsuspecting Uber driver.

"Josh. Right." He lets go of my arm and runs his hand back through his stupid wavy long hair which looks like it was just styled by some celebrity hairstylist. Yep. He wakes up like that even while rocking a hangover. I hate him.

"Look, last night was crazy. I don't know what happened. I was watching you dance with...with *him*. I got carried away tipping back the bourbon. I don't remember much after that. I thought I was...I don't know. I don't remember anything with Alison. That's never happened to me before. I'm...I'm sorry. I wanted to be there for you last night."

"For *me*? You don't have to worry about me ever again. My immaculate V-jay is a thing of the past." I wave him and my sore, ex-virginal vagina off. "You're off the hook."

"You...with...?"

"That's right." I turn and continue walking. "I'm off to graduate school all grown up and devirginized. And you were right. It was amazing! The release was exactly what I needed. So liberating."

We've finally reached my cottage. I want to run inside, lock the door, and be away from D: his smoldering eyes, his touch, his scent, his magnetism.

"And Josh was so attentive and gentle and..."

"You fucked *him* last night?" he barks, his jaw clenching. He looks like he's getting ready to explode. Good. He deserves it since he did such an excellent demolition job on me.

"Isn't that what you wanted, what we planned? For me to find the right guy? A guy who would be there for me? Devoted to me?" I reach for the doorknob.

My stomach lurches. Why am I lying to him?

"Wait. Pip. Please? I'm sorry. Sorry I got so drunk last night. I wanted..."

"No. Don't apologize. It's all good." I hate the way

the anger on his face seems to have given way to a wounded look. And more than that, I hate the way I'm beginning to feel pity for him.

"Is it? It doesn't seem like it is. Are you okay? Are *we* okay?"

"We're fine." But I ask you? How can we be fine? How can I let this slide? He pillaged me last night. Not only my V-Jay but my heart and soul, as well. And he doesn't even remember. The crazy thing is, he's the one I would've asked for advice on how to deal with this situation and now I can't even do that. And then it occurs to me; I'll never be able to talk to my friend the way we did before. The ache in my heart deepens when I realize the full consequences of my reckless actions.

"I have to go. I'm in a hurry." I step into the cottage.

"There's a home game Thursday night. You'll be there, right?"

"I...no...I have a lot of schoolwork to catch up on. This weekend has really set me back, and I start at the new clinic this week. I'll be swamped."

"You don't intern at night, do you?" He keeps shifting from one foot to the other.

I've never seen him like this: nervous, almost pleading with me to forgive him. But he doesn't even know what he's asking me to forgive and I'm not sure it's even his mistake to have to forgive. I think it's mine.

I knew what I was getting into, what I was asking for. He was always honest with me when it came to who he was or how his past had left him scarred. No. That's not exactly true. He told me time and again how he felt— or should I say, didn't feel anything when it came to his liaisons with women. But he never told me anything about his awful childhood beyond his mom dying and his dad abandoning him. Still, I knew what he had endured wasn't good.

I overheard Dak talking to Batt one time when the guys were sophomores. It was one of the first times they stayed at our Malibu house. They were in Dak's room. They didn't know I was in the hallway. The polite thing to do on my part would have been to keep walking and not listen to their private conversation. But all courtesy went right out the window when I heard them mention Wolfe. I couldn't get my feet to move. I stood cemented on the spot like Nancy Drew on a snooping caper to find out everything I could about D.

As captain of the Bernard team, Dak was concerned about Wolfe's behavior when it came to socializing and women. He knew Batt's parents had taken Wolfe into their home when he was around fifteen. I guess he figured Batt could give him some insight into Wolfe's conduct. Dak was responsible for handling any conflicts the guys might get into off the ice. Although none of the guys were saints, *including* Dak, he thought Wolfe's over the top sexcapades might cause problems.

Batt explained what happened between his father and Wolfe and how Wolfe ended up as Batt's stepbrother. He didn't go into too much more detail. Batt said it wasn't his place to disclose any more than that. It was Wolfe's life and his choice to tell Dak about it or not. I don't know if D ever told Dak the rest of his wretched story. But knowing how close all the guys grew to be, I'm sure he did. Nevertheless, D never told me what he had to do to survive.

But I've surmised the things he needed to do to survive on his own. I can't imagine what it would be like to have to live without the love and support of anyone, let alone on the streets of a vast, unforgiving city. I'm sure the painful experience must have had an effect on Wolfe's ability to give and take affection.

I thought he just needed an understanding friend to help him learn how to love again, and since I dubbed him as mine the first time I laid eyes on him, I was self-important enough to think I could be the one to do it. How arrogant I was to think I could change him or to think he even *wanted* to be changed. How foolish to think I could rescue him like some injured puppy.

"Pip?" D's voice reminds me he's still waiting for an answer to his question. "I can send a car to pick you up. You don't even have to drive to the game. You can study in the limo on the way."

"No. I...I just need some time." My words come out in a trembled whisper. I need time to wrap my head around what happened and figure out where we go from here. Or if we can even go anywhere from here.

"I don't get it, Pip. What..."

"Goodbye, D. Good luck on your season." I close the door before he has a chance to respond. I'm sure he's confused and hurt. At the moment, I can't seem to care about his feelings.

My legs give out from under me. I slide to the floor. Pulling my knees into my chest, I wrap my arms around my legs, squeezing myself into a ball. How could I have been so stupid? I knock my head back against the hard door, once, twice.

The crocodile tears don't wait for me to be in my Uber ride home. They're unleashed with a sob when I realize D was right about everything. I wasn't able to have sex with him and walk away like it was nothing or deal with him continuing to be with other women. I want more from him than that. Another loud sob comes with the admission, he was also right about me being a little fool. I wanted something he doesn't have to give.

Maybe that's why I've let D break my heart so many times in the years I've known him. Or maybe I've broken my own heart, let him in when I knew how he felt or *didn't* feel about everything.

This time it's too much. I can't let myself be hurt like this anymore.

Chapter Fourteen

WOLFE

"What's going on, bro? You okay?" Batt asks as I throw my disheveled tux into the back of the Bronco.

"I'm great. Just a dead man walking here," I mumble. "She fucking sleeps with the dickhead and then gets mad at me for having breakfast with Alison. Have a nice season? What the hell does that mean?" I fling my duffel bag into the truck. "Is she planning on moving to another planet? Because that's the only way she's going to avoid seeing me for the whole fucking hockey season."

"What are you grumbling about? Who slept with what dickhead and who's moving to another planet?" Batt scratches his head.

"What?"

"You said..."

"No one. Nothing. I gotta get the fuck outta here." I slam the hatch closed and go around to climb into the driver's seat. I should've flown here. Why didn't I fucking fly here? Now I've got to drive two and a half torturous hours with just me and my thoughts. Who am I kidding? I didn't fly because I thought Pip would drive back with me. It would've given us two and a half alone time hours. I was looking forward to having her all to myself.

I tug my hair back into an elastic band. I'm regretting leaving the top off the truck because I thought Pip would love riding back with it open. Now all I want is to be encased inside it for the damn long ride home—away from the pain in the ass world and everyone in it.

I don't know what the hell happened. Pippa danced with the douchebag. Then we danced together—me and Pip, not me and the douchebag. And then...and then...I don't fucking remember. I slam my hand against the leather covered steering wheel.

"Yo, dude," Batt says from the passenger side door where he's still standing. "Can you give me a lift back?"

"Back where? Thought you had a car service lined up?" Shit. I love him and hanging with him, but he can read me like a book. I don't want to talk to him about this, at least not until I figure out what the hell I'm talking *about*.

"Cancelled it. Decided I wanted to spend some quality time with my little brother." Without waiting for me to say yes, he tosses his bag in the backseat and hops in the truck.

"Little brother?" I scowl at him. I fucking hate when he calls me his little brother. "You know you're only like a month older than me, right? Not to mention, an inch shorter."

"Thirty days is thirty days, dude. And I make up for that inch in other places." He waggles his brow. "Let's go. We have a long ride home."

"Malibu's kinda out of my way, bro." I need to be alone. Not to think, but to call Pippa and get her to talk to me. Tell her I didn't have breakfast with Alison. Find out why she's angry.

"No worries. I'm not going to Malibu. I'm staying with you for a couple days."

"You're...you're what now? I thought you needed to get back to the studio." What the hell is he talking about? Batt never takes off. Never. He's the poster child for Type A workaholics because he's sure no one can do anything as good as he can.

"Dude. I'm the COO, for chrissakes. Garrett can run things without me there. He has a big enough staff to run the damn White House. I can take off a few days to stay with my pain in the ass little brother if I want to. Besides I haven't had a chance to see the shiny new penthouse you bought on that zillion dollar contract you got with the Winds." He buckles himself in. I guess *my* pain in the ass brother is coming to stay with me for a few days.

"It's not a zillion dollars...but it'll do," I grumble. Other than never wanting to experience the kind of need I did when I lived on the streets, I give zero fucks about the money they give me to play hockey. My agent would stroke out if he heard me say I'd play for nothing if I could afford to eat and have a roof over my head. Still, if they want to pay me enough to buy a four-million-dollar condo, I'm not dumb enough to turn it down.

Turning the key, the engine roars to life. I throw the gear shift into reverse. Before it's completely stopped I slam it into drive. The tires respond with a loud screech and a cloud of burned rubber. Every guest waiting for a car turns to check out the lunatic leaving half his tires on the pavement.

"Whoa, dude." Batt reaches out and braces himself against the dashboard. "Take it easy. I have to get back to the studio eventually. I'd like it to be in one piece when I do."

Heading toward the 101, Batt's words about my contract resonate inside my wind-blown head. It occurs to me, as it has before, he could be playing professional hockey too.

As one of the best forwards on the Bernard team and in Division 1 hockey, he had offers from several teams. But instead, he chose to follow in his dad's footsteps and get into the movie industry. He accepted the offer from Dalt's brother, Garrett, and moved to LA to help run the studio they took over when their scumbag father was hauled off to prison for sexual assault and a boatload of other charges.

With Batt's help, they were able to turn a thriving studio into a billion-dollar industry. Still, I wonder if he's ever regretted the decision to leave hockey. I don't know how he did it. It's the most important thing in my life. The only thing I can't live without.

But then it hits me like a punch to the gut. It's not the only thing I can't live without. In fact, it's moved over and taken second place in my life, second place to Heaven. My life would suck if she weren't in it.

"You okay over there?" Batt yells over the gusty wind whooshing past our heads. "Why so quiet?"

"You ever regret giving up hockey?" I blurt out the thought. "You could be playing in the pros now too."

"Nah. Don't worry about me, man. I'm doing okay for myself. I make *almost* as much as you." He laughs. He's so full of shit. He makes more than me.

"I don't mean about the money, dipshit. I mean, you were really good, and you loved the adrenaline rush on the ice as much as I did. Don't you miss it?"

In my peripheral vision, I can see him tilt his head to one side like this is the first time he's ever considered the question. "I don't know. I miss it sometimes. I still play in a rec league, though. So, it's all good. Anyway, I found something I love more."

I glance over at him. He's grinning like he found Shangri-La and the rest of us are missing out. "Before you came along, I tagged after Dad to almost every movie set and location he was on to direct a film. I loved watching him take control, putting the whole thing together, getting the best from all the performers and people behind the scenes. Just getting the whole thing to work. And when I saw the finished product, I remember thinking Dad was a wizard, pulling everything together, making magic."

"So, you decided you wanted to be the next wizard?" I laugh. "Makes sense. I always knew you had a god complex," I rag him.

"Yeah. Something like that. I guess." He chuckles. When I glance at him, he's got a contemplative look on his face.

"Shit, man. I'm sorry. I didn't realize...I mean, I didn't consider how I was taking his time away from you."

"Who? Dad? Nah. You didn't. After you came to live with us, I finally had the brother—the *little* brother—I always wanted." He snickers.

"You're such an ass." I shake my head, keeping my eyes fixed on the freeway and traffic ahead.

"No. Seriously. Once you were a part of the family, I wanted to spend time with you. I didn't need to be Dad's shadow anymore. I had a brother. I wanted to hang with him as much as possible. Watch out for him. Teach him everything he knows but not quite everything *I* know." Even with the taunting words, his candor shakes me. *Jesus. Where are my Wayfarers? This wind is making my eyes water.*

I pull my sunglasses off the visor and slip them on. I never thought about any of this before because I was too busy wallowing in my own sad story to realize the obvious.

I've always been grateful for the way the Battaglias opened their arms and welcomed me into their family. But my stepping into the picture must have been as big a life-changing event for Batt as it was for me. And yet, he took on the role of my *big* brother without hesitation. Open arms, open heart. I guess because he never objected to me moving in on his territory, it made it easy for me to take everything he did for granted. I'm such a schmuck.

"I mean, sure. You had some issues at first. You were an even bigger ass than you are now, but you eventually worked things out. And now you only annoy me half the time rather than all the time." He laughs and smacks me on the back of the head.

"Gee thanks, asshole." He succeeds in making me feel a little less schmucky.

"Anyway, I had already fallen in love with the movie business. Hockey was always going to be second place in my life. And when you fall in love with something so right, you don't let it go. Ever. No matter how many distractions or other things get in the way." I can feel his eyes drilling into me. As I said, he can read me like a book. "You going to tell me what's going on? Or do I need to pummel it out of you like I did when we were kids?"

"Pummel me?" I give him a sideways look. "We're not kids anymore, bro. And I think the cushy executive job you have has taken its toll. Made you a little paunchy." I reach over and tap his stomach, which is as rock hard as it's always been. But I'm not about to tell him.

"Oh yeah?" He shoves my hand away. "Maybe we should hit your glitzy gym when we get back to your place. We'll see who's paunchy."

"You're on." My relief at having distracted him from my issues is short-lived.

"Is something going on between you and Heaven?" He gets right to the point I was hoping he wouldn't reach.

"What are you talking about?" I scoff, trying to sound like it's the most ridiculous thing he's ever said.

"C'mon, bro. I've known for years how you feel about Heaven. In fact, I think there are only three people

on this planet who don't know how you feel about her."
He counts off on his fingers. "Dak, Heaven and you."

I do a quick double take at him. I've never shown any
feelings for Pippa other than friendship. Except for our
Mutual Masturbation Night—which he doesn't need to
know about.

"That's right, little brother. You're in love with her.
Everyone knows it," Batt states with smug certainty.

"Get the fuck outta here. You know I don't do love. I
can't..."

"It's not that you can't. Sure. You have commitment
phobia. What guy doesn't until the right woman comes
along? The woman they can't live without. The woman
they think about every time they take a breath. Problem
is, with you, you think you don't deserve love, so you
push it away. But you do, bro. No one deserves it more
than you." He keeps talking, like everything he's saying is
apparent.

"Did you take a crash course in psychology when I
wasn't looking?" I shake my head.

His psychobabble is laughable. Sure, I love Pippa...as
a friend. Even in that capacity love's a big deal for me. I
figure it's the reason why I think about her as much as
I do.

It's not unusual for a friend to be concerned about a
friend. Right? To think about them several times a day:
wondering what they're doing, wondering what they
would think about something *I'm* doing? Like, would
Pip like the color I had the condo painted. Or does she
like her sheets tucked under in a tight fit the same way I
do. Big deal. So what if I lose my concentration when I

think about the way she looks up at me with her sweet smile or her sly little grin?

Batt's ridiculous. Does it mean I'm in love with her just because sometimes when I'm in the middle of a practice drill my mind flashes to her bright-colored eyes and the way they spark with fire when she gets annoyed at me? Or if there are times I have to smile when I think about the way she can eat a whole vegan pizza all by herself? Or if I sometimes have to adjust myself when thinking about her? *Not an easy task when wearing goalie gloves and a shit ton of padding.* But in love? Me? No way.

Love cuts you open, leaves you vulnerable, results in pain, hurt, betrayal. The only ones I've cracked open for —slightly—since I was a kid, are the Battaglias. And even though they gave me nothing but unconditional love and support, it took me a long time to trust them, to believe I deserved them. No. I don't fall in love.

"It doesn't take a psychologist to know the things you did when you were a kid weren't your fault. You did what you had to do to survive. They didn't make you a bad person: someone unable to love or undeserving of it," Batt continues his amateur analysis.

I swear to God the guy can read my mind. "And to prove my point, I'm pretty sure Heaven's in love with you too. She seems to think you deserve to be loved. Not many guys are lucky enough to have a woman like Heaven fall in love with them." Even without looking over, I can feel the way he's looking at me like he just recited some truth from the Bhagavatam.

"You know you're bat-shit crazy, right? Pip isn't in

love with me. It's just a schoolgirl crush. She's had one for me for years. And I'm sure as hell not in love with her. She's just an infatuated kid, for chrissakes, and I feel responsible for her. I look out for her. Nothing more." *Except for when I jerked off while watching her finger fuck herself.* Yeah. I'm going straight to hell.

"A kid!" Bat scoffs. "For a computer whiz, you are one dumb motherfucker. Have you looked at Heaven lately? Have you noticed the way *she* looks at *you*? There *is* someone in this car who is bat-shit crazy, but it isn't me."

His words blow through my mind with the same force as the wind blowing past us. Sure. I've looked at Heaven. I've noticed the gorgeous woman she's become. Maybe that's why I can't stop thinking about her, why she's all I see when I close my eyes, why she invades my dreams every night. I thought I was dreaming about her last night when apparently, I was fucking Alison.

I'm not proud, but I'm not the one who made the human male this way. Sometimes, any wet hole will do when we're desperate. And that's all this is: I'm desperate because I'm craving a girl who is off-limits.

"So, what's going on?"

In love. Ha. My smug ass brother thinks he knows everything.

"Hey. Asshole." Batt punches my arm.

"Ow. What the hell, man?"

"I asked you a question. But you're off in Heaven Lee Dreamland somewhere. What happened this weekend?"

"I...I don't know...I..."

"Did you fuck Heaven?" he blurts out.

"Christ, Batt."

"What? I'd ask if you made love to her. But knowing you and the dramatic way you left the resort—without her—I'm assuming there was no romance involved."

"I didn't fu...sleep with her. I was watching her dance with the dickhead. I went a little over the top with the bourbon. I got drunk."

"You got jealous." He hits me with the stark comment.

"Jealous? I don't get..." Wait. I'd never been jealous of anyone or anything in my life. I didn't even know what it meant to be jealous. Was I jealous?

"Yeah. Okay." I blow out a breath in resignation. "I suppose I was jealous. I remember getting her away from Dr. Douche and dancing with her. But I don't remember anything after."

"What do you mean you don't remember anything after?"

"Am I speaking a different language? I mean, I. Don't. Remember. I didn't even remember how I got back to my room. When I woke up in the morning, I thought I had been dreaming about Pip...um...like I'd done before."

"You were dreaming about fucking her," he states flatly.

"Jesus. What is with you and your point-blank comments?"

"That's what you were doing, right?" I give him a quick, murderous glare. "Well?" My threatening glare doesn't faze him.

"Yes! Okay? I was dreaming about fucking her!"

"Huh. If that's how you look out for your friends, I'm glad I'm your brother, *not* your friend," he taunts.

"Fuck you."

"And then what happened?" he persists while wiping a gleeful tear from his eye. *Ass.* I'm glad I can be his amusing entertainment for the afternoon.

"You want the nitty gritty details about my dream?"

"No, dumbass," he scoffs. It seems not even my even-tempered, jovial brother can take the level of stupid I've managed in the past forty-eight hours. "What happened *after* the dream?"

"Alison knocked on my door in the morning and explained it was her who had gotten me back to my room and...and...you know." I push the hair, which has escaped the elastic, off my face.

"Who the hell is Alison?"

"She was a waitress at the reception. The..."

"Oh. Right. The big-titted, friendly blonde. Should've known," he sneers.

"What the hell is that supposed to mean?" I'm in no mood for one of his lectures on morality and how to treat women.

"Just that you never miss one." I give him another sideways glare. "Nah, I get it. She was gorgeous and obviously into you. But I saw the way you were glowering at the dude who Heaven was spending time with at the reception. I figured you'd get in there and get your girl. Instead, you let her go, and you go fuck some random chick." He sucks in a deep breath and blows it out.

"I don't know what the hell happened. It's all a blur. And then Pip was all mad at me this morning when she saw me with Alison. I don't get it. She's seen me with other chicks a hundred times. Anyway, she's for sure not in love with me like you claim. She fucked the douchebag last night." My anger reaches venomous levels at the declaration and thought. Pip fucked someone last night. She gave up her virginity to some random asshole.

My neck and head are beginning to feel like they're being squeezed in a vise. Between the residual bourbon pumping through my blood vessels and trying to figure out what the hell happened last night, I'm wound up like a spring.

"Heaven slept with that guy?" I can hear the skepticism in his voice.

"Yeah, and she had no problem gloating about it when she told me."

"You really are such a dumbass. No way, dude."

"No way what?"

"No way would Heaven ever sleep with that guy or anyone else. I told you, bro. She's in love with you." Apparently, Mr. Smartass understands women way better than me. At least he seems to think he does. "Been in love with you for years. *You* may be whorish enough to sleep with another chick to take the place of the woman you're in love with but Heaven's not the type to sleep with some random guy when you're the only one she wants."

"Thank you so much for the rave reviews of my character." I shake my head. "But for your information, she told me herself she slept with him. She even described how good it was, how fucking sweet and gentle..."

"Before or after you told her about Alison?"

"What?"

"Keep up here, bro. Did she tell you she slept with him before or after you told her about Alison?" His exasperated tone is getting on my last nerve.

I'd do anything for this guy, have his back every second of every day. But right now? I'm thinking I should've had 412 install an eject button under the passenger seat.

"*After* I told her about Alison. I had to tell her. She saw me with Alison in the lobby."

"I'm tellin' ya, you really *are* one dumb motherfucker when it comes to women." He laughs.

"You think? When the fuck did you get so smart when it comes to chicks?"

"You just spent the weekend with the girl who's been in love with you since she was a kid. You were at a wedding, in a romantic setting. Walking down the aisle together, stealing her away from another guy on the dance floor, and saying God knows what to her in your inebriated state. Then when you see her in the morning, the first thing you do is flaunt the random girl you fucked. Throw it right in her face. Dumbass." He shakes his head. If he thinks I'm a dumbass now, imagine what he would think if I told him what I did with Heaven in her room the night before the wedding. "She didn't fuck the other guy. She just wants you to think she did." He waves his hand as if throwing away any possibility of Pippa fucking Dr. Douche.

"Are you saying Pip lied to me?"

"I'm saying she wanted to hurt you as much as you hurt her. End of story." Evidently, if Batt says it's so, it is.

189

I look over at him again for a few more seconds than I should. The driver of the car in the lane next to me lays on his horn, alerting me to the way I'm veering over. Thank fuck for trained goalie reflexes. I swerve to get back in my lane.

Batt reaches for the dashboard again. "Eyes on the road, dipshit."

"Man." I grip the steering wheel with both hands and squeeze it with such force, I'm surprised it doesn't disintegrate in my hands. I wish it was my own stupid brain I was squeezing some sense into. "If that's true, if Pip lied to me about sleeping with him, she must really be hurting." My stomach roils in a wave of nausea. I left her there alone. I swallow the bile in my throat and think about Batt's explanation.

Pip was fuming this morning. And she said goodbye like she was never going to see me again. She couldn't even look at me. Maybe she is in love with me. I know what you're thinking. Oh, right. She can't stand to look at you means she's in love with you? It's not as crazy as it sounds.

It's the only explanation for how angry she is with me for hooking up with Alison. If she weren't in with love with me, she wouldn't care. Indifference, not anger, is the opposite of love. I may not be an expert at love, but I am an expert at indifference.

I can't remember one name of the countless women I've hooked up with since college because they were all just a means to an end—the end being a needed release, nothing more. Afterward, if they said they never wanted to see me again, I'd hold myself back from saying thank you—not wanting to be a total dick. If they said they hated me, I'd get dressed and be on my merry way. I couldn't care less one way or the other.

But with Pip, I care. I care to the point my heart hurts thinking about how I left her with that disappointed, wounded look on her face.

My ping-ponging thoughts and emotions have me so fucking confused my brain feels like it's on a tilt-a-whirl.

"Relax, bro. You got this," Batt assures me like he can hear my mixed-up brain spinning. "We'll figure it all out when we get back to your place. Heaven's a special woman, and she loves you. You'll find a way to get her back. You two belong together."

A memory flashes through my mind. *We belong together*. I said the exact same words last night. *Shit*. I grimace. Did I say those words to Alison when I was dreaming about Pippa? I press my index finger into my left temple and move it in massaging circles. *Stupid. So stupid*. The more I remember about last night, the worse it gets. I should have put the eject button under my own seat.

Chapter Fifteen

HEAVEN

Asshole. Dickhead. Cocksucker. I was wrong. There is no better way to express hostile emotion than curse words. Especially when some big jerk has ripped your heart out.

After my purging word expulsion, I blew out a huge cleansing breath. Did I feel better? Nope. Which is why, to the uncomfortable concern of Rob, my Uber driver, I continued to sob for the first thirty minutes of our ride back to Long Beach. The poor guy kept asking me if I was okay, offering me tissues and water. At one point he even offered me a Slim Jim. I guess he figured if he could get me to eat or drink something, I'd have to manage normal breathing rather than gasping for air in between sobs.

When I finally settled down, I simmered in various stages of awareness. Heartache. Regret. Shame. Self-loathing. I eventually circled back to roiling, seething anger at D.

I dumped the whole fiasco right in his arrogant lap. How could he have treated me the way he did? How could he have forgotten it was me? How could he have even considered the possibility of having slept with someone else only one night after what we did in my room? And does he remember the things he said when he was savagely deflowering me? Does he think he was saying them to Alison? How could he have treated our friendship so callously? The questions kept tumbling one after the other through my mind. And the only answer I could come up with was, I hated D—or I was trying to—for doing this to me, to us. It was the only way I could alleviate the overwhelming hurt.

I had ridden the emotional roller coaster for the two-hour drive. And by the time Rob pulled up at my bungalow, I was a tossed and turned wreck.

Perhaps it's the reason why, as the next day's bright morning sunshine begins to stream through my window, all I want to do is stay curled up in a ball cocooned by my cozy, protective bedcovers never having to deal with another human again. Unfortunately, what I *have* to do is get up, put on my big girl scrubs, and get my miserable carcass to my new internship at EliteCare Physical Therapy.

To add to the Greek tragedy which has become my life, the gods—aka Dr. Alice Freeman, the university clinic director—have seen fit to place me at the world-class facility which takes care of elite athletes from the pro teams in the LA area.

I should be jumping up and down like I won the

million-dollar jackpot. It's the dream placement facility for most interns, especially if they're focusing on sports therapy. In my case? It's the sour icing on the cake to the past week. The culmination to the past four days which were already pretty rotten.

EliteCare is the facility which rehabs the Santa Ana Winds' players. In other words, I'll be treating D's teammates—those on the IR list, anyway. Not a very good start to keeping my distance from D, which is my plan. At least until I can pull myself together and speak adult again, rather than blubbering-broken-hearted girl.

Most of the guys on the team know me and know D and I are good friends. I can't deal with any jokes, questions, or game highlights concerning D right now. My only hope is that all the Winds' players remain healthy and uninjured for the next few weeks. I'll be moved after six weeks to an in-hospital urgent care department for my next round.

Of course, it's not the only reason I want the guys to remain uninjured. They're decent guys who eat, sleep, and breathe hockey. And I would never want any athlete on any team to get hurt. But knowing hockey and the way those decent guys love to pummel each other on the ice, and just in case I won't be granted the wish for every elite athlete in the LA area to be kept injury free? I'm going with self-centered, self-preservation mode and praying for a mere six-week reprieve for Winds' player injuries.

Before I leave for the clinic, I check my phone for the seventy-billionth time only to be disappointed by my empty message folder. Not one word from D. I don't want to talk to him, anyway. But I wouldn't be opposed to a few groveling words on his part. *Ugh.* I hate men, at least six-three goalies with long beautiful hair and eyes that pulverize my panties.

"I have four evals and two humongous offensive tackles here all at the same time," Dr. Mackenzie Monroe—or Mac, as she prefers to be called—blows out a huge breath and tugs on her drooping ponytail to pull it back up into place. Dr. Mac is the director and current doctor on staff at EliteCare.

"I'll let you handle a couple of the evals. None of them look like anything too serious: sprains, strains. A frozen shoulder might be the worst of them. Sorry to throw you into this craziness your first week here but we're short staffed with Tammi out on maternity leave, Dr. Joe traveling with the Ducks, and Dr. Madelyn with the Chargers this week. I didn't expect the morning to be this busy. I've got a few more PTAs coming in this afternoon. For now, though, it's you, Penny, and me."

"Evals. No problem." A week into my internship and I've been thrown into the water without a life preserver, so to speak.

I love the fact Mac trusts me to do the evaluations— at least on some of the minor injuries, for now. She always takes time with the patients I've evaluated before we start treatment on them anyway, even if the condition is minor. It's a requirement for any eval done by interns.

Still, the evaluations give me a chance to hone my diagnostic skills, while really getting to know the patients.

Elite is a bustling clinic even on so-called slow days. The state-of-the-art gym, Olympic size pool, full body cryotherapy chambers, and best sports therapy DPTs in the state are some of the reasons every professional and college team in the Southern California area send their athletes here. Not only for acute or chronic injury care but for prevention, strength, and conditioning training as well. Some of the DPTs here rotate weeks traveling with professional teams.

It's the clinic of my dreams, the place I'm hoping to land a job when I get my doctorate. And the non-stop pace has kept my mind off a particular goalie who will not be named. One week and so far my prayers have been answered—no injured Winds' players.

"You've been doing a great job, Heaven. I'm so grateful they sent us an intern with your knowledge and expertise. I don't know what I would do if I had to lead an intern around by the hand while at the same time dealing with our patient numbers."

"Whatever you need, Mac. I can handle it," I assure her.

"I'll spare you handling the linebackers. It seems the bigger they are, the louder they whine." She smirks.

"Serious injuries?" Mac is the most skilled and compassionate DPT I've worked under. I'm a bit surprised by her seeming insensitivity to the football players.

"Sprained thumb and a sprained ankle." She quirks a brow. "But they bellyache more than the female high school soccer player I have rehabbing a post-op torn ACL." She shakes her head.

"Oh. I see." I smile. I completely understand. Most athletes I know could have a limb hanging off and still want to continue playing. But I *have* seen a few hockey players as big as trees moaning over things as minor as a hangnail. "You sure you don't want me to work with them? I can handle a little abusive griping this morning." I chuckle.

"No. I got it. I know my guys. They need to believe they're the center of your universe. These beautiful monsters require a little extra attention and TLC. It's taken me years to figure out how to deal with the professional athlete, especially the male professional athlete. Women are much stronger when it comes to dealing with pain. You know what they say, it's the reason women are the ones to have the babies, or the human race would have become extinct." She laughs. "You'll learn how to deal with the professional male athlete and all his quirks and eccentricities over time."

My mind immediately segues to D and figuring out how to deal with our complicated relationship.

"But I love working with them. I wouldn't trade my job for any other one in the world." Mac's words bring me back to my current professional duties. "We better stop yakking and get to work, or we'll be here until ten o'clock tonight."

The day continues at a hectic pace. The phrase, 'thank God it's Friday' holds new meaning for me.

To my credit, I only glance at my phone twice. Once at lunch and now, after sliding my weary ass into my car.

My heart skips a beat when I see the number three next to my message folder. But I have to swallow the lump in my throat when my heart takes a dive into my stomach.

The texts are from Nikki asking me how I'm doing and wondering why she didn't see me at the home game this week. Even though I'm disappointed not to see D's name attached to the texts, Nikki's concern is sweet. I can't keep hiding from her. I'll answer her when I get home. Although, I don't know what I'm going to tell her. I'm sure I won't be able to disguise the gloom in my voice. A whole week without one word from D and I'm still having trouble breathing when I think about him.

"Hey, girl," Nikki chants over the phone. Hal keeps nudging me with his head. He's not getting my undivided attention as I sprawl on the couch after work and he's not happy. "Where ya been? We missed you at the last game. I was getting ready to send out a search party."

"Sorry I haven't called. I started the new internship at Elite. It's been crazy."

"Yeah? How's that going? You sound...tired."

"It's intense. Non-stop. But I love it. I'm learning a ton, and it keeps my mind off... it keeps me so busy the day rushes by in a blink."

"Hmm. You sure you're okay? I thought maybe something happened." I can hear the skepticism in her voice. Nikki and Tracey have developed this tag team skill to see through everyone's BS. But I thought since Trace is still on her honeymoon, maybe Nikki wouldn't have her full-on Sherlock Holmes powers.

"Happened? No. What would have happened? Nothing happened." Great. Could I sound more like I'm hiding something?

"Well, considering the way you bolted from the resort without saying goodbye and then a certain goalie burned half his tires on the pavement leaving, also without saying goodbye, me and Trace figured something happened between you two." The dynamic duo strikes again.

"No...I...we...he..." And that's all I can manage to sputter before I begin spewing tears again like an unlocked fire hydrant.

"I knew it! What did the dick for brains do?" Nikki demands.

"Nothing. He..."

"I'll be right over. Dalt left for the away games. I'll pick up Chinese takeout. The nanny has popcorn and a Disney movie lined up for the kids." I don't even get a chance to argue before Nik adds, "But more importantly I have two large bottles of wine with our names on them. One red. One white."

I breathe out a huge sigh. "That sounds wonderful, actually. I could use the company," I concede.

"And about ten big glasses of wine, I'll bet," Nikki states.

"Yeah and that." I manage a smile.

"I'll grab another bottle."

Nik's a great friend and the perfect shoulder to cry on to give me some much-needed advice on how to deal with a hockey player's frozen heart. She and Dalt went through some crazy times before finding their way into each other's arms forever.

"I'm calling for an Uber. Give me forty-five minutes."

"Okay," I manage to sniffle out.

"Make that thirty. Hang in there. I'll be right over."

When the call disconnects I'm cheered, looking forward to Nikki's company. But then it occurs to me. I'm going to have to explain to her everything that went down at the wedding between Wolfe and me. I'm so embarrassed by the way I behaved: drinking too much and then sleeping with D, knowing he had also been drinking way too much and wasn't thinking straight. I'm so ashamed of my poor judgment.

But it's too late now, in more ways than one. Not only did I make poor choices last weekend, but I also agreed to let Nikki come over and console me. She's already on her way, and knowing Nik, she won't give up until she's heard the whole sordid story, and then she'll offer to castrate D for me. I manage another smile when I think about how worked up Nikki can get. For a little thing, she can be very sassy and determined.

I should probably talk to D and work this out before I tell anyone else about it. What happened isn't all his fault. I was a more than willing participant. I dove in with both legs wide open knowing D's MO. I have to accept the residual heart and V-Jay ache I was left with.

Maybe Nikki will share her wine for half-truths because I'm not ready to tell anyone how totally stupid I've been.

Chapter Sixteen

WOLFE

"I've seen high school kids do more presses than this with more weight. Do another one," my pain in the ass brother goads me. He's supposed to be spotting me. But with his arrogant arms crossed over his arrogant chest I'm not sure how much help he'd be if I dropped the 250-pound bar across my neck while grunting out my seventh rep.

"Am I being tortured for something?" I grumble, dumping the weighted bar onto the rack.

"It's been a week. You haven't made one attempt to contact Heaven, asshole." Batt slaps my sweaty forehead, Three Stooges style.

"Get..." I try to smack his hand away but every muscle in my body is spent. He moves faster. "What the fuck, dude?"

"What are you waiting for, *dude*?" He throws a towel across my face.

"She didn't even come to the game this week, and she hasn't called or texted me, either," I mumble. *She must be really mad...and hurt.*

"Aww. You poor baby. Don't be such a thirteen-year-old girl."

"You know, you can be a real asshole sometimes. How do you know what I'm doing when you're not breathing down my neck?" I growl at the meddling know-it-all. "I'm trying to figure out the right way to go about this. What do I say to her? Sorry for fucking some other chick when it was you I wanted to be fucking?"

"At last. A look into the way that bizarre thing you call a brain works. You're a regular Lord Byron."

"Fuck you."

"Seriously. You're pathetic when it comes to talking to women. I'm not sure why the ladies love you so much."

"Because I don't waste time using my mouth and tongue to *talk*. It's not my *words* they love. I can explain it to you sometime if you're ever interested in finding an actual woman and giving your fist a break." I smirk.

I use the towel to wipe the sweat off my face and throw it back at him. He swats it across the room before it hits him.

"Real funny. You know you're a pig?" He shakes his head in disgust. "But somewhere deep, deep, *deep* down, I know there's a sensitive, caring human being in there. There has to be. I read somewhere once that the woman you want reflects who you are. And you want Heaven. She's as good and caring as they come. Stop trying to define everything. Go for it. Go get her back."

"I'll think about it. Maybe when I get back next week. I'm going to hit the shower."

"Is it going to be one of those extra-long try-to-get Heaven-out-of-your-system showers?"

"Fuck off, Batt." *And yup. It probably is.* "And now that you mention it being a whole week, when the fuck are you going home?" I don't really want him to leave, and he knows it.

We haven't been able to spend time together like this since college. I didn't even realize how much I missed hanging out with him. Not to mention—even though I'll never admit it to him because I'd never hear the end of it—his emotional support this past week has been a godsend. Also, he's a lot smarter than me when it comes to interacting with other humans, particularly female humans.

I miss Pip. My thoughts are a mess. I can't think straight, can't seem to function without her. I have such a need to be with her, to talk to her, even when there's nothing to say. I just want to be near her.

And every time I start to curl up into a lump like a sniveling teenager, Batt pulls me back to life saying something like, *"Do you love the girl, fucktard? Then get the hell up and fight for her."* Dude's so compassionate. Isn't he? But he's right. I have to talk to Pip. I'm not sure what to say. I'm shit at expressing emotions. I need some time to figure out a game plan.

"You know you'll miss me, *little* brother, and the gourmet meals I've been cooking every night," Batt answers the taunting question I forgot I asked.

"You're right. I'll miss the meals." I laugh and drape

an arm around his shoulders as I push the elevator button for my penthouse's second floor.

I had the entire first floor set up with a state-of-the-art gym and use the second floor for living quarters. The place is big enough for three families to live comfortably and never see each other. It's too big for me. I never noticed before. Ever since this past weekend, though, it feels empty and...lonely.

"You should adopt a dog," Batt says as the elevator door opens into the large entryway. It's as if he read my mind about the place being too big and empty.

"Yeah. Right. And what do I do with it when I'm on the road during hockey season? Like starting tomorrow. I'll be away all week."

"Hire a dog sitter. This is LA. There are more people here you can hire to spoil your pet than there are to take care of your kids."

"I don't know. Maybe," I mumble. I head for my bedroom and the long shower I'm looking forward to. *Pippa would love it if I adopted a rescue dog.* Except she might never know because she may never speak to me again.

"And bro, while you're *thinking* about Heaven?" He air quotes around the word thinking. "Try to think of something nicer to say than 'I'm sorry for fucking another chick when I really wanted to fuck you.' That's cold, dude. Unfreeze the ice cube you call a heart and tell her how you feel. Be honest. Be sweet. Heaven's in love with you. It won't take volumes of poetry. Just be you. Uh...no. Wait. Check that. You're a fucking idiot most of the time. Be the you hiding inside that meathead of yours."

"Fuck you, bro," I grumble again. My vocabulary is somewhat repetitive when I'm around my asshole brother. He laughs as I slam my bedroom door.

I strip off my sweat-drenched clothes and drop them on the bathroom floor. *Be the me I have hiding inside.* That's the problem. There is no other me deep inside. I'm a broken leftover shell of a guy. Only when I'm with Pip am I a better man, a better person. But what do I have to offer *her* besides a big empty penthouse and a big broken me?

My mind drifts to the times we've spent together and how perfect she is. She brings a calm to my life I've never found anywhere else. Her beautiful, smiling face fills my thoughts and my heart pounds faster as I remember what we did at the resort and the vivid dream I had afterward.

I turn the full body jets in the shower on high. Stepping in, I let the hot water hit me full force. I drop my chin to my chest and allow one jet to beat against the back of my neck in an attempt to alleviate the pressure building in me, the same way it does every time I think about her. But nothing ever eases it. Not even when I take matters into my own hands and stroke myself into a powerful release. It's getting to be a pathetic substitution for the real thing.

But then it occurs to me. Maybe, what I need to do is learn to be the better man she brings out in me, the one she used to see in me. Be that man even when I'm not with her. I have to prove to her I can be a decent guy.

More importantly, I have to prove it to myself. Prove I can be the kind of man who deserves a woman like Heaven.

Chapter Seventeen

HEAVEN

Another hectic week at Elite is over. My body is in remote mode when I drop my computer bag next to the sofa and drag myself into the kitchen to grab a glass of Cabernet before heading back to the living room. I turn on the television as I pass it, put my glass down on the coffee table, and take a face-first swan dive into the sofa. It was a late night at the clinic. I'm beat.

But the Winds/Stars game is about to begin. Nikki was kind enough to remind me in about twenty texts that D is starting tonight.

I somehow managed to get her to stop asking me questions during her visit last weekend. I told her about my drunken activities with D in my cottage. I did *not*, however, tell her about my further humiliating rendezvous with D in *his* cabin. and his bourbon-soaked amnesia regarding it.

Maybe our three-bottle wine consumption kept her

from being her usual perceptive self. Hopefully, she bought the masturbation pas de deux as the only reason I was feeling miserable about seeing D with Alison the day after the wedding. Problem is, finding out about my intoxicated interaction with D has somehow fueled Nikki's matchmaking engines. She's more confident than ever D and I belong together.

Groaning when my cell phone rings inside my bag, I stretch to reach for it without moving from my prone position. The annoying tingling sound vibrates again.

"Ugh. Make it stop." I dig into my bag. My fingers know right where to find the cellular nag. I pull it up to see who's calling and sure enough, there's Nikki's beautiful, sassy face—blue bangs and all—sticking her tongue out at me and flipping me the bird. I don't even remember where we were when I snapped the cheeky photo. It's Nikki to a tee.

"Are you watching?" She doesn't bother to say hello when I swipe the accept button.

"Yes, Nik. I'm watching," I mumble into the sofa cushion.

"Wait till you see him play. Dalt says Wolfe's been on fire at practice. So focused. Not one female-involved extracurricular activity. Dalt says Wolfe hasn't even gone out with the guys all week. Just practice, training, hitting the gym, and home to bed. Dalt says he's like a new man. He's even sworn off drinking." I don't say a word while Nikki continues to convey Dalt's acclaim of D's virtuous behavior.

"Hello? Heaven? Are you there?"

"I'm here," I yawn the words into the phone.

"Are you sleeping?" she asks with an indignant scoff.

"How could I possibly be sleeping while you're blathering about the honorable Damon Wolfe?" I yawn again.

"Don't you dare go to sleep. Your man is starting. You have to watch," She demands.

"He's not my..." No point in arguing. It will only drag out this conversation. I really want to get off the phone, drink my wine and pass out until Monday rolls around again. "I'm watching, I'm watching," I assure her.

"Good. Have to go. I don't want to miss Dalt when he skates around the ice to warm up. His ass looks amazing, even on television, when he's doing cross overs."

"Yup. Dalt has one amazing ass." I smile into the phone. But Nikki disconnects the call before I finish my sentence.

Sitting up, I don't waste time savoring the wine's aroma or the taste on my tongue. I take a long swallow, enjoying instead, the warm fuzzy sensation it induces right down to my toes. It's almost as good as the tingling sensations I got when D had his lips and hands all over me. *Nope. Not as good as that.* But much more dependable and a lot less heartbreaking.

I haven't heard much from D or about him, other than Nikki's recent praise. The team was away this week. Happily, there were no injured Winds' players requiring care or rehab.

While away, D sent two texts with three words. *I miss you.* Nothing else. I didn't tell him I missed him too. Even though I do. So much. My return texts were only to wish him luck in his games and to congratulate him on starting tonight.

I pick up the remote and click to the NHL channel broadcasting D's game just in time to hear the announcer introduce the Winds to the ice and see the beautiful-ass parade gliding across my screen.

"Dammit. Why do hockey players have to have the best bodies?" I shrug and let out a huge sigh. But my breath catches when my favorite ass glides past, the one I could pick out in a beautiful-ass lineup.

I cross the room and sit cross-legged on the floor in front of the television. Touching the screen, I use my fingers to follow D around the ice until he takes his place at the net.

Right from the opening face-off, the game is in over-drive. The puck gets traded back and forth between teams. But with both goalies playing with catlike reflexes there's no score when the first period ends.

When the second period starts, the competitive aggression on the ice is seething. The puck is passed to Dalt, and the sparks begin to fly. He kicks it ahead, chases it to the side boards, and a Stars defender smashes Dalt into the boards.

The next time the puck is passed to Dalt along the boards the same defender skates toward him. As he's about to smash into Dalt's left shoulder, Dalt flicks his left arm up in the air, sending the Stars player flying. He takes a hard, crashing seat on the ice, and the Dallas fans in the arena explode, booing, jeering, and hissing like a metal pot in a microwave.

I'm nervously chewing my nails when the puck is

passed and flies down the ice toward D. I see it happen almost before it does. D dives, sprawling himself out. In a flash, he wiggles across the goal on his stomach like a fighting scorpion deflecting the puck with his right pad. Then he's up, both legs spread out into a front split, twisting to the left and then the right to repel the puck. I can see the pained grimace cross his face even through his mask. To add to the calamity, I'm not sure if it's an accident or on purpose when a Stars forward comes sliding knee first and full force into D's thigh. I gasp when D flops onto his back, writhing in pain.

Running my hand over the screen again, I imagine I can soothe him with my touch through the glass. "Oh God, D. Get up. Please get up," I whisper to the liquid crystal display. But I know he won't get up because he's hurt and in pain and I can't do anything to help him.

Suddenly my view is obliterated when the whistle blows and the screen fills with green and grey jerseys. Both teams' benches have emptied. A full out brawl has broken out in the crease.

I'm screaming at the television like a crazy woman. "Get out of the way! Where's D? Someone help him!" It takes only moments—which seem like an eternity—for the refs to stop the brawling and the team doctor and trainer to get to D.

After they carry D off the ice, I don't know how long I stay seated on the hard, living room floor sending texts to D to see if he's okay, before I pass out in exhaustion right on the spot.

Chapter Eighteen

WOLFE

When I come hobbling into EliteCare on my crutches for my evaluation and rehab session, it's the first time I've seen Pippa since the wedding. She's a goddess even in scrubs with her hair pulled up in a messy bun. I have to remind myself to breathe.

There were several missed texts from her before I could get to my phone after they carried me off the ice at the American Airlines Center.

HEAVEN

Are you okay?

Please let me know if you're okay.

Have they given you a diagnosis yet?

D, tell me what's going on?

With the last one, I could almost see her standing there with her hand on her hip reprimanding me for not getting back to her fast enough and for being foolish enough to strain a groin muscle. I smiled to myself imagining her lecture to me about all the proper ways to stretch and warm-up to avoid the injury. But my smile quickly faded when the whistle blew and we lost to the Stars 1-0.

I managed to get off a short text to her in between the prodding, poking, and x-rays.

> I'm fine but the game is fucked. I'll see you on Monday.

Now, as I settle into a chair in the reception area, I can see Pip standing in the hallway at her office door having an animated discussion with another doctor. Every once in a while, when the music being piped into the waiting room goes into a softer refrain, I catch a few words.

"Sorry, kiddo. This one's all yours. I'm swamped."

"But I can't," Pippa protests.

"Sure, you can. It's a Grade two strain. It's already been..." The music picks up again. I can't hear the rest of Dr. Joe's sentence. But I see Pippa shaking her head.

They're obviously discussing who is going to work with me and by the dread on her face, I'm guessing Pip has drawn the short straw.

"I don't get it. Most women and some guys would give a week's salary to get to work on Damon Wolfe's adductor muscles." Dr. Joe chuckles. But Pippa isn't smiling.

The dread has morphed to sheer revulsion when I catch part of her answer. "...all theirs, but I, on the other hand, am trying to stay away from all hockey players' adductor longus muscles. If you...

Dr. Joe lets out a big laugh at Pippa's statement. "Sorry, again, kiddo. But you're in the wrong profession if you don't want to work on hockey players' thighs."

Thankfully there's no one else in the waiting room at the moment to hear his comment. But when Pippa realizes their conversation is a little louder than is appropriate she glances down the hall. When her gaze lands on me, her face turns rosy red.

I wiggle my fingers to wave hello and shrug my shoulders at the awkward situation. She stomps into her office and slams the door without returning the wave. But a second later the phone buzzes on the front desk. Carmen, the receptionist, lets me know a PTA will be right with me. I'm sure it was Pippa calling her, sending the PTA to get me. It gives Pip a few more minutes to avoid seeing me.

"Hi, Wolfe. You're in room four today. Let me help you," the PTA enters the room and offers her assistance to help me up. "Look at you. What did you do to yourself?" the overly friendly PTA asks.

"I got it," I grab my crutches and hoist myself up ignoring her hand. "I had a little mishap in the last game. Nothing serious."

"Bet you could use another massage," she whispers and gives me a wink. *Another massage?* Do I know her? What did Carmen say her name is? Nancy? Mandy?

"My Jacuzzi tub is up and running again and I just

got a whole new supply of essential oils," she continues to whisper while escorting me into room four. "And *honey*," she adds, wiggling her brows up and down. *Honey?* Oooohh. Yeah. I remember the oils and honey.

"Thanks, Sandy. I'll take it from here." Pippa enters the room behind us as the PTA, whose name apparently is Sandy, helps me up onto the examination table. Hopefully, Pip didn't hear *Sandy's* offer. I don't want her to think I initiated it or that I'm interested.

"Okay. See ya later, Mr. Wolfe," Sandy says in a more professional tone. But when she adds, "Call me if you need anything. Anything at all," I'm not sure if she's talking to Pip or me.

"That's it for now, Sandy. Thanks, and close the door on your way out," Pip instructs her.

When the door closes, Pip stands in front of me with her hands in her pockets, her iPad tucked under her arm. We both stare at each other for a moment. I'm not sure what to say; how to tell her everything I want her to know.

She's the first to break the silence, blowing out a big breath. "Nice to see nothing keeps the infamous Damon Wolfe down. Not even a strained groin." She slides the iPad from under her arm and begins tapping the screen.

Damn. I don't want her to think I'm interested in Mandy. "No. Pip. I wasn't..."

"It's fine." She stops me from explaining. "I'm happy you feel well enough to...to...date. I just need to ask you some questions before we do the physical evaluation." She's happy I'm well enough to date? Doesn't sound like a woman who's wallowing in heartbreak. "I already have your personal information since you've been here before and we keep all the Winds' players info on file. So, let's get right to the injury and how it occurred."

"I thought you saw how it occurred. I got all your texts the second I hit the locker room." *And you seemed way more concerned than you're pretending to be now.*

"I did see it happen. We were watching the game from home. But I need to hear it in your own words for the records." *We* were watching? Who the fuck is *we?* She couldn't have been watching with the douche. *He* never got into the sport. Fucking loser.

"Sorry I didn't answer your texts right away. They were diagnosing the injury. I couldn't get to my phone."

"No problem. Sorry about all the crazy texts. I had a little too much wine and...well, you know how silly I get when I've had too much to drink." Shit. She was drinking with Jackoff. *Yeah. I know all too well what you're capable of doing when you've been drinking.*

"I...uh...I don't even know Mandy. I mean, I didn't remember her." *But now that she reminded me, I remember the interesting things she can do with oil and honey.*

What in the hell am I doing? *Pull yourself together, dude. This is Pippa. You practically grew up together. Why are you talking about Mandy? Say something meaningful.*

She shakes her head and gives me a strained smile. "Sandy."

"What?"

"Her name is Sandy. I see some things never change. Let's get back to your evaluation, shall we?" She forces another smile. Somehow, I'd feel better if she slapped me or yelled at me or didn't speak to me at all. This creepy smiling thing seems...well...*creepy* and indifferent.

"Things change. I've changed. Have dinner with me tonight. I'll show you how much I've changed." I reach out to touch her, but she moves away from the examination table and pretends she didn't notice.

"Sorry." Her apology has an underlying you-pathetic-chump-not-a-chance-in-hell-am-I- having-dinner-with-you tone. "I'd love to, but I'm super busy with school-work and clinic notes I have to catch up on." She doesn't look at me when she blows me off, just keeps punching things into her iPad.

"You have to eat, Pip. How about I bring takeout to your place?" If she wants me to beg, I can do begging. "You can take a few minutes to eat and get right back to your work." I may be sounding a little too needy because I am. I need her.

And then it hits me as if someone smacked me in the forehead. If I didn't know better, I'd think Batt was in the room. The smug ass was right. I'm in love with Pippa. Completely. Totally. Inexplicably. It's not just her body—although I definitely want that knockout body. I want all of her in my life: her smile, her wit, her sass, her strength, her vulnerability, her compassion. I miss her the second we're not together. I want to be with her all the time. She's everything I thought I'd never have, everything I thought I never wanted.

There it is. I don't know how it happened, how Pip became the center of my universe. Maybe I fell in love with her a little the first time she blew my mind with her storybook princess looks. Or the first time she challenged me to a competition and beat my ass at whatever it was. Or the first time she smiled up at me with those sparkling eyes. Or maybe it's everything about her rolled up into one beautiful little package. She's crept inside my heart and soul and melted all the icy vows to stay away from emotions, attachments...love. I belong with her and to her, totally, completely. And she belongs with me. Why didn't I realize it before now?

"That's sweet but I can't. Thanks, though." Pip's further rejection bursts my love bubble.

She's treating me like you treat the people you're trying to let down gently. You know, the clingy, stalkerish types you're not the least bit interested in, but you're trying not to be a total dick, so you shoo them away with a nice thank you.

No way. This is me. She can't fool me with her façade. I saw the panic and fear on her face when she was trying to talk Dr. Joe into treating me. *And* I saw the anger and mistrust in her eyes when her glare landed on me in the waiting room. She's far from uninterested. If she didn't care about me, she wouldn't...care.

But I'm so fucked. I've fallen hopelessly in love with the girl I've done everything in my power to convince never to love me.

I'm going to treat this as another challenge between us. Game on. I'm going to show her how I feel. Show her what I want, what *she* wants, and how spectacular we can be together. I've never been a quitter. But this time, we both win.

Chapter Nineteen

HEAVEN

You know the Dolly Parton song, *Here You Come Again*? Sure you do. Everyone does. Once you hear it, the tune is on autorepeat in your head for a week. Think about the lyrics. Can you hear them? Well, that's what it's like every time I see D. Every. Damn. Time. I have to stop it. I have to stifle the racing beat in my heart and vagina whenever he's in the same room as me.

I'm *a strong, powerful woman in control of my own destiny. I'm a strong, powerful...*I'm a professional. I can do this. I *will* do this. I can treat Damon Wolfe for a groin strain. I can check his range of motion, stretch his adductors, and do an ice massage on his inner thigh without the slightest flutter of my ovaries. I *can.*

I absolutely, positively will not succumb to his gorgeous face, sigh-worthy body, and mind stupefying smile. I can't play this game with him anymore. I may be a strong woman, but my heart is a stupid, weak fool. I won't let D crush it ever again. My brain is in control from now on.

"Let's do some passive motion tests. Lie back on the table, please. Let me know if and when the movements cause pain," I instruct D in my most professorial tone.

"I feel pain," he states.

"I haven't done anything yet."

"I feel pain because you won't have dinner with me." He gives me the half grin which he knows causes every panty in the area to moisten. But since mine are the only panties in the immediate vicinity, and I am now immune to Wolfe and his fever-inducing tricks, my panties will not be affected by his charms today or ever.

"As your therapist, I would be going against my own recommendations for recovery if I were to allow you to go to dinner. Initially, you're going to need to rest and keep ice on this," I continue to instruct him while I begin the tests. "Then we can begin with a few simple exercises. We should be able to get you back in the game in a few weeks, maybe less if you follow all my instructions."

"I definitely want to get back in the game. I'll do whatever you say, listen to every command," he says in a stupid seductive tone while touching my hand, the hand I'm using to hold up his bent leg.

I apologize to all the health gods, Hippocrates, and whoever else we doctors are supposed to recite vows to for what I do next. Sorry, but I can't seem to help it when the range of motion test I'm doing on D goes slightly beyond passive causing him to let out a pained yelp. After all, I'm still only an intern. I haven't honed my gentle touch skills yet. Right?

"Oh. Did that one hurt?" I coo in pretend empathy.

Okay. I'll admit there may be a slight conflict of interests here and maybe I shouldn't be treating my arrogant, pain in the ass, HAF ex-friend. But I promise I would never do anything which would increase his injury. And I am very good at keeping promises—unlike someone else in this room.

"Ow. Fuck yes, it hurt. Can you take it easy?" D whines.

"Of course. I would never want to do anything to hurt *you.*"

"Listen, Pip. I—"

"Let me get an ice pack. Stay there. I'll be right back," I interrupt him and slam the door behind me.

Leaning back against the door, I take a few deep breaths. *Be still my beating vagina.* This is ridiculous. Why do I still want him? He's conceited, cocky, a repulsive womanizer and...we've been friends for years. I can't treat him like a stranger forever. I should tell him the truth but let him know nothing sexual is ever going to happen between us...uh...again.

I'm a strong, powerful...blah, blah, blah. I'm not so strong and powerful. I'm scared to death to feel everything I'm still feeling for D. *Get out of your vagina.* Right. Time to practice some good, strong psychic self-defense.

What was I doing? Oh. Right. Ice pack.

———

"I'm back. How we doing?" I ask D in a rehearsed, cheery, health provider voice as I reenter the treatment room. He's still lying on his back, one arm draped across his eyes, the other hand applying pressure to his inner thigh.

"I don't know how *you're* doing, but *I'm* hurting like a bitch," he grits out from under his arm.

"The ice will help. Let's get your...um...those..." Oh. My. God. I have to get his pants off. I should've had him do it before he laid down. They're sweatpants. He could have easily slid them off while he was standing. I should've had Sandy do it before she left the room. Now that he's lying down he's going to need assistance. Should I call Sandy in to help him? *Brilliant, Heaven.* That wouldn't be awkward at all. Get someone in here just to slide his baggy sweatpants off. I bet he'd love it, though, if I did get Sandy to remove his pants. *Damn. This is so unprofessional.*

"You still there?" D peeks out from under his arm and reminds me I'm supposed to be helping the injured patient lying on the table in pain. "I'm looking forward to any relief you can give me. This thing is really throbbing," he groans.

Throbbing. Dear God. Did I just sigh out loud? I'm sure my mind has already broken every ethics rule in the book. I see a vision. It's me, no longer in school. I'm living on the beach...as a bag lady. I shake my head and clear my thoughts. I will not get kicked out of school.

I place the ice pack on the side counter. "Let's slide your pants down. They're pretty loose. You don't have to move too much. Just lift up slightly so I can get them down past your...so I can get them down."

D grimaces while lifting his butt off the table and I

slide his pants to his ankles. Oh. My Freaking. Word. He's commando! Is he kidding me?

I force myself to look away but not before noticing he's definitely not a grower. Even in its inactive state, his penis is *huge* and lying across his *injured* thigh. I know I'm not supposed to be assessing his penis. But look at it. Have you ever...? Never mind. Not the time or place

Taking the thin blanket from the foot of the table, I unfold it, drape it over him and pull it up to his waist. Thank goodness D's arm is still covering his eyes. He doesn't notice me noticing his...gifts.

"There we go. This should keep you comfortable. It's a little chilly in here," I offer, as a sweat droplet slides down my back. I glance over at the digital thermostat. It's 66º in here. So why am I sweating like I'm in a sauna?

"Sorry about the commando thing. It was too painful to bend my knees to get my briefs on. Baggy sweats were all I could manage." His apology sounds sincere. I don't think he did it on purpose to shake me.

I know how painful it can be to bend or raise your leg even slightly when you've had a groin strain. Besides, he didn't know I would be the one treating him. On the other hand, maybe he thought it would be *Sandy* removing his pants. No. This is D. He doesn't need to do anything raunchy to get a woman to notice him. He just needs to breathe, fully clothed, and heads turn in his direction—both male and female.

"No problem. I know it can be very hard in this situation...uh...I mean...hard when you're bending...I mean... I didn't even notice." Oh for god's sake. I am definitely getting booted from this program. My parents will be so proud. *"Sorry. Your daughter has been thrown out and can never practice in any health profession because she's an inappropriate perv."* Sounds about right.

D moves his arm off his face and gives me a little smile. Not a cocky grin but a sweet smile, like he sympathizes with the battle going on between my professional brain and my slutty vagina.

"This will feel a little cold at first, but it will help alleviate the swelling...I...I mean...the inflammation and pain."

"No problem." D chuckles. "I'm an expert at this. I grew up using ice packs."

"Really? You needed that much cooling off in the area, huh?" I laugh. Whatever. This is D. We've been teasing each other with sexual innuendos for years.

"Very funny, smart ass. I meant I grew up using ice packs *every*where on my body. Hockey is a tough sport."

For a moment, it almost feels like old times, pre-wedding-from-hell-weekend. Until I slip the ice pack under the blanket and slide it up his thigh. It runs smack into his reposing penis and just like that we're *all* less than relaxed. Me, D *and* his penis, jump. Really? Can a penis respond even when being confronted with an ice pack? Yes. Apparently, it can.

D cringes. I pretend I don't notice the unintended encounter and begin circling the ice over the injured adductor muscle. D's eyes roll back in his head. He lets out a sigh as I continue the ice massage. And then, he begins moaning.

"Mmm. Oh yeah. Right there. Like that. Feels so good. Mmm. Don't stop."

For. The. Love. Of. God. What is this? A test? A test I'm failing miserably. Sweat droplets begin to form on my brow and don't even get me started on what's going on between *my* legs. And *then*, I see it. The blanket raising into a tent-like shape.

"Okay. Times up." I yank my ice pack filled hand out from under the blanket.

"Already?" D groans. "I don't think you did it long enough."

"Yes. It was long enough." *What is happening?* All my words have become crude references to penises. "I have to check on another patient. I'll send someone in to do your ultrasound treatment. I'll come back when you're done to go over recommendations for tonight and get you set up for another appointment tomorrow," I rattle out in a rushed barrage.

Scurrying out the door, I hear D call to me, "Wait. Pip. I'm sorry. I couldn't..." But I don't hear the rest. I run down the hall, fly into my office and slam the door behind me.

"I'm a weak, powerless woman who craves Damon Wolfe like a junky craves Crack," I sigh out in a whisper.

Chapter Twenty

WOLFE

It's said it took God seven days to create the world. Well, if he can create a whole universe in a week, I figure two weeks is enough time for *me* to get a woman to forgive me and go out with me.

For almost two weeks I've been coming to EliteCare for rehab. I watch Pip as she moves around the clinic with confidence. Seeing her handle patients with proficiency and tender care, you would think she already has her doctorate.

I'm feeling great. The crutches are gone. I'll be in playing shape in no time. As I said, Pippa has the magic healing touch. Uh, not exactly *touch*. Not with me, anyway.

She sets me up in the Cryo chambers, works with me in the pool, prescribes exercises, and then instructs me on how I should be doing them. Sadly, though, after my unintentional enthusiasm during my first visit, Pip never does any therapy which requires touching my body. Any massage or electro-therapy treatment is handed off to another doctor or assistant.

Can I help it if God had a sense of humor when he was doing all that creating? Or maybe it was the last thing He created on the seventh exhausting day: penises. Maybe he was worn out when He created the overly sensitive, highly responsive appendage. It's not my fault I get hard every time Pip touches me. I'm a guy, and she's a beautiful woman I happen to be in love with.

I decided I needed to do something to melt Pip's clinical heart and get her to agree to go out with me. So yesterday, after I left Elite, I had a thank-you slash please-forgive-me-gift delivered to the clinic: five dozen white roses. It had a simple note included.

Thank you for taking such good care of me. You're going to be an amazing doctor. I'm sorry for everything. Please have dinner with me Saturday night.
Love, D.

I was going to put **all my love, D** but it seemed like too much.

Today? As I look around the reception area? It's like someone vomited roses all over the clinic. There are rose-filled vases all over the place: on the receptionist desk, on the tables in the waiting room. There's even a bunch in the bathroom. I didn't think about how small Pip's shared office is. No one would be able to get in the door if they put five dozen roses in there.

"Jesus. It smells like a funeral parlor in here. What the heck is going on?" Dr. Mac exclaims when she walks in the clinic's front door. I wasn't thinking about the overpowering scent this many roses would produce, either. I'm a virgin when it comes to this stuff. I've never given a woman a forgive me gift before.

"Mr. Wolfe sent them as a thank-you to Heaven." Nancy tips her head toward me and throws me right under the bus.

Dr. Mac whips around and glares at me. "Sweet. But next time, Wolfe, a simple thank-you note will suffice. This is a clinic, not a bordello," she says, and continues walking through the reception area. Geez. It's like I'm being reprimanded by the principal. And who the hell uses the word *bordello* anymore?

Mac stops and turns around. "Or better yet. We'd all love some tickets to a Winds game," she suggests and then disappears into her office.

See how it goes with women? Try to be a nice guy, and now I'm going to have to send an apology gift to Dr. Mac for my apology gift to Pippa. This forgiveness stuff is complicated.

"Ready for you in the gym, D." Pip comes down the hall to escort me from the waiting area. "By the way, thanks for the beautiful roses," she says as I walk with her to the gym. "You didn't have to do that." She smiles and a faint blush warms her cheeks. Yes! She's smiling and softening up toward me again. I told you. I'm no quitter.

When I want something, I figure out a way to get it. Note to self; apology gifts are the bomb!

She pushes open the gym door. "It's my *job* to take care of you." She reverts back to her curt tone and deflates my victory celebration. "To be clear," she continues while holding the door open for me. "You could send me the entire contents of the Dubai Miracle Garden, and I would not go out with you. I am not having lunch or dinner with you at a park, at the beach, on a rooftop or on the moon. Nowhere. Not now. Not ever. So, save your money."

"Not in a box or with a fox or in a house or with a mouse," I mumble my sarcastic remark.

"That's right, Dr. Seuss. Now you've got it." She purses her lips and lifts a brow. "Get on the treadmill."

Okay. Time to pull out the big guns. Pip's no ordinary girl. Flowers and candy won't do the trick. I'm going to have to think outside the box. I need to do something really spectacular to get back in her good graces. Something no other guy would think to give her. And then it hits me, the thing most important to her, besides school and surfing and beating me in competitions.

Chapter Twenty-One

HEAVEN

Oh no he didn't. He's the devil. He knows just what to do to tempt me. Sitting on my desk when I get to the clinic the next afternoon, is a big manila envelope. Inside the envelope is a thank you letter from the Best Friends Animal Society thanking me for my twenty-thousand-dollar annual contribution. I would say it's a mistake, but I know it's not. It's exactly the kind of thing D would do to soften me up—and it's working. The big jerk.

Best Friends runs the nation's largest no-kill sanctuary, their focus being animal welfare. Their goal is to find homes for unwanted pets and to ensure there will never be another homeless pet. It's an organization near and dear to my heart and the donation is much needed. I'm sure the generous donation will be put to good use.

Next to the large envelope is a small white one. Inside is a simple folded note.

Please have dinner with me. I'm so sorry for everything.
Love, D.

I brush a lone tear off my face.

Love, D. Exactly the problem. I'll admit, just considering his invitation sounds like a dumb move on my part. I will also admit, the first day Wolfe came to the clinic after his injury, I panicked and said I had to keep my distance because I still wanted him in ways I shouldn't. I know I said I would only see him on a professional basis. And now, after this sweet, devilish gift in my name, I'm thinking about going to dinner with him.

Let me explain, make my case, so to speak. Things have been going really well at the clinic. While I've been treating him, Wolfe has behaved like a perfect gentleman, no more inappropriate reactions. He sent me roses to apologize for the massage incident–albeit, enough to build a float at the Rose Bowl Parade. He's been following my treatment recommendations to the letter, without complaint. And now this thoughtful contribution to Best Friends. He's really trying. And since the infamous weekend, I've realized a few things

I enjoy being with D. I miss him when he's not around. We enjoy each other's company. We make each other laugh. We have fun together. Most importantly, I've accepted the fact D is *never* going to be a relationship kind of guy and I am *never* going to be a one-night stand kind of girl. This eye-opening revelation may be the only good thing that came from our night together.

Having come to these sensible, level-headed understandings, I've decided I shouldn't throw away an important friendship just because we shared one night of really stupid mistakes—okay, two nights.

I know what you're thinking. You can't go back to being *just* friends once you've been intimate. But I've chosen to look at that dreadful night as a two-pronged experience. The first prong was hell. But the second prong helped me understand our diverse views on relationships. I've also come to this realization: D not remembering the event is a good thing.

If I can put it behind me—forget it ever happened—it will be like it *didn't* happen. We can hold onto our friendship. As I said, no sense in losing my friend over a weekend of bad decisions.

Sure, I won't deny there's still a teensy magnetic pull between me and D, especially after the masturbation incident which D *does* remember. But lots of friends dance the Sexual Attraction Tango with each other. It's just typical playfulness. It doesn't mean anything. It took some soul-searching heartbreak on my part to figure this all out. I get it now. I can handle it like a mature, professional woman: not some manic teenager.

Sounds good, right? Or maybe...I'm totally fucked.

WOLFE

"The contribution in my name was too much, D. But it was very thoughtful." She gives me the sweet smile I've been missing. "And I know Best Friends will certainly put it to good use. But...I don't..."

"C'mon, Pip." I stop her before she can turn me down again. "Please, just have dinner with me. I'm sorry for everything: The drinking too much, the jacking off in front of you, the hooking up with what's her name afterward. You have to forgive me." Christ. I sound like a whiny little bitch. But she's making me crazy. She still hasn't said yes, and I'll never be able to top the Best Friends contribution. I thought for sure it would be the offer she couldn't refuse.

"Will you shh? There are other patients here. They don't need to know all the sordid details of my life," she loud whispers.

I glance around the gym. There's only one other patient in here. Mr. George Gilbert, a cantankerous, retired, investment banker. He's been here every day I've been here for rehab. He's always on the treadmill. Although, if he walked any slower, he'd be going backward.

I've tried talking to him several times, but the only thing I got from him was, "Aaie? What are you saying, boy? Speak up. Why does this whole damn generation mumble?" He's like a hundred and fifty years old. I don't think he could hear a meteor blasting through the roof and landing smack dab in the middle of the gym.

"Mr. Gilbert can't hear a word we're saying." I shake my head at Pip.

"I'm not so sure about that," Pip whispers like she's plotting a crime. "Last week, Sandy was working with him in here and talking to another PTA telling her about her weekend and some guy she hooked up with. She was whispering so quietly the other PTA had to ask Sandy to repeat herself when she described the guy's...um...short-comings. Before Sandy could go into her reprise, Mr. Gilbert yells out, "Take a trip with me to Paris, honey. I'll show you some equipment you'll never forget.""

"No fucking way." My belly laughing causes me to stumble as I step up onto the elliptical. Pip reaches out to stop me from falling. But I get myself together before she touches me. I don't want to have another unexpected incident with *my* equipment if I end up in her arms.

"Yes way. I think Mr. Gilbert is holding out on us." She chuckles.

This is good. We're laughing, joking. More relaxed. Almost like we were before. But she still hasn't agreed to go to dinner with me.

"I miss you, Pip. I miss us," I grunt as I continue my climb to nowhere. "You're being silly. Just have dinner with me."

Shit. Shit. Shit. I almost had her, and I blew it. Let's take a brief pause for some advice to all you guys out there. If you're trying to melt a woman's heart, get back in her good graces, get her to like you again, never, ever, *ever* refer to her as silly.

"What did you call me?" Pip's not whispering now— or smiling. "You think I'm being silly? It's silly to be upset about us...um...doing what we did and then you... sort of...hooking up with Al-i-son? Her name is Alison! You should at least remember the woman's name you... you...did things with after we...did things." She's so angry it's like she's speaking in Morse Code.

"No. No." I stop climbing long enough to think about how to answer her without getting my head bit off. "I don't think you're being silly." *I don't understand what the hell you're talking about, but I don't think you're being silly.* "I just meant..."

"You just said I was silly. So, which is it, D? Am I silly or not?" She's got her hand on her hip and she's tapping her foot, waiting for me to come up with the clever words which will dig me out from the hole I've created.

Problem is—again for you guys out there—you can't dig yourself out from a hole. Remember. The more you dig, the further you sink into the hole.

"I...I..." The sweat is dripping down my neck, and it's not from the exerting climb I was doing.

"He's an asshole. Dump him and fly away with me to Monaco. I don't think you're silly. I think you're gorgeous and I have a private jet," Mr. Gilbert yells across the room.

Pip and I stare at each other in wide-eyed shock. After we've had a minute to process what the hell just happened, we simultaneously burst into laughter.

"O...okay," Pip sputters out while holding her side in pain from laughing. "As a thank you from all the homeless animals, I'll have dinner with you. I suppose one dinner won't hurt the doctor-patient relationship. But I get to pick the place."

"You got it. Anywhere. I mean, I don't have a private jet, but maybe I can borrow Mr. Gilbert's." My big smile spreads across my face. And my next thank you gift is going straight to Mr. George 'No-Filter' Gilbert.

Chapter Twenty-Two

HEAVEN

I picked the perfect place to have dinner with D. It will be like it was, pre-weekend from hell. Just two friends hanging out, having fun. I'm ready when D knocks on the door because I don't want to invite him in. No sense in tempting fate...or my vagina.

"Am I early? You're not dressed," D greets me—or rather, *doesn't* greet me—when I open the door.

I look down, scanning my body to make sure I'm not experiencing Early Onset Dementia. Did I forget to put my clothes on? Nope. Fully covered—except for my arms—in a short sleeve silk top and jeans. It's a balmy November evening, even for LA. No need for long sleeves.

"What are you talking about? You're right on time, and I *am* dressed."

"Oh...guess I'm a little *overdressed*." D shoves his hands into the pockets of his sports jacket. "When you said you wanted to pick the place I assumed it would be…'

"What? You thought I would pick somewhere we would get two nibbles and a check requiring a month's salary?" I bite back a smile while assessing his attire. I can't stop myself from scanning him from head to toe. He's ridiculously beautiful. I squelch the impending thought, *he looks scrumptious* in his navy sports jacket, white open-collar dress shirt, and grey dress pants. *Nice. He looks nice.* Not scrumptious.

"You should know me better than that, D. I require some good old greasy food to maintain the energy required to whoop your butt. Hang on. Let me grab my purse." I turn to get my purse from the kitchen counter. "You look very nice, though." I glance over my shoulder.

"Whoop my butt? I thought we were going to dinner?" he calls after me.

"We are. We're going to a place I can do my two favorite things: eat unnecessary amounts of artery-clogging food and beat you at every game we play." I saunter past him with a contented smirk, pulling the door closed behind us.

I can't miss his shiny red vintage car parked two spaces down the street. "I'm pretty sure those are *not* your favorite things to do," he says in a smug tone while opening the passenger side door for me.

I stop short. My leg raised in midair to climb into the truck, my hands clutching the door frame on either side. Panic sweeps over me. Does he remember? Or is he going to bring up the night I drank too much and behaved like an idiot? Other than my telling him I never wanted to think about it again—on our walk to my parents' cottage, the morning after—we haven't discussed *not* talking about it. But since we *haven't* talked about it, I thought it was an unspoken mutual decision *never* to speak about it. God. Nervous energy is racing through me, making my thoughts tangle together.

D places a hand under my elbow to help me up into the truck. I step back and brush his hand away. "What do you mean?" I blurt out the indignant question.

"What do you mean, what do I mean?" He chuckles.

"What do you mean they're not my favorite things? How do you know what my favorite things are?" I bite out.

"I *mean*, I've known you long enough to know surfing tops your Favorite Things To Do list. But since I didn't bring my wetsuit, I don't think we're having dinner on our surfboards." His brow pinches, and he shakes his head. "Geez. Relax, will ya? What's the problem?"

"Um. Nothing. On second thought, I'll drive." I stick my palm out, waiting for the keys. If I'm driving, I won't be able to behave like a nervous ninny, overreacting to every comment he makes.

"What? Why? You know, you're being extra weird, even for you." He clamps his fist around the keys.

"No, I'm not. You don't know where we're going. So, give.' I wiggle my fingers for the keys in a come-hither motion.

"So, tell me where we're going, and then I'll know." He crosses his arms over his chest, still clutching the keys.

"Stop being such a stubborn jerk, D. I want to

surprise you. What is it? You don't trust me to drive your precious car? Maybe this whole dinner thing was a bad idea after all." I turn toward my house. No maybe about it. This was a terrible idea.

"No. Wait. Of course, I trust you to drive my car. You had a great teacher. After all, I'm the one who taught you how to drive a stick." He scratches his head like he's confused and holds the keys out to me.

Hmph. Good thing he doesn't remember how he taught me to drive *his* stick. Or *didn't* teach me, as it were. I snatch the keys from his hand.

I don't know. Maybe I was wrong. Perhaps we can't go back to being playdate buddies. Not if everything he says sounds like a sexual innuendo to me because I can't forget what it felt like to come apart while watching him do the same. Or because I *can't* forget what it felt like when D mercilessly pounded into me.

I'm terrified. I can't be with D the way I want to. But I can't be without him.

Chapter Twenty-Three

WOLFE

"Yeeesss! Win-ner and champ-i-own. Boom! Take that, you looza." My victory celebration may be excessive, but it's required if I want to maintain my balls, which are diminishing every second we're here.

Pip's brilliant restaurant idea for a dinner date, or whatever we're calling this excursion, was Dave and Buster's. I thought she would pick some quiet, pretentiously expensive restaurant as payback for the way I've been bugging her to go out with me.

I should've known better. I should've known she'd pick the one restaurant where we could eat in between her beating me at every damn game in the place. Doesn't matter what it is: *Mario* and *Sonic*, *Ghostbusters*, *Fish Bowl Frenzy*, the girl whoops my butt—as she put it.

So, when my last ball swishes in, and I beat her at *Super Shot Basketball* by ten points, I'm razzing her and celebrating like I just won the NBA finals, jumping up all around Pip and fake shooting like I'm sinking imaginary basketballs.

"Yeah. Woot. Woot," Pip's tone is flat and sarcastic as she slow claps. "You managed to win one game. You *do* realize you're like a foot taller than me, right?"

"Go, ahead. Make your excuses," I taunt, grabbing my jacket from where I had tossed it so I could play without any restriction, and her purse, which is lying next to it.

"Okay, Karim Abdul. Let's eat. You shouldn't be jumping like that yet, and I'm starving." She snatches her purse from me and pushes me out of her way.

"Aww. Did the wittle pip-squeak burn up all her reserves trying to beat the big, strong man at basketball?" I fake pout and then cross box into the air to continue my celebration as the current Dave and Buster's alpha basketball hero.

"Yes." Pip turns and sticks out her bottom lip, imitating my pouting. "I burned up all my energy *letting* the big man-child win." She pivots and walks away.

For a moment her words don't register. All I can think about is her full, luscious, strawberry tasting lip, begging for me to bite it and then lick it. And then it hits me.

"Wait. What?" I chase after her. "You did not *let me* win. I beat you fair and square." *Right? I beat her. Didn't I?*

"Of course, you did,' she says matter-of-factly as she slides into a booth. It's in an area where there are no arcade games. The immediate quiet is a welcome sound to my thumping eardrums.

"You little monster." I slide into the seat next to her without thinking about it. "You did not let me win. You're just saying that because you can't stand losing to me."

She opens a menu. "Yes, Wolfe. You're the biggest, baddest *Super Shot* player in all the land," she mocks me, without taking her eyes off the menu.

"That's it, Andersen. You are so going down." With a swift move, I slide over, pinning her against the wall. "We'll see who's the baddest." Without giving a crap about our current location, I begin tickling Pip in the spot I know she's most sensitive—just under her ribs.

Pip is squirming on the slick vinyl seat, causing her to slide down onto her back. She tries to push me off her and swipe my hand away while giggling in sporadic squeals, "D, stop!"

Our juvenile playtime continues for several seconds until an intrusive throat being cleared distracts my mission to torture Pip with tickles and wrap myself up in her warm musical laughter. Pip bolts straight up in her seat. I use the hand I was tickling her with to give a nonchalant tug on her shirt and pull it down into place, covering the silky skin our wrestling has left exposed. I'd rather be pulling her top off and tickling her nipples with my tongue, but I'm reasonably certain the waitress wouldn't approve. "Can I take your order *now*?" her indignant tone and pursed lips are evidence she's not amused by our antics.

"Pip? You ready to order? Or should we find a dark corner to finish working up our appetite?" The waitress's mouth drops open. I'm pretty sure the pole up her ass moves higher. Pippa's cheeks warm to a blush. I'm waiting for Pip to reprimand me for my crass remark. I couldn't stop myself, though. The way the stuffy waitress is glaring at us, you'd think we were screwing in the booth rather than just having some fun.

"No, thank you." Pip smiles, lifting her menu. "Let's wait until after we eat and then find somewhere to screw off the calories," she adds without taking her eyes off the menu. "Um...let's see...I'll have an extra-large sweet potato fries, a large onions rings, and a double black bean burger. Thanks." She hands the menu to the stunned waitress. "Babe? What would you like?" Pip asks while running her hand up my thigh in a long stroke. Have to admit, I'm kinda stunned myself.

"Uh...yeah...I'll have all the pre-game appetizers and a triple bacon burger." I hand over my menu.

"All...all of them? That's a lot of food, sir," the waitress stutters out.

"Yes. *Sir,*" Pip purrs in my ear. "I'm going to have to take *extra* time to burn all those calories off for you." *Jesus Christ.* I don't know what she's doing. But my dick is standing at attention hoping she's serious.

"Any...anything to...to drink?" The flustered waitress wipes a hand across her brow.

"No!" Pip and I shout simultaneously. "I mean, I'll have unsweetened ice tea," Pip answers in a calmer tone.

"I'll have the same." I bite back a smile. Guess neither of us wants an alcohol-induced repeat-wedding-weekend performance.

"Could you rush our order, please?" Pip asks. "I don't think I can wait much longer to fuck my boyfriend." She smiles demurely at the waitress, who drops her pen and order pad. I'm almost beginning to feel sorry for her.

The waitress, whose cheeks have flamed to crimson, retrieves her pen and pad and scurries off without saying a word. Meanwhile, my throbbing erection is ready to punch through my pants.

Not sure how the waitress is going to handle our little show. Either she'll bring our food in record-breaking time, or she'll call the cops and have us arrested.

"What the hell was that?" I sputter out in a laugh.

"Sorry. I couldn't take her judgmental attitude." Pip slides down the bench, putting space between us.

"No. That was great." I reach over to touch her shoulder, but she leans away.

"I think you'd be more comfortable on the other side of the booth." She tips her head to direct me to the other side. And my sexy, teasing, friend is gone, replaced by my polite physical therapist.

"Okay. Sure. No problem." Grabbing a folded napkin from the table, I shake it out and hold it over my crotch as I stand. Because my cock is having a *huge* problem moving away from Heaven.

"So...um...this is nice. I've missed you." I readjust myself under the table in an attempt to get comfortable.

"You've seen me almost every day for weeks. How could you miss me?" She purses her lips. I stare at them for a moment. They're in a perfect configuration to be kissed. Long and hard.

"D?'

"Huh? Oh...yeah...but not like this. Not like we used

to before...I mean..." Her elbow is propped on the table, her chin resting on the palm of her hand. She tilts her head a bit and studies me. Doesn't say a word, doesn't help me out, just watches me squirm in my seat.

The nervous waitress shows up with our drinks and nearly throws them on our table while running past. You'd think she doesn't like us or something.

"Um...so you still seeing the animal dude?" I ask and take a long swallow from my ice tea. The question I swallow along with the icy drink is, *are you still fucking Dr. Dickhead?*

"Who?" So, this is how she wants to play it, pretend she doesn't know what I'm talking about.

"You know. What's his name? Jack?" *Jack off.* "Jason?" *Jiz head.*

"Oh. You mean Josh. No. I haven't seen him since... um...since I started at Elite. My schedule is too hectic right now for socializing."

"Thank fuck," I mumble out on a relieved breath into my glass.

"What?"

"Huh? Oh, nothing. I was just saying, I can understand. I see how crazy busy you are at the clinic. Too bad, though. He seemed like a nice guy." *And I'd sprain my other nut to keep you busy for another month or two and away from him.*

"Oh, really? You thought he was a nice guy." She smirks.

"Yeah. He was okay. If you like that type. I mean, not the right type for *you*. But..."

"Hmm. And here I thought you didn't like Josh.

245

After all, you did threaten to rip his arm off, along with a few other threatening pleasantries."

"What? No, I didn't." *Wait. Did I? Pip and I were sitting at the bar and...*

"Um...never mind." Pip interrupts my thought process. "He knew you were drunk. No hard feelings."

Maybe I shouldn't have brought up the douche. But I need to know where we stand. Where *I* stand. If she was still fucking the asshole, I don't know what I would do.

Our food is delivered to the table by two guys carrying trays loaded with everything we ordered.

"Wow. We ordered a lot. Looks good. Let's hurry and eat." Pip begins shoving fries in her mouth like she's never seen food. But I think it's an attempt to stop talking, to shut down again.

Nope. Not going back to being awkward around each other. "You want to hurry and eat so you can burn off the calories by having your way with me like you told the waitress?" I give her a wry grin while popping a fry into my mouth.

Without missing a beat, she swallows *her* fry, runs her tongue along her bottom lip in a slow, sweeping tease and says in a soft voice, "I *am* going to burn off these calories while having my way with you." *Holy fuck.*

The ice cubes rattle in her glass as Pip sucks down her ice tea. The provocative comment and her sucking lips wrapped around the straw have my hopeful dick twitching again.

"How's your leg feeling?" She continues teasing the straw with her tongue.

"My leg is fine," I blurt out. *What the hell does she have in mind?* I'm dying here.

"Good. Because I'm about to humiliate you in *Dance Dance Revolution*. Best, most fun way in the world to burn off calories." She gives me a smug grin and bats her lashes.

Fuck. Yup. My leg is fine. My balls, on the other hand, are turning bright blue. Not to mention, she knows damn well I'm terrible at the stupid dance game. But I guess I won't complain. I'll willingly take the loss to have the chance to watch her sweet ass—in those tight jeans—doing all the hot moves she's mastered for the game. It's not as good as finding a dark corner to work off the hundred zillion calories we're eating. But beggars can't be choosers. Until she's the one begging *me*, that is.

Chapter Twenty-Four

HEAVEN

"I'll admit he's an idiot most of the time. But I think it's sweet the way he sings to Trace."

"Sweet? He's acting like a fucking fool—again. What is his obsession with singing his drippy heart out in front of people?"

It's Karaoke night at the Flying Puck. Dak and Trace are staying at Dalt and Nikki's for the weekend. They just got back from their honeymoon-slash-Save All the Coral trip. Since it's a rare night when the guys don't have a hockey game, and everyone's here, we decided to make a night of it. Karaoke is another checkmark on my Favorite Things To Do list. We're seated at a table in front of the stage.

D's recovered from his strain but continues to come to the clinic almost every day to use the gym. Good news is, he and I are back to our friends hanging out status like we were before The Incident—which as far as I'm concerned, shall never be discussed as long as we both shall live. I've been having a sadistically great time at beating him in arcade games, surfing competitions, miniature golf, bowling—any activity which doesn't require being alone with him. Although, Karaoke isn't a competitive activity, it keeps us surrounded by other people. Precisely how I want it, to keep me from making any more foolish mistakes. Bad news is, Wolfe detests Karaoke.

He wanted to get a blanket and lay on the beach—just him and me—to "stargaze." Stargazing alone with D sounded much too hazardous for my heart's health. After some pretty-please, begging on my part, D reluctantly agreed to come here.

My goofy brother is up there being all gooey, singing his trademark song for Trace, the same one they danced to at their reception: *Tracey* by The Cufflinks. Everyone in the bar is having a blast because as much as I hate to admit it, Dak has a great voice. It's not the first time he's done something like this. He did the same thing when they were in college to get Tracey to forgive him for yet another stupid thing he did. Stupid things must be in our genetic coding.

Tracey, as well as every other woman in the place, is swooning over the big dope. Meanwhile, Wolfe is gagging over the "asinine" spectacle my brother is making. Wolfe's word, not mine.

"You should totally try it, D. It's so much fun. It's liberating getting up there singing your heart out."

"Oh? You mean like the liberating, letting go,

vibrating higher, thing you did at the resort?" He lifts a brow and gives me a smug grin.

"No. Absolutely nothing like that." I give him a smug grin right back and lift my virgin ice tea in a mock toast. I've continued my moratorium on alcohol, at least whenever I'm around D.

I'm told D hasn't had anything to drink since the reception, even when he's not with me. Guess he's a stronger person than me. Nights alone with my girls, Trace, and Nik, are all about major wine consumption and unending girl talk.

"Hard pass. I will never get up there and do that shit." He shakes his head at Dak, who's oblivious to D's disapproval. "Pfft. Wearing your heart on your sleeve. It's demoralizing," he mumbles into his lemon water.

"Our turn!" Nikki shouts when Dak is finished. "C'mon, Trace, Heaven. Let's rock this place." Trace jumps up without any coaxing. Nik grabs my hand and tugs me from my chair. "We'll have these guys comin' in their pants." She takes a long pull from her beer and slams her mug down.

"Um...no. Nik, I don't think I should..." I try to protest because I don't *want* D 'comin' in his pants' or anywhere else which concerns me. I've been doing my best to avoid all forms of D's *coming*. We've managed to repair our friendship. It's the only way we work.

"Come on, bitch. It'll be fun." Nikki doesn't give me a chance to finish my objection. She leans in and whispers, "If not Wolfe, maybe you can take another one of these hotties home with you. Look around. The place is wall to wall hot cocks."

"Nik!" I screech. I swear I will never get used to her non-filter.

"Oh, c'mon. You know what they say. Use it or lose it," she preaches as she drags me toward the stage. Trace is already up there picking a song for us. "I'm afraid if you don't get laid soon your pussy is going to seal itself closed —*forever*. Or at least, the first guy in there is going to have to plow through the cobwebs."

"You know you're completely warped. Right?" Thank goodness we're far enough away from the table, Wolfe can't hear her.

"Maybe. But I can't let my girl waste the best fucking years of her life. And I do mean *fucking* years. So many men. So little time." She pulls me up the stage steps.

"What are you saying? Stop teasing my sister-in-law." Trace laughs when we join her on stage. "You know you're full of shit, Nik. You haven't even looked at another guy since the day you and Dalt fell in love."

"Oh, I've looked. I'm married, not dead," Nik states in a droll tone. Trace shakes her head at the flippant comment. "Don't worry. Looking is as far as it goes. I mean, *look* at Dalt." Nik turns and blows a kiss to the man we all know is the love of her life. "Why would I need another guy? Dalt's fine as hell, sweet, considerate, loyal, respects me, loves me unconditionally *and* he makes beautiful babies."

"Exactly," Trace agrees with a relieved sigh.

"And the fact he has a nine-inch cock as thick as a beer can doesn't hurt, either. Well...sometimes it hurts. But in a good way."

"Eww! You're disgusting," Trace and I groan through our laughter.

"Okay, bitches. Here we go." Nik hands us microphones. Apparently, she's finished her Nik's Warped Lessons in Love 101 lecture.

When the intro to our music begins and the words to another classic sixties' song, *He's So Fine* by The Chiffons, roll across the big screen, I figure what the hell. Might as well give in and enjoy the time with my girls.

But when Nik and Tracey begin singing to their soulmates, which leaves me awkwardly glancing at Wolfe while I sing, I'm not sure this was the best idea after all.

Chapter Twenty-Five

WOLFE

"Thanks for doing this. I had a great time. I owe you one," Pip says, as we walk toward my car.

"No. It was fun actually. I had a good time." I don't tell her I could have fun testing devices in a Medieval torture chamber—if she were the one doing the torturing.

"As long as you don't have to be the one singing." She chuckles as she climbs into my truck.

"Yeah. As long as that." I smile and close the passenger door.

"You have a great voice, though. I loved hearing you sing," I say as I slide behind the steering wheel.

"Really?" She looks at me like I have two heads. "Karaoke must be in our genes." She laughs. "My mom and dad met at a Karaoke bar when they were in college. Dad said he couldn't hear or see anything or anyone else in the packed bar when my mom began singing. He said his knees melted as well as his heart when she sang *Feel Like Makin' Love*." She wrinkles her nose as if thinking about her mom singing the provocative song and her dad's reaction to it smells.

"Mom begged him to let her tell us the whole story about the infamous night. But *I* begged him to put the big kibosh on that idea." She shakes her head. "You met my mom. You know how revealing her story was probably going to be. I wasn't ready to be damaged for life thinking about my parents getting it on in a car or back alley or something." She grimaces.

"Your parents are a trip." I chuckle, remembering the yoga episode. "Especially your mom. Must be nice to be so uninhibited and open."

"I guess. It's sad though, in my case, the apple fell far, *far* from the tree." She lifts a shoulder and drops it.

"Nah. What are you talking about? You're my vibrating-higher-Pip." I reach over and brush her hair back off her face. She trembles when my fingers feather across her cheek. "And I loved the way you were singing to me tonight."

"Oh...I..." She squirms in her seat and looks around like she's searching for the escape exit.

"Seriously. I was the luckiest guy in the bar to have you singing to me. Thank you."

I can't hold back another second. As I lean over to kiss her, I swear she's leaning toward me too. Like gravity drawing two electrons toward each other. But then, also like two similarly charged electrons, we're pushed away from each other when Pip says, "You're welcome, but we should get going. It's getting late." That's my relationship with Pippa in a nutshell. We have the same negative charge toward each other, repelling us from getting together.

"Sure, no problem." I sit up straight behind the wheel and turn the key in the ignition. The truck roars to life. "Do you want to take Nik and Dalt up on their invite for a nightcap before heading home?" I *don't* want to go to Nik and Dalt's.

In the past few weeks, Pip and I have spent almost every day together, whenever we have some spare time. It's been wonderful to have her back in my life. But in all these weeks we haven't spent ten minutes alone. I want to be alone with her. I want to tell her how I feel, how I think we should take our relationship to the next level.

"I'm pretty tired.' She lets out a small kitten-like yawn. "Sorry. But A few hours with Nik can be exhausting. I love her to death, but her energy is contagious—and draining." She blows out a big breath.

"Yeah. Nik's another free-spirited, uninhibited girl. You seem to be surrounded." I chuckle.

"I know. Maybe the universe is trying to tell me something." She smiles through another yawn.

After buckling in, Pip sinks down into the seat. She rests her head back and closes her eyes. The dim parking lot lighting streams through the windshield and washes over her in an amber glow. Even here, sitting in a truck, with her eyes closed and completely relaxed, she looks like a Botticelli painting.

I don't know what the universe is trying to tell *her,* but it's telling me to reach over and caress her cheek, run my hands through her long, silky hair, kiss her pink pouty lips. But I don't dare listen to the universe. We've finally gotten back to the place where we're having fun together, relaxed around each other. I don't want to ruin it. I want to hold on to whatever time she'll allow me to spend with her. But I definitely don't want the night to be over.

"You know what I just realized?" I didn't *just* realize it. I've been thinking about it forever. But the timing was never right. Not sure if now's the right time either, but here goes.

"What's that?" she asks without opening her eyes.

"You've never seen my condo. All this time I've been here, you've never been to my condo."

"Um...no...I guess I haven't." She glances over.

"Why don't we stop there? I'd love your decorating suggestions."

She wrinkles her nose. "I don't know anything about decorating."

"Your place looks amazing."

"Ha. If that's what you're going for, just put everything you love around your condo and you'll have my decorating expertise. That's what I did in my house."

"Exactly why I want you there...uh...to give me some ideas. You up for it?"

"Um...I don't think..."

"It's the first time in my life I've owned a home, and you're the only one I want to show it off to." I place a hand on her knee. She stares down at her leg through narrowed eyes as if some alien creature landed on it.

"O...okay...sure." A nonchalant shove of my hand off her leg is added to the reluctant affirmation. "Why not?"

She shrugs. "It's Saturday, I can actually sleep in tomorrow. Take me to your lair, Milord." She laughs and snuggles down into the seat again.

I throw the truck into reverse. My nerves begin racing along with the engine.

"Wow. This is amazing," Pip says in awe as she walks around admiring my gym. "Now that you're finished with therapy, I don't know why you bother coming all the way to the clinic. You have all the same equipment here."

"There's someone at the clinic I happen to like spending time with." I smile. She needs to know how important she is to me and how much I enjoy our time together.

"Aww. That's sweet, D. I'll tell Mr. Gilbert how you feel about him. Maybe he'll offer to take *you* to Monaco for dinner."

"Real funny, funny girl. I think it's time for the spanking I was about to give you at Dave and Buster's before we were interrupted." I stalk toward her. She laughs and runs behind the treadmill.

"No! D, don't you dare," she says in between giggles. I keep right on prowling toward her.

"D, I swear if you take one more step, I'm going to..."

"What? What are you going to do, funny girl?" I chuckle. She squeals when I reach the treadmill. We dance around it, moving back and forth in opposite directions as she tries to keep it between us and avoid me.

When she makes the wrong choice and moves the same way I do, I grab her around the waist. She lets out a little scream as I spin her around in my arms. We're both laughing as she pounds on my chest and tries wiggling herself free. When she finally gives up the playful struggle, she collapses into my arms.

The skirmish has left us gasping for air in between giggles. With each heaving breath, her tits press into my chest. She looks up into my eyes, and when those gleeful pools of blue hit me, game time is over.

"I hope you know CPR because you take my breath away," I whisper.

I don't give her time to come back with another pickup line. Instead, I close my lips over hers with a gentle touch, giving her a choice to let me kiss her or push me away. But then the most wonderful, beautiful, sexy thing happens. The corners of her mouth tip up and I can feel her smiling against my lips. She lifts up on her toes and presses her lips more firmly to mine.

"Heaven," I whisper into her mouth.

In a moment, our kiss goes from soft and tender to hard heat and frenzied grasping. My hands go straight for her ass and pull her into me. Her arms wrap around my neck like she's hanging on for dear life. Our tongues are in and out each other's mouths in an overexcited dance. We exchange moans.

"Fuck. Heaven. I want you," I groan.

She whimpers and stops kissing me, placing her palms against my chest. "Wait. D. We should stop." *God. No! Please don't make me stop.*

I touch my forehead to hers. She's looking straight

into my eyes with her exotic blue ones—the ones that had me by the balls the first time I looked into them.

"If that's what you want, Gorgeous. Whatever you want. Just tell me." Her eyes glaze over at my soft words.

"I...I want..." I don't think she even blinks as she keeps staring into my eyes like she's searching their depths for something. "Um...I want to see the rest of the condo." She drops her gaze and sighs.

We're still wrapped up in each other's arms. I dread letting her go. The thought occurs to me; I may never have her in my arms like this again.

She pushes away from me and extends her hand out for mine. "C'mon. I can't wait to see what you've done with the place." She smiles.

Taking her hand, I thread my fingers through hers and stare down at our connection there for a moment. I look up at her and smile. "Okay. Let's go. I want to see if you like the color I had it painted."

We remain hand in hand in the elevator for the few moments it takes to get to the second floor. The short ride is spent in what feels like an eternal awkward silence. When the door finally opens, Heaven moves to exit the elevator. I tug her back.

"Hey, Pip?" She turns, waiting for my comment. "I just want you to know, you felt perfect in my arms."

She looks at me for a second and says, "You did too."

Pippa gasps when I push the remote and the blinds open to reveal the floor to ceiling windows in my living room and the view beyond. The moon's reflection is dancing on the surf below. The white sand glitters in crystal pinpoints.

"This is so beautiful," she whispers, like her voice will disturb the tranquil scene. "It almost seems like I could reach out and hang on the tip of the moon from here."

I walk up behind her and circle my arms around her waist. "Please don't," I say to her reflection in the glass. "I like having you right where you are."

She sighs and leans her head back against my chest. "What are we doing, D?" She tilts her head to look at me.

"Something I think we've both wanted to do for a very long time." I feather a kiss on her cheek. "But nothing, if you don't want to."

She turns in my arms and puts her palms on my chest, securing the barrier between us once more. "I'm scared, D." *God.* The concerned look in her eyes hits me square in the heart.

"Of what, baby? Tell me what I can do to make it better."

"That's just it. I'm scared of you." She tears me apart with her troubled look.

"Of *me*? You don't have to be scared, Pip. I would never pressure you. If you're not ready, I can wait."

"It's not that. It's what you can do to me. I don't think I can handle this."

"Listen to me, Pip." I sweep her hair back, behind her shoulder. "I know I've been a fool. I'm so sorry for all the time I've wasted, for all the time we could have been, *should* have been together. I thought I was doing the right thing for you. If I hurt you while I was trying to

deny my feelings for you, sorry isn't a big enough word."
A lone tear escapes her shimmering eyes. I catch it with
my thumb.

"I'm sorry for what happened in your room at the
resort. No. I'm not sorry for that." Her brow pinches in
confusion. "I'm sorry we didn't take it further. I wanted
to. I wanted to so much. But then you were with what's
his name. I thought he was better for you. I wanted you
to be happy, and you looked really happy with him." She
closes her eyes, shakes her head, and blows out a breath.
Shit. I reminded her about the other guy she fucked. Is
she wishing she was in his arms rather than mine? Everything I was feeling as I watched her dance with him
washes over me again.

When she looks up at me, I swear I can see our life
together in those pleading eyes. "But then I couldn't take
seeing you with another guy. Thinking about you with
someone else got me crazy. I kept trying to numb away
the feelings with bourbon. The only thing I succeeded in
doing was to get so fucked up I didn't even know what I
was doing. I can't remember most of what I did. All I
know is, I really fucking messed up because I wanted to
be there for you, for us."

"No. D, we..."

"It's okay. I get it. I understand why you did what
you did. He was there when I wasn't, and if you still want
him, I'll let go. It will kill me, but I'll do it because all I've
ever wanted is for you to be happy."

She strokes her hand down my cheek. My stomach
tightens as she stares into my eyes. I hold my breath for
the few seconds it takes her to answer. "I've never wanted

anyone else but you. I still don't," she says in a soft voice. I turn my head and place a gentle kiss on her palm.

"Pip," I breathe out against her skin. "Mmm. You smell so damn good like...what is it...caramel and..."

"That's my Bum..."

"Bum cream," I finish her sentence. She gapes at me in wide-eyed shock tinged with panic. "We've had this conversation before." She sucks in her lips and doesn't answer. "At the reception."

She drops her gaze and says in a quiet voice, "Yes. When we were dancing,"

"And I said I...I wanted to *eat* you. Fucking hell." No wonder why she was panicked. I brought back the horrible memory. Now I know why she was angry with me the next day. I must have been a complete thoughtless ass at the reception.

"I'm so sorry, Pip. I don't know what else to say about my behavior. Please forgive me. I wanted things to be different. *I* wanted to be different."

She looks up at me and whispers, "It doesn't matter. That's all in the past." We hold each other captive with our eyes.

"You tell me what you want. Whatever you want, that's what I'll do. I would never do anything to hurt you. I'm happy just having you here, in my home, in my arms."

"Oh, D." She shakes her head. "I know you would never do anything you were aware of...I mean, you would never do anything intentionally." She tilts her head back, pinches her eyes shut, and grimaces like I'm already hurting her.

Fuck. What the hell happened that night? What else did I say to her? I don't know what to do, what to say now to make her understand what I feel for her. Hell. I don't even *know* what I'm feeling. I only know she's a part of my life I can't lose.

She stares straight ahead into my chest rather than into my eyes when she says, "I've realized a few things recently, D You were right about me. I can't...you know... sleep around. And you can't...well...I know how you feel about relationships and monogamy." She glances up. "It hurt too much to be with you and...I mean...it *would* hurt too much to be with you and then have you be with someone else the next day. I don't want to be hurt. I...like you said...I deserve someone who's going to respect me, someone I can trust. I guess I'm a one guy kind of girl, after all. Guess that's what I want."

The liquid need in her eyes grips my heart and twists it. She's voicing all the reasons I haven't touched her before now, all the things I've told myself time and again when it comes to being with her. But things are different now. We're different now. I would never hurt her. Never.

I place a finger under her chin and tip her head back. I need her to look at me when I say what I'm about to say. "I understand. I feel the exact same way. I do respect you, and I promise you can trust me. I want to be that guy for you. Unless...unless you want someone else." *Christ.* If she says she wants the dick head, I don't know how I'm going to handle it. How am I going to live without her?

When she doesn't answer, I take the opportunity to add, "But if it's me you want, then it's just you and me.

No one else. Whatever happens, I would never hurt you. I'd destroy anyone who did. Trust me, Pip," I whisper. "Let me..." I decide to tell her without words how I feel.

I cup her cheeks and capture her lips with mine, trying to let my kiss finish the half-spoken promise. I pour everything I have into the kiss. She responds with a helpless cry and then slips her tongue into my mouth. In seconds it's all heat and tongues clashing. It's no longer soft and flirtatious. This is all hunger and savage need. We keep kissing and nibbling and ravaging each other's mouth.

God. She tastes familiar, but at the same time like everything I've never had, like everything I never knew I wanted. Until now. I'm crazy with desire and so hard with the need for her, I'm sure my cock could drill through steel. But if this is all I can have, I won't make a move to take it further. I'll just keep kissing her forever.

"Heaven," I whisper against her kiss-swollen lips.

"D," she gasps my name on a breath. Her hands slide under my t-shirt. Pushing it up, she stops long enough for me to raise my arms to allow her to tug it over my head.

A wry grin curves her lips as she stares at my chest. She leans in and licks down my pecs and around my nipple. When she sucks it into her mouth and continues teasing it with her tongue the room around me blurs.

"Holy fuck," I breathe out, my gaze fixed on her. "Wha...what are you doing, Gorgeous?"

She looks up, smiles, and mumbles with my nipple still in her mouth, "Everything. I'm going to do everything."

I can't hold back another second. Hope this isn't her favorite blouse. I push her back and rip her shirt open. She giggles when buttons go flying everywhere. Her pink lace bra is hot, but I'm not interested in any obstructions between us. It takes flight, seconds after her blouse. I scoop her up into my arms and rush toward my bedroom. The need to feel her naked against me is uncontrollable. Although I intend on having her on every surface in this place, I don't want our first time together to be on my living room floor.

Chapter Twenty-Six

HEAVEN

As we walk into his gigantic bedroom—which is somewhere around the size of most LA apartments—a small lamp on his night table comes on, automatically casting a sultry glow around the room. I take a nervous glance around. The decor is contemporary in black and grey tones, the walls stark white. My entire cottage would probably fit in this space.

D lays me gently on the bed. As I lie back, uncertainty begins to take hold again. He said I could trust him. He said he would never hurt me. If he only knew how he's hurt me already.

But this is different. He's different. This isn't the same Damon Wolfe, the aloof, insensitive, loner. This is D, the complex man he keeps hidden inside. The sensitive, caring man I've caught glimpses of throughout our years as friends. The boy who captured my heart so many years ago.

I hold out my arms in an open invitation. I just need to feel him in my arms for reassurance. This is right. This is perfect.

He climbs over me and captures my lips in a kiss. When my breasts press against his bare chest, I moan into his mouth at the overwhelming sensation: lips against lips, soft skin against hard muscle, racing heartbeat against racing heartbeat. I slide my hands down his back, at last having the opportunity to savor every smooth, hard muscle.

He kisses a trail down my neck and then across my collar bone. My skin prickles in chill bumps, definitely an inaccurate description, since rather than being chilly I'm burning up. He moves further down to my breast and sucks me into his mouth. A soft gasp escapes my lips. His tongue flicks over my hardened nipples. I push my chest up in a wanton need for more. He chuckles against my skin.

"Your tits are perfect. I fall asleep at night thinking about these tits. I could spend a lifetime worshipping them." He moves to my other breast, licking, nibbling, and then sucking on the nipple. *Oh my.* He certainly has a way of using his words...and tongue.

"That feels so good." My body trembles along with my words. I grip the bedcovers in an attempt to steady myself.

"That's just the beginning of what I'm going to make you feel,' he says, and continues kissing and licking a trail down my stomach until he reaches the top of my jeans.

He pops open the button on my pants and slides the zipper down. Standing up, he tugs my jeans off and drops them on the floor. His fingers skim the elastic on my lace panties. They join my jeans on the floor before I even realize they're off me.

He's a man on a determined mission. He's also the only man who has ever undressed me. Call me crazy, but it's almost more seductive than the way he was licking me.

For a moment, lust-filled, silver Wolfe eyes penetrate my soul. Except for his spectacular bare chest, he's fully clothed in jeans. While I, on the other hand, am totally naked, lying spread eagle across his bed like a human offering. His wintery, heavy-lidded eyes sweep over my body. I'm being scrutinized by a demi-god. I'm sure he must be able to see the way every part of me is quivering. I've never been this vulnerable, this exposed to anyone. It's intimidating and embarrassing. I move to cross my arms over my chest.

"Don't." D's command stops me mid-movement "You're gorgeous, Heaven, like every artist's vision of Venus. Don't ever cover yourself." *Ever? Like never ever? Pretty sure a girl could get arrested.*

"I need you to do something for me, baby," he says, his hands stroking my thighs. I shudder at his touch. I glance down, unable to miss the enormous bulge in his pants. *Do something for him?* Pretty sure I know what he wants me to do. But I don't know how to do anything. Except for the one hit and run night with him, I'm a complete neophyte at this stuff.

"O...okay," I stutter, my nerves taking hold again. "Wh...what do you need?"

"I need you to let me taste you." He licks his lips. My whole body responds in an unintentional clenching plea.

"Taste me? You mean you want to..." I glance down at myself. I'm unable to say the words. *God.* I'm such a semi-virginal dimwit. I don't know anything about anything. I've never even let a guy go down on me because I was too busy saving myself for the perfect guy—*this* perfect guy.

"Yes." He pulls me to the edge of the bed and drapes my legs over his shoulders, giving him a bird's eye view of my lady parts. "Every. Single. Inch. Of you." *Well, this is interesting and a teensy bit disconcerting.*

But then he begins talking to...my vagina, apparently. Because he looks straight into my core when he says, "I want to taste you." He places a light kiss on my left inner thigh. "Lick you." He licks and kisses my right thigh. "Suck you." *Dear God.* All discomposure vaporizes and lands between my legs in the form of wet pleasure. Dropping my head back, I close my eyes and bask in his words and the warmth pulsing through me.

I'm sure the way he's sucking on the soft flesh of my inner thigh is going to leave a bruise. The thought drifts through my lust-muddled brain, *it's fine with me if he leaves bruises on my entire body if this is what it feels like to get them.*

"I want to feel you come on my face," he says while continuing to stare into my most private place. Just like that. Like it's the most normal thing in the world to be explaining to my V-jay what he wants her to do. And then he takes a long lick down my center.

"Oh!" I buck so hard from the sensation caused by

his tongue on my throbbing clit, it's only thanks to D's quick reflexes I don't take his head off with my pelvis. "Sorry. I..." I bite my lip.

Looking down, seeing D's beautiful face between my legs, his long, sexily disheveled hair and his heavy-lidded eyes eating me alive with desire, is enough to make me come without any further stimulus. I tangle the bedcovers around my fingers and hold on, preparing myself for the next thing he's going to do to me.

"Relax, baby." D gives me a lazy smile and places a soft kiss on my leg. "Have you ever had a guy go down on you before?"

"No, I...I'm sorry for being such a rookie." I blow out a breath.

"A rookie?" He chuckles and takes my legs off his shoulders before standing up.

Nooo. I inwardly protest. I've ruined the moment being a complete nervous ninny, know-nothing.

He leans over me and places his palms flat on the bed on either side of my head. "Heaven," his tone is no longer soft and sultry. Instead, he sounds like a professor about to lecture me for turning in a late assignment. "My beautiful, naïve, sexy as fuck girl." *Well...no professor has ever lectured me like this.* "I have been dreaming about this moment with you forever," he continues.

"You have?"

"Yes, I have." He cups my cheek with one hand, and all I want is for him to keep touching me—everywhere. "And the only thing that could possibly make me happier than to finally have you here, in my home, in my bed, is to know I will be the first man to make you feel everything I'm about to make you feel when I fuck you with my tongue."

"Oh...I..." My entire body flushes in heat.

"So, is it okay with you if I continue to taste you? Because you're so fucking sweet, I can't wait to get back to eating you." He stares at me, the muscles in his arms flexing from the way he's holding himself up. *Jesus. They're like flesh-covered tree trunks.*

"Y...yes. It's okay," I stutter.

"Okay. Good." He leans in and presses a hard kiss to my lips. He nibbles my bottom lip and then soothes it with his tongue. "But you have to relax, Gorgeous." His words become soft and caressing again. "Because I'm going to take my time and savor you like a fine wine. Nice and slow until you explode your sweetness all over my tongue. Got it?"

"Yes. Yes. I've got it." I'm nodding like a bobblehead. *Oh. My. God.* I'm dripping wet, quivering like a leaf, and so turned on I may begin flying around the room.

He trails kisses down my body again, sliding down as he goes. When his head is between my legs, I'm mortified by how wet I am. Kneeling on the floor, he bends my legs and places my feet on the bed.

"Mmm," he hums and slides a finger inside me, sending shivers throughout my body. "So wet. So soft." *Oh God.* I clench around his finger. Tensing every muscle, I try to keep my hips from jumping off the bed.

"Relax," he repeats, whispering against my swollen lips. He slides another finger into me, working me, lighting me up. "I'm going to lick up every drop of this sweetness."

This is nothing like the night at the resort, the night D doesn't remember. This is slow, seductive, cherishing.

Sliding his fingers from me, he continues to follow through with his promises. "Let me take you somewhere you've never been before," his breath whispers over me.

"Th...that almost sounds like lyrics to a song, D," looking down at him, I coo in pleasure.

"Then let me make you sing." *Damn.* Who knew my cynical friend was a poet, as well as a legend in bed?

He pushes my thighs apart, spreading me wider, giving him access to every part of me. Then he parts my lips and circles his tongue around my throbbing clit and I'm no longer on his bed. I'm soaring, then free-falling as he continues to lick and suck me. Using his tongue to fuck me deeper, he presses his thumb to my needy clit. I tangle my fingers through his hair, tugging him toward me. My hips once again push up, this time in an unrestrained reflex to grind against his mouth and ride his magnificent tongue.

He takes me to the edge and then brings me back. Savoring me, as he promised. "Oh God. Please, D. Please." I bite my lip to hold back my begging outburst. He looks up, his tongue still working me, his gaze dark with molten desire.

"Does that feel good, baby?" His deep voice vibrates through my entire body.

"Oh. God. Yeeess!" My hips circle against his mouth to help confirm my statement.

"Then don't hold back. Tell me what you want. I'm all yours to command."

He nibbles at my clit. I'm writhing and groaning and begging, "Ahh, God. Please. Please."

"Please what, baby girl? What do you want?" He delves back into me with his magic tongue. I swear I see rainbows and shooting stars.

"I want to come. I have to come! Please."

He pushes two fingers into me, taking over for his tongue long enough for him to say, "There's only one thing I want before I let you come."

Jesus. What is he saying? "Don't stop," I moan.

"When you come, I want you to really let go. Scream for me, Heaven."

And then he goes back to licking and sucking and drinking me in. Yup. Damon Wolfe has the most incredibly talented mouth and tongue, which he is using to say and do the most wonderful, dirty things.

He said he was mine to command, but at this moment I'd do anything he asked. And I do. I play all his requests. When I reach the point where I'm about to ignite, I sing out, "Your tongue deserves the MVP award!" No shame, because it's the truth. I scream his name, chant prayers, groan sounds I didn't know I had in me.

My whole body shakes as I come apart, consumed by sensations I didn't know were possible without burning up and completely disintegrating. When I come down to earth, I have no desire to move or speak or come back to reality. I'm a sated jellyfish. No control over my body.

"Hey. You okay?" I believe that's the smiling voice of the man whose tongue just blew my mind, tickling my cheek. Although, I'm unable to open my eyes to confirm my belief.

"Mmhmm," the only response I can manage.

"Can you move?" The warm voice pours over me and melts me even further into the bed.

"Auhn uh." I succeed in shaking my head and giving a contented grin.

Two strong arms scoop me off the bed. I moan in protest. Then I'm on the bed again, my head on a pillow, covers being pulled over me.

"Thank you," the seductive voice feathers across my lips. "Your sweet pussy deserves the MVP award too." And just like Sleeping Beauty, his soft kiss brings me back to life.

"D." I open my eyes and sigh against his lips. He tastes like my sex and caramel body wash.

"Hi there. Thought I lost you for a minute." He smiles. "Stay right there. Don't move."

"Mmm. I have no intention of moving, ever." I wriggle, belying my declaration.

"Definitely don't move like that." He stands up. I groan in disapproval. "Yet," he adds the afterthought. "I'm going to get us a snack."

As I look at him, I realize he still has an iron rod straining in his jeans because he hasn't had any satisfaction. "But you're still..." I push up on my elbows and glance at his crotch.

"I have your favorite cereal. How's that sound for a late-night snack?"

"My favorite cereal?" What is he talking about? That huge thing bulging against the unforgiving denim has to hurt.

"Yeah, those maple wheat things you like."

"I thought you hated those sugary things," I say to his back as he moves across the room to his dresser.

"I've acquired a taste for them, along with other sweet things." He looks back and gives me his sly grin and *my* crotch area clenches.

"Let me get outta these jeans first." He pulls sweatpants from a drawer and in one quick move kicks off his jeans and briefs. *Sweet Jesus*! I'm looking at the back of a naked god. If I'm a so-called vision of Venus, he's Bandinelli's *Hercules*. Every angel in heaven must have been working overtime when they put him together.

He's impossibly chiseled. His hulking shoulders are so broad, I could spend several pleasure-filled hours admiring them. His wide back vees down to a perfect trim waist and his muscular ass is a blessing which deserves a lifetime of adoration.

Right now, though, there seems to be another *large* area which is in pressing need of attention. He slips on his sweatpants, turns, and adjusts himself. The head of his unsatisfied gigantic cock is peeking out over the waistband. He casually adjusts himself to no avail, because now his rock-hard erection is pointing right at me through his loose pants, like a divining rod.

"Here you go. Slip this on while I get the cereal." He hands me a t-shirt. "The remote is on the night table if you want to pick something to watch. I'll be right back," he says and makes another nonchalant move to adjust himself before walking out the bedroom door.

Is he kidding? He wants to watch television and eat

cereal while he's still...uncomfortable? This is not the same man who had gotten himself off and left me with nothing but an "I'm coming so hard" and a snore. This was a guy who wanted to take care of me, give me everything without a care for himself.

I think I'm falling in love—and it's terrifyingly glorious.

Chapter Twenty-Seven

WOLFE

This is a new, nightmarish predicament. Saying I'm uncomfortable doesn't begin to describe the distress I'm in. I make another useless attempt at soothing my disgruntled cock because tonight is about Pip.

This is all fairly new to her. It's obvious she's nervous and frightened. After the way I behaved in my drunken stupor while dancing with her at the reception, I understand her apprehension. But I want her to know she doesn't have to be worried. I'm going to give her everything she needs, everything she wants, with no expectations for anything in return. Until she's ready. Until she's so sure, she's begging me.

"Sorry, dude." I look down at my frustrated cock, which is beginning to get the 'it's not happening' message. But we'll *both* have to get over it because Heaven is the most incredible woman I've ever known and worth every second of my *hard*ship. I'll wait as long as it takes.

My dick twitches, as if in protest. "You've had a lifetime of satisfaction, dude. You can hang in there for a while." *Christ.* Apparently, since all my blood is between my legs, I'm losing my mind and having a conversation with my own dick.

When I open the bedroom door, I'm struck dumb and nearly drop the tray I'm juggling. Pip is standing next to the bed, her hand on her hip. The t-shirt I gave her is tossed on the bed, and she's still completely, gorgeously, brain-stupefyingly naked. She wiggles a come here finger to me.

"I...I have our cereal." I stutter the comment like a nervous teenager who's seeing a naked woman for the first time. "And...and two glasses of almond milk." I swallow hard because my gaping mouth has gone bone dry and could use some of the disgusting tasting liquid.

"Put it down and come here." She gives me a lazy smile. My cock is in full on attention again.

What the hell happened to the hesitant girl I left in my bed only five minutes ago? This woman is all certainty and confidence, the same woman who rides a surfboard as if it's an extension of her body and beats me in every competition.

I take her advice and place the tray on the desk before I dump its contents all over the carpet from the way I'm shaking. "Wh...what are you doing, Pip?"

She tilts her head and gives me a smug grin because she answered the same question a few minutes ago.

"Everything?" I check just to make sure I have it right.

"Yup." She pops the P and...prowls, is the only word I can describe the way she's moving toward me as if she's about to claim her prey. She pushes me against the wall and drops to her knees.

"But I need you to do something for me." She licks her lips. She looks up at me through languid eyes.

Holy fuck. "Wh...what do you need?" If she says she needs me to sing *Twinkle Twinkle Little Star,* while standing on my head, I'm good with that. I'd do anything for her at this particular moment. But my anxious cock and I are hoping she has something else in mind.

She grips the waist of my sweatpants and slides them down my legs. *Fuck me sideways.* My cock couldn't be any harder or more swollen. For a second, when it swings in her face, I'm worried it might take her nose off. But she just tilts her head and stares at it for a moment as if she's observing some strange creature she's never seen before.

"Uh...is that normal?" She continues studying my cock. The tiny crease she gets between her brows—whenever she's really thinking about something—appears. My cock thumps against my stomach like it's answering her.

"Is what normal, baby?" Apparently, she's never gotten up close and personal with a throbbing dick.

"It's so impossibly long and...thick."

I can't keep myself from chuckling. "I don't know. Maybe a bit more than average."

But then, she licks her lips again, looks up, and hits me with her bright blues while saying, "I need you to let me taste you too." I swallow my laughter and find out I was wrong. My cock *can* grow bigger and harder. And it does. "But I have a problem," she adds and chews on her bottom lip.

Fucking hell. Please, God. Don't tell me she's not going to do what I thought she was going to do. Yeah. Definitely going to hell with a prayer like that.

"A problem?" The words come out in a shaky sputter. I said I could wait until she begged me but this is too much. I'm the one about to do the begging. What is she doing? Is this payback for all the times I rejected her requests to vanquish her virginity?

"Uh huh." She keeps eyeing the iron rod throbbing against my stomach and continues to work her lip with an anxious nibble. "I want to do this." She strokes my cock with her fingertips. It jerks at her touch. An electric shock shoots straight to my balls. I close my eyes and hold my breath. *Jesus Christ.* She's going to make me come with one look and a touch.

"But I've never done it before. I might need your help—tell me what to do. I don't want to hurt you."

For the guys out there. Are you seeing this? I've got this naked, gorgeous, sexy as fuck woman kneeling between my legs—a woman I've wanted with every hormone in my body but have been restricting myself from touching for years. She's looking up at me with imploring eyes—a color blue no human has the business having—as if her mission on earth is to worship my cock. But *she's* concerned it won't feel good for *me*. Have I painted a vivid enough picture? I pride myself on stamina. But in this case, with Heaven on her knees touching me, I'm one hand-stroke away from blowing my load in her sweet face.

I gulp down some much-needed air. "Baby. There isn't anything you could do to me that would feel bad." I stroke my fingers through her silky hair.

With my reassurance, she wraps a hesitant hand around my shaft, leans in, and licks the precum off the tip. Next thing I know, my dirty prayer has been answered when the entire head is enveloped by her soft lips. She flattens her tongue on the sensitive spot under the tip and licks at it like a kitten. *Fuuuck.* And then, like I'm her candy, she's licking and sucking up and down my length. My head drops back and hits the wall behind me. But I don't feel anything except her soft, warm lips working me.

It seems to take only seconds for Pip to become the world's best blow job giver. Seriously. If there's an award, she deserves it. She takes me in, inch by inch as far as she can, licking and sucking and moaning as she goes and then uses the moisture her tongue leaves to stroke and twist her hand up and down my shaft. She slides her mouth off my cock and gives a tender nibble and lick to my balls.

My legs shake, and my knees begin to buckle under me. I press my palms against the wall to hold myself up. When she licks from my base up to the tip and laps her tongue just under the head again, the room around me blurs. My entire body bucks as she keeps working me.

"*Fuck* me," I growl. Tangling my fingers through her

hair, I begin thrusting into her sweet, warm mouth and she matches every pump, sucking me in. *Christ.* I'm so hard I'm going to choke her, but I can't hold back. "Ahh, fuck yeah. Just like that. Just like that," I groan. "Where did you learn to do that?" I blow out a heavy breath.

She looks up at me and blinks her long black lashes and answers me with a smile and a gratified "mmmm." The sight of her sucking me so deep and the vibration from her lips sends a hot rush through my body. I'm on fire, and I'm going to explode.

Fuck. I pinch my eyes shut and grit my teeth, desperate to control my body, to hold back. But she's too fucking good at this, a natural. She definitely didn't need any instructions from me. Yup. She deserves all the awards.

"Pip. I can't...ah, ah shit, I'm gonna..." I'm grunting and groaning like I'm about to detonate, while trying to pull out of her mouth. This is her first time. I don't know how she'll take me coming in her mouth. Not to mention, I don't want to gag her with how fucking hard I'm about to come. But I swear to God, the woman has more powerful suction than my Dyson and she doesn't let up.

She starts working me faster, harder, her head moving up and down as she eats me like she's starving. When I let go and explode with the power of a firehose she keeps swallowing and moaning and drinking me in until I stop pulsing hot jets down her throat.

She takes one more, long lick down my shaft, sits back on her legs, sweeps her tongue over her lips and says,

"Yum." No shit. *Where has this woman been all my life?* Oh yeah. She's been offering me her virginity for years, and I've been saying no. What a complete dumbass.

I bend down and scoop her up into my arms. She wraps her arms around my neck. I take a moment to hold her, cradle her against me. Nuzzling my nose into her hair, I breathe her in. Then she nestles her head under my chin. "I may have been wrong," I whisper into her hair.

She tips her head back. "About what?" A worried expression crosses her face.

"I'm thinking you should never, ever stop reading those trashy romance books you read." I smile and kiss the top of her head.

"You are such a jerk." She laughs and gives me a light punch to the shoulder. "I really don't know why I put up with you."

"Mmm." I nibble down her neck. "I know why I put up with you." She sighs and melts into my arms. "I'd love to do some swoony, literary, romantic gesture: carry you across the room and throw you across the bed. But unfortunately, my pants are tangled around my ankles. I'd probably trip and..."

"Put me down, you caveman hockey jock." She kicks her legs and giggles. "I can walk to the bed, and you can serve me my after-delicious-sex meal, in bed."

"Your what?" I chuckle and kiss along her sweet neck.

God. She's delicious. I didn't think it was possible, but she's even more beautiful with her pink, swollen lips, flushed skin, and tousled, sexy hair. And although I just had the best fucking orgasm of my life, I'm getting hard again just thinking about being balls deep inside her.

"You know. My cereal," she blows out in exasperation. "I'm starving."

"Yes. I could tell." I nibble on her lip. "Me too."

Chapter Twenty-Eight

HEAVEN

"You better put that t-shirt on, or I won't be eating cereal for a late-night snack." D puts me down and tugs his sweatpants up.

I hurry my naked ass to the bed to grab the shirt. "You're beautiful, you know," he says behind me.

"Thanks." I quickly pull the shirt over my head. Even though he's seen every part of me—intimately—and he seems to like what he sees, the assurance I was feeling a few minutes ago evaporates. I'm not comfortable prancing around on full display. I slide onto the bed and lean back against the headboard, taking a minute to admire all his perfection. "You're pretty gorgeous yourself."

He crosses the room, eating up the space between us in an instant, bends down over me and says against my lips, "Are you from Tennessee? Because you're the only ten I see."

I shake my head. "I just can't get enough of your corny pick-up lines." I giggle.

"And I just can't get enough of you." His soft lips brush against mine. "I'll never get enough of you."

Oh man! He knows all the right words and how to use them to get me all hot and bothered. Running my hands over his sculpted chest, I can't believe I finally get to touch him. "Me either." I lift my eyes and meet his direct silver gaze. It heats me down to my core. I'm aching for him with an impossible need. I want him to touch me, want his lips on me—everywhere. I want him inside me.

"I'd prefer to eat you again, but our cereal is getting soggy." He gives me a lazy grin and walks over to retrieve the tray from the desk. I whimper as he leaves.

I've waited for this for years, but somehow now, it seems as if everything is moving too fast. These feelings are too powerful. Does he feel the power too or am I in this alone? I need to take a step back, slow things down. I won't be able to handle it if this is just another one-night stand for him and he moves on to someone else tomorrow.

"What do you want to watch while we enjoy our gourmet meal?" He hands me the remote.

"Talking about late night, it's getting really late. I should probably be heading home." I don't want to leave. I feel wonderful, all warm and tingly. I never want this feeling to end. I'd like to stay cuddled next to him, wrapped up in his arms all night. *Take a step back. Slow down,* what little sensible mind I have left, warns.

I need to heed the warning. This is probably the first

time D has ever had a woman in his own bedroom, having one here all night may be too much to expect. I don't want to leave, but I have to take some care—even if it's too little too late—to protect my heart.

He flips the covers back and stretches his massive body out next to me on the bed. "Don't leave, Heaven." He trails kisses down my arm. "Stay with me. I want to hold you all night, wake up next to you in the morning. Stay with me, please." His soft words envelop me, warm me, and shroud any tentative, practical thoughts.

"I want that too." I touch my fingertips to his cheek. D rolls over and straddles my legs. His revitalized cock is tenting his sweatpants. He grips me around the waist and slides me down onto my back, under him. His lips are on mine. Our tongues tangle together in and out of each other's mouth, lapping and tasting, like we're trying to swallow each other.

"Do you feel what you do to me?" My shirt is pushed up around my waist. I'm not wearing anything under it. He rubs his hardened length over me where I'm wet and needy. Even through the thick fabric, I can feel his heat.

"Oh God." I wriggle under him and try to spread my legs wider to welcome him inside me.

"Not yet, baby. Not yet." He moves off me. I'm left cold, trembling, and confused.

"Let's eat and watch some Netflix." I'm sure the look I'm giving him must be that of a confused, abandoned puppy. He gives me a warm, tilted smile. "We have forever, Gorgeous, and I want to make this special and be sure *you're* sure."

Forever. We have forever. It seems as if he's feeling

something here too. Something more than the usual hit and run Wolfe is famous for. I want to believe he is. I *have* to believe he is. Because I *am* sure. He's all I want.

"So, what are you up for? Action? Horror? Fantasy? *Romance?*" D asks and scrunches his nose at the last suggestion.

Since fantasy is my second favorite genre, I decide to spare him the romance. "I love fantasy. Do you?" I say in between mushy, milk-soaked cereal slurps.

"Of course. Best computer graphics. And I have a thing for dragons." He swallows a spoonful and pushes a button on the remote. A gigantic LED screen on the wall comes to life. "What'll it be?"

"Have you ever seen the *Merlin* series?"

"Merlin?"

"You know. Camelot, knights, magic, lots of dragons, and *Bradley James*." I don't mean to breathe the name out on a heavy swoon. But I can't help it. I've been fangirl crushing on the actor for years.

"Who?" D purses his lips to one side.

"You know," I insist. "King Arthur. The round table. There are also lots of bloody battle scenes and swordfights."

"Now you're speaking my language."

He takes my empty bowl and places it, along with his, on the tray. He hands me a glass. We gulp down our milk and put the empty glasses on the tray. D makes a face like the milk tastes sour. He slides the tray onto the night table.

Propping some pillows along the headboard, he rests back against them, then stretches his arm out and invites me into its strong shelter. I cuddle down into him and lay my head on his chest. My head moves up and down with his breathing. I can hear his rhythmic heartbeat thumping in a comforting steadfastness. He drapes his arm around me. I'm warm, protected.

"Let's see what these knights and this *Bradley* dude have." His chest rumbles under me when he sniggers.

We watch in silence for a while. But then I can't help myself. Even though I've seen this series three times, when Arthur, aka Bradley, pulls off his shirt after beating the villain in a swordfight, I let out an unintentional sigh.

"I know you didn't just sigh at another guy while you're lying on my chest." D's playful voice rumbles in my ear.

"Of course not." I smile.

"*Pip-pa.*" He places a finger under my chin and tilts my head up to look at me. "Did you just sigh at that little piss ant?"

"No. Of course, I didn't sigh at him." I suck in my lips to keep from smiling. "And he doesn't look like a piss ant to me," I mumble under my breath.

"I see how it is." He flips us over. I'm on my back pinned under him. He tickles under my shirt until I'm gasping through my laughter and screaming for him to stop. "You're into the guy with the biggest, fastest sword."

"No!" I screech and try to push his hands away. "No...not the *fastest.*" I chortle out in a gulp.

"Oh, just the biggest, huh?" He stops tickling me and presses his growing hardness against my leg once more.

"Yup." I stroke his hard arousal through his pants. "Just the biggest." He lets out a growling sound. "Of course, I don't have much to compare it to." I smirk.

"Is that so?" He pushes my shirt up and nibbles on my nipple, then laves at it with his tongue.

I arch into him and spread my thighs further apart, trying to give him access to the place I want him. "Please, D. I want you."

His eyes scrunch closed in a frown and his jaw clenches. "No, baby." His voice is strained. "Not y..."

I frame his face with my hands. His eyes open and he looks straight into mine with his molten searching gaze. "Yes. Now, D. All I've ever wanted is you. We've waited long enough."

"Heaven," he whispers my name like a prayer. "Are you sure?"

"I don't want to wait another second. And you can't tell me you don't want this too." I slip my hand into his pants and stroke his hard shaft. He's like hot velvet over iron. He lets out a raspy groan and presses the blunt head into my hand. Then he's up on his knees. One knee lands on the remote. He yanks it out from under his knee, presses the power button and throws the remote across the room. He rips the shirt I'm wearing in half and licks and kisses a frenzied trail up and down my body.

Our mutual desperation is all heated chaos. I push his sweatpants down, frantic to feel him naked against me. He kicks them off. Reaching over to the bedside table, he takes something from the drawer.

My chest heaves in breaths, wild with anticipation. Closing my eyes, I try to calm my breathing. In. Out. In. Out. I hear D tear open the wrapper. I open my eyes in time to see him slip the condom over his huge erection.

He holds me captive with eyes filled with such need it's almost unsettling. Pushing himself up with one arm, he uses his other hand to grip his shaft and rubs the tip over my wetness. Every muscle tenses in expectation, remembering the pain the first time he plowed into me.

But then he whispers, "My Heaven."

His reverent voice sweeps over me, washing away my anxiety. I hook my feet around his thighs and grasp his arm. He uses his knees to spread me open even further. I lift my hips. Then he thrusts, gently, pushing his heavy erection into me. I gasp, but then blow out a relieved sigh. He's inside me, stretching me, and it doesn't hurt. It feels...strange, but...wonderful. I shift to accommodate his thickness. I can feel him everywhere, and I moan.

He stops moving. "Are you okay?" His voice is raspy, almost desperate.

"Oh yes," I groan in pleasure.

He lowers himself and pushes deeper into me, filling me.

"Ahh, fuck. *Fuuck. Heaven,*" he groans, pulls out a little, then pushes back in. This time his strokes are measured, deliberate but tender. This time he knows it's me and it feels like what I've always imagined making love should feel like.

Captured by the strange new feeling of his massive

girth filling me, pleasure sizzles through my core. I arch into him. Greedily wanting even more. Finding a rhythm, I move my hips, matching his, thrust for thrust.

"Oh God. Yes. Yes. I had no idea. No idea," I moan. Everything has become scalding wet heat. My entire body is shaking. Uncontrolled energy crackles through every cell. He's so deep inside me, and it feels amazing.

"Ohhh, D." I moan as pleasure rocks through me. Every time he pulls out and plunges back in, he buries himself deeper inside me. But somehow, even then, it's not enough.

My legs are shaking as I wrap them around his waist, push my hips up to meet his and beg, "More. Please, D. More. Harder." I don't know if it's physically possible. I only know I'm dizzy with desire and my body is craving more. And even as I'm pleading with him, to get me to the climax my body longs for, I'm clenching around him, never wanting this to end, never wanting to let him go.

His thrusts become harder, deeper, more urgent. He tips his head back and bites his lip. His brow pinches. "Ahh. Ahh. Christ. *Fuck*. Sorry. I wanted to go slow but... Fuck. *Heaven*," he moans like he's feeling all this for the first time. "Too fucking good."

"Oh, God. Right there. Right there, D. Don't stop. Don't go slow. Fuck me." I keep throwing out unrestrained demands like my life depends on it.

I close my eyes. When he does what I've begged for and pounds into me, with each deep thrust, I'm lifted on a scorching wave of pleasure, chasing something I've never had. The sounds of moaning and wet skin slapping wet skin fill the room.

I want to remember every sound, every breath, every sensation. But overwhelming need swells inside me, building, taking me higher until I'm coiled tight. I continue to rocket toward a place I've never been before, chasing a release with such ferocity it might shatter me. I dig my nails into his shoulders, holding on for dear life.

The climax rips through me as I come in an explosion of pleasure, the intensity beyond anything I've ever imagined. My mind splinters. *Ecstasy.* I become a trillion shooting stars, a white-hot comet rocketing across the sky. I chant D's name over and over and scream filthy words which can't possibly be coming from my mouth. I ride wave after blissful wave, whimpering and breathless.

When I open my tear-filled eyes, I see D gritting his teeth. His neck muscles are straining, his eyes are screwed shut, his lips a taut grimace. His chest drops closer to me, and with one more, hard thrust, he groans in shuddering pleasure and growls out, "Heaven."

He collapses onto me. I can feel him throbbing, still pulsing inside me as he completes his release. We're both panting and gasping, covered in sweat, seemingly paralyzed in mutual pleasure.

But then he grunts, pulls out, and moves off me. Cold air prickles my sweat-soaked skin. D tugs the condom off and walks into the bathroom. A panicked thought grips me. *This is it. We're done.*

After a moment, which seems like an eternity, he comes back into the room and slides in next to me under the covers. He lays on his side facing me, his head propped up on his hand. I turn on my side to face him.

He leans in, rubbing the tip of his nose across mine. The simple gesture wraps me up like a warm blanket.

"Hi." His voice is soft, comforting.

"Hi."

"Are you okay? Was I too rough? Did I hurt you?" His warm breath brushes my lips. His concern soothes mine.

"In order of your questions." I smile and run a finger down the length of his beautiful, perfect nose. "I'm wonderful. No, it was incredible. And no. You were amazing."

"That's funny." He places a soft kiss on my lips.

"What's funny about that?" I kiss him in return.

"Because you took the words right out of my mouth. That's exactly how it was for me. Why the fuck did you make us wait so long, Pip?"

And then we fall asleep wrapped up in each other's arms. It's the loveliest sleep I've ever had.

Chapter Twenty-Nine

WOLFE

I'm dreaming about Pippa again. My aching cock is hard enough to chop wood. I have to wake up. I reach down to stroke myself, seeking some relief. I'm startled when my hand lands on a smaller, softer one. Pushing my eyes open, I force myself to wake up. And then I remember. It's not a dream. Pip's really here and... she's on top of me, straddling my hips. She has her hand wrapped around my throbbing cock, stroking it up and down in a steady rhythm. Her fingers are like magic, causing my cock to get thicker and harder with every stroke. *Holy fucking Christ.* For a "rookie" she has some skilled hands.

"Pip?" I rub the sleep from my eyes to be sure I'm seeing what I think I'm seeing and then glance over at the alarm clock. Five-fifteen a.m. I'm not going to ask her what she's doing. I'm pretty sure we're still working on the "everything" she wants to experience. "Is ev...everything okay?" My breath hitches when she fondles my balls one at a time and then slowly strokes up.

As she stares at my rock-hard cock with wonder-filled eyes, she teases the tip and rubs the moisture on the slit around the head. I clamp my eyes shut and bite my lip. *Fuck.* She's driving me wild, making me lose every sliver of self-control with just her touch.

When I open my eyes, she's staring at me, her wide-eyed bright blue orbs filled with awe as if she can't believe she has the power to make me respond like this. Then she leans over and runs her tongue over the glistening head.

"Oh *fuuuck.* Pip.*" My hips jerk in response. A guy could get addicted to that tongue.

"Mmmm." She wiggles against my thighs. I want to let her have the control. But I can feel the warmth dripping from her, and I'm dying here. She keeps watching me like she's cataloging every reaction.

"I'd like to try it in this position. Is that okay?" She chews on her lip. Is she kidding me right now? It's fucking adorable how she thinks she needs to ask permission to suck me off or give herself to me.

But then it occurs to me. She's never done this either? What the hell did the douchebag who was lucky enough to fuck her for the first time do with her? Wham, bam, thank you, ma'am? What an asshole. He gets a gift like Heaven's virginity, and he doesn't take the time to savor her, worship her in every position possible. But even though I regret—for her sake— she didn't get to have a notable first-time, I'm selfishly happy as hell I'm the one who gets to have all these firsts with her.

"Sweetheart, you can do whatever you want." She

runs her hands over my pecs. My stomach muscles clench. A pleased grin tugs at her mouth. She sweeps her hands lower and traces the hills and valleys of my abs. I. Am. Hard. As. Fuck.

"Give me a second, baby, to get a condom." I start to reach toward the night table, but she puts her hands on my chest to stop me.

"No. Wait." If she's changed her mind, I'm going to have to take a quick trip to the bathroom because if I don't find release soon my engorged cock is going to have permanent damage. "Can we leave it bare? I mean... without a condom? I'm on the pill. I want to really feel you inside me."

I've never gone bareback in my life, a safety habit I learned at a young age and continue to practice. But I know Pip is clean and I know she's seen my health records at the clinic. So, she knows I'm clean.

"I've never done it without a rubber before," I say aloud as I'm thinking about it and realizing this will be a kind of virginal experience for me too.

Pip's brows pinch and she tilts her head like my statement is the most puzzling thing she's ever heard.

"I told you, baby. Whatever you want. And I can't think of anything better than to be deep inside you, touching every part of you with nothing in between us."

Gripping my shaft, I brush it back and forth over her silky entrance. Her eyes roll back in her head. She rocks forward, begging for me to push into her. But before I have a chance to, she repositions her knees, spreading herself wider and then pushes up and drops down on me with a quick thrust. We both cry out at the sensation.

I'm deep inside my Heaven. The pleasurable double-entendre darts across my mind. *My God.* It has never felt like this. Never been this good.

I can't take my eyes off her as she pulls up and then gradually lowers herself, clenching around me like a vise. She's whimpering and groaning as she slides up and then slowly lowers herself, taking in every inch of me. Her eyes are pinched closed, and she's running her tongue along her bottom lip as if she's relishing every movement, every sensation.

"That's it, baby. Ride me." The pressure in me keeps building as she keeps contracting around me.

I grab her ass and press her soft, plump cheeks together, increasing the pressure against her inner rippled flesh. She makes little mewling sounds and twists down, taking me deeper. Every time she pulls up and drops down, her perfect tits bounce. I run my thumbs over her puckered nipples and then crunch forward and suck one into my mouth. She gasps and rocks forward, pushing her tits further in my face. I lick and suck one and then the other and continue massaging them, giving them the attention she's craving. But then, she plants her hands on my chest, bracing herself. She rocks back and forth, moaning as my cock presses against her swollen clit.

"Oh God, D. I'm...I'm coming." Her body shudders as she chases her release and begins to lose all control. I grab her hips and move her up and down on my shaft as I thrust up into her.

She arches back and grinds down on me. I know when the orgasm grips her because her muscles clench around me like she's trying to milk my cock. When the climax rips through her, she spasms in pleasure and keeps riding me as if she's riding a tumbling wave. She's moaning my name and making the sexiest fucking sounds I've ever heard. My stomach tightens and heat rolls down my cock. Then she groans and collapses onto my chest like a rag doll. Like she's wrung out and doesn't have anything left to give me. But she's about to find out she's wrong.

I flip her onto her back. I'm still inside her, still throbbing in urgency and her tight pussy is still trembling. Hand to God, I've had my fair share of women... ah, more than my fair share, but this is beyond anything I've ever had. Nothing has ever felt as good as Heaven does. It doesn't matter what she does, how she touches me, how she moves, it's like lightning bolts shooting through me, setting me on fire. She's so tight. So fucking good. And the sensation of being inside her without anything between is almost too much.

HEAVEN

"We're not done yet, my sleepy girl. It's my turn," D rasps out in a growl.

I mumble something even I don't understand. I think I'm trying to tell him I can't. But nothing is working. Not my brain. Not my mouth. Not my body. I'm completely spent, used up, my bones are Jell-O. I knew being with D was going to be earth shaking, but this is galaxy shaking.

He thrusts deep inside me. "Ooooh." *Goodness.* My hips make an involuntary circle and I grind against him. He's like the Pied Piper, enticing me to follow his lead, even though I didn't think it was possible to move.

"You feel that? You feel how fucking hard you make me?" He pulls out almost all the way and pumps into me again, hitting a spot which sends sparks out to every neuron in my body. A guttural moan pushes up from deep in my core and comes out loud enough, I hope the neighbors don't call the cops.

"That's right, baby girl. You feel how deep; how lost I am inside you?"

I try to say yes. All I can manage is a nod and a "hmmm." I can't even get my eyes open. The sensations are overwhelming. I'm still throbbing from what I thought was the orgasm to top all orgasms and yet, each time he pistons into me, liquid fire surges through my body. I want to tell him it's too much. It's almost painful...in a good way. The pleasure is insane, intense, almost crippling. But my traitorous body wants him, needs him, like an addict craving more, chasing the high.

"You know what that means?" He continues to stroke in and out.

"Ahhh." *Dear Lord.* He's fucked me into stupidity. I am never going to be able to put a coherent thought or sentence together again.

"It means I'm going to fuck you hard. Hard and deep," his words come out in a desperate rasp. "Are you ready for this, sweetheart? It's going to be fast. But I'm going to fuck your tight, wet pussy so hard you're going to see God when you come on my thick cock. Do you understand me, Pippa?"

"Yes. I understand," I almost growl in longing and wrap my legs around his waist.

"Are you ready for me?" I look up. I'm burning up in his liquid silver gaze, molten with desire.

"Yes. Yes. I understand. Do it, D. Now. Do it." I'm begging like a shameless hussy.

He shoves my legs up. My knees are up by ears, opening me up to him even more. Plunging into me, he fills me to the core with his long, hard sex. He pulls out slightly and rams back into me, pounding into me with hot, driving hunger. I attempt to lift my hips to meet his surging thrusts, but D is pressing down on my legs, keeping my knees pushed up toward my head. I'm unable to move. He's in complete control as he keeps slamming into me with relentless, hard strokes. All I can do is clench around him in an effort to hold him inside me, to never let him go. And every time he slams into me we simultaneously gasp as we continue to fuel each other's pleasure. It's torment. It's ecstasy.

I'm consumed with wild energy, bucking and writhing under him, while he tries to hold me in place. I watch him as he pumps into me, his face taut, his neck veins bulging, every godlike muscle straining. His powerful beauty is surreal.

I arch up as tension coils in me. I'm consumed in blazing pleasure as the white-hot climax rips through me, I feel D stiffen and then with one more deep thrust and a savage grunt he explodes into me. His body jerks hard as his hot violent release gushes into me.

Our bodies keep shuddering in mutual waves of pure heat and pleasure. D keeps pulsing what seems like unending jets of warmth into me. When we're finally spent, anesthetized by overwhelming pleasure, D moans and rolls off me. We're on our backs, both of us covered in a sheen of sweat, both of us gasping for air. We don't speak, as we gulp down every molecule of oxygen in the room and our heartbeats attempt to resume normal rhythms.

After a moment, D reaches out and entwines his fingers in mine. "Jesus Christ. Jesus Christ, Pip," his words come out on a heavy breath.

I drop my head to the side to look at him. It takes me a second to focus through my orgasm-muddled eyes. His carved chest is heaving up and down. "That was...it was... I think I l—" He rolls on his side and begins peppering my face with soft kisses. "Stay with me, Heaven. Stay with me forever," he whispers.

The words fall out of my mouth before I realize I'm saying them, "Oh, D. I love you so much."

He continues covering my face and neck with soft kisses, making me feel cherished, precious.

"Be right back," he says against my cheek.

The sun hasn't come up yet but the light on the night table is still on, casting a soft glow in the room. D gets up. I watch as he walks across the room to the bathroom. His back muscles flex and glisten with sweat as he moves. He's stunning, too perfect to be real. If I'm dreaming, I never want to wake up. Although, the throbbing soreness between my legs assures me this is definitely not a dream.

D comes back to bed with a warm moist cloth and sits next to me on the bed. I haven't moved a muscle. I'm not sure I can.

"Sorry. But you make me crazy. Are you okay?" he asks as he cleans me with soft, soothing strokes.

"I'm good," I push out on a sigh. "A little sore, but it was beyond wonderful."

He tosses the cloth. It lands in a laundry hamper across the room. Stretching out next to me, he pulls the covers, which are crumpled in a heap at the foot of the bed, over us. Then he scoops me into his arms. My soft body melts into his hard curves. D wraps his arms around me and holds me tight against him as if he's afraid I'll disappear into thin air. But I won't because I'm his more than willing prisoner.

He doesn't return my words, though. He doesn't say he loves me. And as we drift off to sleep, molded together in a perfect fit, the thought skitters across my mind, *please don't break my heart.*

Chapter Thirty

HEAVEN

I awake to the smell of deliciousness. For a moment I forget where I am and how I got here. When I roll onto my back, the twinge between my legs reminds me.

"Mmm, D." Remembering last night's sex marathon flushes me in heat from head to toe. I revel in memories: D's hard body pressed against mine, his glorious tongue and huge sex pushing into me, marking me as his. "Mmmm," I repeat, with a catlike stretch.

"Hey, kitten. Hope you're hungry and that sound means my attempt at breakfast smells good enough to eat." D is standing in the doorway leaning against the frame. He's wearing loose sweatpants, which hang low on his trim hips, no shirt. The lovely vee-shape lines where his abs meet his hip flexors are taunting me as they point down to the most magnificent penis in the world— at least, I think it is. I'm somewhat lacking in comparative research. *No. It has to be the most magnificent. There couldn't possibly be a better one.* D's arms are crossed over his chest, accentuating their size and girth. Maybe he can spoon feed me because I may never get out of this bed again. Food, water, and D. What else could a girl ask for? On second thought, who needs food?

"Good morning." I roll onto my side to face him and prop my head on my hand. "Hey, D. You know what I was thinking?"

He saunters toward me and sits down on the edge of the bed. "What's that, Gorgeous?" He strokes my hair off my face.

"Remember when you said you wanted my opinion on the color you painted the condo?" I chew on my lip for a second.

"It was last night, Pip. I haven't had that many concussions. I remember." When I don't say anything, he asks, "What? You don't like it?"

"No. It's great. Very clean. Very contemporary." I chew on my lip again.

He must sense my hesitation when he glances around the room and asks, "So, what's the problem?"

"Well...you do realize the walls are all white, right? Every room...white." I wrinkle my face in an I'm-so-sorry-to-tell-you-this gesture. Maybe he's color blind.

"What?" He chuckles. "No, they're not. Stop kidding around, Pip. Our food is getting cold."

"D." To make sure he can hear me, clearly, I sit up, pulling the covers around my chin. "Every room is white. I mean, I like it. It looks good with your black and gray décor."

"Pippa." He shakes his head in exasperation. "The

woman at the paint store helped me pick it out. It's called Misty Storm or Stormy Mist or some shit like that. She even offered to come over and make sure it matched my furniture. Why would she offer that if it was white? White matches everything."

"Hmm. How old was this woman?" I ask while trying to keep a straight face.

"I don't know. Twenty, thirty. I didn't ask to see her ID while I was buying paint."

"And did you let her come over...to *match* your paint?"

"No. I didn't have time. I had practice. But she wrote her number down on the receipt if I wasn't happy with the color. Why? You want to talk to her?" Men are such simple creatures, aren't they?

"The paint is white." I push him off the bed with my feet and stand up. "Now, could I have another shirt, please, since you shredded the one I was wearing last night? And then let's go eat. It smells delish and I'm starving. I seem to have worked up an appetite last night." I grin and flutter my lashes at him.

He throws me back onto the bed and stretches out over me. "You little smart ass. I'm starving too, and there's something else around here that's delish and good enough to eat." He kisses down my neck.

"Oh no, you don't." I push on his shoulders. "Not until you feed me. It's the rules," I tease him.

"I think the rules are *dinner* first, babe." He chuckles and brushes the tip of his nose across mine. "But we broke all those rules big time last night."

"Then you can at least feed me the morning after Walk of Shame Breakfast."

"No deal. There will be no walk of shame anything around here. But I do intend on feeding you breakfast, lunch, *and* dinner, while I snack on some sweetness in between."

"Is that right?" I slide my hands into his pants, grip his ass, and squeeze—as best I can since it's not easy to squeeze hard muscle. He rolls his hips into me. I'm the one who ends up moaning and arching into his thickening shaft. He responds with a devious chuckle.

"Oooh. You do realize you can't hold me captive here? I have to go home at some point today," I pant out the meager rejection while my hips are practically screaming 'keep me here forever.'

"Why? My pantry is well-stocked. We have everything we need to survive here for months." He rubs his palm over my boob and then teases the puckered nipple between his fingers. I know there are a million logical reasons why we can't stay here for months, but, I can't seem to think one rational thought.

"You do not play fair, Wolfe. You know I can't think straight while you're feeling me up." I look down and watch him lavish my girls with kissing, licking, and sucking. My head tilts back, and my eyes flutter closed.

"Okay. You win," I mumble in blissful senselessness. "I'll give up my PT career, and you can give up your hockey contract. We'll live off sex forever."

He pulls his mouth off my tit with a pop. "Way to kill the mood, Andersen, with that smart, practical brain I like so much." He gets up and walks across the room to his dresser, leaving me frustrated and panting.

"So, it's my brain you like me for?" I grumble while my body continues to swoon.

"Of course. What kinda guy do you take me for?" He throws a t-shirt as he walks back toward the bed and it lands across my chest. "Did you think I only loved you for those perfect, plump, kissable lips?" He bends over me and kisses my lips. "Or those gorgeous round, lickable tits?" He drags the shirt across my chest. The friction causes my already sensitive nipples to pucker further. D licks at one hard peak and then the other. "Or maybe you thought I only liked you for this warm, tight little cunt." He slides a finger into me where I'm once again dripping with need for him.

"Mmm," he hums. "You might be right. This sweet pussy is right up there with your brain when it comes to all the reasons I like you." He tugs me up into a seated position. "Now put the shirt on, Gorgeous, and let's eat breakfast so I can spend the rest of the day fucking you on every surface in this *enormous* condo."

I finally manage to stand my speechless, befuddled-self up. When I have the shirt halfway over my head, my arms tangled in the sleeves, D gives me a light smack across the ass. I jump and let out a yelp.

"Oh yeah. I forgot to mention that round, fuckable ass." He grabs one cheek. His fingers have no problem sinking into my soft flesh. I pull the shirt down over my head. "Nobody has an ass like this." He licks his lips and kneads my ass cheek.

"You are the devil, Damon Wolfe." I shake my finger at him.

"And you're my Heavenly angel." His mouth tips up in a sly grin.

"Nevertheless, there's only one reason I like you." I grab his swollen shaft through his pants. He blows out a breath at the unexpected invading touch. "It's this long. Thick. Fuckable. Cock." I follow up each adjective with slow strokes up and down.

"*Fuck*, Pip," he groans and pushes his fabric-covered erection into my palm.

"Now let's eat so I can have *my* way with *you*." I smirk and sashay my way out of the room, swaying my hips as I go.

"Ahh. Fuck," he moans behind me. I can only imagine the way he must be adjusting his disgruntled penis. A satisfied grin crosses my face as I make my way to D's restaurant-equipped kitchen.

"You little minx," he calls out with a laugh. "I'm going to have to fuck you even harder today to teach you a lesson."

"Promises, promises," I call back.

"My kingdom for a coffee," I groan as I look around the high-tech, stainless-steel appointed kitchen for a simple coffeemaker. Every appliance is commercial grade, and there are double everything: two six-burner stoves, two enormous ovens, and a *walk-in* refrigerator. Seriously? Who needs a walk-in refrigerator unless they're preparing state dinners? Wait. I misspoke. There's a regular built-in refrigerator as well. A regular, *double-wide* built-in refrigerator. This kitchen is insane.

There's something delicious smelling warming on one of the million-dollar stovetops. Maybe the stove cooked the food all by itself. Because if I had a kitchen this high-tech I'd expect it to robotically whip up meals —Jetson-style.

"Is Cappuccino okay?" D walks in behind me. I take a quick glance over at him to assess his current situation. It looks like he's got the over-excited-penis-thing worked out.

"Cappuccino sounds amazing. Did you order out?"

"Nah." He crosses the room and turns on another stainless-steel contraption which has about a thousand knobs and several tube things. "Batt insisted I needed one of these frou-frou things when he was staying here," he yells over the loud grinding noise. Apparently, the space-age looking thing grinds the coffee beans before brewing them.

"It makes espresso, Cappuccino, and even regular old coffee. He said he couldn't drink the swill coming from my Keurig. I thought he went out to buy a simple brewing coffeepot and he comes back with this shit." He waves his hand at the machine and blows out a breath.

"He even ordered me a case of organic coffee beans. I swear to God the pain in the ass has one too many X chromosomes." D chuckles as he works the device like an experienced barista. Steamed milk and a cinnamon sprinkle later, he hands me a perfect Cappuccino with a frothy heart swirled on the top.

"This is beautiful. Almost too pretty to drink." I stare down at the cup and try to keep *my* puerile heart from reading too much into the frothy artwork.

"Go ahead. Taste it. I used cashew milk." I take a sip and moan at the warm lusciousness. "My little moaner. I'm already an expert at your moans." D smirks. "I'd say that means you like it."

"I am not a moaner," I protest. D stares at my mouth as I lick the foam from my top lip.

He takes the cup from my hands, places it on the island, and tugs me into his arms.

"Oh, you're a moaner and a whimperer." He traces my lips with his tongue. "And a screamer." He nibbles my bottom lip. "And a little wildcat when you're coming."

Right on cue, I whimper, and he laughs. "See?" He grabs my ass and kneads it. "Now let's eat this mediocre food I've prepared so I can get back to making you scream my name." Once again, he leaves me in a dizzy haze as he releases me and turns to the stove to flip the warming omelet.

"Can I help?"

"Nope. All done. Have a seat. I'll serve you."

I sit at the granite island, which is roughly the length of a football field. There are twelve stools along one side. It occurs to me this condo is either designed for a huge family, a boutique hotel, or a guy who intended on doing a lot of entertaining. *I wonder how many other women he's entertained here.* I clutch my hands around the coffee mug at the thought and sip at the silky, warm comfort.

D serves me a plate piled high with a veggie omelet and bacon. *Vegan* bacon.

"Wow. A girl could get used to service like this." I chomp down on a healthy bite of omelet. "This is delicious. And you made vegan bacon."

"Trying some new things." D quirks a brow as he scoots in next to me with his full plate.

"I don't get it. The guys always said you were a disaster in the kitchen when you were in college."

"I didn't have any interest when I was in school," he explains while eating. "Anyway, Batt's a gourmet cook. He prepared meals for us almost every day. Now that I live alone it's time to learn how to adult."

"A man who can cook has so many other *interesting* talents and claims to be here to serve me." I let out an over-exaggerated sigh. "I may just have to keep you, Hockey Jock."

"Oh, you're stuck with me now, Pip-squeak. I can't promise the cooking will always be good, but the other talents are all yours."

Okay. This is definitely no hit and run. D sounds as if he wants to give this, whatever it is, a long-term try.

"How did you learn to cook?" I ask in between forkfuls and hopeful thoughts.

"Anyone can cook if they really want to. If you can read, you can cook. Follow the directions. No big deal. And Batt taught me a few tricks when he came to stay with me after we...I mean..." He stops mid-sentence and slides his food around his plate. "Batt stayed with me for a little while after Dak's wedding." He glances over and shrugs.

"Really? You must be special. I thought Batt never took off. He didn't even take off when we all went on the ski trip to Big Bear. How did you manage to get him to agree to that?"

Batt never, ever, takes off. Everyone knows that. I don't think he would take off if he severed a limb. He'd tell the doctors to stitch it on fast because he has to get back to the studio.

"It was his idea. He thought I needed...I mean...he wanted to see my new place." D offers a reticent explanation for Batt's visit.

Hmm. Maybe D needed some brotherly comforting after we parted on not so good terms. Or perhaps I'm reading too much into a simple visit from his brother. Either way, I need to tell him what happened that weekend. I can't keep it from him if we're going to have a relationship built on honesty and trust.

"D...about that weekend. I need to tell you something. The reason I..."

"It's okay, Pip. I get it. I understand why you were angry. I behaved like a complete jackass at the reception. And I should have never done what I did the night before when you were feeling your alcohol. I don't blame you for not wanting to ride home with me." When he looks up at me from under his dark lashes, for a moment I see the hurt little boy in those beseeching eyes, rather than the hard-edged man. "But if it's all right with you, I don't want to talk about it right now. I just want to move on from my moronic behavior and enjoy this day together. I can't promise I'll never behave like a moron again, but I finally have you here with me. I don't want to dwell on all the stupid things I've done in the past. Okay?"

"I...okay." I shrug. His heartfelt sincerity dissolves my determination to tell him what actually happened. The behavior he's apologizing for is trivial compared to what he's doesn't remember. I'll have to tell him eventually, but I don't want to ruin this day either.

"It must have been nice to spend time with Batt." I change the subject while finishing off the omelet on my dish. "In college you guys were all together every day, playing hockey, living together, hanging out. I wish we could all spend more time together. Everyone's so busy adulting these days."

"Yeah. I miss being with my bros." He brings his plate to the sink and scrapes food remnants off into the disposal. "But right now," he comes back, picks up my empty plate, and dumps it in the sink. No scraping required from my dish. I can eat my weight in food. And I usually do.

Pulling my chair away from the island, D finishes his thought, "I have a great big sunken bathtub complete with a hundred massaging jets which has your name on it."

"D, I told you. I can't spend the entire day lounging around your house."

"Why not?" He bends down and nibbles my earlobe. "It's Sunday Funday. And I know all kinds of fun we can have together." He licks just under my ear and dammit, I whimper again. My head drops back against his shoulder.

"Um...well..." *For Pete's sake. I can't get my brain to function when he's touching me.* He continues to trail kisses down my neck and then pushes the t-shirt off my shoulder and nibbles and kisses there. *Shirt. Clothes. That's it!* "For one thing, I don't have any clean clothes here."

"Sweetheart." The corners of his mouth tip up in a roguish grin. "You're not going to need any clothes for the kind of fun I have in mind." He nips at my neck.

"Mmm...well...Sheldon has to go out and they all need to be fed and..."

"I'll get someone to go over and take care of the fur babies," he whispers against my skin.

"You do not play fair. I have classes bright and early tomorrow. And don't you have a road trip coming up this week?" I half-heartedly protest as he continues to lavish my neck and shoulder with attention.

"I was thinking," he stops kissing and nibbling me and sits down next to me, "you should come with me." He strokes up and down my thigh. I love how he can't seem to stop touching me. But the way my brain shuts down and my body responds to his touch is not helpful when trying to have a sensible conversation.

"Come with you where?" My mutinous legs open wide with an automatic invitation to come right in.

"On the road trip. Four different cities. I can get you a suite in the hotels we're staying in. I'm not ready to leave you for a whole week." He strokes higher, causing the all too familiar clenching my V-Jay does whenever he touches me—or looks at me, or breathes on me, or, hell, whenever he's within a hundred-mile vicinity. She seems to be her own personal Wolfe-radar-tracking device.

I clamp my wanton legs together. "I can't go on your

road trip. I have a full schedule of classes next week leading up to my interning at the Acute Care Center. Besides, you're just coming off the DL. I don't think Coach Donnelly would be too happy about the distraction."

He blows out an exasperated breath. "Okay. Fine. My levelheaded, sensible, delusion-shattering Pip-squeak." He hops up and sweeps me off my chair. "Then you're spending the whole day as my prisoner here. I'll take you home in time to get a good night's rest."

He carries me into the en-suite bathroom—which is almost as big as his four-hundred square foot bedroom—and stands me up in front of the double, black marble vanity. In the middle of the room is a rectangular, black sunken bathtub the size of a small pool. As D promised, it has hundreds of shiny chrome jets.

"Don't move," he instructs. I follow his command as he moves to turn the faucets on in the bathtub. Four streaming waterfalls in each corner begin filling the massive tub. D pours something into the water. *Mmm, lavender.* He flips a switch on the wall. The water begins to froth with bubbles.

"Now," he says as he stalks back to me, "I can't promise you'll be able to walk when I get you back home." He slides my shirt up. I raise my arms overhead to assist him in taking it off. "But I can promise it will be worth it." He spins me around and pushes me against the cold countertop.

He drops his sweatpants and kicks them off. He looks up and stares at our reflections in the mirror. I immediately recognize the predatory lust in his silver gaze. And then he glides his fingers down between my ass cheeks and into my already dripping center.

"Oh, God." My eyes close and my head drops back against his chest.

"Open your eyes, Gorgeous. I want you to watch what I'm doing to you." His words come out in a raspy demand. He uses his leg to spread my thighs further apart and continues to plunge two fingers in and out.

I drop forward onto the unforgiving marble, I'm like hot putty in his hands. The cold surface is a relief to the heat flaming through me. He removes his fingers and pulls me back against him. His swollen thickness is aligned at my center. I grip the countertop in an effort to keep my legs from collapsing under me.

"That's right. Hold on tight," D whispers and wraps his arm around my waist to clutch me against him. He plunges into me with a slamming thrust. Lights glitter behind my eyelids. I gasp at the deep intrusion. "Told you I was going to punish you for teasing me this morning. Didn't I?"

"Yesss," I groan and wiggle my ass further against him.

"You like when I pound into your tight pussy, don't you?" His words are like gasoline on an already raging fire.

My repeated yes comes out in another pleasured groan. I raise my head to look at our reflections. My heavy-lidded eyes are almost impossible to keep open. But I do as D instructed and force them open to watch as he slams into me. His heated gaze is wild with pure desire as he continues to pull out and pummel back into me.

"I love the way this tight cunt feels when I'm fucking it." He whispers his filthy endearment in my ear. My entire body vibrates as he drives into me, working me into a frenzy.

In the short time I've been with him, I've come to understand one thing: D is not a gentle lover. He likes to be in control. But D and I have built our friendship on competition. As much as my body hungers for release in his powerful arms, it's time to set the record straight. I give him a mischievous grin and clench, squeezing around his throbbing shaft.

His eyes squeeze shut. "Ahh. Fuuuck. Pip. Shit. What you do to me." His rhythm becomes more frantic, jack-hammering me over and over against the unforgiving stone counter. He's right. I may be bruised and unable to walk tomorrow but holy smokes it is definitely worth it. He's deep inside me hitting that newly discovered wondrous spot again and again, sending me hurtling toward the edge.

He grips my hips, pulling me hard against him and with one more powerful thrust he growls my name. We come together, bucking and groaning. His hot release thunders into me. D folds over me in exhaustion, his chest thumps against my back as our hearts beat in a mutual thrumming cool-down. But somehow, he manages to keep us both from collapsing onto the floor in sated feebleness.

He pulls out, his spent shaft still semi-hard. His warm juices drip down my legs as he turns me around, gathering me in his arms. I nestle into him, circling my arms around his waist and resting my head against his heaving chest. We stand there for a moment, wrapped in mutual warmth, panting in contented bliss.

At that moment he changes from the aggressive, powerful man fucking me, to the sweet, protective lover. His deep voice rumbles in my ear when he whispers softly, "I love you, Heaven."

Chapter Thirty-One

WOLFE

Her legs are still trembling when I kneel down and clean her with a moist towel. I pick her up, carry her to the tub, and lower her into the soothing warm water. She's going to need the comforting warmth and lavender bubbles after the way I've been working her. But I can't help myself. It's as if my cock and I are both trying to make up for lost time.

"You're getting in with me, aren't you?" She looks up at me with her flushed face and sparkling blue eyes. And I know I'm beyond fucked when it comes to this woman. My feelings for her go way beyond this unbelievable sexual attraction we have.

Of course, I'll get in the tub with her. What guy in his right mind would say no to this gorgeous woman inviting him into a bubble bath? But no matter what she asked, I'd never say no to her. I'd do anything for her, give her anything, stay with her forever if she'll have me.

"If there's enough room for me." I brush some bubbles off her face.

"D, there's enough room for your whole team in this tub." She giggles. I swear to Christ my heart skips a fucking beat at the sound.

"I'm all about teamwork, sweetheart." I smirk, climbing into the tub behind her. "But if even one of those assholes came anywhere near this tub with you in it, he'd never play hockey again."

"No worries. If one of your teammates got anywhere near this tub with me in it, I'd be the one making sure he never *played* anything again." She slides back between my thighs and lays her head against my chest. Circling my arms around her waist, I close my eyes and wonder how I got to be the lucky bastard who gets to have her in my arms.

"I've been telling you for years I can take care of myself, D." She tilts her head and looks up at me. "You just never believed me."

"I believed you." I sweep her long hair to one side and kiss her soapy shoulder. "I've always known you were strong enough and smart enough to take care of yourself. I just wanted to protect you from...me." The confession comes out with a big exhalation. Because she's pressed against my chest, she rises up and down in the water in sync with my breath as if she's a part of me. And she is...a part of me I'll never let go.

"You never needed to protect me from you. I'm a big girl. I can handle you." She's running her hand up and down my thigh while smiling up at me and my dick is beginning to thoroughly enjoy her *handling*.

But I have to focus. It's the perfect opportunity to get things out in the open. Before we get any further into this relationship, she needs to know the whole truth about my past. I don't want secrets between us.

"Pip." I thread my fingers through hers. Not only because I want to be holding her hand when I tell her about the things I've done but because I need her to stop stroking my leg so I can think straight. "There are some things about me you don't know."

"I know everything I need to know." She nuzzles her nose under my chin. I want to say fuck this, pull her onto my lap and fuck her so hard I'll forget my bullshit past. After all, it *is* the past. I'm a different person now with a totally different life. Maybe I shouldn't risk telling her and losing her. After she knows, she may decide to walk away from me because my skank past is too much for her. But I can't be the one to make that decision for her. I have to tell her.

"No, you don't." I turn her around so she's facing me. I pull my legs out from under her. If she's straddling my hips, I'll be balls deep inside her before I get the first sentence out. The jets are still pumping. The soothing lavender oil I dumped in the water for her is still bubbling. I reach over and turn off the faucets and consider turning off the jets too but then decide to leave them on. Something about the rhythmic sound and warm silky bubbles gives me comfort and courage to continue telling her my sordid tale.

"I know you were living on the street when Batt's dad found you," she whispers and reaches for my hand under the oozing froth. She tangles her fingers in mine again.

"Dak told you."

"No. He didn't tell me. He would never betray your trust."

"Hah. He wouldn't betray my trust, but he'll tell you I'm a dirtbag anytime my name comes up."

"Yup. Pretty much." Her lips tip up in a slight grin, and she shrugs. "The only reason I know about Mr. Battaglia finding you is that I kinda eavesdropped when Batt and Dak were talking about you at our house one time."

"Oh great. I was everyone's pity case and topic of conversation."

"No, D. It wasn't like that. Dak was concerned about you and wanted to know what he could do to help. Batt told Dak he would have to talk to you if he wanted to know any more because it wasn't his place to tell him. I assumed since you guys were all so close, Dak did talk to you about it. But I never asked any questions, and he never told me anything. And I don't need to..."

"I need you to know," I interrupt her. "I need you to listen to me. Don't say anything. Just listen, because if you stop me, I won't get through this."

"Okay." She slides away from me. A waterfall jet streams down her back. She does a little wiggle to get into a comfortable position where some of the water is streaming down her hair and some of it is running over her shoulder, cascading over her tit like clear satin over silk. She's a dreamlike vision stretched out before me, willing to accept whatever I have to tell her. Flawless beauty that doesn't deserve the crap I'm about to lay on her. But she does deserve the truth. "I'm listening," she announces.

I take a deep breath, swallowing hard to get my head back into my sleazy storytelling task.

"When I was nine, my mom and I were in a really bad car accident,' I begin. The sound of skidding tires, crunching metal, and my mom's scream resonates in my head. I rub my temples, trying to quiet the loud memory.

"I'm so sorry, D. Don't..."

"I'm okay. Please let me finish." Pip bites her bottom lip. Her eyes glaze with unshed tears. I realize my words came out gruffer than I intended. "Sorry, babe. I haven't talked about any of this in a long time, but I need to talk about it now. I need to tell you."

"Okay." She stretches her legs out and places them on top of mine. Having her silky skin against mine is an added comfort. I'll share my bullshit story with her and then it won't be a constant nagging silent obstacle between us anymore.

"I was in the backseat and didn't have a scratch on me, but my mom got pretty messed up. The impact shattered her pelvis, fractured a couple vertebrae in her neck, and left her with a severe concussion. The doctors didn't even know if she was going to survive at first because they weren't sure about brain trauma.

"She survived, but when she came home, she was in constant pain. Some days she couldn't even get out of bed. The only way she could function was by taking pain meds. After a while, she had to increase the dosage. It was the catalyst to her prescription med addiction, a vicious downward spiral. The more she took, the more she needed. I came home from school one afternoon and found her on the floor in her room. She was cold and stiff, lying in her own vomit."

"Oh my God, D. I..." Pip begins, but I give her a pleading look because I really need her to let me get through this. "Oh. Sorry." She runs her fingers across her lips like she's zipping them closed. I bite back a smile. Even while reliving my darkest day, she brings sunshine to the situation.

"Anyway, my dad was devastated. He couldn't get over her loss. She was his whole world. He was madly in love with her, and she was just as in love with him. The difference was my mom loved me too. He only wanted me because he knew it made her happy to have a baby and he wanted to give her whatever he could because he couldn't afford to give her material things. Even as a kid, I felt the way he treated me like an intruder in their lives. He only put up with me for her sake.

"When she died, he blamed me because she had been picking me up from hockey practice when we got in the accident. He never forgave me and didn't want anything to do with me. He spent every day drunk out of his mind, trying to erase his pain. He lost his construction job, walked around like a zombie, completely out of it. We could hardly afford food. Every extra penny we had went to buy his whiskey. One night, when I was thirteen, he went out to get another bottle and never came back."

Tears are streaming down Pip's face. Her breathing is stuttered as if she's holding back sobs. I fucking hate that I'm doing this to her. Especially since I told her I wanted this to be a chill day without any bullshit drama concerning my past behavior. But I can't keep this shit from her any longer.

"I was placed in foster care. But the first family I ended up with was worse than living with my negligent father. I heard my foster parents talking one night. They were going to make me sleep with them. All three of us. Together. I was thirteen fucking years old." Pippa gasps but clamps her hand over her mouth, trying with everything in her not to make a sound.

"I climbed out the window. Ran away and never looked back. I ended up on the streets. I figured even that was better than being the sex toy for some perverted couple. It didn't take me long to realize I had something I could use to make money. The ladies seemed very interested in my looks. Guess I looked older than my age. I got some fake ID and used it to get into places I was too young to be in. I began to make decent money servicing older wealthy women. Enough to buy equipment and get back into hockey. Then Dad...I mean Mr. Battaglia, found me and well, the rest is history." I take a few deep breaths. My brow is covered in sweat. It feels like I just ran a marathon, but strangely restorative, like a heavy weight has been lifted.

"All this time I've been pushing you away because I had so much sordid baggage. I'm a scarred mess. And your life is perfect. You're perfect. I didn't want to drag you down into the gutter with me."

Pip is wiping the tears off her face and squinting from the bubbles she's splashed in her eyes. But she doesn't say a word. For the first time, I can't read her face.

I don't know what she's thinking. Is she thoroughly disgusted? Is she pitying me? As much as I don't want to lose her, I rather have her disgust than her pity.

"Pip?"

"Hmm?"

"Can you say something? I'm dying here."

"Oh. Sorry. Can I talk now?"

"Yes. Talk. I'm done. Now you can talk. I need to know what you're thinking."

The bubbles lap against her beautiful tits as she crawls toward me. She straddles my hips and brushes my hair back off my face. She presses her hands onto my chest and begins unconsciously tracing my muscles while she expresses her opinions on my fucked-up childhood. Her fingers on me are calming, soothing and—since I'm a guy and she's a beautiful naked woman sitting in my naked lap, touching me—dick stimulating.

"I'm not perfect, D. No one is. We all have our demons." She cups my cheek and I turn my head to place a gentle kiss on her palm. "I'm so sorry the adults in your life, the people who were supposed to take care of you and protect you. were the monsters you needed protecting from. No child should ever have to go through what you did. I know I don't have to tell you it wasn't your fault your mom died. It was an accident, and the prescription med addiction is an epidemic too many people have had to deal with. But you were a little boy having to make decisions and choices most adults never have to make." Her glistening blue eyes are filled with compassion and love. She is, honest to God, the most beautiful person I have ever known, ever seen in my life. I swallow the huge lump forming in my throat because no way am I going to start blubbering like a baby and add that level of humiliation onto my already overwhelming shame.

"It's true. I don't know what it feels like to be you, to have had the harsh past you had. A past that broke you a little bit, broke your heart a little bit. But it doesn't matter to me if you have scars. It never mattered to me that you thought your heart was too broken to love."

"Oh, baby." I tilt my head to kiss her, but she pushes my face away.

"No. Now I need *you* to let *me* finish." She gives me a sweet smile.

"Got it." I hold my soapy dripping hands up in surrender to confirm I won't touch her until she's done.

"None of that ever mattered because I wanted to give you all my heart to heal yours. With everything we went through, I couldn't give up because I loved you beyond any fault you or anyone else thought you had. I had some idea of what you must have faced as a teenager alone, trying to survive. But look at you now. Look how far you've come. I'm so proud of the way, with the Battaglias' help, you worked hard to become the man you are today." She drops her head and won't look at me. Here it comes. The gentle let down. The *'But I had no idea how bad it really was. I love you, but there's no way I can be with you.'* Every muscle in my body tightens, bracing myself for her next words.

"The thing is...I never cared about who you fucked or what you had to do to get here. I only ever cared about you. I love you, D. I always have."

I wrap her legs around my waist and tug her against my chest. I don't care if she's done talking or not. My lips capture hers. She hooks her arms around my neck. And she returns the kiss, tangling her tongue with mine. Jesus. This girl can kiss. She puts everything she has into it. I could live off her kisses. Between our hungry give and take and her declaration of unconditional love, I'm in full on arousal. I may be in this state permanently as long as she's around.

I clasp her hips and slide her closer toward me, lining my erection up with her entrance. She lets out a soft moan when she feels my shaft press against her wet pussy. Gripping her soap covered ass cheeks, I lift her and guide her down on to my cock as I slowly sink into her. Even in the slippery, bubbly water, she's so damn tight. She gasps when I push into her but then settles down onto me, clenching around me. We keep kissing and breathing each other in as I thrust my hips up and guide her hips up and down on my shaft in slow, controlled movements.

This is much more than fucking. I can actually feel the overwhelming sensation growing in my chest. We're making love.

Her legs begin to tremble and her muscles tense. I know she's about to come apart. Her pussy spasms around me as she grinds down on me, shuddering and moaning my name. I push up with one more deep thrust and let go, exploding warm jets into her.

We rock together in each other's arms in the pulsing water, reveling in the after-effects. I whisper, "I love you, Heaven. Always."

Chapter Thirty-Two

HEAVEN

The term Sunday Funday has a whole new meaning. As D claimed, we've had very little need for clothing.

After the bubble bath, he carries me into his enormous shower. It has more shower heads protruding in all directions and at all heights than people have body parts. Some are pulsing some are pouring down like rainwater. It's like standing in the middle of a tropical rainforest if rainforests were made from black marble.

D pours shower gel onto a cloth and washes my body from head to toe in slow, caressing circles. Then he does the same with my hair, working the shampoo through it with his fingers. The entire time he keeps whispering loving endearments to me. And even though he's brought me to innumerable mind-blowing orgasms in the last few hours, this is the most seductive thing I've ever experienced. Once again, I'm dripping with desire for him.

He takes one pulsing shower head with a long hose from the wall. I tip my head back. He showers water over my hair and body and then between my legs. Oh God. The pulsing sensation is yummy. I let out a whimper as the warmth sweeps through me and the tension builds in my stomach.

D drops the shower hose and spins me around. He plants my hands against the damp marble and peppers kisses down my body. Dropping to his knees behind me, he spreads my legs apart.

"*D*," I moan. He's right. I've become an incessant whimpering, moaning, needy hussy. I didn't even know it was possible to climax so many times in one day and it isn't even noon yet!

"I can't get enough of this delicious pussy and its sweet juices," D murmurs and presses his face between my ass cheeks. Oh. My. God. His tongue circles my clit, and when he begins sucking, hello shooting stars. I circle my hips back against his mouth, riding his glorious tongue and the waves of the building climax. When I crash over the edge, I do exactly what D requested last night. I sing out, chanting his name like a Benedictine monk singing a Gregorian hymn. My legs begin to melt under me. D presses his hand to the small of my back to hold me up and finishes eating me out from behind. With as many times as D refused to have sex with me in the past, who knew he would turn out to be a giver with a capital G?

Nevertheless, it's my turn to give back. The

remainder of our shower is spent with my returning the favors: washing his magnificent sculpted body and long sexy hair and then dropping to my knees to suck off his deliciously, suckable cock.

After the shower I call Brett, my Anatomy lab partner, and offer him everything short of an organ, to go over and feed Hal and Sheldon for me. Wolfe, the turtle, is fine for the day without me. Sheldon has a doggie door to an enclosed area in the backyard and Hal has a litter box. But if they don't eat all day, they may eat each other. Brett still has a key to my house from the last time he took care of the menagerie for me when I was away at Dak's wedding. While he's reluctantly agreeing, I hear some very expressive female moaning sounds in the background. I think I interrupted Brett in the middle of *his* Sunday Funday. But he only lives a few blocks away from me in an apartment house filled with male graduate students. It would take me half the day to drive from D's to my house. I'm going to owe Brett big time. I'll have to agree to be the one to dissect the cadaver in lab for the rest of the semester. He can be the note taker. It's the least I can do.

With my fur babies' care accounted for, D and I spend the rest of the day in robes. D orders out for lunch and dinner. And I'm not one bit ashamed to admit we eat both meals in bed while watching several more *Merlin* episodes. I don't sigh anymore when Bradley aka Arthur comes on the screen because in between eating our food I have my very own knight in shining armor using his magic *sword* to take me in positions I didn't even know existed and bringing me to orgasm after orgasm. Can a person die from too many climaxes in a day? If so, I'm willing to take the risk because oh what a wonderful way to go.

***

"I'm not inviting you in. Don't even bother to turn the car off." I gulp down some much-needed air when we finally unlock our lips. I would rather kiss D than breathe, but we both have serious obligations to fulfill in the morning. Therefore, breathing is going to have to be a priority for now. I'm going to get out of this car and go into my house alone.

"Aww, just two minutes. I'm not ready to let you go," D whines in protest.

"D, it's already ten o'clock. We both know two minutes isn't a possibility. If you come in, I'm going to keep kissing you, and then you're going to keep kissing me, and then one thing will lead to another, and we won't get two minutes' sleep."

"Sounds amazing," he mumbles against my neck in between nibbling at my skin.

"Mmm, D. You have to stop. I need to put on my big-girl-responsible-pants and say goodnight. And I can't do it if you're kissing me, or touching me, or…" I glance down and how is it possible for him to be erect? It can't be humanly possible to have that many orgasms in one day and be up and at 'em already. I'm convinced he is definitely part superhero. But I, on the other hand, am not. And in order to attend classes tomorrow, I sorta have to be able to walk.

"I'd prefer it if you'd take *off* your big girl pants and let me taste you again." He licks under my ear. I let out a sigh, recalling his super-human tongue's capabilities.

"No." I muster what little resistance I have left and push away from him. "I'm going inside now, and you're going home." He gives me the cutest pouty face, which on him looks sexy as hell.

"A whole week. How will I survive?" he gripes.

"It's only six days, D. We'll be so busy we won't even notice. And BTW, you *better* survive. I've given him a year's worth of attention today." I glance back down at his crotch area. He needs to write out his diet and exercise plan and sell it worldwide. Every man—and some women—on the planet, would thank him.

"No worries, babe. He's not interested in any pussy but this one." He slides his hand between my thighs and even through my pants, the pussy he's referring to clenches.

"Good night, D." I push his hand away before I grab it and drag him all the way to my bedroom.

"I'll be back early on Saturday to get you."

"To get me?"

"Did you think I forgot it was your birthday?" Oops. Maybe *he* didn't, but I did.

"I'll pick you up at seven. I'm taking you to dinner, so don't make any plans. And I'm choosing the restaurant this time." He shakes his head. "No loud, over-crowded, greasy spoon."

"Oh, darn. I was looking forward to beating you at *Super Shot*." I open the car door.

"Forget it, sweetheart. Never gonna happen.

Wouldn't even let you win on your birthday." He gives me his tilted sexy grin. I'm thinking about closing the car door and climbing onto his lap. But I don't because at least one person in this car has to be a responsible, boring adult.

I hop from the truck and walk to my door. I unlock it but before I can get inside, D calls out, "Pip." I turn to look at him. A big smile crosses my face. Although we've spent twenty-four intimate hours together, when I look at his beautiful face and panty-melting eyes, I can't believe he's finally mine.

"Yes?" Raising and dropping my shoulders, I let out a contented sigh.

"Wear something nice. I'm going to wine and dine you *before* we fuck this time." He throws his truck into gear. I watch from the doorway as he drives away.

Closing the door behind me, I'm greeted by my not-so-happy furry friends.

"Sorry, guys, but it couldn't be helped. I've been super busy falling in love with the most wonderful guy in the world."

As I climb into bed sated with warm, fuzzy feelings and already counting the hours until next Saturday, my phone chirps with an incoming text.

WOLFE

I miss you already.

> I miss you too.

> This was the best day of my life.
> Thank you for spending it with me.

Geez. Even from long distance, this boy has the ability to make me tingle. Before I have a chance to answer, my phone rings and D's face lights up my screen.

I swipe to answer. "Hey. Are you home?"

"Yeah. I'm in bed. But I'm lonely, and the bed is really cold. How am I going to sleep without you?" D's gravelly bed voice has me regretting sending him home.

"You've been sleeping without me for twenty-six years," I answer through a smile because I'm totally loving that he's missing me too much to sleep. "And anyway, you wouldn't be sleeping if I was there."

"You got that right. I'd be licking you, everywhere," he hums in a soft voice. A warm flush spreads over my body. I rub my legs together to sooth the empty ache for him.

"Mmm. This was the best day of my life too. Thank *you* for spending it with *me*." I snuggle under my covers.

"It's a good thing you liked it because we're going to be spending lots more days together and I wouldn't want you to be unhappy." I can hear the smile in his voice. "Where are you?"

"I'm in bed. And it's lonely here too," I lament in a soft voice.

"Oh man. You're killin' me, Pip. I shouldn't have let you go," he groans. "I'm hard just hearing your voice and thinking about you in bed."

"Mmmm. Me too," I close my eyes and moan my

response. But then it occurs to me what I said. "I mean, I'm not hard. I'm…"

"Wet," D corrects me, his voice almost a growl.

"Yes," I whisper. My cheeks warm at my confession.

"Are you thinking about me there with you? Touching you?" His sultry words continue to flame my need.

"Mm-huh." I roll onto my side and close my eyes.

"I'd love to be tasting your pussy right now, running my tongue over your clit, sucking on you."

"Mmm, D."

"Are you touching yourself, baby?"

"Yes," I purr.

"If I were there I'd slide a finger inside you, then two and work you while I circled your clit with my tongue. Can you feel it?"

"Mmm. Yes. Oh God. Yes."

"I love hearing you moan for me. I'm so fucking hard right now thinking about you touching yourself. I want to bury my cock deep inside you."

"D. Oh God. I'm…I'm…" I come apart using D's seductive words and my own fingers. While I'm still trembling and trying to regain some semblance of lucidity, I hear D groan and growl a raspy "fuuuck."

The phone line goes silent. I can't believe we both climaxed. I thought phone sex was a myth. I didn't believe it was possible to climax just from talking to someone over the phone. *Holy Mary Mother of God!* Even from twenty miles away, this guy gives mind-blowing sex. Who knew robocoitus could be so…stimulating?

"Are you there, Pip?" D asks in a post-sex graveled voice.

"I'm here," I force my brain to engage and say actual words.

"You okay?"

"I'm wonderful," I coo and tug a pillow into my arms, pretending it's D I'm wrapping my arms around.

"I'll be thinking about you while I'm away. And I'll call you every night to talk you to sleep. Okay?"

"Yes. Please."

"And when I do, I want you to pretend it's me touching you." For Pete's sake. He's getting me all hot and bothered again.

"I will. And D?"

"Yes, baby?"

"Good luck on starting in the net next week."

"Will you be watching?

"Of course."

"Then that's all the luck I need. Good night, Heaven."

"Good night, D."

I disconnect the call and place my phone on the night table. Tugging the pillow tighter into my arms I fall asleep thinking how perfect everything is. I've never been happier in my life. But you know what they say about things being too good to be true. Whoever *they* are, they're right.

Chapter Thirty-Three

HEAVEN

"Wolfe seems off. What's going on?" Nikki gripes.

The Winds are playing the Sharks, or should I say sort of playing the Sharks. The score is 4-1. D can't seem to do anything right. I'd say it's because he's just getting back into things after his injury, but he started Tuesday night, and he was on fire. Nothing got past him. Two days later, he looks like he's never played in the goalie position before. Every time he reads the situation he makes the wrong decision. One goal was scored through the five-hole. D never makes that mistake. Never. A moment ago, a Sharks forward took the puck down the ice through a sheet of Winds' players. He flew right up to the front door challenging D. Once again D made the wrong decision when cutting the angle. The score is now 5-1.

"I don't understand." I'm seated on the floor on a

pillow next to the coffee table. Nikki is writhing in agony on the sofa, holding a throw pillow over her eyes to avoid watching the latest failed challenge on Wolfe's part.

I refill our wine glasses because I'm closer to the bottle and our half-eaten pizza.

No Friday classes and next week off in between internships, means mid-week wine drinking is on the okay-to-do-list. I was starving when I got home from class. Nik texted and offered to bring pizza if I supplied the wine while we watched the game together. But watching the way the game is falling apart, I can't take another bite. However, I can take more wine. Lots more wine.

"What's happening?" Nikki wails as she peeks out from behind the pillow when she hears the horn designating yet another scored goal.

"I don't know. Something's up. Maybe his leg is bothering him."

"What did he say when you talked to him? Did he say it was?" Nik is aware my relationship with D has taken the fast track to paradise since the last time I spoke to her. She knows he's been texting me non-stop since he's been away. I haven't disclosed the contents of the X-rated texts. But if I know Nik, she would be more than interested in the contents and using it to give Dalt some pointers on sexting. Although, from the things she's told me, she and Dalt have a very *non-boring* sex life and he doesn't need any tips.

"I didn't talk to him today."

"Well, what did he say last night?"

I knew something was off when he didn't call me last night. He hasn't missed a night since he's been away, phone sexing me to sleep. I tried calling him, but he didn't pick up. Then I sent him a good night text but didn't get an answer. I convinced myself I was being silly reading something into it. He was probably hanging out with his teammates. Perhaps he fell asleep early. It was a long week on the road playing and traveling. But now I know I was right to be concerned. Something is definitely wrong.

When Coach Connelly replaces D in the net, the camera follows him to the bench and catches him throwing his gloves and mask on the floor at his feet in frustration. As the camera pans in on Wolfe's face, one analyst makes some snide comment like, "Looks like the wolf didn't come out tonight."

"I'll say," the other commentator adds with a chuckle. "Seems their superstar is way off his game tonight."

"Oh, fuck you!" Nikki yells and throws the pillow at the screen. But then, when the camera pulls back, I see it. I see D turn and say something to *her*. No. It can't be. I must have imagined it.

"What the hell? Did you just see what I saw?" Nik sits up and leans toward the television.

"I don't know. What did you see?" Please, God. Don't let her say what I think she's about to say.

"Wasn't that the skanky blonde waitress from Trace's reception sitting behind the Winds' bench? You know, the one Wolfe hooked up with."

"I...no. What would Alison be doing in San Jose?

You must be seeing things." I choke out a chuckle because I thought I saw her too.

"Rewind it. I know it was her. Maybe that's why Wolfe's head isn't in the game. The douchebag is hooking up with that slut while he's away."

I pick up the remote and clutch it in my hand. I can't bring myself to press the rewind button. "That's ridiculous, Nik. He hasn't seen her in months and we..."

"Give me the remote." Nikki grabs it away from me. My insides are tumbling and spinning like an Olympic gymnast is doing a floor routine in my stomach.

Nik hits rewind. When she gets to the point where D turns and says something through the Plexiglas to the bouncy, gorgeous blonde behind him, the gymnast inside me decides to toss the pizza I ate, up and out. I make a beeline for the bathroom in time to hurl my dinner into the toilet.

"I'm so sorry, babe," Nik says from the doorway. She comes in and flushes the toilet. Sitting next to me on the cold tile floor, she brushes my hair back. "He's an asshole. He doesn't deserve you."

"It can't be. Nik." Using the back of my hand, I swipe under my runny nose. "He said he loved me. He said always. He's told me every night since he's been away. He couldn't have been lying."

Nikki gets up and takes a washcloth from the shelf. She runs it under the water, wrings it out, and returns to her place on the floor next to me.

"Oh, sweetie," she says, wiping the cloth over my face and stinging eyes. The damp coolness is a relief. "Sometimes these hockey fuckers are...fuckers."

"No. It's a mistake. We're jumping to conclusions. D would never hurt me like this." *Of course he would. He's done it before.* Just because he had his dick inside me—innumerable times—doesn't mean he isn't the same old Wolfe with the same old MO.

"When D calls tonight he'll explain everything." I'm not sure who I'm trying to convince, her or me. I fight back the tears burning my eyes.

"Maybe he will." Her words are soft. She's trying to be soothing like my mom used to do when one of my pets died. Nik, being a mom herself now, knows the perfect tone to use.

"He will," I insist.

"I hope so, for his sake as much as yours, because Dalt is going to kick his ass all the way back to Santa Ana, and Dak is going to castrate him when they find out what he's done to you." She wipes the cloth across my forehead. It helps to soothe the pounding in my temples. "And then Dalt is going to kick his ass *again*. I might even put my two cents in."

My heart skips a beat when my phone chirps with an incoming text message. I left it on the coffee table. I jump up and practically fly into the living room. I'm beyond relieved to see Wolfe's name pop up on my screen. Until I read the message.

WOLFE

Won't be able to make it for dinner Saturday. But we need to talk. I'll call when I get back.

Oh, God. No 'I love you.' No 'I miss you.' 'We need

to talk' can only mean one thing. I think I'm going to be sick again. But before I can get to the bathroom, Nik walks into the room with her phone pressed to her ear.

"I'm with her now. Yes." Every time the person on the other end says something, Nik glances at me.

"Yeess, Dalt. Why?" It's Dalt, and they're obviously talking about me.

"What? Is this a joke?" Dammit. If it's about me why doesn't she put it on speaker so I can hear what he's saying?

"Motherfucking motherfucker." Nik looks like she's just seen a ghost or heard one. When she looks at me with what can only be described as wide-eyed panic, the floor seems to drop out from under me, and the room starts to spin. I hang onto the nearest piece of furniture to keep from falling over.

"What's wrong? Is it D? Is he okay?" Nik holds up a finger. My whole body is shaking, waiting for her to answer.

"Yeah. I will." Dalt says something on the other end. "I won't. I'll bring her home with me."

Nik's voice softens, "Me too. So much." She slides her phone into her pocket. The brief silence in the room is deafening. I've never known Nikki to be at a loss for words. This is bad. She can't find the words to tell me whatever it was Dalt just told her.

"What is it? Tell me."

"Maybe you better sit down," Nik suggests, using her soothing mommy tone.

"I don't want to sit down, Nik. Tell me what happened," I demand, much like a spoiled three-year-old.

She crosses the room, and taking my hand, leads me to the sofa. I collapse onto the couch in a huff, and she sits next to me.

"That was Dalt," she states the obvious. I'm ready to pull my hair out, or maybe her pretty blue bangs.

"Yes. I know. Nikki, for heaven's sake, what did he say?"

"He...it's Wolfe...he..." she scrubs a hand over her eyes. "I am so going to kill that motherfucker," she mumbles.

"Nikki, please. Tell me what's going on."

She sits up straight and blows out a big breath. "That *was* Alison we saw at the game. Apparently, Wolfe has seen her since the wedding weekend."

"He...no. I don't..."

"She contacted him while he was on the road and met him in San Jose." I've never seen Nikki like this. She's shaking almost as hard as I am.

"And he hooked up with her." I finish the nauseating statement for her.

"Yes...well, no."

"Jesus Christ, Nik! Either he hooked up with her, or he didn't. Which is it? Stop coddling me and just tell me."

"It's much worse than that."

"Ha. What could be worse than that? Did he..."

"She's pregnant." I tilt my head and stare at her mouth waiting for the smile, the laugh, the 'gotcha just kidding.'

When it doesn't happen, I coax her. "Stop kidding around, Nik. That's not funny."

ELIZABETH HARTEY

"He's going to marry her, Heaven."

I jump from the sofa like I've been hit with an electric shock. "What the hell are you talking about? That's ridiculous." I wheel around like a trapped rat looking for an escape. *Wake up, Heaven.* This has to be a nightmare. I can't breathe, can't catch my breath.

"Calm down. Just breathe," Nikki stands and puts her arms around me. But I push away, flailing my fists at her, taking my anger out on the messenger. She holds her hands up, allowing me to take my aggression out on her but not letting me land a punch.

"You're lying. Why are you lying to me?" I keep yelling and thrashing until I'm physically and emotionally spent. After a moment, I fall into Nikki's arms, sobbing.

"He can't be getting married. He doesn't even date," I wail in between sobs.

"I'm so sorry, sweetie," Nik says while she strokes my hair. "She wants to keep the baby, and he doesn't want to abandon them. Shit. This is all my fault."

"What...what do you m...mean your fault?" I take a step back to keep myself from saturating her shirt with tears any more than I already have. "How can it...it be your fault?" The words come out in hiccoughs as I try to catch my breath.

"Well...mine and Tracey's fault." Nik shrugs and hands me my full wine glass. She reclaims her seat on the sofa, picks up her wine glass, and takes a big gulp. I follow her lead but chug my entire glass in one long swallow and put the empty glass down before I throw it against a wall.

346

"It was us who tipped the lead singer at the reception to play those songs."

"Songs?" I swipe my nose again.

"We saw the way you and Wolfe looked at each other. We thought all you needed was a little shove in the right direction. So, we asked them to play *The Wolf*. We knew it was his ringtone on your phone. We figured it would get his attention and yours. And when you were dancing together, we told them to play *Say You Won't Let Go*. I mean, who can resist that? It's the sexiest falling-in-love-song ever." She takes another long swallow, finishing her wine but reaching for the bottle and refilling our glasses to the brim. "If we hadn't interfered, maybe this whole thing between you two would never have started. And then he hooked up with Alison instead and..."

"He didn't hook up with Alison. Not at the wedding, anyway." I flop down into a pod chair. The chugged wine is beginning to take effect.

"I thought you said..."

"It was me."

"What?"

"He hooked up with me. I helped him back to his room. He was really drunk, but I didn't realize how drunk. Or maybe I did. I'd just wanted him for so long, and...one thing led to another and we...hooked up." I lift a shoulder.

"But I thought you said Wolfe was with Alison?"

"The next day he didn't remember what happened or who he was with. Alison told him it was her and he believed her."

"What do you mean he didn't remember?"

"As I said, he was pretty drunk. He didn't remember it was me and I was just too humiliated to tell anyone how stupid I had been."

"But you were a...a..."

"A virgin. Yep. It was...interesting. D thought I slept with Josh that weekend."

"What did he say when you told him the truth?" I look down at my hands and pick at my cuticles. "Heaven? You told him the truth, right?" I glance up at her and grimace.

"I meant to. I was going to. I was waiting for the right time."

"Oh, Heaven. You should have told him what a lying, scheming skank she is."

"You see? It's not your fault or Tracey's. It's mine. If I had told him..."

"No, you don't. No blaming yourself. If Wolfe had kept his wandering dick in his pants, this wouldn't be happening. "

"How pregnant is she?"

Nik's brows pinch together. "Completely?"

"I mean, how many weeks?' I shake my head. If she's trying to be funny, I'm not in the mood.

"Oh. She told Wolfe she's ten weeks."

So, he slept with her right after the wedding. Probably the next day to thank her for taking *care* of him. Or maybe he was seeing her when he was coming to the clinic begging me to go out with him. And what happened to him '*never*' fucking without a condom? I let my head drop back onto the chair. I've been so stupid, so naïve.

"This cannot be happening. Not now. Not after..."

"He's not worth it. There are a million other guys out there who would give their left nut to be with you... to love you."

"Jesus, Nik. I've spent almost half my life loving him." I pull my knees to my chest. Wrapping my arms around my legs and resting my forehead on my knees, I continue to cry, this time silent tears. How could he do this?

"Are you okay?"

"No," I sniffle, keeping myself curled up in my self-protecting ball. I may never be okay again. "How long will it take for this stabbing ache in my chest to go away?" My sniffling escalates to full-blown blubbering.

"All right. That's it. Get your stuff." I look up in time to see Nikki polish off her wine and stand up. "You're coming to my house for the weekend. No good sitting here and crying over spilled sperm," she declares, placing her glass on the table. My sweet friend has such an interesting way with words.

"No. I'm fine." I sit up, wipe the tears from my eyes, and guzzle more wine.

"You don't look or sound fine," Nikki taunts. I'm sure what must be a very red, splotchy, swollen face and gasps for air are belying my statement.

"I've got several more bottles of Moscato to drown my sorrows in. Go home and enjoy your babies."

"Are you kidding? My babies are a miraculous blessing, and I thank God every day for them." Nik looks toward the ceiling. "But Chloe is becoming a hellish diva. She's driving me out of my mind. If I didn't know better,

I'd swear she wasn't mine. All she wants to do is dress up like a princess and pretend she's being rescued by a prince. She won't even *look* at a soccer ball. I mean seriously, where the hell did she come from?"

"Maybe she'll play hockey," I sniff and offer my meager conciliatory suggestion over my wine glass rim.

"Oh, my fucking word. God forbid. Bite your tongue." Even through all my misery, I have to smile at Nik's earnest protestations. I'm sure she would be thrilled if her daughter wanted to play hockey. She's just trying to support me in my current hockey-player-hating mood.

"I bought her a mini-me black leather jacket," she continues her rant. "I thought she would be thrilled to dress like mommy. You know what she said?" I bite back another smile and shake my head. Thank God for Nikki. She can bring humor to the darkest situation.

"I quote, 'eek, no Mama. It's a-twhoasis.' Can you believe it? Not only does she hate soccer and black leather, she throws around words like atrocious. At three-years-old! I won't even be able to converse with her by the time she's ten." I don't know how she does it. She actually has me laughing into my glass.

"You're coming home with me. Tracey and Dak are coming for the weekend, and Dalt will be home early Saturday. The kids are going on outings with the nanny, so you'll have some peace during your stay. I can't believe I ever argued with Dalt about hiring her. I don't know what I would do without her. She's like Mary-fucking-Poppins without the cool accent."

I consider her invitation as I finish off my wine. I'm

not sure how many glasses I've had, but since I'm not numb yet, it hasn't been enough.

"I have a fully stocked wine cellar. We can get blissfully, mind-numbingly blottoed," she adds as if she read my wine-pickled mind.

"I'll be ready in two minutes." No sense in sitting here alone wallowing in misery. Being with my friends will help keep my mind off Wolfe and my hands off my phone to call him. I don't ever want to see him or talk to his lying ass again. It's like someone drilled a hole straight through me and removed a piece of my heart—the piece that belongs to him. How do I live without it?

Chapter Thirty-Four

WOLFE

I knew my past would come back to bite me in the ass. But I didn't want it to destroy Heaven in the process.

I drop my bag on the bedroom floor and collapse onto my bed. I grab a pillow and sink my nose into it, hoping I can still smell Heaven on it. Dammit. I forgot the cleaning lady was here and changed the sheets.

Staring up at the ceiling, I realize Pip was right. It's plain old stark white. Empty. Blank. Nothing. Just like I am without her. Just like my life without her is going to be because I fucked up royally.

Images flash across my mind: Heaven here in my bed, in my arms, her giggling, her under me, her moaning and breathing in stuttered breaths when she came apart. I squeeze my eyes closed and try to hold back the tears. I can't. I've lost her. But even worse, I've hurt her, broken her. I took the love of this beautiful woman, knowing I didn't deserve it. Allowed myself to love her, knowing she was much too good for me and then I destroyed her.

My God. I didn't know it was possible to love someone like this, to love her more with every breath I take. But with every one of those breaths, it's like a blade piercing my heart. I can't live without her. But I can't abandon my child. I refuse to be the same kind of absentee, crap father my father was. A kid needs a father—a father who's there and loves him...or her.

My head is throbbing in confusion. I'm being pulled in two different directions. With every heartbeat, I hear Heaven's name, and yet my mind tells me I have to be there for my child. There's no way to make this right.

I wish I had a magic wand to erase my existence from Heaven's mind. I'll spend every day, for the rest of my life, living off the memories: her smile, her warmth, her love and the excruciating agony that comes with her loss. But if I could spare *her* one tortured second, I would.

Dalt called a few minutes ago and said Heaven already knows. He said she's staying at their house and she's in pretty bad shape. Of course, she is. That's my MO. Decimate every beautiful thing I touch.

He suggested I come over now because Dak's not there yet. Dak's going to go ballistic when he sees me. I don't blame him. I should have stayed away from her. I should have kept my hands and dick away from his sweet sister. But I want to spare Heaven the drama the confrontation with Dak is going to cause—at least for now. I've caused enough drama in her life, and the timing couldn't be worse.

It's her birthday. Instead of celebrating with her like I

ELIZABETH HARTEY

planned, this betrayal is my fucking birthday present to her.

I want to scoop her up in my arms and run far away. Find an island somewhere, just her and me, block out the world, forget everyone and everything. But that's a dream. Our reality is a fucking nightmare. Christ. Why didn't I stay away from her? Yet, I wouldn't give back one second of the time we've shared together.

Even though I don't know what I'm going to say to her, I have to pull myself together and go see her. Although I have zero words to make this right, she deserves some kind of explanation.

———

"What the fuck are you doing here?" Nik opens the door and gives me the well-deserved callous greeting.

"I have to see Heaven," I explain with a nervous shrug.

"No, you don't. You don't ever have to do anything again when it comes to Heaven, you asshole. In fact, the only thing you have to do is get the fuck off my front porch."

"Nik, I understand you hate me. I hate myself more than you ever could for hurting her. But if I have to pick you up and physically move you out of my way so I can get to Pippa, I will."

"I would love to see you try it. You dic..."

"It's okay, Nik." Dalt walks up behind her and places his hands on her shoulders to keep her from punching my lights out. I'm grateful for his intervention because

354

there's no doubt in my mind Nikki could do it. "I told him to come over."

"You invited this douchebag to her birthday celebration? Are you fucking kidding me?" Guess I'm no longer Nikki's favorite goalie in the NHL. I can relate. I'm not even my favorite goalie on this porch.

"I didn't invite him to the celebration, Nik," Dalt mumbles through clenched teeth, as if I won't be able to hear him from a foot away. "I told him to come and see Heaven. They need to talk. *She* needs to talk to someone or she won't even come out of her room for her own birthday. She needs...him."

"Well, she can't have him, can she? Since he decided to stick his dick in that skank and get her pregnant." Nik is talking to Dalt, but her growled words are directed at me.

"Okay, babe. I know you're looking out for your friend, but they're going to have to talk eventually and isn't it better for her to talk to him here, surrounded by friends, where she can have moral support?" Dalt circles his arms around Nikki's waist and I find myself envying him being able to hold the woman he loves.

"Whatever," Nikki reluctantly agrees. She and Dalt step to the side and I walk into their enormous foyer. "Wait here," Nik commands and gives me a narrow-eyed glare before stomping up the staircase which looks like something right out of *Gone With The Wind*—the California, white marble version.

"You really fucked up, dude," Dalt informs me, watching the stairs until Nik is far enough away she can't hear him. "What the fuck were you thinking?"

"I wasn't thinking. That's the problem."

"You better have unicorns and rainbows coming out of your mouth when you talk to Heaven because she's pretty wrecked," Dalt continues.

"I know. Fuck," I rub my hands over my face. "I don't know how the hell this happened."

"You don't? Should I give you a quick lesson on the birds and bees, dickwad?" He shoves my shoulder. I get the distinct impression he's holding back with every nerve cell in his body from punching me.

"Christ, Dalt. I'm so in love with Heaven. The last thing I want to do is hurt her. I was going to ask her to move in with me. But now...Alison is keeping the baby. I have to stand by her."

We both glance up the stairs when we hear mumbled voices coming from somewhere upstairs. A few loud 'no's' echo down the stairs.' I'm sure it's Pippa telling Nik she doesn't want to see me.

"You don't have to marry her just because she's having a baby, dude." Dalt shakes his head. "I mean...if you don't love her," he clarifies, because Nik had his baby before they were married. The difference in their situation was Dalt and Nik were madly in love. They had a few minor obstacles to kick to the curb before finding their happy ever after.

"That's what Batt said too. But I'm having a kid with her, man. I won't abandon the kid, be an absentee shit father."

"Then I don't know what to tell you, bro. Except this is one serious cluster fuck."

"You think?"

His astute information is interrupted when Nik comes halfway down the stairs and says, "Okay, dickhead. You can come up. But if you say one word to upset her more than she already is I'm throwing your ass off the balcony—the second story balcony. Understood?"

"Completely.'

Just then, Chloe, Nik and Dalt's daughter, comes racing into the foyer and circles her little arms around my legs.

"Hey, sweetheart." I bend down to give her a hug.

She places her tiny hand on my face. "Uncew Woof, ahw you heaw to wescoo Aunt Heaben? She's cwyin'. Ahw you hul pwince?" I look up at Dalt because I haven't learned how to decipher Chloe's toddler speech, yet.

"She wants to know if you're here to rescue Aunt Heaven...if you're her...uh...prince." Dalt scratches his neck.

"No, honey. Uncle Wolfe is no prince," Nik answers from the stairs.

She's got that right. "No, Chloe. I'm not here to rescue Aunt Heaven because she doesn't need rescuing. Girls don't need men or princes to rescue them. They're strong enough to take care of themselves."

"Dey ahw?" she asks in wide-eyed wonder.

"Yes. They are." I give her an assured smile. *As long as they stay away from assholes like me who decimate their hearts and all trust in humanity.*

She ponders my statement for a moment before declaring, "Otay. Good."

"Come on, Chlo." Dalt reaches his hand out. "Let's go have a snack."

"You wanta snack too, Uncew Woof?"

"Not right now. Thanks, Chlo. Maybe later."

"Otay." She wraps her arms around my neck and says in a loud whisper, "I wuv you, Uncew Woof. Don't be sad." And then she latches onto her dad's hand and walks away. I swallow past the lump forming in my throat.

"You break their hearts at every age, huh, asshole?" Nik sneers when I stop at the step below her, waiting for her to give me directions to the guest room Heaven's in.

"Give me a break, Nik. I didn't mean for this to happen."

"Then I guess you should have kept your dick in your pants, huh?" I pinch my eyes shut and grimace at her words, which are like a punch straight to the gut.

"Aw. Don't tell me I hurt the big bad Wolfe's feelings? Impossible. You have to have a heart to have feelings." She nearly spits the words at me. "Third door on the left."

I have a heart. I know I do because just like the Tin Man, I can feel it breaking. But my broken heart doesn't matter, not to Nik *or* me. The only thing that matters is Heaven, and what I've done to her.

I continue up the stairs. "Don't forget what I said, dickhead," she calls to my back. "If I hear one sob I'm throwing your ass over the balcony."

When I reach the third door on the left, my hands shake as I give a tentative knock. As much as I want to see Heaven, I'm hesitant. One, because I've fucked up our life together. And two, I'm going to want to hold her and kiss her and never let go. But that can't happen now.

There's no answer, no sound in the room. I check to make sure I counted the doors correctly since this hallway is about the same length as the corridor in the Ramanathaswamy Temple. No wonder everyone comes here to hang out on holidays. Dalt and Nik own a palacea Newport Beach palace.

I wanted to give all this and more to Pip, give her everything and anything she wanted. While I'm brooding over the sad fact I'll never be able to share anything with her, never have a future with her, now, the bedroom door clicks open.

Pip opens it just enough to peer out. Her face is splotched red, and her eyes are puffy and swollen. Fuck. I did this to her. But even though she looks like she's been crying for days, she's the most beautiful thing I've ever seen. I have to stop myself from pushing the door open and taking her in my arms.

"What are you doing here?" Her voice is quiet, flat. As if someone has sucked the life right out of her.

"Can I come in?" I say softly, afraid if I speak too loudly, she'll shatter into a million broken pieces.

She doesn't say a word, but walks away from the door, leaving it open. I assume it means I'm not welcome, but I can come in. I walk in and hesitate for a moment, not sure if I should close the door or leave it open.

"Close the door," Pip makes the decision for me. She's standing at a large window which takes up almost the whole wall and apparently looks out over the ocean. She continues to stare out the window, giving me her back.

"I wanted to see you."

"Why?" she asks, her breath fogging the window.

I walk toward her but stop before getting close enough to touch her. I've lost all right to touch her.

"I...I'm sorry, Pip. I didn't mean for this to happen."

"You played horribly the other night," she states, ignoring my apology. Her voice is robotic, nothing like my vivacious Pippa. But then, she's not my anything anymore.

"I know. I had a lot on my mind."

"Hmm. I suppose so."

"Listen, Pip. I know I've made a lot of stupid mistakes. Recently, the most stupid. But I want you to know I meant every word I said to you. Every word was the truth. I love you. I'm in love with you. Always. I..." She turns and begins walking toward me. My breath hitches and I can't finish my sentence. When she stops, just inches from me, my heart races. Every cell in my body is crying out to kiss her. I can almost taste her sweet lips on mine.

I fist my hands at my sides waiting for her to make the first move. And then she does. It happens so fast I don't see it coming. She swings her arm around and slaps me with such force I'm knocked back a step. Rubbing my jaw and shaking my head, I take a moment to clear my vision and process what she's saying.

"Don't! I can't listen to any more of your lies," she seethes.

I stand frozen in place, rubbing my stinging cheek. I deserve much worse from her for what I've done. But I've never lied to Pip. I never would. Although, I'm sure, telling her would be little conciliation since I managed to knock up another chick.

"It's not a lie. I love you with all my heart," I whisper.

"You love me with all your heart, but you're marrying the girl you got pregnant." She shoves both hands against my chest, and I take another step back.

"I swear to God, I don't know how it happened." I run my hands back through my hair and squeeze hoping I can squash my idiotic cranium between my palms.

"What do you mean, you don't know how?" she yells and shoves me again. "How could you do this? How could you do this?" She's crying as she keeps pummeling my chest and then she collapses into my arms and sobs into my shirt.

I wrap my arms around her and stroke her hair. "I'm sorry, Pip. I'm so sorry. I don't know what to do. I love you so much but...I can't abandon my kid."

She continues to sob and tremble, her face pressed into my chest while I try to soothe her with useless comforting words. It doesn't matter how many times I tell her I love her. My actions have destroyed her, have destroyed us.

After a moment, she tilts her head back and looks up me. All I see in her beautiful tear-filled eyes is anguish. The anguish and pain I put there. My God. What have I done to her?

But then she pushes away from me, swipes her hand under her nose, and says, "I'm good. You can go."

"Wh...what do you mean?"

"I've had a few days to think about this. When I saw Alison sitting behind you at the game, it felt like I had been hit by a Mack truck. But after I allowed myself time to think I realized some things."

"Shit, Pip. I didn't invite her to the game. She just showed up to tell me..."

"It doesn't matter." It's unsettling how flat and emotionless her voice has become. "I chose to be your friend, but I didn't choose to fall in love with you. From the first moment I saw you, all those years ago, it seemed to be...beyond my control. And ever since, I've tried to convince you to love me in return, to show you, *you* deserved to be loved. I poured my heart out to you because I didn't think or care about my happy ending, I only cared about my happy journey with you. When the journey hurt, sometimes, I let it. I lived with the occasional pain if that's what it took to be with you because somewhere along the way I forgot *I* deserved to be loved too. I was worth more than rejection, more than heartbreak."

"Pip, please. I..."

"You broke my heart again. But I've let you tear my heart in two so many times I've lost count." She tilts her head as if she's actually trying to remember how many times I've broken her heart. "And every time it healed, it would beat for you all over again. And I'd think, 'this is enough for now, because if I keep loving him he'll see and he'll know this is right.'

"I guess that was the problem all along. It's *not* right. We're just not meant to be together. For *you*, this was a tricky, complicated relationship and for me, it was...just love. But I'll never let you do this to me again because I have a good heart and I won't let you break it ever again."

Every word is an ice pick plunging into my heart. She's right about everything. I should have told her I loved her a long time ago. I was supposed to make her happy, take care of her, love her—always. Instead, I've siphoned away her joy, left her empty and broken.

"It's funny, really. Something good has come from all this heartache." She forces a joyless smile.

"I only know I love you and there's nothing good about any of this." I run my fingers back through my hair.

"Oh, but there is. You've finally made me realize a very important thing. I *am* worth it. I deserve to be loved completely, without any uncertainty." She turns and walks toward the door.

"Pip, please forgive me." This can't be happening. I can't be losing the best person I've ever known, the only woman I will ever love. I swipe the tears off my face, and it occurs to me she's stopped crying. It's as if someone flipped a switch and a different Pippa took her place, a cold, lifeless version.

"I can't do this anymore. It's too much. I'll probably miss you forever. But I'm going to have to try to live without you. I was young, but I had a life before you and I will definitely have one after you. One of these days you won't be the first thing I think of in the morning and the last thing I think of before I fall asleep."

My shock and confusion must be written all over my face. She can't believe anything good has come from this situation or our relationship has only been heartache.

"It's not so surprising. I've been drowning in your uncertainty for too long. Now, at least, our future or our *non*-future is certain. I know this is going to hurt for a long time. But I'll get over it, eventually." She opens the door and stands there holding the doorknob.

I stare at her, dumbfounded. I came here to talk but I'm speechless. I can't beg her forgiveness when I'm walking out of here and marrying another woman. I don't have the right to ask for her continued friendship when I've betrayed her unremitting loyalty. When I don't make a move toward the door, Pip reiterates her dismissal. "Good-bye, D. Please don't call me or text me anymore. Please let me be strong enough to get over you. If you really do love me...let me go."

Chapter Thirty-Five

WOLFE

My intercom buzzes with a call from the reception desk. "Fuck off." I'm not interested in interacting with humans. I can't even stand my own company as I sit at my absurdly long kitchen island and polish off my third beer.

The box buzzes again. "I said, fuck off!" I shout to the inanimate object on the wall. But the dumbass at the front desk apparently can't hear me through the building's cement and steel structure and buzzes again.

"Okay, asshole. I'm coming. No Christmas bonus for you this year," I mumble and stomp to the intercom. "What?" I push a button and yell into the box.

"You have a visitor, Mr. Wolfe," Tony's voice booms through the steel speaker. He's a good guy and a diligent doorman. But at the moment, a major pain in my ass.

"I'm not home," I snarl.

"It's Mr. Andersen, sir. He says it's an emergency." Dak? Shit. Did something happen to Heaven? Before I have a chance to answer, I hear a scuffling sound and another familiar voice booms from the speaker.

"I'm coming up one way or another, asshole. Give this guy the green light and save him some trouble." Dak has obviously taken the phone receiver from Tony.

It occurs to me if something had happened to Heaven, I would be the last person Dak would notify. He's come here to have it out about what's gone down between Pip and me. I have to face him sooner or later, may as well be sooner. He deserves an explanation as to why I betrayed him *and* his sister.

"It's okay, Tony. Let him come up."

"Are you sure, sir?" I can hear the apprehension in Tony's voice. Dak must be fuming. "Yeah, Tony. It's fine."

Two minutes later, it sounds like my door is about to be pounded off its hinges. Taking a deep breath, I open the door but before I have time to open my mouth to greet my buddy—ah, my ex-buddy—I'm knocked on my ass. You know those little birds that fly around a cartoon character's head when he's been pummeled? Well, I can now attest to them being real.

"You motherfucking, cocksucking asshole!"

"Hey, Andersen." I rub my jaw and greet him from my current position on the floor where I'm lying on my back.

"I told you to stay away from my sister. Didn't I?" He walks in and stands over me.

"I'm sorry. I..."

"Get up, you asshole, so I can knock you down again," he growls.

I push myself up and hold my hands out to keep him at arm's distance.

"I know you're angry, dude, and I get..." I don't have a chance to finish my sentence before he clocks me again with a right hook. I stumble back but manage to stay on my feet this time.

"Listen, bro." He doesn't listen. Instead, he lands an uppercut straight to my chin.

"Don't call me bro, shithead. I'm not your bro anymore." Okay. I get it. He's pissed off. I deserve his wrath but I need him to stop punching, or I won't be able to put together a coherent thought.

"Bro...I...I mean, Andersen, I deserve this and much more, but if you punch me one more time I'm going to have to punch you back, and I don't want to do that. I want to explain..."

The fucker punches me again. "You don't need to explain, dickhead." But I keep my hands fisted at my sides to prevent myself from retaliating. He has every right to pummel me into oblivion.

"What's to explain? You fucked my sister and then dumped her. I knew you were a whoring scumbag, but I thought you at least had the decency not to treat Heaven in your shitty whoring way." He takes a step toward me but I back up to keep him from landing another punch.

"Nah, man. You don't understand..."

"Oh, I understand. I understand my naïve, caring

sister has loved you unconditionally for years and it still wasn't enough to keep you from treating her like garbage." He takes another swing but I duck, and his arm sweeps the air over my head.

"I love her too, goddammit!" I yell. "If you would just let me get a word in here."

"Ha. Right. You love her. So, you take her virginity and then go out and fuck some other chick and get her pregnant. Pretty shitty way to love someone." Dak glowers at me like he's getting ready to rip my head off.

But then he runs his hand over his hair and says quietly, "She's destroyed, dude. She won't come out of her room, won't eat anything, won't stop crying. Christ. I had to remind her to breathe when she was telling me what happened. She was a virgin, for fuck's sake. How could you do this to her? She's done nothing but love you since she was a kid."

"I know she has and I've loved her...wait. What are you talking about? I know I'm a pig, but Heaven wasn't a virgin when we slept together. She had already been with the douchebag doctor you fixed her up with. She slept with him when they stayed at the resort for your wedding."

"You're an even bigger dumbass than I thought you were." Dak shakes his head.

"Thanks for the commentary, dude. But what the fuck are you talking about?"

"She never slept with Littner. It was *you* she slept with at the wedding, you fucking idiot."

"What? No. I had way too much bourbon but...I was dreaming about Pip and...Alison...she came to my room the next morning, and...she said it was her." He can't be right. He must have misunderstood Pip.

"Pip would have said something. She would've told me." Right? "I wouldn't..." But then I envision Heaven's face flushed with longing and I hear my own words. '*I think I've been waiting for you my whole life.*' Fuck me!

"Come on, fucktard. You take a woman's virginity, and the next morning, you not only forget, but you think it was some other woman. You think Heaven was going to hang around and explain it to you? I don't even know why she took your sorry ass back afterward. And then to top it all off, you go fuck the other chick and..."

"Shut up!" I need him to stop talking. I need to process this.

"What did you say?" His chest heaves like a raging bull who's about to attack.

"I said, shut the fuck up." I put my arm up to hold him back. "Are you saying I didn't fuck Alison that night?"

"Are you deaf as well as stupid, dickhead? I just told you. You fuc...you slept with my sister that night. And I'm going to fucking ki—" At the sound of my maniacal laughter, he swallows his latest threat.

"What the fuck are you laughing at? Have you completely lost what little mind you had?"

I've never kissed a guy before, but there's a first time for everything. I grab Dak's pretty boy face between my hands and kiss him smack dab on the lips.

"What the fuck?" He pushes me away from him and swipes the back of his hand across his lips. I'm surprised he doesn't shout *'yuk, dog germs'* and spit on my floor, Lucy-style. "What the hell are you doing?"

"Andersen, my man, in the past forty-eight hours I have been called a jackass about five hundred times, five-fifty if you count the guys I'm not even friends with. But at this moment, I could kiss every single one of them."

"That's great. Now that you've slept with almost every woman in the country, you've had a mid-life revelation concerning your sexual proclivities?" He smirks.

"No, bruh." I laugh and walk toward him. He steps back and holds his hands out to keep me away.

"Thanks, but I'm good," he says with a nervous stutter.

"You're adorable, dude. But only one kiss per friend." I snicker at his apprehension. "What I'm trying to tell you is, I never slept with Alison!" I feel like Ebenezer Scrooge on Christmas morning when he finds out the spirits saved his nasty ass.

"Oh yeah? So, what is it? Like a miraculous immaculate conception?" Dak sneers and shakes his head at me.

"I'm pretty sure Alison is no immaculate anything. But if she's pregnant, it sure as shit isn't mine. The only time I slept with her—I *thought* I slept with her—was at your wedding. If it was Heaven, then the baby can't be mine." I'm gonna do a cartwheel right here in my foyer. Wait. Do I know how to do a cartwheel? No. No, I don't.

"Let me get this straight." Dak pushes his fingers into his temples and shakes his head like he's clearing cobwebs. "You're a professional hockey player, with a gazillion dollar contract and just as many women comin' in their pants for you and you didn't have Alison take a paternity test to make sure the baby was yours? No. Wait. To make sure she's even pregnant?"

I grimace and raise my shoulders. "I assumed she..."

"For fuck's sake, Wolfe. You put everyone through this, especially Heaven and you..."

"Holy shit, Heaven! I took her virginity and...I'm going back to Dalt's. I have to see her." I turn in a circle looking for...something. What am I looking for? I look down. Right. Clothes. I don't have anything on but sweatpants.

"Hold up, dude." Dak puts his hand up traffic-cop style. "I'm not letting you go over there and break her heart again. According to Nik, she hasn't stopped crying since you were there this morning, and we're supposed to be taking her out for her birthday tonight."

"Where are you taking her?"

"What the fuck do you care? There's no way I'm letting you ruin her birthday any more than you already have."

"Dude." I chuckle. "It's so damn cute how you think you're going to keep me away from Heaven now that I know the truth."

"You think so, asshole. I'll show you cute.' He comes at me again. This time I take the first punch, and *he* lands on *his* ass.

"Sorry, brotha. But just because I let you get in a few cheap shots protecting your sister's honor doesn't mean I'm going to let you keep doing it. Besides, it's my job now to protect her honor."

"What?" Dak leans back on his elbows and looks up at me, all dazed and confused.

"That's right." I reach out to help him up. "Whether you approve or not, I'm going to be protecting and loving her for the rest of our lives." Dak latches onto my hand, and I tug him up. "If she'll have me. Now, come have a kiss-and-make-up beer with me and tell me where the hell the birthday celebration is."

Chapter Thirty-Six

HEAVEN

"We'll have a round of Passed Out Nakeds for both tables," Nik yells to the waiter, over the music and the current girl performing. It's Karaoke night at the Flying Puck. Nik, Dalt, Dak, Tracey, Batt and half the Santa Ana Winds team decided it was the perfect place to celebrate my birthday. Not sure why the heck the Winds' players are here. Maybe Dalt invited them—every player except the only one I want to see—the one I told a few hours ago I never wanted to see again.

"Oh no, Nik. I'm not drinking those." I don't even want to be here, let alone drinking shots which are potent enough to remove paint.

They insisted I had to come out and celebrate. I'm in no mood for celebrations. But Nikki can be very persuasive when she wants something and when she has Tracy as her sidekick, it's a done deal.

"Ah. Yes, you are, girlfriend. After the night I drank

Jäger shots at the Thirsty Whale and went crazy on Dalt in his car in the parking lot, I swore I would never drink it again. That was three years ago, and I've kept my promise. But I'm breaking the moratorium just for you, in honor of your birthday." *Please don't do it for me.* I've recently learned my tolerance for alcohol is somewhere on the level of a premature, newborn mouse and results in catastrophic behavior.

"That's right," Trace adds her two cents. "We are getting shitfaced tonight, and then we're going to sing our little hearts out."

"Yeah. Come on, sis. Join the party. Karaoke is your favorite thing. And it's your birthday," Dak reminds me for the forty billionth time. How could I forget? It's the day which will go down in my history book as the Birthday from Hell.

The waiter shows up with two trays of the toxic shots made from equal parts Bacardi Rum, Cuervo Gold, Jägermeister, Peppermint Schnapps, and trouble with a capital T.

He places one tray down on our table and brings the other to the table next to us, the table where the Winds players are seated. Seriously. Why are these specimens of God's creative abilities here? They're pretty but as lethal as the shots being raised in cheers around our table.

I'm following Nikki's lead and declaring a moratorium, not on Jäger—although that's not a bad idea. I'm reinstating my resolution to stay away from all people who wear hockey pads and are deficient in an X chromosome.

"Happy birthday to the best sister in the world!" Dak

raises his glass. I know he's feeling sorry for me if he's toasting me without one sarcastic remark. I can't take everyone treating me like a baby bird with a broken wing. I just want everything to be normal.

When everyone calls out my name in response to the toast, I look from face to face. I get a sharp pain in my chest. My heart actually hurts because the one face I want to see isn't here. I find myself wondering if anything will ever be normal again.

I thought this was going to be the best birthday I've ever had because I would be spending it with Wolfe. Still, I can't deny it's sweet and comforting to have my family and friends around me doing whatever they can to help me get through this.

"Oh, what the hell." I raise my glass and down the venomous swill. *Jesus. It burns!* But by the time Tracey raises her toast to me—the *third* toast and round—the sluice goes down fairly smooth, and I'm feeling pleasantly numb.

"Time for a birthday performance," Nik calls out. I sit there—a stupid-drunk grin stretching my lips—waiting to see which one of my Jäger-happy friends is going to volunteer. When everyone starts chanting the name Heaven, I look around to see where this Heaven person is they're encouraging to sing. Oh yeah! Silly goose. *I'm* Heaven. They want me to sing. And yup, you guessed it. I am more than ready to sing my lungs out.

I saunter my way to the stage...at least I think I'm sauntering. At this point, I can't feel my legs. Remembering to get the mic and tell the guy in charge of the music what I'm going to sing, I take center stage. Whistles and catcalls reverberate off the walls. I tug up on the skintight, body-hugging white dress the girls insisted I wear. It has off the shoulder straps for sleeves. Its demi-push up cups are dangerously close to allowing my girls to spill out the top.

"Now, now. All you naughty hockey boys out there need to quiet down," I purr into the mic, which only causes them to whistle louder. "That's right, ladies. We have been blessed with a plethora of hot Santa Ana Winds' players here tonight." The room explodes with cheers and swooning oohs and ahs. "Oh. But don't be fooled, ladies. Stay far, far away. These guys are like Foxglove...*really*. They're beautiful, but they will destroy your heart." The whistles coming from the Winds' table morph to hisses and boos. "Wow. How quickly they turn on you." I chuckle. "Look at me, being all Mrs. Maisel up in here. Maybe I missed my calling." That gets the audience laughing again and the chant "sing, sing, sing" sweeps through the room. *Okay. I've got this.*

When the music starts and the lyrics to Dua Lipa's *New Rules* roll across the karaoke screen, I begin singing like I wrote this song, like I can feel the words right down to my soul. By the time I'm finished strutting around the stage—or stumbling, depending on your perspective—and belting out the song like my life depends on it, everyone in the bar is on their feet chanting "encore," and I'm feeling pretty freaking good about myself.

Until another song, which I did not choose, begins playing and a familiar voice, behind me, starts singing the lyrics to *I Say A Little Prayer*. The room goes wild, especially the hockey players. I turn slowly, certain this is a

Jäger induced hallucination. *You have got to be fucking kidding me.* Apparently, Passed Out Naked shots contain the same liquid Alice drank when she fell down the rabbit hole.

I turn back toward the audience. Why are my friends cheering and clapping? Even my overprotective brother is freaking smiling!

My tormentor walks up next to me, looking right at me as he sings the bridge to the song telling me he loves me and there's no one else but me. I blink and shake my head to make sure I'm seeing what I think I'm seeing. I'm angry as hell D showed up here when I asked him to stay away from me. At the same time, my broken heart skips a joyous beat.

"What are you doing?" I loud angry whisper over the deceitful lyrics.

He moves the mic away from his goddamn beautiful lips and says through a smile, "I'm vibrating higher, singing to you. Singing with you."

"I'm not singing with you. I told you to stay away from me."

D ignores my comment. He continues to mesmerize me with that damn smile and bewitching eyes. The words to the chorus roll across the screen and D closes the space between us. He looks down at me. I'm consumed, absorbed into his magnetic quagmire.

"Sing with me, Pip."

I can't pull my gaze away from his as I raise my mic and the lyrics fall from my lips. But after a few too many 'forever and evers' and 'together togethers,' and excessive cheers from my soon-to-be ex-friends, I'm jolted from my hypnotic state. I remember I can't be singing love songs with him, professing our eternal love. He belongs to someone else.

I run from the stage. I don't know where I'm going. Anywhere to get away from D. I end up running down a back hallway which leads to offices and stock rooms.

"Pip, wait." My tormentor catches up with me and tugs me back.

"Leave me alone. Why are you doing this? Get away from..."

He pushes me against the wall and crashes his lips onto mine, interrupting my fuming protests. I ball my fists—one of them still clutching my mic—and pummel his chest. "I hate you," I cry into his mouth, but I don't stop kissing him.

"I love you. Always," he whispers against my lips.

"Get away from me. I don't want you to kiss me," I groan against his soft lips.

"You're a little liar." He smiles and swallows my lies. He grinds his erection against the spot I can't keep from wanting him. My body moves with his. And then I remember. No. I can't do this. He isn't mine. He's marrying someone else.

"And you're an asshole!" I push his face away from mine, but he keeps my body pinned against the wall with his.

"In so many ways," he agrees while clutching his hand over his cheek where my nails gouged his god-like face. "But not in this one. Alison isn't pregnant."

DAMON

"How lucky for you. You dodged a bullet—this time. But I still don't want you kissing me or touching m..."

"Goddamit, Pip! Will you shut up and listen to me? I never fucked Alison!"

"Are you seriously yelling at me after...wait. What did you just say?"

"I *said* I never fucked Alison. She lied about having sex with me, being pregnant. The only time I slept with her...*thought* I slept with her was the wedding reception night." I soften my voice and touch my forehead to hers. "But it wasn't her, was it? Why didn't you tell me?"

"You didn't remember. You thought it was someone else," she breathes in a hushed, apologetic tone.

"Jesus, Pip. I'm so sorry. I'm sorry it was...I thought it was a dream. I dreamt about you so many times before."

"Does this mean you're not going to marry Alison?"

I put a finger under her chin and tip her head back. Her liquid blues pierce my soul. I'm drowning in them, and I never want to be rescued.

"I'm not going to do anything with Alison or anyone else ever again. The truth is I haven't been with anyone else since the night we...since the night you introduced me to Sheldon and Hal." It's like every muscle in her body uncoils when she drops into my arms. I can feel her stuttered breath as she lays her head against my chest and cries silent tears.

"And don't forget Wolfe, the turtle." Even through her tears, I can hear the smile in her words.

"I haven't forgotten Wolfe, the turtle. And I get it. You named him after me because he was another lost being hiding inside his broken shell." She doesn't acknowledge my deduction, but she doesn't deny it either.

"Listen to me, Pip." I keep her wrapped up in my arms and stroke her hair as I try to put into words all the things I want her to know. "I think I've been searching my whole life for something that was missing. No matter how much I did, no matter how much I had, it was never enough to get rid of that empty feeling. Except when I'm with you. It's like you bring colors to my life I've never seen before. And even when I'm not with you, you make me smile. You're the first thing I think about in the morning and the last thing I think about before I fall asleep." I repeat the words she said to me only a few hours ago. "You're all I think about every minute of every day.

"I love your compassion for all the broken things— especially me." She giggles in between her tears. "I love how you beat me at every damn game we play and tease me about it afterward. I love the way you eat the crust off your pizza first because it's the best part and you don't want to be too full to eat it. I love how you call me out when I'm being an ass but stick by me through all my crazy. I love how you can't pick a favorite color because you think there are too many beautiful colors in nature to decide on just one. I love how you cry at animated movies like *Bambi* or *Dumbo*. I love your cheesy pick-up lines. But most of all, I love the way you let your love for me grow in slow baby steps until it was certain and strong. While I, on the other hand, was too stupid to see what was right in front of me. I had to have everything burn and crash down on my head all at once to realize what I had and what I almost lost."

I take a step back and cup her face in my hands. I want to drink her in. "I know I don't deserve you. But marry me anyway." I pull the ring I was getting ready to toss into the ocean from my pocket. "I bought this while I was away. I was going to give it to you when I got back."

I open the velvet box to offer her the three-carat blue diamond ring. "I chose it because it reminded me of your eyes, only not as beautiful." The eyes I'm referring to go wide in shock and glaze over with tears—hopefully, happy ones. "Stay with me forever, Heaven. I love you. Let me spend every day for the rest of my life proving to you I can be the man you've always seen in me."

"Oh, D." She throws her arms around my neck and holds on as if she'll never let go. And that's just fine with me. My heart is hammering inside my chest to the point I'm sure it's going to break through my ribs and lay itself down at her feet.

"But you're wrong." Oh shit. She's going to say no. She's going to walk away from me, and I'm going to be lost without her; inside my broken shell forever. "I didn't love you in baby steps."

She tilts her head back to look at me. I brace myself for the knockout punch to my heart. "My love for you crashed down on me the first time I met you. From that day on I belonged to only you, completely. So, yes. Yes. Yes. Yes." She peppers kisses all over my face with every kiss. I pick her up and spin her around.

A lifetime of weight has been lifted off my shoulders. I'm sure in my elation we're going to lift off the floor and take flight. But my excitement is distracted when somewhere in the distance I hear thundering applause, cheering, and whistles. And then I hear my name being chanted like my hockey bros do when they're cheering for another bro.

Only then do I realize Heaven still has the damn mic clutched in her hand and the entire audience in the Flying Puck heard every word we said—every word *I* said. I will never live it down.

But I give zero fucks. My teammates can break my balls from now until forever because I'm the lucky SOB who gets to love Heaven Lee Andersen and I'm good with everyone in the world knowing it.

"Happy Birthday, Gorgeous. I love you. Always," I whisper against the lips I will never stop kissing as long as I live.

Epilogue

DAMON

Three Years Later

"'I could feel every ridge, every vein as I licked his rock hard, pulsing, heat-seeking missile. When I reached the bulbous mushroom tip, I began to suck as hard as I could, and when he exploded his molten juices down my throat, I gagged. But he tasted like roasted marshmallows, and I wanted to swallow every bit of his gooey love seed'.*

"Eewwah. This book is just awful." Pip throws the book onto the blanket next to us.

I chuckle and turn my head to press a kiss onto my beautiful wife's gigantic pregnant belly. "It's not the worst one you've ever read to me."

In her current state, one of her favorite pastimes is to lay on the beach and read to me. And of course, Pip's favorite thing to read is romance. I don't mind, though, because I'm the fortunate recipient of her heated response to the juicy love scenes.

Sometimes, since this is our own private beach—the one outside the twenty-acre estate I bought when we got married—we have our own private reenactment scene.

"Ugh. It's pretty bad. I may never eat a roasted marshmallow again." She giggles. My head bounces against her belly.

On the days she reads to me, *my* favorite pastime is to lay my head on her stomach and listen, not only to the story but to the muffled, gurgling sounds of our baby inside her. I can't believe this is my life.

"The babies need some exercise. Why don't you throw some sticks for them to chase?" Pip suggests.

"Be right back," I whisper against my baby mama's belly to the him or her growing inside and then plant a kiss on her lips. "Don't move, Dr. Andersen. I'll be right back, and we can eat our picnic lunch."

"Hey! That's Dr. *Mrs.* Wolfe to you," Pip calls out as I run to the shoreline and collect some sticks to throw for the *babies*; the babies being the menagerie of rescue animals we've adopted since moving into our spacious new home.

Last count, we had: seven dogs, six cats, one pot belly pig, two parrots, three turtles, an iguana, and a partridge in a pear tree. Actually, although we *do* have a pear tree, we *don't* have a partridge in it. But I'm sure we would if Pip found one who needed rescuing.

It's the reason I bought this place. I wanted her to have the space to adopt all the creatures needing her love.

No one knows better than I do how she can take in broken, damaged strays and love them back to life

"Throw one near Sheldon, D. He can't keep up with the other dogs," Pip calls to me.

I glance back and take in the vision of my pregnant wife—still rockin' a teeny string bikini— stretched out on a blanket. It's the most gorgeous sight I've ever seen and continues to make my knees weak and my cock hard.

There are still some days I go down a dark road thinking about my past. But when I'm not feeling good about myself, Pip pulls me back. She reminds me who I am now and what I have. She's brought me back to life and makes me a better man, every day.

I don't know how or why I deserve all this, why I've been so blessed. But I thank God every day for giving me Heaven and in two months, our baby. As I said, I'm the lucky bastard who gets to love Heaven Andersen—now Heaven Wolfe—for the rest of my life. But the most amazing thing is, she loves me, unconditionally, in return.

HEAVEN

See the massively huge pregnant woman stretched out on a blanket in the beautiful, California sun, smiling from ear to ear? *Yup.* That's me again, Heaven Andersen Wolfe. Now you know my boring/not so boring love story, the journey to my happily ever after. And here comes the beautiful reason for my HEA.

"Hey, babe. I was thinking," my gorgeous husband stretches out next to me on the blanket. I still get chill bumps every time I see him or hear his voice. I can't believe he's mine and I'm his. "I don't think you should travel with the team anymore. It might be too much for you and the baby." He rubs his calloused hand over my baby bump—uh, my baby *mountain*—and nuzzles his nose into my neck.

Even now, with one touch, I'm wet and ready to straddle him. Pregnancy hormones are fantastic for one's sex life. Although, a husband like D doesn't really need much assistance in getting me hot and bothered.

"I'm pregnant, D, not handicapped," I protest while running my fingers through his long silky waves.

"I know, babe, and I love having you as the team's DPT when we're on the road so I never have to leave you but..." He bites his lip like he's afraid to finish his sentence.

"But what?"

"But...um...you're getting kinda...um...large and immobile."

"What?" I click the T off my tongue. Pregnancy hormones also tend to make you want to bite off the head of the person who's the reason you're the size of a small whale.

"I...I mean...you're getting close to the end and I think you should take it easy. Take care of my girl and our baby." He nibbles my earlobe and trails kisses down my neck.

I let out a huge sigh. I'm so stupid in love with this

guy I can't even stay mad at him when my hormonal chemistry is raging at DefCon 100.

"No worries." I suck in a breath as D continues to lavish kisses down my chest. "I already worked it out with Mac. I won't be traveling with the team until after the baby is born."

"Awesome. You need to take it easy for the last couple months."

"But you'll miss me while you're away next week, right?" I give him a teasing pout.

He licks one of my nipples right through my bikini top and my hips jump off the blanket begging for more.

"Mmm. Can you touch me so I can say I was touched by an angel?" he moans. *Oh, God.* I adore his stupid pick-up lines. "Let's go back to the house. I want to take care of my girl right this second."

Yup. I'm a very lucky girl. And if I've learned anything over my years growing up with D, I've learned some very important things besides the fact I deserve to be loved completely, without any uncertainty. Love isn't always easy. Sometimes it can hurt and be a real struggle. But when you find the right person, don't give up, despite their so-called flaws. Hang on for the ride. We all have flaws. It's what makes us human.

Oh. One more unsolicited chestnut of wisdom? Don't be afraid to be the one who loves the most. No matter what happens, you'll never lose if you share your love.

The more love you give, the more love you get in return. I don't know who said that. Um...maybe the Beatles. Whatever. It's true.

I didn't think it was possible, but I fall in love with D a little more every day, and he returns my love tenfold. And when you're lucky enough to fall in love with your best friend and blessed enough to have his babies, it's the happiest happy ever after any girl could ever ask for.

Before You Go...

If you enjoyed my book please take a second to leave a short review. These reviews help me as an author be found by other amazing readers like you.

Thank you so much! :)

CROSS CREASE PLAYLIST

Pink Julia Michaels
Don't Be a Fool Shaun Mendes
Love the One You're With Stephen Stills
Run Away Bruno Mars
Your Side of The Bed Loote
Tracey The Cufflinks
Dancing With A Stranger Sam Smith
The Wolf The Spencer Lee Band
Say You Won't Let Go James Arthur
Girl You'll Be A Woman Soon Urge Overkill
Will You Still Love Me Tomorrow Carole King
One Night Christina Perri
Here He Comes Again Dolly Parton
Say Something I'm Giving Up On You Cristina Aquilera
He's So Fine The Chiffons
Feel Like Making Love Roberta Flack
Don't Know What It's Like To Be You Shaun Mendes
I Can't Make You Love Me Bonnie Raitt
New Rules Dua Lipa
I Say A Little Prayer Dione Warwick
The End The Beatles

Acknowledgments

First of all, I want to thank Limitless Publishing. If not for the amazing team at Limitless, my book babies wouldn't have the chance to travel out into the world. I'm forever grateful to them for giving me the opportunity to realize my dream.

To Toni Rakestraw, my new editor. Thank you so much for polishing my manuscript and making it shiny and perfect for my readers. It's been one of the most pleasant editing experiences I've ever had—once I got my program to work correctly. LOL. I know some of my incorrect dialogue grammar makes you crazy but my characters insist on talking like that. So, blame them.

To all my girls, Jordan, Taylor, Elyse, Rachel, Jackie, Ronnie and Kristina. I couldn't ask for a better street team. Thank you for all the constant support and helping to spread the word about my books. Can't wait to see the photos of you guys holding this book in some beautiful location.

Thanks to the girls at DreamWorks for loving my characters as much as I do. I'll try to get my book boyfriends out to you a little faster in the future.

To Michelle Lancaster. Thank you so much for the beautiful photos. Your photography is inspirational. Here's to many years working together.

To Darren C. Thanks for the hockey lingo. Your humor helped shaped the personalities and conversations of the Bernard Boys.

A big thanks goes out to all the bloggers, reviewers, and booklovers who spend so much of their precious time spreading the word about my books out of the goodness of their hearts. There are not enough ways to say I love you.

Of course, I want to thank my family for putting up with me when I'm in writing mode. I tend to get just a teensy bit grumpy when someone interrupts the creative flow. But I would never be able to do this crazy thing of writing books if not for your constant love, support and inspiration. So, thank you for loving me unconditionally —as Wolfe would say.

Most of all, thank you to all my readers. There would be no point in doing this if no one ever read my words. I am so grateful to all of you for buying, reading and reviewing my books. I've spent so much time creating the characters in this series they have almost become part of my family. I love that you love them as much as I do. Wolfe and Heaven hold a special place in my heart. I hope they will touch your heart as well.

Until next time, happy reading.

See you between the 'covers.'

Love,

Elizabeth Hartey

About the Author

As a lover of the northeast United States, Elizabeth moved with her husband to the Poconos several years ago to open a Chiropractic Clinic. Four children and a menagerie of animals later, she has finally found time to fulfill her lifelong dream of writing novels. A dreamer at heart, romance is the genre she spends most of her time writing and reading into the wee hours of the morning. When not juggling work responsibilities and writing, she enjoys hiking the beautiful hills and woods around her home, swimming, knitting, travelling, and spending time with her family. She is an avid hockey fan, which means she has to compromise with her husband, one night of hockey for her, in exchange for one night of football for him.

Website:
https://www.elizabethhartey.com
Newsletter:
http://eepurl.com/cZCEuL